DAYS OF DECAY

Mia Watson

Chapter One

Then

Outside the corner shop, the two teens stared begrudgingly at the sorry states of their wallets.

"Maybe we can pawn off that ring of yours," Kit remarked as he pointed to the silver, floral ring that wrapped around Asha's middle finger.

She gasped, mocking shock, and held her hand protectively over it before nudging him hard with her elbow. "I've literally had this for a week and you're already trying to sell it for alcohol."

"Oh, come on, I'm sure *Mamasita* wouldn't mind," Kit grinned as he rummaged desperately in his jean pockets for any hidden cash.

Asha's hazel eyes rolled instantly. "When will you stop sexualising *mi mamá?*"

"Never," he replied, his freckled nose scrunching in a smirk.

She frowned up at him. "She would kill you if she knew you were the reason her Mexican, family heirloom lived in a pawn shop mere days after being gifted to her eldest daughter on her 18th birthday."

Kit shook his head, amused. "Isobel would *never* kill me. I'm the son she never had."

"You are something else…" Asha mused, reaching into the deep crevices of her bag. Her fingers brushed over something that felt very thin, and very crumpled. She grabbed it immediately and whipped it out, her eyes bursting wide.

"Yes!" Kit shouted before snatching the £20 note from her grasp. "We can get a nice bottle for pres."

Asha promptly plucked it back. "*I* can get a nice bottle for pres."

He shrugged, not looking too disappointed. "Is that really how you treat your best friend?"

"Yes, and that's why you're my best friend over anyone else."

"You don't count Ella as your *bestie*?" He asked, pushing the door to the shop open and walking in.

Asha followed him, keeping as close as possible to him as the guy who ran the shop had a penchant for younger girls, especially ones who wore what Asha was wearing at that very moment. "No, she's my sister. I was *forced* to spend my life with her. You're a choice."

"I feel so privileged," Kit remarked, moving Asha in front of him as they walked further down the shop, his glance pointed behind them for a brief moment before he looked ahead again to the shelves of enticing bottles.

"You should." Asha's focus stuck fast onto the variety of drinks in front of them. She reached out for a pink bottle of gin and after checking the price, pulled it from the shelf. "This will do."

"Okay, but I need to mix it with coke. What will the boys think if they saw me chugging that down?"

4

Asha's frown re-appeared. "What the fuck is wrong with you? Honestly. Your toxic masculinity will be the death of you. It's 2023, we're drinking it with lemonade."

"Fine," he agreed, "I'll get over myself just this once."

"Since when did you become so agreeable so fast?" She questioned him with a thick, dark eyebrow raised high.

"Since I can't be bothered to fight with you, and since we're going to be late to this party if we don't hurry up!" He said, swiping a 2L bottle of lemonade from the bottom shelf and walking towards the cashier.

Asha scoffed and hurried alongside him, gin and money in one hand while the other hand rummaged in her bag for her ID.

When they reached the pay desk, Kit purposefully stood in front of Asha and presented all of their goods on the counter before sticking both of their IDs out to the man.

The man in question was in his fifties, had a gut the size of a beach ball, a top that was splattered in questionable stains and a leering sneer across his bulbous face. He'd owned the store since Asha could remember. The neighbourhood kids throughout generations bonded over their disgust of him; it was a strange act of comradery.

"£19.50," He spat, his eyes wandering.

Kit handed him the note.

There was one other thing the teens in the town shared, and that was the fear of the abandoned house on the hill on the outskirts. Which was where the party was being held that evening. Yes, they were all scared shitless by it, but it made it the perfect place to party as loud and as hard as they wanted, without drawing attention from the police.

—

5

They were out of the shop faster than their legs could carry them, not bothering to wait for a bag. In their haste, the glass bottle slipped from Asha's hands as she stumbled out onto the street. Luckily, Kit had freak-like reflexes and caught the thing swiftly before it smashed on the ground along with their hopes of getting smashed that night.

"What would you do without me?" He questioned her, with a cocky grin upon his handsome face.

Asha sighed as she pulled out her lipstick from her bag. "Live happily?"

He gasped and smacked at her hand just as she was applying a precise swipe of lipstick, making her paint her cheek with red instead.

"You… absolute…prick," Asha muttered angrily, standing perfectly still which made Kit feign panic and begin running down the street. "Oh no you don't," she said to herself before hurriedly shoving the lipstick back and taking off after him, not bothering to pull down the short skirt that was riding up as she gave Usain Bolt a run for his money.

*

Asha preferred to remember that night the way it was, before the world changed. But there was only so much she could remember before it became a literal hell.

It was around one in the morning when she finally arrived home in the taxi. Her head was spinning and the kebab in her stomach churned relentlessly. She was grateful to finally be out in the open air instead of trapped in a moving vehicle.

Kit was nowhere to be seen - he'd disappeared halfway through the night presumably with some girl. So, she was facing sneaking into her house alone rather than going through Kit's broken backdoor and sleeping there. Her mamá wouldn't mind, Asha had learnt it from somewhere, hadn't she?

The keys in her hands made the most amount of noise as she spread them apart attempting to locate the right one. Before long though, she managed to open the door and stumble into the dark house, ready to collapse on her bed.

But something pricked her ears instantly. It was a faint sizzling sound.

That was when the smell of cooking meat invaded her senses, making her stomach do even more flips.

She didn't call out to anyone. Instead, she took in a few deep breaths and blinked away the drunkenness enough to make her way through the darkness to the kitchen where she could see a tall silhouette cooking next to the small, exposed flame of the hob; their arm was jutting out animatedly to the tune of the music.

She blinked quickly.

It made her uncomfortable, like she wasn't supposed to be seeing it. The smell of meat was overpowering, and it was unlike one she'd ever smelt before. Everything was confusing and all she could do was stand there and watch; she felt like an intruder in her own home.

There was only one person in the house who could fit that silhouette.

"*Papa*?" She asked, her voice wavering.

When he didn't answer, she reached for the light switch.

—

7

The alcohol that was coursing through her body instantly disappeared as she was left in the sobering wake of the sight before her.

Her mother's severed head lay lopsided on the counter, her vacant eyes boring into Asha's like a poison. On the floor was her sister's head. Their bodies were nowhere to be seen.

She watched horrified as thick, oozing blood dropped from the counter down to the wooden floor below with little thuds.

Asha was overcome in ice, freezing her to the spot she stood. She felt like she was going to faint and throw up simultaneously.

Fuck, fuck, what?

Breathing was difficult. All she could think about was what she was seeing. Her basic bodily functions had abandoned her. Fear held her in a steel like grip as she frantically looked around the room. It was then that she spotted the remaining parts of their bodies crumpled together on the floor by the sofa. Large hunks of flesh had been sliced off their limbs. Suddenly, the realisation of what she had been smelling set in.

Pan-fried human.

Her stomach emptied noisily to the floor below.

He turned around then; his appearance throwing her further towards the edge than she thought possible. His skin was so pale it was almost translucent and the veins in his face bulged and pulsed in dark, almost black, blood. Despite its delicate look, it didn't seem too damaged by the scratches that littered his face.

Her mother and sister had put up one hell of a fight.

8

"Ah, *Mija, buena.* You're home," his deep voice broke through her panic, and she tore her eyes from the gore, back to him. "Are you hungry?"

Asha's mind was at war with itself. One part of it wanted to crumple on the floor and howl for her loss, another part could shatter her entire being through fear; and the other part bubbled with a rage she hadn't known she could possess.

A second passed and as he looked at her up and down in the dim light, his face went from pride to frank dismay.

"Oh, *Mija,* you disappoint me," he said, shaking his head as he reached for the kitchen cloth and began to calmly clean the blood off his hands.

"*W-what?*" She managed to stutter. She was surprised she could say anything at all. In fact, she was impressed that she was able to keep herself standing, considering the circumstances. Any normal person would have either collapsed on the floor or fucked off out the front door.

"You were always more like your *mamá.*" His eyes were dead cold, he was gone.

He was quick. She watched on helplessly as he grabbed the kitchen knife and launched it at her with precision. The blade penetrated her side and she crumpled with sheer pain. A hideous warmth seeped quickly from her side.

This can't be happening. This can't be happening.

She saw him run to her then, but before he could reach her, she ducked to the side and pulled the knife from her body. Each and every serration of it cut at her raw flesh on its way out, but it didn't matter. Nothing mattered except for her staying alive.

Hot blood began to spill from her side, wetting the floor as she sprinted off through the house.

There was no way she was dying tonight; it wasn't on the cards for her.

She held a hand over the wound instinctively, trying her best to slow the flow. Her footing was compromised by her blood, and she slipped slightly before regaining her composure, eyes stuck on her ravenous father.

He reached for her, but she yanked her whole body from him as she careened around the corner and down the wide corridor towards the stairs. He growled, his spit flying through his clenched teeth; he looked more frenzied now, if that were even possible.

Her screams got lost in her throat as she catapulted up the stairs with all her muster. She held one hand against her now gushing wound, and the other helped her climb the seemingly endless stairs. Panic had set in, she could feel it wanting to take over her body, but she fought it.

She wasn't going to let it win, not this time.

His heavy footsteps took to the stairs rapidly behind her. He was faster than her, but when she reached the top of the stairs, she quickly spun around and swung her leg out towards him. The side of her foot met with his chest with a thud, and he fell backwards down the hardwood stairs, landing at the bottom with a resounding crack.

He lay there without a single movement; the sight of it sent a chill down her spine and her kebab threatened to make yet another appearance.

She stood trembling at the top, staring down at him while she greedily sucked in long gasps of air. The blood from her side continued to pump out, and her hands were becoming sticky with the redness.

The man who had raised her now lay, still as stone, at the bottom of the stairs because she'd kicked him down there.

She was a monster.

As she cautiously made her way down to him, her mind twisted in a flurry. Memories of her life with him through the years surfaced; his gold tooth shining, dancing with him on her *quinceanera*, learning how to make the perfect tostada.

That was when the tears came.

"*Papa! Shit, shit shit!*" she whimpered as she neared him. She knelt down by his head and rested her hand on his pale cheek.

But then it hit her. He wasn't her dad. He'd killed her mother, he'd killed her sister, and he tried to kill *her*. He was *cooking* them. He was COOKING them.

A sharp breath from the body below snapped her out of her reverie.

She bolted upright before sprinting back to the kitchen, her survival instincts pushing her beyond her capacity. She avoided the sight of her massacred family and instead concentrated on opening the cutlery drawer and pulling out the longest, thinnest knife she could find. She knew deep down there was no easy way of getting out of this nicely. She had to fight fire with fire, no matter the cost. She'd already lost.

When she turned around, he was there.

"Asha, *Mija,* don't do this. I'm your father, *por favour*," he begged, seeming more like the man who had raised her, yet his neck was bent at a severe angle and his crushed spine had him swaying sickeningly from side to side. He wasn't human, not anymore.

"*No, no, no,*" she whispered under her staggered breath as she held the knife shakily in front of her. Black circles started to invade her sight, dizziness began to set in.

She wanted her dad back, she wanted to hug him; she wanted everything to be okay, to be normal. Fear and adrenaline had consumed her energy, leaving her shaking and weak, barely even able to hold the knife out in front of her. She let her cry come out, not caring that it showed her weakness.

She *was* weak.

Her arm wavered slightly, and he took that moment to lunge at her. His face was a mask of rage and hunger, and in that moment, she knew there was no more of him left.

Any ounce of giving up left her body and she stood her ground.

He launched himself at her; his slender finger managing to scratch her from the base of her throat downwards, while his other hand reached for her knife.

Unluckily for him, she was fast too.

She thrust the knife upwards with a crying shout. It lodged itself up through the bottom of his jaw and he halted immediately. She held him there for a second and let his black blood drip onto her trembling fingers.

Everything was still.

The only sound in the room was her ragged breathing. She suddenly felt a harsh burning from her throat all the way down her front, and as she glanced down, she saw that her father's scratch was an open wound, and it was oozing a black blood. She let go of the knife and his body hit the floor with a loud thump.

Tears soaked her cheeks and she collapsed to the floor beside him, her body was giving up on her. She began to crawl towards the front door. She needed to get out of the house. Her side was on fire, along with her throat.

As the blood left her veins, she could feel her life slipping away. The muscles in her arms screamed as she dragged herself to the front door. Once finally there, she reached up with a weary hand to unlock it.

She immediately pulled herself out, the air of the night hitting her like a punch. Its coldness brought some sense of clarity to her, and even the haze of impending death couldn't drown the horror of what she'd done.

She crumpled on the grass, whining before throwing up the rest of her kebab and blacking out.

Chapter Two

<u>Now</u>

The stains on the wooden floor had been the hardest to scrub out.

It was only the second time she'd been back in the last six months. The remnants of dark red blood still taunted Asha, showing her that nothing had really changed since she left the place. She knew it wouldn't have magically disappeared, but some part of her wished that it had. She stared, standing like a statue in the room, the mid-morning sun gracing her face, warming her skin even though she was icy to the touch.

She didn't cry. She couldn't anymore.

Nox had hardened her fragility, turning her into an unfeeling being, stalking the earth for no reason other than to survive. That's what it felt like. There were no parties, no celebrities to insta-stalk, no viral videos to watch. She had no purpose, no-one did.

The virus ended everything Asha knew. The only explanation they ever got was that it was a biological warfare attack. But they never found out where it had come from, only that it was worldwide and all consuming.

She found it unsurprising that the world managed to kill itself through its obsession with war. Letting half-brains and power-hungry trust fund kids into government was the single worst mistake mankind made, and now they were paying for it; those who were left behind at least.

Fucking idiots.

Nox was a horrible way to go. If you contracted it naturally, you suffered a painful flu for three days until your insides began to seep out of every orifice. 60% of the global population experienced that horrific fate.

Around 20% of people were naturally immune to the biological compounds of the virus.

And the rest of civilisation turned into Hunters – highly intelligent, psychotic, cannibalistic, vampire-esque people -, a *pleasant* new addition to the already messed up planet.

It seemed that only the strong adults became Hunters, whereas the weaker population, like the elderly and children, got wiped out. It was some sort of sick natural selection.

Everything happened so quickly that it was impossible to contact anyone. Radio and TV broadcasts still ran for a few days after the initial onslaught, but they couldn't say more than it was a global event and everyone should be with their loved ones. Hardly helpful for Asha who had witnessed and participated in killing those she loved.

A sudden sound from outside drew her attention. She raised her knife, jaw clenched. Her glare stayed hardened at the open doorway.

3, 2, 1.

She breathed a small sigh of relief as a spindly fox eventually emerged into view. She rolled her eyes before striding through the kitchen and to the window overlooking the garden.

The final resting place of her family.

Their graves were still protruding; the crosses Asha had put as the headstones remained strong. So much had happened since burying them, it was hard to comprehend that she'd experienced it all without her family by her side.

Her eyes eventually set on her father's mound. She could forgive him for what he'd done, it wasn't his fault he got sick.

As she gazed blankly out of the window, a tall, faceless figure hopped over the back fence of her garden.

The only saving grace of the whole end-of-the-world thing was the fact that Kit was immune like her.

He jogged across the grass, his whole body and face covered with clothing, until he reached the backdoor where he promptly took off his motorbike helmet and slammed it angrily onto the table next to him.

"No luck?" Asha asked sternly.

"No. *Fuck*," he seethed through gritted teeth. She could see his eyes welling up. He ran a gloved hand through his sweat-dampened curls, clenching his jaw.

She sighed, thinking about the mother and sister who he hadn't seen since the fall. This made it his sixth attempt to find any trace of them. He was convinced that they would come back from their holiday to find him. Asha had her doubts that they had survived Nox, but Kit clung to his faith in them. He needed to believe it, he needed to.

Suddenly, he yelled and flung his fist at the wall, a wince-worthy crack echoed from his bones and he shouted once again clutching his hand.

"*You really need to keep the noise down*," Asha hushed, her eyes warning. "It's the day, they could be around."

Hunters predominantly appeared at night because their paper-like skin couldn't withstand the sun. Even the slightest exposure to it burnt them like acid – Asha was eternally thankful they had a defect. However, it was easier to hunt humans in the day, so they had to cover up well if they wanted a better chance of a meal. Hence why Asha and Kit dressed like them, a disguise.

She picked up Kit's helmet and as she passed it to him; her eyes caught sight of the old newspaper sitting on the table. The headline read 'Global Peace Corporation: An End to World Hunger?'. She internally grimaced and turned away quickly - hunger had become the end of the world in every sense.

Kit groaned as he took his helmet back and looked at the paper too. "Wasn't their existence meant to stop shit like this from happening?"

"Does it really matter now?" she breathed out, defeated.

He shrugged and closed his eyes. Asha *did* agree with him, but she had learnt to live without too much hatred towards their incapability.

There was already enough to be angry at.

"I should've stayed with them," Kit sighed wishfully, looking back towards his house next door.

"And left me to die?" Asha questioned nonchalantly.

"What?" He said, his brow creased.

17

"If you hadn't found me that night, I would have died. You know that," she said, straightening her black dress over her thick tights.

"Let's just stop talking about that day, alright?"

"Alright... We should go," Asha suggested, one hand gripped on her knife, the other on the strap of her khaki backpack.

"Wait, I swiped this from Crazy Sock Lady next door," he said quickly, pulling out a plastic bottle of honey from his pocket.

Asha reached for it and immediately squeezed the sweetness onto her tongue, swallowing it slowly in its thick gooeyness. She smiled slightly at the feeling.

"You should keep the bottle, you're wasting away, Ash," Kit said, a concerned look across his face.

"Well, I'm sorry that I can't eat takeaways all the time anymore," she spat back before sucking down some more honey.

"Just saying,"

He was right, she had lost a lot of weight since Nox. He had too, but he'd still kept his muscles. He worked out as best he could. Asha didn't have the energy to, or the will power. Her body reflected the stress filled, traumatised and broken girl she felt like. She dreamt about being healthy and strong again, but it was merely a fantasy. Not one likely to come true, what with their diets consisting of scarcely found tinned foods and honey.

"I also got these," he said, brandishing a large pair of steel scissors. "Your hair's growing back."

Asha turned to glance in the long mirror on the wall, it was true, her hair was getting longer.

In the beginning, she decided to hack off most of her thick wavy locks, which usually tickled her lower back. She thought she'd feel liberated and headstrong, like girls did in the countless books and movies she'd devoured. But it didn't make her feel any better. What it did, was it showed her a version of herself who existed only in Nox. Her shoulder length bob and middle parting was her new identity. A way to make sure that the girl she used to know would never have to live through the new world.

"That gives us something to do today. We also need to get more petrol for the generator," she said.

"Plus, we can play Monopoly," Kit suggested. "What's the score? 55/45 to me?"

"You wish," Asha grinned, poking at his ribs.

She internally cringed at the thought that playing board games and getting petrol was her life now instead of smuggling pills into the clubs and getting drive-thrus on a Friday night.

"Come on then. Let's go home," he said before donning his helmet once again and heading to the front door.

Home. Home was no longer the four walls she stood in. Home had become the derelict house on the hill just outside of town, the one they had all feared. The truth now was that it was a blessing in disguise, it had saved them.

The first week in the house was one that felt like years to Asha.

Kit had found her passed out near her house on the verge of death that first night. He took it upon himself to grab everything useful he could from both their houses and haul it all –including her lifeless body- up the hill to the place where he knew no-one would be. Why he took them there? She wondered that too, but he never told her. She could only imagine he had seen or done some things that told him life as they knew it was over; home wasn't safe.

Her stab wound was the first obvious problem, but he cleaned and stitched it up before it became any worse. Then things spiraled. Nox survivors still went through the debilitating flu that eventually killed the others who weren't destined to be Hunters. Kit suffered horribly through it, all the while trying to heal Asha and her unique problem.

Her scratch burnt her and filled her body with the virus in a more intense way. She had a fever far higher than his and her insides felt like they were melting.

She squirmed and screamed for five days straight before Kit tried to end it.

Blame couldn't be put on him of course. After all, she was in a kind of pain that didn't look like it was letting up, and for all he knew she was only going to die in agony or become a Hunter anyway. He was vulnerable and recovering from the flu; he was at risk with her screeching down the house.

So, she wasn't really surprised to find herself waking up from an already disrupted sleep one night to his hands over her mouth and nose, tears streaming down his reddened face.

She remembered struggling for a few moments under his force, but after that, she just let him do it. As far as she was concerned, death was her only escape from the pain and heartache that had consumed her every cell.

But he couldn't do it.

He let go soon after she gave up struggling and just sobbed next to her on the mattress.

She tossed and turned the rest of the night wishing he'd finished it.

Now, she was happy that he didn't push through. She felt relatively normal, despite the strangely darkened blood running through her veins. She didn't feel any more psychotic than the world had made her; she wasn't one of them, she was sure of it.

Her hands reached for her black floppy hat, sunglasses and grey handkerchief before assembling them on her head, shielding her from the sun, and from any oncoming Hunters. She then gave herself one last look-over in the mirror before stalking out of the house and joining Kit.

They walked the streets, the bright sun casting two dark shadows, matching their dark attire. The wind picked up, it was cold, and it just reminded her that the winter was coming and that they would soon be up against another war, swapping their weapons from knives to fleece blankets. She shivered but kept her attention on the road in front of her. Her eyes glancing over the skulls and decomposed heads that were strewn around.

Hunters didn't like the heads.

They didn't bother her, not anymore. The only thing that would make her uneasy, would be seeing a fresh head; that meant danger was close by.

She was suddenly halted by a blood curdling scream in the distance. *I thought too soon.*

She turned to face Kit who was already grabbing for her hand and pulling her towards a nearby bush. He crouched down and dragged her with him. She barely found balance on her heels before he threw his visor open and pulled down the bandana covering her mouth. She took her sunglasses off, and her steely eyes met with his.

"Look or leave?" He asked, a little waver painting his voice.

She licked her lips and gathered her breathing, her stare holding his. The adrenaline that coursed through her veins was something that she had begun to crave. She stammered for a second longer as she thought about the soul whose wretched scream still rung around the air. They needed help and there sure as hell wasn't anyone else who was going to do it.

Survivors were a rarity. She and Kit had been alone throughout most of Nox; they preferred it that way. Less people meant less risk; they only ever needed each other. But they didn't have the choice to be selfish, they didn't have the luxury of staying in their comfort zone.

Moving on is a part of life and being scared tells you that you are alive.

With a heavy heart but fire running in her veins she drew a breath.

"Look."

Chapter Three

"What's our play here?" Kit whispered as he stood up. His eyes darted from her to their surroundings, trying to pinpoint direction.

"I don't know... find them first, then decide. We don't wanna be outnumbered. We can't put ourselves at serious risk... unless you're in the mood to fight?" Asha said, her narrow stare going to Kit who seemed to be fidgeting more than usual.

He thought for a moment with a wicked smile before shaking his head, mouth dropping. "We can't if there's no chance of winning. Though I do always want to fuck a Hunter up."

Another cry flew around the air, this time followed by unintelligible pleading from a man.

"Did you only bring your axe?" Asha asked, her heart beating a little faster now.

"Yeah, I didn't think we'd run into trouble. We haven't for weeks," he shrugged, looking a little frustrated.

"It'll have to do," she said, twisting her bag to her front and inspecting the inside. "I've only got my knives," she sighed, annoyed.

"Is this a good idea?" Kit asked, suddenly seeming worried.

"When do we ever have good ideas?" Asha grinned. "I got you," she said holding her hand out to him to shake.

"I got you back," he said, taking her hand and shaking it with muster.

The first thing they needed to do was find out exactly where the screams were coming from.

It seemed simple enough, but with English, terraced housing and countless alleyways, the puzzle became harder to solve.

They walked with pride; calmly, chins held high and hands absolutely *not* ready to attack. If there were Hunters around, they had to at least try and fool them. To them they'd be just a couple of fellow cannibals wandering the streets for their next meal. Although, how that helped with a plan to rescue the poor people, Asha really wasn't sure. All she knew was that they needed to get to them, for any hope of their survival.

They followed the ever-increasing yells with vigilant ears, their search finally coming to halt where the road broke into a crossroads. Asha caught a glimpse of a man kneeling on the tarmac, his face was puffy and crimson; she could see the tears dripping from his chin as he looked upwards. Her view was blocked from the rest of the scene by trees and buildings, so she located the nearest house that overlooked the crossroad and ran silently to the front door. There was too much chance of getting caught if they made noise, so she knelt down and pulled out the twisted hairpin from her bra and worked it through the keyhole.

Time wasn't on her side and as the cries became frantic, breathy and almost accepting of death; she could feel herself beginning to sweat. She whipped off her sunglasses and held her ear up to the keyhole, niggling the pin until it clicked open the lock.

A child's plea for help invaded her ears and her heart stopped.

Asha twisted the door handle and flung it open before racing on tiptoes through the house towards the living room to look to the road. The house itself stank of mould and damp; she averted her eyes from the family photos scattered around.

The scene through the large bay window played out before her. A mother, a father, a daughter; death. There were four Hunters. They looked manic, and even though their clothing covered every inch of them, their manner gave enough away. What looked like the leader was pacing joyfully around the family who were all sat in a line trembling on their knees.

The survivors had no weapons. The mother looked like she'd taken a severe beating, far more than what the father looked like and the younger girl... her hair stuck to the side of her face with red. Hunters were much like cats toying with their food before finally putting them out of their misery. It was the enjoyment that got Asha the most; she could see one of the Hunter's shoulders bouncing up and down while another pointed and threw their head back in response. They were laughing at them. Blood boiled in her. How had humanity come to this? Humanity had become a joke.

Kit pulled off his helmet and sighed.

"The fuck are you doing?" Asha whispered with urgency, taking down her handkerchief.

"I'm sorry," he began with sarcasm dripping, "but have you seen what's happening out there? There's more Hunters than people. We'd be screwed." He looked at her with wide eyes, he was sweating.

She looked to the hardwood floor, studying the cracks before letting out a long breath. As much as she hated it when it happened; Kit was right. The world was different now and getting used to it was half the battle.

Decisions like this broke her.

Back in the real world she couldn't even make a decision about what outfit to wear on a night out, let alone something like this. Did they leave the family for the taking or did they try and save them whilst simultaneously putting themselves in danger too?

"Max!" The mother yelled until her voice became raw.

Her husband wasn't answering; he just shook his head, letting tears hit the ground. The girl – who seemed around fourteen- was shuddering so hard she was finding it difficult to kneel up straight. One of the Hunters kept shoving her into place with their foot as they giggled.

Asha was frozen, unable to comprehend an action. She could feel Kit's heavy presence beside her, his head towering high above hers. She glanced up to him, his eyes were fixated on the girl, his jaw clenching and the veins in his forehead pulsing.

Asha took off her hat and held it against her chest. Her breathing slowed as her eyes stayed transfixed on the two groups of desperation. The only sound in the house was their hearts beating and their breath slowing. There was nothing they could do for the family, not unless they wanted to die too. They *were* being selfish, but they had no *choice*.

The mother placed her hands in prayer and began chanting to the sky, the girl stayed very much silent. Everything felt still, numb.

-Click-

Asha's entire body jolted to the sound that came from behind them, and as she swung around awkwardly on her heels, she saw him.

"Yeah, we got a couple of *Chameleons*," the Hunter said into a walkie-talkie with a snarky tone.

She hadn't realised it, but she'd dropped her hat and her knives were already out in front of her, braced to attack. The Hunter was draped in grey camouflage protecting every slither of skin.

She was alert but didn't dare make a move, not yet.

"I caught 'em 'bout a mile from here, tracked 'em. Thought they were clever just like the rest of the *Pures*. Fucking idiots," he said into the device.

"*You got the others with you?*" A voice stirred from the walkie-talkie.

"Yeah, they're on their way in case these rats decide to run." Even though she couldn't see the Hunter's mouth, she knew he was smirking. "Big rats mind you. Kill the others, we'll get these. We'll be eating well tonight," he slimed.

A final collective screech came from the other side of the window, followed by muffled gurgling. Throats slit, and they were next.

Time slowed down and Asha's mind began to kick itself into a flurry. *Find a way out.* Her eyes darted from the evil in front of them, to a clear route past him to the wide-open door. *But didn't he say there were more waiting for them? And won't the other four join in on the chase too?*

They were dead meat walking.

A sudden movement came from beside her along with a roar of anger. Kit's axe swung through the air, stilling straight into the Hunter's neck. Sunglasses now off, the pale man's eyes bulged so much she thought they'd pop out.

His hands swung to the wooden handle and pulled it free from himself unleashing a river of darkened blood. He tried to suck on the air, but he couldn't; instead came pathetic splutters.

They weren't about to hang around to see him truly go, so Kit lunged for his axe and began to make his way to the door. His gaze turned to Asha quickly with a slight nod before flattening himself against the wall by the door, checking the coast was clear. She hopped over the convulsing body of the Hunter and padded her way to the door frame, her knives causing indents in her palms. She leant against the opposite side of the door and looked out to the open. She couldn't see anyone, but they had to move immediately otherwise they'd be trapped.

A pinching thought came to her. "We can't go home," she whispered. "They'll find us, and we'll lose *everything.*"

"So, we run as far away as possible, for now," Kit ordered. Though he sounded hardened, his eyebrows were turned up and his eyes were glistening.

He grabbed her hand and pulled her out into the now volatile surroundings, and they began to run. They had no protection, no disguise. They were there for the taking.

Footsteps appeared on their tail.

Run.

Kit led the pair up and over fences, through gardens and finally towards the woodland park. Asha's lungs threatened to give up on her after ten minutes of non-stop running. She made a mental note to herself to work on her stamina, if they made it out of this alive of course.

Before long, they had lost them and reached the end of the park. With no more sign of the Hunters, they collapsed onto the leaf scattered ground, rolling and grabbing at their burning sides. Kit coughed violently beside her, and Asha just stared up at the trees against the bright sun, trying to steady everything from her body to her mind.

Nearby, a car engine hummed.

Air caught in her throat as she rushed back into a standing position. They had a car; of course they had a car. She glared at Kit, there was no way they could outrun a car. But they could weave through more houses, they could disappear.

"Get up," Kit ordered. He then pointed over towards the lake. "We stay away from the road. We can probably lose them through those trees and into the old school building."

"Right."

I can do this.

Their legs began to carry them once again, destination: not being murdered.

The car seemed to be getting closer, almost like it was paralleling them on the other side of the trees.

Hunters knew everything about humans, they knew their nature. That's what made them such intelligent killers; they knew their coding, their patterns, their outcomes. They were going to find them no matter where they ran. The only way they could ever escape them was to defeat them. That was one important thing they'd learnt since the beginning of all this. There was no *beating* them, there was only *ending* them. They had to end them. They had to end all of them.

Asha was lost in her train of thought as they started to run past the lake. But she was quickly brought out of it when Kit was swept from right in front of her and thrown into the lake by a seemingly invisible force.

What the-?

Without a thought, she jumped in after him, quickly clocking the Hunter who was wearing unusual, white attire holding her best friend below the icy waters. She waded rather awkwardly to them and brought her thinner knife up in the air before plunging it straight through the top of their head with a loud grunt.

The Hunter froze immediately, and Kit spluttered to the surface only to look wide eyed to behind her, prompting Asha to turn around to be faced with a jumping figure of black.

She let out a gasp and held up both her knives to the sky. The body fell on her blades, crushing her down to the lake's slimy bottom. Asha couldn't move and the shock of everything had her mouth open and drinking down the lake water. She opened her eyes; all she could see was murky green water as it consumed her.

Luckily, the heavy bulk of Hunter was quickly shifted, and two hands reached for her. Kit yanked her up to the surface with an exasperated breath. She choked on algae and spat out the remaining water lodged in her throat.

"Are you hurt?" He asked quickly, his heavy breaths leaving clouds in the air. He looked concerned as he twirled her around. He should have been more worried about himself; a bloodied gash boasted above his right eye.

She went with his movements for a second before pushing his arms away. "I'm fine, I'm fine," she said, though her wrists were hurting, and the blinding-cold was making her ache. "We need to get out of here." There was no telling how close the others were.

She shoved her knives into her bag, swam the brief distance to the water's edge and hauled herself out, cursing the season. If she was cold before, she was intolerably freezing now. Nights out without a jacket in winter hadn't been enough training for this. If they didn't get to warmth, they'd surely die of pneumonia, which would be ironic considering the circumstances.

"Come on, if we cut through the school and then over the bridge, we'll be home," breathed Kit as he hoisted his body up and out of the water.

"Home? We already agreed not to go there," she urged, dragging him into the trees for cover. "We can't lead them there," she shivered, whipping off her gloves - they were making her too cold.

"You wanna bet any of these other houses have a fucking generator? We need to get warm," he growled, rubbing his arms.

"Those two just came out of nowhere. We could be *surrounded,* Kit."

"…And we might not be," he looked around before meeting her stare. "The first guy said there were others, and I'm guessing we just killed them. And maybe the ones with the family stayed with them. They had to take their bodies some place safe, or others would steal them."

He had a point, and they'd been standing there talking for a minute without hearing a sound, not even a car.

31

"Maybe they've escaped with their loot. Them being nearby was just a coincidence," he said before motioning his hands to the lake. "They're gone. The others are too," the last bit left his voice wavering slightly.

"Let's just get the fuck out of here," she groaned; she was beginning to feel the cold biting into her bones. All she could think about now was getting into their lukewarm basement so she could feel something other than burning cold against her skin.

The journey was a slow one, what with the two of them being on acute guard of their surroundings, and numb limbs refusing to move them at a normal speed. They passed the school without an encounter, but every minute that passed, Asha felt less sense of her body. Kit was a shuffling mess by her side, he had a bit of meat on him, but nothing was enough to bear the cold. He wiped at the blood that kept dripping into his eye. She'd have to stitch that up probably.

Just as she thought she couldn't take any more of the outside, they turned the corner to the house on the hill. They couldn't get there fast enough; both of them grappling up the grassy hill on all fours to race there.

Kit yanked open the thick wooden door and Asha fell into the hallway revelling in the mild warmth of the boarded-up house. As she did so, however, her silver ring tumbled off her finger and rolled along the worn wooden floor. She quickly crawled to it before it fell through a gap and shoved it back on her finger. It was far too big for her now, meaning she spent a lot of time chasing after it. She refused to not wear it, she needed to feel close to her mamá.

Kit shut the door as quietly as possible and clicked down the large wooden lock, securing them from the outside world. He dropped to the floor and breathed out slow, steady breaths.

Asha glanced to him and couldn't help but start laughing. It was an uncontrollable and unexplained laughter, the kind you got in the minute silence at school. She looked at Kit through joyous, tear-filled eyes and he looked at her like she was crazy. But after a second, he started chuckling, and soon enough he was in fits of laughter too. Two minutes went by of utter madness.

Then came the knock on the door.

Chapter Four

Their laughter halted immediately.

Dread spilled into Asha's heart, and she suddenly felt sick. She glanced to Kit, but he was already staring at the door, his hand reaching for his axe. *Who could it be?* There was no way in hell a Hunter would use such politeness, they'd just knock down the door and attack. Which meant it must be another human or a '*Pure*' like the Hunters called them. But then what if it was a Hunter trying to trick them? Either way, someone had found them, they'd found their home.

"*Kit!*" Asha urged, keeping her voice below a whisper.

He looked to her and she shook her head hard. He shook his back like he was dismissing her. She frowned and let her eyes roam to the door.

Three more heavy knocks came.

She had forgotten about the icy coldness that had seeped through her clothes and into her flesh, the only thing she could feel was anxiety and it was making her chest hurt.

"Let us in!" It was a man and he sounded desperate. "*Please*, we know you're in there, we saw you go in," he said.

Us, we? There was more than one of them. Asha blinked, unmoving from her position on the floor. She then slowly reached for her knives and held them against her sides as she shuffled as quietly as she could towards Kit.

"Look," another voice came through, his voice thick with a South London accent. He took a calmer approach. "We can help you."

34

Help us? She felt Kit's hand go to her side and she looked at him in distress. They were trapped. There was nothing they could do except get up and face whoever was out there. They would break their way in sooner or later; the wood was rotten and barely held itself together anyhow. But this was their home, this was their safe place. It was all ruined now, tainted.

"*Come on, Max, let's leave them be for now,*" a kind, female voice said.

Familiarity shot through Asha like a bullet.

"*Did she just say Max?*" She breathed out quietly.

Kit looked confused for a moment before piecing it together. They were the rest of the dead group, the luckier half. The man at the door was who the woman was calling to and that's why the man didn't answer her. She was calling for backup; but they never came. They weren't Hunters, they were like them. They were survivors.

"*We need to find the others!*" The first man's voice came again. He sounded younger and less gruff than who she guessed was Max, the second voice.

Asha couldn't let them head back out there, not with Hunters nearby, and not with the likely possibility of finding their friend's heads on the road. She couldn't let that happen. And she wasn't about to let rare survivors get themselves killed, not a chance.

Shuffling footsteps began making their way down the hill. With a sharp intake of air, she quickly hauled herself to her feet, dropped her knives and raced for the door. Kit tried to grab at her ankles to stop her, but she already had a hand on the lock. She pulled it off with a grunt and thrust the door open, its hinges squeaking loudly in the cold air.

"Wait!" She cried, clocking the four people with their backs to her.

They weren't wearing anything over their heads; they were exposed to the sun which meant they *were* like them; they were safe. She felt relief wash over her, and yet sadness filled her faster than she could bear. All four turned quickly on their heels to face her.

Time to bear the bad news.

"Your friends," she began before taking a deep breath and sighing. "They're dead. I'm sorry."

She watched as their demeanours dropped, like the air had been sucked from their lungs. All but the lanky blonde girl who was probably just a couple of years younger than her; she seemed almost relieved. The tall, burly, shaven-headed black man who she instantly thought to be Max, looked over to the blonde girl and put his hand on her shoulder in a sympathetic way, but she shrugged him off with a roll of her eyes. He sighed heavily; Asha could feel his anguish even from where she was standing.

"The young girl?" The other man asked, his voice cracking. He was skinny with auburn hair that licked the bottom of his neck. He wore thick-rimmed glasses with the lenses missing.

Asha nodded her head mournfully, suddenly feeling Kit's presence beside her. "I'm sorry," she said weakly while rubbing her hands on her arms, the cold was burrowing in again.

"Oh god, those poor souls," the kind voice came from an older lady who had flowing red waves of hair, a bright contrast to the bleak surroundings. She seemed older than Max, who looked to be in his early forties, yet her skin was flawless. "*Daisy…*" she cried making her way over to the blonde girl with open arms.

The girl, Daisy, closed her eyes and just let her hug her. She must have been related to at least one of the dead; it would explain the attention she was getting. But her exterior showed otherwise. She seemed fucked off at the sympathy she was receiving. She had long, wispy blonde hair which shielded her from the outside world. Her angular cheekbones suited her.

Asha felt a pang in her chest, and it wasn't from the cold. This was exactly the reason why she and Kit had stayed away from the notion of a group. Loss was inevitable. But despite that thought, she wanted to help them. She knew as well as everyone else around her what it was like to lose someone close, and she knew that even a simple pick-me-up was enough to make at least a little difference. They had food and drink, and they had a sort of warm place to sit. The least they could do was invite them in for the night, let them recover and have a small amount of safety.

Something Max had said suddenly came to her mind again.

"I'm sorry for what's happened, I really am," Asha's teeth started to chatter, she knew she had to get inside quick, "but you said you could help us. What did you mean?"

Max nodded his head and walked closer to her, his back hunched. She noticed his greying facial hair when she stopped in front of her. "Maybe if we talked inside it would be safer?" He asked, his eyebrow raised slightly. He had this almost cockney charm to him, she felt strangely safe and at ease around him.

"Whoa, hold on," Kit held his hand up towards Max's chest, he stopped.

"Sorry?" The burly man replied, his charming exterior holding strong.

"You can't just expect us to let you in and play happy fucking families," Kit exclaimed. "For all we know, you could be *Reapers*," and with that, he shot Asha a piercing glance and she glared back.

Reapers were people who were immune but kidnapped and sold other immune people to Hunters in return for their safety – like a tax the mafia would set.

But these people couldn't be Reapers, they had lost their friends, Hunters wouldn't have killed their own workers. Besides, they didn't look the sort; they were too mismatched and expressive of emotion. Something that Reapers lacked was humanity, after all, any person with who would knowingly entice and betray a fellow person to their death was no human at all.

"Kit, I don't think-" Asha started but he interrupted her.

"And how the fuck are *you* going to help *us*?" He pushed, his stance strengthening.

She gauged Max's reaction expecting him to assert himself before Kit, but he just looked down, shook his head and smiled, like he was disappointed and frankly amused by his offence. Even though their eyelines matched, Kit seemed smaller somehow.

Asha took the moment and looked past Max to the others in his group, trying to get an idea of them. Daisy was looking off into the distance with her arms tight across her chest. The red-headed lady stared on worriedly at Max and the skinny man stood beside her, his hand on her shoulder. They weren't evil, you could just see it, they were just like them. And even if they *were* Reapers, there were four of them, they'd get inside anyway.

"We're going somewhere safe, where this doesn't exist," Max explained as he straightened himself up, maybe to seem more in charge, which worked because Asha found herself looking up to him in awe.

The first thought that came to her mind was about how cliché it was. In all the movies she'd seen, there was always a 'safe place' that the hero had to get to. But now, actually being in an apocalyptic reality, the mere whisper of a safe haven stirred her curiosity and her hope.

How could such a place be real?

She couldn't believe him, but a large part of her jumped for joy at the idea of a place where people weren't eating each other. She'd thought about it before, about a place which had been spared from the sickness, but it was always a dream, a stupid fantasy. Now, someone was right there, telling her it was real. The skinny man walked forward to stand next to Max.

"He's right," he affirmed. "He works there."

Asha stared at both of the men in front of her with a furrowed frown. She was confused and torn between believing in such a place and telling herself it was impossible. Suddenly her scar started to itch so she let her fingers go to it, relieving the discomfort.

"Christ!" the skinny man breathed hurriedly, his eyes sticking fast to her neck, to her black scar.

Kit quickly batted her hand away from it and pulled up her top to cover it again. The skinny man looked to Max who looked back at him with a slight smile.

"When did that happen?" The man asked, his voice quiet and impatient as he pointed to her neck.

"Six months ago," Asha admitted, studying the two men in front of her, suddenly feeling vulnerable, like an animal in a zoo.

There was a moment of heavy silence that followed her answer. She didn't know what was going through their heads, but they seemed perplexed and elated at the same time. She felt uncomfortable as she was scanned and scrutinised by strangers. Everything in her just wanted to go inside, get her icy damp clothes off her and play a game with Kit; but instead, she was faced with a different path.

They looked at her now with a sense of victory.

"We can help you," Max repeated himself. "And the rest of the human race."

*

The basement felt a lot cosier with the four extra bodies to contribute their heat. Asha was grateful for it because even after taking off her clothes and changing into dry ones, she was still shivering violently. She sat with her legs crossed on the mattress on the floor along with Kit who was annoyed because she let the others in.

The others who -after formalities- she now knew as Max, Daisy, Leo and Piper, were gathered on various pieces of furniture and floor space. Before discussion went down about their future, Asha had gathered some of the food and drink they had and distributed it between everyone. Daisy wasn't interested in her food apparently as she hadn't touched a thing, but the others were appreciating it, scoffing their energy bars and gulping their fruit juices. Asha gingerly nibbled on her peanut bar, too excited and unnerved to eat. Kit didn't seem to have an appetite either as all he did was sit with his arms rested on his knees, not taking his eyes off the others.

"Thank you for this, we appreciate it," Piper smiled gesturing at her food. Her voice was fairy-like.

"It's the least we could do," she replied. And it really was, they'd lost half their people after all.

"So, are you going to tell us what's going on, or are we just going to sit and have a lovely lunch together?" Kit pestered loudly and Asha rolled her eyes.

He really knew how to bring the tone down.

Max squeezed his juice carton and sucked up the rest of it before pulling it from his lips and wiping his mouth with the back of his hand. "You know something Kit; you got a real big attitude, and it ain't gonna get you anywhere."

"I tell you what's not gonna get me anywhere, you wasting my time."

Asha sent a hand flying into Kit's chest; he recoiled and let out an annoyed gasp. It seemed to shut him up enough to let Max speak.

"Look, it don't matter if you don't like me, 'cause I don't care, alright? I think the world is past holding grudges, don't you?" He paused for a second, gathering breath. "There's a place called Harbour. It's off the coast up north on an island. That night, we closed the docks and we killed whoever turned into one of 'em. We lost almost everyone in that purge. When everythin' was secured, I put myself forward as a Finder. There ain't many of us, but we go out to the mainland to try to find Pures."

It was all too much to take in. If what he was saying was true, then that meant there was somewhere they could be safe, somewhere they could live normal lives once again.

41

Asha couldn't help the hope that rose like wildfire in her stomach.

"As it stands there are about four 'undred of us there. I've been on mainland for about two weeks now. An' as you can see, I ain't barely found anyone. I'm hoping the reason for that is 'cause everyone's become better at hiding themselves. But I doubt that's the case." He looked saddened, his brow creasing and his large hand rubbing his shaven head. "But, now we've found you," he smiled. "And you've just given us more than you could ever know."

"Again, with the fucking mystery!" Kit moaned loudly.

"Will you shut the hell up?" Daisy spat. Asha was surprised at her interjection; she looked more annoyed than Kit did; it was the first time they'd heard her voice. "We're trying to help you, you arrogant, bloody arsehole. Just fucking listening to you makes me wish we never stopped at this shit-hole. Like you're worth saving or something."

Kit stood up then, his face fuelled with anger. Everyone became tense for a brief second, but he just turned to the wall and punched it with an angry grunt followed by a small cry. He took to pacing then while rubbing his hand of the pain. The second time that day where his knuckles had taken the brunt of his rage.

"*Drama Queen,*" Daisy muttered, rolling her all-encompassing eyes.

"Maybe you should shut the fuck up. Who gave you the moral high ground anyway?" Kit jibed.

"How about everyone shuts the fuck up!" Asha shouted, getting too anxious over the situation.

42

"Everyone let's just be thankful we're all alive and together, please," Piper begged, her red hair falling over her shoulder. She was definitely the type of lady who did yoga and grew her own vegetables. Asha could bet she had children who she doted on. *Had.*

"Enough with the fuckin' bickering, alright?" Max's voice boomed around the basement and Asha shot him a glance to keep it down. He gave her a taught nod before lowering his voice. "You want answers, I'll give 'em." Kit huffed and folded his muscular arms but let Max continue. "The fact that you're immune like you are, Asha, means we can advance toward a proper cure and put an end to all this... We've already developed something to help stave off the effects of the infection, but to actually cure someone, we need the DNA and blood of, well, a real immune person; and in this case, that'd be you."

"Y-you need my blood?" She questioned, her voice shaking from all the new and confusing information.

"Yes, and other things too. Don't be scared, they ain't gonna kill ya. They'll just need samples for testing," Max responded.

"I need a piss. You guys got a toilet round here?" Daisy asked, her upfront manner was growing on Asha. She was certainly braver than the dark-haired girl was, it was something that she admired in her. Her question did however throw her off guard slightly, seeing as they were discussing the future of the world and how it lay in her blood.

"Uh, yeah, go up to the main house and turn right, there's a room in there. It's not exactly pretty," Asha advised.

43

The plumbing went relatively quickly after the world turned into a hot pile of shit, so they had to make do. There was a bucket, toilet paper (if they were lucky) and a large hole outside to dispose of their business. Dignity had been long forgotten. And hygiene? Let's just say the rainy English weather was their best friend.

Asha missed baths.

Daisy didn't thank her -not that she was expecting it- and just skulked her way out of the basement door.

"So, you're telling me that if I get to Harbour, they can make a cure and we can turn everything back to normal?" She asked, her heart hammering to the tune of new hope.

"With a lot of work, yes," Max nodded his head, a clear air of confidence in his eyes.

"Well, what the fuck are we waiting for then?" Kit proclaimed, his hand still rubbing his now badly bruised knuckles.

Max sighed as he rubbed his shaven head. "As much as I'd like to go now, there's no point. The boat won't be there for a week."

"What bo-" Asha began to ask but was cut short.

"There's a boat that comes to pick up Finders. We all get three weeks to search for people before we have to go back. There's one port and one day when it'll be there. We usually have radios to talk to them but mine, and my replacement, got trashed. So, in normal cases, I'd be on that thing like a bloody cheetah telling them to come early. But, until we find another radio to contact them, we've got some time to fill," he sighed again, deeper this time.

Asha glanced at Kit who seemed a little calmer now, he caught her eye, and he bit his lip before tilting his head towards the corner of the room. Her eyebrows creased but she eventually got that he wanted her to come over and chat. He walked to the boasting bookcase, and then stood waiting for her. She tiptoed her way across to him giving Max a reassuring smile before standing by Kit.

"I don't know about this," he said, his voice laced with unusual worry.

"Kit, I-I know you want to protect what we have here, and us. But how long were we meant to live like this, hmm?" She said, her voice barely making a peep. "It couldn't have lasted forever. There's a place where we can be normal again," she urged.

"I like it here," he stood his ground, being as stubborn as ever.

"We could save everyone. Cure the sick,"

"Like those fucking things deserve to be saved after what they've done," he protested, his face twisted in disgust.

"We're doing this," Asha ordered, unwavering, her heart thumping against her ribs.

He was quiet for a moment, but she could feel the hum of life coursing through his veins; he was nervous. "I'll sleep on it."

"Good," Asha smiled, knowing full well that he was going to agree with the changes, he just had to make it seem like he was in charge, that it was his decision.

She turned to the rest of the room and made her way back to her seat on the mattress. One of the springs popped up against her and she quickly adjusted her seating, making room for Kit to join her.

She glanced around the room, feeling oddly happy about the company they had. Piper was staring happily at her, Asha smiled softly.

"This place is so interesting!" The redhead smiled gracefully.

"Thank you, there's a funny story about it actu-" before Asha could finish her sentence, a shrill scream pierced the air along with a sickening crash. Goosebumps coated her skin and panic engulfed her brain.

Daisy.

Chapter Five

There was something so painful about Daisy's scream, that it resonated deep within Asha, rippling through her like a lightning bolt. Her immediate reaction was to see what Kit was doing. It seemed to be her reaction to most things in life, *what would Kit do*? He just stood dead still, along with the rest of their newly found friends. Piper's eyes bulged like something just shot through her heart. Leo swallowed loudly and Max clenched his jaw before suddenly racing towards the door.

Shit.

"We're not losing anyone else!" He yelled as he bustled out of the room.

With a sharp breath, Asha followed quick on her feet, almost tripping up the stairs from the speed. Hurried footsteps rang behind her, and as they reached the main house, she ran to Max who had turned down one of the dusty hallways. He launched himself into one of the abandoned rooms.

There, they found her.

"Right, everyone back up. This whole thing could collapse," Max ordered. They all shuffled back to the outskirts of the room. Asha craned her neck to see where the blonde girl was.

Daisy -who was swearing incoherently- was curled up in an unusually vast space between the floor and the ceiling of the basement below. It looked like the rotten floorboards had given way under her, despite her tall yet tiny frame.

Asha assessed Daisy from where she stood. She came across something worrying. Daisy had her hand pressed against the fleshy part of her forearm; blood pumped from beneath her fingers. She'd been cut by something on her way down and Asha quickly spotted the culprit; a rusty nail within a floorboard - it dripped with deep red.

Max reached out his hand for Daisy to take but she refused and shook her head stubbornly. For a girl who'd just fallen through a house she looked more irritated than broken.

"I can't get to you, you gotta take my hand," Max urged, keeping his voice quiet but steady. Then he realised the problem. "*Ah,*" he said under his breath. "Okay, you just gotta reach up, I need to get you outta there, alright?"

She nodded her head slowly before reluctantly freeing her bloodied hand and holding it up to Max. He gripped her just under her elbow and yanked her up; Leo helped bring her onto the floor. She let out a pained grunt as they laid her down. She quickly put her hand back to stem the bleeding, but on her way up the wound had spilled a faint-worthy amount of blood, and it showed no sign of letting up.

"I'm fine," she huffed, but her face was showing a vulnerability that threatened to melt her icy front.

"I think that's the opposite of fine, Daisy," Asha said, her eyebrow rising.

The blonde girl gave her a scowl.

"Everyone out of the room," Max said before lowering himself to Daisy. "I'm gonna pick you up and you better not squirm," he demanded.

She rolled her eyes but didn't protest. He had no trouble lifting her up; it was like he was

48

picking up an empty cardboard box.

Asha couldn't help but watch as blood dripped onto the wood below. *Tap, tap, tap.*

"I'll need all the medical stuff you have!" Piper demanded as they all rushed down to the basement with Max leading.

Asha nodded and branched off the main basement to the large room at the back of the house. Kit followed her, probably not wanting to get involved with the emergency at hand. She clicked open the door hurriedly and quickly lit the large candle in the entrance. Her arms stretched out, guiding her way through the dark room. When she reached the back, she sank to the floor and rummaged through their 'doctor's bag', which was essentially every medical thing they'd collected over the past six months.

"This is bad. Did you see how deep that cut was? I wouldn't be surprised if she bled out by the time we get back in there," Kit said, pacing around, arms folded.

"Shut up," Asha retorted. He was distracting her.

Most of the stuff they had was useless for now like painkillers and thermometers. They did have bandages and a sewing kit which they would definitely need. But antiseptic... She flicked away boxes of plasters and pulled out the one TCP bottle they had; it had but a drop left. *Typical.*

She knew that the five pharmacies in their town had been picked clean, not even a cough sweet littered the floors. That was what happened when the world fell into disease and disorder, people panicked.

Without antiseptic, Daisy would get an infection for sure, and they didn't have the medicine to fight it off. She would most certainly die. Asha clenched her jaw and gripped the entire bag before sprinting to the others with Kit hot on her heel.

When they got to the room, Daisy had been laid on their bed, her skin was white as a sheet and her eyes were closed - she was shaking profusely. Piper sat next to her, her fingers working at tying a t-shirt underneath the wound. She was keeping her arm high above her head, but the blood kept coming, rolling in multiple rivers down her arm. The cut was extensive; raw flesh as bright as a rose glistened under the makeshift tourniquet. The mattress was becoming soaked in blood and a metallic taste coated Asha's mouth.

"*She's losing too much blood*," Piper said, her voice was hushed as if trying to keep the information from Daisy whose breathing had increased tenfold; a prominent sweat blanketed her forehead. "Her blood pressure is decreasing rapidly because of it. She's going to get blood poisoning." The redhead looked worried as she glanced back to Daisy. "She needs antibiotics, insulin and vasopressors. Do you have any of those?"

Asha shook her head but passed the bag to Piper still. Kit quickly swapped places and held Daisy's arm up while Piper pulled out what she needed from the doctor's bag. Once she was finished, she sat on her heels and sighed, her fingers easing the pressure between her eyes.

"Even if I sow this up and clean it, the infection will take her," she breathed sadly. "There's no point in trying unless we get what she needs."

"There must be something in this fucking bag!" Max bellowed as he snatched the thing from Piper. She let him and gave Asha a reassuring look while he began flinging all the useless stuff across the room. "I'm not losing her! You hear her? We can't lose her."

"All the pharmacies are bare," Asha interjected. "Our only chance at getting anything close to *vasso-*?" She quickly looked to Piper for clarification.

"Vassopressors," she offered, a kind smile on her lips. She swapped places with Kit once again.

Asha nodded her head in thanks. "*Vassopressors,* is if we go to the hospital in the next town. It's the only place that might have what we need," she said, her eyes fixed on Max for his response.

"How long by foot?" He asked.

"About two hours," she replied. "But with those Hunters out there, who knows how long it could take us."

"We've got a chance to save a person's life. I say we go," Leo joined in, adjusting his pointless glasses.

He was right; even if it meant risking their lives in the process, they needed to keep every sane soul alive, otherwise they had no chance of recovering the world as they once knew it.

They had to go to the hospital.

"Whoa, hold on a second. We can't all go. We need to decide who goes and who stays," Kit moaned, making a somewhat fair point.

Someone had to stay with Daisy, if not two people. And either one out of Kit or Asha had to stay to protect their home. But the question was, who?

"I'm staying," Piper said, her face firm. "I was a nurse; I need to be here with her."

"What about when we get to the hospital? How will we know what to get?" Asha asked, worried at the prospect of leaving the medically trained person behind.

"I'll make you a list," Piper smiled wearily before rummaging around for something to write on.

"Well, I'm going," Max announced, his arms crossed against his hard chest. It made sense; he was a seemingly natural leader, and he was the guy whose job it was to save people from this hell.

Asha looked to Kit to wager his decision. She hated the idea of being split from him, but it was the only way, and he knew it too. He gave her his 'I dunno' face and she rolled her eyes.

"I'll go," she eventually said, stopping him from having to make a decision.

She was faster than him anyhow and he'd taken a knock to the head earlier. Maybe she was their best shot. He looked a little apprehensive, and a distinct look of worry washed over his face.

"Wait, Ash," he said, striding towards her, his hand finding its way on her shoulder. "Are you sure? I-I dunno how I feel about this, " he urged, she could see the fear in his eyes, screaming out to her.

"I'll be fine," she assured him. He always tried to be the stronger one but more often than not, it was Asha who came out on top. "Honestly."

He clenched his jaw and bore his stare straight into her. "Be careful," he said before leaning into her ear to whisper. "*If things go bad. You can take him; I know you can.*"

52

What he said scared her slightly. Did he really think there was a chance that Max would turn on her? She gave him a puzzled look before looking at the large, hulking man. He was strong, muscly, fearless. She didn't know why Kit thought she had the ability to take him on. That bash to the head had definitely done more than just cut him.

"I'm coming too. More the merrier, right?" Leo said. "Kit can do a well enough job at keeping these two safe, right?"

"Sure I can!" He huffed, standing up straight and puffing out his chest.

"Right, so that's sorted then," Max said before taking a deep breath. "Me, Leo and Asha will go to the hospital. Get your bags ready; essentials only," he commanded.

"Here's the list," Piper chimed as she passed Asha an old, crumpled receipt. "I couldn't write a specific antibiotic, but I wrote anything with 'cillin', 'cycline' or 'floaxcin'. Try to get the last two, just in case she's allergic to penicillin." She pressed her lips together and gave Asha a tight nod before returning her attention to the critical blonde.

*

They dressed themselves appropriately –Asha in dark skinny jeans, and a grey hooded cloak, Max in a black Shearling jacket and Leo in a thick Parka- and packed their bags with all the stuff they needed. Then it was time to say goodbye.

That was the problem nowadays; a simple goodbye could mean forever.

Dread began to grow in Asha's stomach; a nauseous concoction swelling back and forth. She felt sick about the possibility of leaving her home and best friend for the last time. *No,* she thought, *you'll make it.* She let that thought engulf her into a sense of security; it helped a touch with the idea of leaving.

"You sure you'll be okay? I can go instead if you want?" Kit asked. He looked pale, exhausted.

"Shut up, okay? I'm going. You need to stay here and guard. Besides, you've probably got concussion from that fall in the lake. It's better if you stay here anyways," she shrugged, trying to bombard him with reasons he should stay, so that he'd feel more at ease letting her go.

Truth be told she was terrified of being out there without a friend. It was all happening so fast; it unsettled her. Just this morning she and Kit were perfectly adjusted to their life in the basement. And now they were being thrown into all sorts of different scenarios, with talks of a safe place, a cure, of immunity. It made her head hurt, but she had to go with the flow if she wanted to survive. And yes, it was scary. Change *was* scary. But ultimately life was a nonstop journey of change. There was no way of stopping it. whether it led to bad or good. And in this case, she was hoping and praying for the latter outcome.

Piper put the finishing touches to the cut, closing it. Asha made her way over to Daisy, the reason for their daring escapade, and gently smoothed her matted hair.

"Just hang in there," she whispered. The blonde girl looked sickly, like she didn't have much time left. Asha breathed a small sigh before standing herself up and nodding to Max.

He returned the motion and clapped his hands. "We're leaving."

They marched their way up the stairs, she, Max and Leo. Kit followed close behind, leaving Piper in the basement with Daisy. As they approached the door, Asha gave Kit a long hug, making sure to hold onto the moment. She then pulled away and gave him a small smile and he smiled back quickly before looking to the floor. Her heart dropped slightly as she swallowed the lump in her throat. She was stronger than this. She held up her chin, pulled out her knives and took a deep breath.

It was time.

She cracked open the door and took a quick look outside. The air seemed still and from the first look, the coast seemed clear. She put up her hood and took a step into the world. Max's large stride came up behind her and she felt immediately sure of their ability to do this…until a voice of uncertainty came from the doorway.

"Uh, on second thought," murmured Leo, who stared out to the surroundings, his eyes wide. "Maybe I-I…"

"Cat got your tongue, Leo?" Max sighed slowly; his disappointment clear as he glanced back to him.

"Not that, no, not exactly. Anyway, you two will be faster, right? And, plus, Kit isn't fully capable of really looking af-" he stammered before Max butted in.

"Just go back inside," he said lowly. "You're wasting fucking time."

Asha gave Leo a glare, her eyes dark. How could he be so fearful? With that kind of attitude, she wondered how he'd managed to stay alive as long as he had.

She briefly thought about all that she'd had to endure since this all started. Her body rocked from the memories, but it was because of them she was who she was today. Surely Leo had been through a similar experience, how did he still back away at the sign of danger?

She felt angry at him, she wasn't entirely sure why. Maybe it was because deep down she was scared, scared of going out there with one man short. Or maybe it was because she couldn't stand to see someone cower away when another person's life was at hand.

"Cheers for lowering our chances, *coño*," she spat.

Leo looked confused at her Mexican insult and then defeated before giving them a mumbled 'sorry' and retreating back into the darkness of the house. Asha's eyes lingered on the wooden door for a moment before she felt Max's hand touch her shoulder.

"Time to go, Kiddo."

The journey to the hospital was surprisingly uneventful. As night started to fall, however, Asha's nerves did start to creep in. Even so, they managed to avoid any run-ins with the Hunters, which she was extremely thankful for because after the day they'd had, all her energy had been used. She would struggle in a fight.

Night had fully dawned on them by the time they reached the hospital's entrance. The whole place was deathly still. It felt sinister, like it didn't want them there. Her mind flitted to the countless horror movies set in abandoned hospitals and she shuddered. All of a sudden, the building was even more daunting. She wiped her brow of sweat and looked to Max for the next step.

He surveyed the vast building, his eyes landing on the huge revolving glass front door.

"Could it be this easy?" He murmured quietly.

His large hand pushed gently against the glass as Asha stood by, her hardened eyes glancing from him to the all-consuming darkness that seemed to inch towards them like a fog.

A loud click resonated in the silent air and her breath stilled, waiting for movement from around them. They stood quietly for a beat before deeming it safe to push through into the hospital.

She looked to Max who pulled his finger to his mouth and made a 'shh' gesture before giving her an awkward smile, which she found herself returning as she followed him inside.

Apparently, it *was* that easy.

Asha whipped out her torch and Max did the same. She flicked it on and what shone before her was a large sterile reception left in disarray. She didn't dwell on the haunting feeling; they had a task to complete. They made quick work on finding the first storage cupboard. Max shifted the door open, her mouth dropped. It was empty. Completely bare, like it had never been filled.

"Shit," Max muttered under his breath.

"*En serio?*" Asha whispered before shooting off down another corridor to another cupboard.

Empty.

Quiet panic spun around them as they began to tear through every storage unit
they could find. Empty, empty, empty.

Everything was gone.

They stood in a stunned state after what seemed like the hundredth empty drawer. Asha tried to comprehend how every last morsel of medicine had disappeared from such a large hospital. They couldn't even find shitting paracetamol. It was bizarre.

"What do you need?" A distant voice asked from the darkness.

\

Chapter Six

They turned around swiftly. Asha held her torch and knife out shakily in front of her. Both their beams landed on a guy who stood at around 6 feet; he wore a grey t-shirt, a dark green jacket, and black jeans. More notably, he was wearing a creepy old-fashioned gas mask. It obscured his face completely. His hands were covered by black gloves too.

He was hiding his skin, which would usually leave Asha to believe he was a Hunter. But it was dark, there was no need to cover up. She was left confused by his appearance, and equally as confused at the offer he had laid on the table.

Max began to walk towards the guy who took a slight step back before standing his ground.

"What do you mean, boy?" Max questioned; his voice sounded rougher than before somehow.

"I have everything," the guy mumbled through the mask. One of his hands went behind his back, like he was reaching for a weapon.

The burly man stepped forward defensively.

"Max, wait," Asha urged. He looked to her and took a step back to be with her once again. She didn't want any conflict; she just wanted the medicine and to get out of there. She looked to the gas-masked guy. "What's your name?" She asked.

"Finn Thorne," he answered quickly but with uncertainty, like he wasn't supposed to say it.

Asha was still for a moment, judging the situation along with Max. Could they trust the perfect stranger? In times like that there wasn't really an option.

"Right, well, *Finn Thorne*, how about you take off that mask? We're not gonna hurt you. And it ain't the day," Max ordered.

Finn hesitated for a moment; silent and unmoving. He looked like something out of a nightmare, the kind of thing that would chase you until your lungs burst and you shot awake with a scream. A few more seconds went by before he began to fiddle with the gas mask. He wiggled it off, and underneath was a boy who looked around eighteen.

He held up a hand against their light, but Asha could make out his key features.

His skin was lightly tanned, and he had this chestnut, messy hair which stuck up in light peaks. From behind his hand, she could just about see his face; he had these almost quaint lips and a pert nose all of which lay under squinted golden eyes. Moles scattered across his face.

She felt an unusual flutter across her chest, a foreign feeling, an unwanted feeling. Of-course she knew what it was, attraction, lust. But she pushed that aside. The most important thing of all was his skin; he was Pure, and he was alone.

"That's better," Max grinned, giving him a solitary clap of the hands.

"Listen, I'll give you what you need," Finn said, his voice a lot clearer now, though he looked a little nervous. "But I need to ask you some questions first."

Asha was a little thrown by this. They had all the weapons they needed to bring him down in one easy attack. Who did he think he was?

"What?" Max asked, taking a threatening step closer to the honey-eyed boy.

"It's just what I ask everyone," Finn chirped, holding his hands up in defense.

"So, a lot of folks pass through here?" Max asked, his voice taking a more serious tone.

"Not anymore. In the beginning, there were lots… I haven't seen anyone in a while."

"*Mierda*! Would you hurry up with the 'all important' questions? We don't have fucking time," Asha urged.

"Okay, okay," Finn started. "What are your names?"

She let out a deep breath. "I'm Asha; he's Max, next question."

"What are you here for?" He questioned the pair.

His boyish looks made him seem more fragile and far less intimidating than the mask-wearing guy they'd first met. It didn't help that he seemed to be trembling slightly, but for all Asha knew, he might have been cold.

"One of our group is dying from blood poisoning. In fact, in the long time we've been speaking, she's probably *died*," Asha huffed. This boy - although hot - was getting on her last nerve.

Finn's face dropped slightly, and he clenched his jaw. "Sorry, follow me," he said before turning his back to them and walking further into the darkness of the hospital corridors.

They followed.

61

"What's with all the questions, Thorne?" Max pestered him as they walked.

"Some people are here for the wrong reason, that's all."

"And what's that supposed to mean?" Asha asked.

She noticed she was being particularly hostile towards the boy, and part of her hated that, but she couldn't help it. She was tired, hungry and down on her luck. She just wanted the medicine, and to be back in her bed. The other part of her, however, held a strange need for the boy, something that she decided to ignore; using all the effort she had.

"It means they come for a high or they come for enough drugs to knock out a person. I just want to make sure stuff goes to the right people is all," Finn replied, exasperated.

"Right," Max pondered. "And what if they *do* want those things? What do *you* do about it?"

Finn -although scary with the mask- didn't seem like a particularly strong kind of person. He wasn't scrawny, in fact, Asha had noticed muscle pushing through his grey t-shirt before, but he didn't seem very capable of fighting. He seemed like a pushover. All Max had to do was ask him once to take off his disguise and he did it. She was full of thoughts about the weak boy in front of her; that was until she noticed what was in his belt.

A gun.

"I deal with them," Finn replied shortly, barely giving them a look back as he strode ahead.

She nudged Max and pointed at Finn's gun. Max nodded his head in acknowledgment but didn't seem too bothered by it.

She thought about it, Finn didn't really seem like a threat, besides, he could have killed them before they'd even seen him, and yet here they were.

She heard Max pull his bag quietly over from his shoulder and unzip it. Looking over she immediately saw what he had in there. There were at least three guns. She was concerned about Finn having one already, but Max too? A feeling of fear crept into her, being outnumbered in weapons was not good news for her. Besides, when did England become as loaded as the fucking cartel?

If things did go wrong, she'd be caught in the crossfire. She'd be done for. She tried not to think about that possibility and just concentrated on following Finn who seemed to be heading for a dead end. Once Max was satisfied with what Asha had seen, he zipped his bag back up and slung it over his shoulder with a slight grunt.

They stopped at what seemed like nothing. Asha shone her light around them; there were no doors, no windows, just a huge metal wardrobe. Her eyebrows clinched together, and she turned her light back to Finn who was standing perfectly still. He took a little breath and let it out almost like a whisper.

"Tell me what you need, and wait here," he ordered lightly.

"What? Why?" She asked, annoyed. *Stop, matona.*

"Just stay, please. I won't be long," he said, his voice shaking slightly.

Asha was getting a little tired of him being so in control, like he owned the place or something. He'd stockpiled everything in the hospital and now he wouldn't even let them in his secret den.

Oh shit, here we go.

"You can't just take everything for yourself, you know. That's playing God! Who the fuck gave you the right to be in charge? Everyone deserves to be helped, who are you to make the decision between life and death?" She shouted, not meaning for her voice to be so loud. It echoed uncontrollably around the desolate building.

Max placed his strong hand on her apparently trembling shoulder, and she halted her rant. "Just let the boy get us what we need," he said, his teeth clenched. "Where's that list, Asha?" He asked and she could almost hear him smiling through his teeth. He was trying to apologise for her actions, like a husband covering for his out-of-control, drunk wife at a quiet dinner party.

She shoved her way out from his grip, delved into her bag and pulled out the list before storming over to Finn and slapping it into his open palm. "Make it quick," she barked.

Finn's eyelids fluttered shut but he opened his eyes after a second with a small smile and turned towards the wardrobe. She noticed he had dimples when he smiled - *Jesus wept*.

Her stare remained on him with her torchlight highlighting his every move.

He clicked open the large steel door and edged his way inside. She made sure to follow his trail with her light. Inside the wardrobe there was a hole to the back of it. That's where Finn ducked into, but before he shut himself off from them, she caught glimpse inside the room that was hidden.

She saw a woman lying in a hospital bed.

Finn covered the hole he'd just come from with a sheet of steel and Asha had to stop herself from barging in after him. She knew she just had to cooperate, and they could leave with what they needed, without someone getting hurt.

She stood for a second when suddenly the smell of rot invaded her mouth and nostrils making her gag. Max coughed to the side of her and spat on the floor. It was a wind of death. The smell made her feel so nauseous that she had to hold her hand over her mouth to stop herself from throwing up. Had that come from the room Finn went into? It must have. There was no other explanation for it. The woman. The woman in bed, she must have been…

"There's a dead woman in there," Asha said to Max who spat two more times on the floor.

"Y'think?" He asked mockingly, wiping his lips with the back of his hand.

A smell like that was something she'd rarely come across. Most of the dead people that she'd encountered had either been fresh or void of their bodies. Also, the majority of the time, they were outside where the air could disperse most of the horrid scents.

But here, tucked away in a room where a body could fester, it was sickening. She couldn't stand to be there any longer. She needed to get some air, but she wasn't about to leave without what they came for.

"We need to hurry back, and we need to take him with us," Max breathed carefully.

"Take him *with* us?" Asha retorted sharply, though her buried thoughts sprung to attention and excited her.

"Yes," Max simply replied.

Asha rolled her eyes and instead let her mind think about why Finn would have a dead woman in the place where she presumed he lived.

He'd obviously figured out a way to hide both himself and whoever that was in there, what with the carefully placed wardrobe and secret entrance. He cared about them. He cared about them a lot. Her heart sunk. Maybe he wasn't as selfish as she'd concluded. He was protecting that lady at all costs. She didn't look like she was dead when Asha caught sight of her, which could only mean that she went recently. Maybe he couldn't let her go. Asha could understand that to a degree, but who would you do that for? He had to have been close to them, really close.

The realisation of what was behind the wardrobe hit her like a two-tonne truck. That was when Finn emerged once again, letting the smell seep back through. He had white boxes piled against his chest up to his chin along with a bottle in one hand. He noticed them covering their noses and he looked back to the wardrobe before setting his eyes on them apologetically.

"Sorry about the smell," he sighed, looking deeply saddened. "Here's what you need," he said as he handed over all the medical stuff to Max who promptly shoved it into his backpack.

"Who is she?" Asha asked, knowing who it was, but wanting to hear it from him.

Finn looked to the floor, his manner dropping. "… She *was* my mum," he looked up to her then with glassy eyes. Asha felt her heart tug as they stood in awkward silence. He cleared his throat and blinked back whatever tears were forming.

"This place had power until a week ago. Backup generator," he paused. "She needed a lot of care, most of which only a machine could give her," he scrunched his nose up and looked up to the ceiling. "She didn't last long once the power went out," he let out a long breath, as if to soothe himself.

"I'm sorry," Asha said, not really knowing how to help.

If it had been the old world, she would have offered him some shots and a much-needed takeaway feast. But this wasn't the old world, it was the new one and death was a daily experience.

She'd become stoic in the face of despair.

He shook his head quickly and rubbed his grief away with rough hands. "Look, you got what you wanted. I hope your friend gets better," he said before turning back to his precious lair.

"Wait, Finn," Max bellowed, stilling the boy. "You need to come with us. We have a safe place to go."

"I've got my place here," he said, giving them a saddened look over his shoulder.

"No, you don't understand," Asha pressed.

"There's a place where this isn't," Max continued. "It's an island off the north coast. No Hunters, no nothin'; apart from a few hundred *actual* people. You should come with us. We need the manpower if anythin'."

Finn shook his head reluctantly. "I'm staying where I'm needed more. But good luck," he simply said before shutting himself away.

Asha ran up to the steel barrier and banged on it hard once.

"They've got a cure! This can all be over; we just gotta get to the safe place. Don't be a prick!" She yelled, trying to make a case even though the decision should have been obvious. Not for this kid apparently because no more noise came from behind his barrier. She let out a few defeated breaths before returning to Max's side; a huge frown blanketed her face.

"No use draggin' a man to where he don't wanna go," he shrugged. Even though it was his job to save the humans, there were always going to be the ones who couldn't leave home, no matter how good the alternative.

"I'll never understand people," Asha sighed.

"Let's go. Who knows what state Daisy is in right now," Max said. "We got everythin' we need."

"Fine," Asha muttered. She was getting tired and the thought of having to run for another two hours really wasn't sitting well with her. Plus, leaving Finn felt wrong and it frustrated her.

Getting out of the hospital without Finn's knowledge of the place added time onto their clock but they eventually made it out. Asha pulled off her hood; there was no point in hiding now. Hunters were about anyway, and the disguise wasn't going to make a difference. The moon shone brightly down on them.

"Lead the way Asha...?" Max said, trailing off like he was fishing for something.

She began to jog, and he kept up with her pace.

"Flores. Asha Flores," she replied. Her lips formed a small smile; she hadn't said her full name in so long. It pulled her back to a time when second names were important, she couldn't help but feel nostalgic. He knew hers, now she needed to know his.

68

Without her having to ask he cleared his throat. "A latina name, I like it. I'm Bennett. Well, Max Bennett. I'm sort of used to being called Bennett," he said, through ragged breaths.

She thought about what he'd said. It led her to think he could have been in the military services. It would make absolute sense. The way held himself, the natural authority he had. And being referred to by his second name more than his first, he was definitely a soldier, or used to be. She was beginning to like Max more and more. Despite his intimidating form, she felt like he could look after her, even dare she say it, more than Kit.

They ran in comfortable silence for ten more minutes before entering the woods. Asha started to develop a stitch, but she ran through the horrible feeling. They needed to get back home and if they could do it in less than two hours then there was more of a chance of Daisy surviving.

She thought about Kit and how he was there alone with three strangers. He wasn't always the best at small talk; he just never knew what to say unless he could think of a snarky remark or be sarcastic. Maybe it was a defense thing.

She missed him.

Asha was lost in her train of thought when she began to hear shouting for help coming from behind them. It was feral and full of desperation. She stopped in her tracks and ducked behind a huge oak tree trunk with Max quickly joining her.

"Look or leave," she asked.

"What?" Max breathed harshly. His face was twisted in confusion as he clutched his chest.

She guessed that only worked with Kit. "What do you want to do?" She pushed, her voice barely a whisper.

"We have to help, save as many people as we can. It's the only way," he replied, catching his breath.

Max looked like he was in pain. He wasn't as young as her and even *she* was struggling with the constant running. He was right though. She nodded her head in agreement and jumped back into the woodland path.

That's when she saw him.

He was running like there was a tsunami chasing him, almost tripping over twice as he careened towards them. The look on his face was of pure terror. His eyes were wide and harrowed, his brow was dampened, and his mouth was contorted into a permanent cry for help.

"They're here!" He shouted.

"*Coño*!" She yelled at Finn, though something deep in her bloomed at the sight of him.

Her attention turned to Max who was already shoving his hand into his bag. She felt rage building up in her throat. That boy was leading those monsters straight to them.

Max pulled out a pistol and smacked it into her chest then took one out for himself. Asha stood in confusion for a moment just staring at the metal object in her hands. She had no idea how to use a gun; Max noticed that pretty quickly and once he'd prepared his gun, he snatched hers, took the safety off then passed it back.

"We're gonna shoot our way outta this one. That boy's got a nerve. Careful with the trigger, it's sensitive."

"I-I've never used—"

"Now or never, Asha."

―――

70

Finn was about 30 yards in front of them bumbling at speed. She counted five Hunters behind him. Two men and three women, one of whom couldn't have been older than fifteen. She braced herself and stood with her legs apart, taking aim at the first woman. Finn eventually reached them and skidded past them against the earthy ground. Hunks of dirt flew around him and he practically choked on his laboured breath as he stilled on the ground behind them.

Asha pushed him to the back of her mind and concentrated on her aim. She was sure using a gun was going to be harder than it seemed in the movies; it made her nervous, and she hated feeling anything less than confident. The saliva seemed to disappear from her mouth. Holding a gun out like this, it was so unnatural that it just emphasised what she'd become, a stranger to her former self.

When the Hunters saw Asha and Max with guns ready, they faltered slightly and reduced their run down to a gentle stroll. Asha's defensive, dead eyes scanned them carefully, noticing features from each of them, like the Beatles shirt one guy was wearing and the pink hair dye that had faded to a dusky rose on one of the women. They all bore the infected skin, which was even more translucent in the milky moonlight. Even so, she couldn't help but imagine their lives before the disease.

One of the guys stepped forward, a bloodied cricket bat in hand; he had a nose ring and a serpent neck tattoo. "Hey, hey, come on now. Who brings a gun to a knife fight?" He laughed.

Her aim went to him.

"Turn back the way you came or die. Your choice," Max shouted, the air dispersed around his mouth in a frosty cloud.

"Ooh, I'm so-o-o-o scared!" The man poked, sticking his tongue out. "We outnumber you Pures. I actually feel sorry for you, especially with that cowardly thing on the ground. But God, you look like you'd make a nice sandwich, something on par with a New York Reuben sandwich, with all those layers of meat. Don't they look good, guys?" He licked his lips. "Daddy's gotta eat."

Asha pulled the trigger.

It hit him in the shoulder, shattering the bone. *Shit,* she was aiming for his head. The gun was difficult to work; her hand ached from the backlash and her ears rang from the percussion.

The Hunter pressed on his shoulder screeching while the other minions began their attack. It all happened so quickly. Asha's fingers worked faster than ever, cocking the gun and shooting. It was an unfair fight; they had firepower. The Hunters didn't have a chance of even reaching them. She took down two of them and Max took the other three. She had to go back to them to finish off the job; her aim was of course not as good as Max's. A single shot to each head sufficed. Somehow, killing with a gun felt easy to her, it was far less personal and less difficult than killing with a knife.

Once she'd finished, she closed her eyes, held her head to the sky and let out a deep long breath. The cool breeze of the night against her blood-splattered skin calmed her.

She slowly came to, and when she did, she looked across to Finn with a solemn stare. He was still on the ground; his face frozen in horror at her. His skin was pale in the moonlight as he gazed at the bodies that now lay at her feet.

There was something in her that switched on when it came to killing, she was all of a sudden confident, unnerved and catastrophically numb. But Finn was enough to pull her out of it.

Anger fuelled her now, she was brimming with it; she was close to blowing.

She clicked on the safety of the gun and slotted it into her belt next to her carving knife. Max began to search the Hunters – presumably for anything useful - while she marched her way over to the boy on the ground.

"I see you put that gun to good use," she spat as she stormed to him.

He looked to the ground, ashamed, before gaining the guts to look her in the eye. Even then, his stare wavered. "It's a tranquiliser gun. I didn't have time to reload it back there."

She rolled her eyes and let out a mocking chuckle as she looked up to the now surprisingly starry sky. "A *tranquilliser* gun? You don't subdue these things; you have to *kill* them! ...You just get better and better, don't you?" She could now add 'twat' to his list of wonderful qualities, along with being tragically indecisive. "So, you changed your mind about coming with us and then as a thank you gift, you thought you'd bring five new friends for us to play with?"

"I'm sorry, okay! I didn't know what else to do!" He cried, literally, his cheeks turning pink. *Don't cry, please.* A boy crying was her kryptonite; he was swaying her.

He threw the gun to the bushes in either a protest or because it was useless now. Either way, he looked like a stroppy child. For such a potential fighter, he was a hundred light years away from being anything but.

"Jesus, get a hold of yourself," Asha muttered and looked down to her middle finger, her ring was dangerously close to slipping off once again, she huffed and twisted it back into place, for now. She was suddenly aware of how fast her heart was beating. Her hand went to her chest and held it gently, easing it to a normal pace.

Finn was making her feel too many emotions all at once. She wasn't sure how to deal with it. She guessed she would run with the inconsistent feelings she had towards him. He was polarizing her mind, puzzling her senses, overthrowing her control. He made her angry, sad, warm, sorry. He was faulted yet he was pure. He was an inconvenience to her thoughts.

He was another day's problem.

"Right, here's the booty," Max grinned as he came to the pair, seemingly happy with what was happening. He handed Asha a hammer that was coated in dark dried blood. She scowled but took it anyway, wiping the blood away in flakes on her jeans. He offered Finn his hand to yank him up and then passed him a crowbar and a small knife. He kept the cricket bat for himself. "Keep your eyes peeled, gunshots ain't exactly quiet. There are probably more Hunters around and if we have the unfortunate luck of running into 'em again, Finn, you need to fight with us. This is what it's gonna be like now, alright?"

Finn nodded sheepishly as he gripped his new weapons tightly. Asha's anger at him still hung high but she could feel herself soften slightly. It wasn't his fault entirely. All he wanted was their help, and sure, it was pitiful, but it was also sincere. He'd obviously never been through something like that and seeing a massacre for the first time was hard for anyone.

They began to run again. Asha made sure to slip into Finn's pace. His face was even redder now, though it mostly flourished in his cheeks. His dimples were more prominent when he pressed his lips together.

She liked them. *Shit.* She really liked them.

"Sorry for being so hard on you," she said, gasping for breaths. Running and talking? Not a good combo. "And I'm sorry about your mum. But it's done, okay? Get a fucking grip."

He seemed to laugh, but she couldn't really tell. "I will," he replied shortly.

*

By the time they reached the bottom of the hill, Asha was soaked in clammy sweat and she was frozen to the core. She sucked in as much air as she could, her lungs burning along with her legs. Breathing quickly only made her choke on nothing. She felt like she was going to pass out, she hadn't eaten properly in at least a day. Her body was running on fumes.

"Come on, last push," Max said, his voice hoarse.

Asha's eyes almost rolled to the back of her head, but she persevered with the steep daunting hill. Every lunge took it out of her, she let out small whimpers as she climbed, not letting them be loud enough to hear. She didn't want the others to think she was weak. She was no longer the sad girl in her kitchen with a knife in her hand and a cry on her lips.

Once she reached the curve of the hill, she could see the house clearly. That was when everything changed and she felt her heart jump into her throat.

75

The front door had been ripped from its hinges.

Chapter Seven

A gasp escaped her lips. *"Kit!"*

Her feet couldn't carry her fast enough. Every thought about how uncomfortable she was, flew out of her head. All she could think about was how she might find her best friend dead inside. She clutched at the grass to help pull her up towards the house quicker.

"Stop!" yelled Max from behind her. "It might be a trap!"

"Asha!" Finn cried out.

She didn't listen and she didn't care to listen. She needed to get in there and see if he was okay. She felt suspended in a horrible turmoil. She couldn't lose him. She cursed herself for not listening to him before. He was right, they should never have let the other group in. He was fucking right and now she might have lost him forever; all because of some remark about a cure.

But then again, the life they were living was something so mundane and fearful it was starting to get on her nerves. And after all, any promise of new life was something to strive for.

She stilled her mind for a moment, realizing she was losing control. There was no point in speculating and putting her body through emotional trauma when it hadn't happened yet. Checking the house was her priority and now her only thought; not her potentially dead best friend.

She practically fell through the open doorway and into the echoing hallway. Immediately she sensed the house was empty, but she persevered. She wasn't even aware if Max and Finn were behind her, all she cared about was finding her Kit.

Her legs carried her quickly as she stormed through the house before racing down the rickety wooden stairs to the basement. She almost tripped at the bottom step, but she steadied herself before running to the main room. It was silent as she ripped open the door. Her eyes scanned the room, everything was as it was, except for the fact that Kit, Daisy, Leo and Piper weren't there. What *was* left behind was the blood-soaked mattress. There was no way someone could lose that much blood and still be alive. Asha's hope for the others' safety was diminishing with each quiet second.

She stood for a moment gathering her thoughts. *The storeroom*, maybe they were hiding in there. She began her sprint down the corridor to the door of the storeroom, which was shut; unlike how she'd left it open before. She felt a smidgen of happiness at the thought of them stowing themselves away in the room. Even so, she still held her breath as she clicked open the door.

The room was in total darkness, but she could still see that it was empty, as in, everything had gone.

The food, the drink, the bedding, everything that they'd kept safe. It was all gone. Her heart dropped; all those excursions risking their lives for the sake of their survival were for nothing. Those Hunter bastards had taken everything. That was one of their many hunting ploys; taking everything Pures needed so that they would have to emerge from their hiding place, straight into their awaiting, translucent arms.

Anger bubbled in her stomach. She took in a deep breath, turning to stalk back through the house, but something in the back of the room caught her eye. She furrowed her eyebrows and tried to make her vision adjust to the darkness, but to no avail.

There was something there on the floor.

She stepped into the room, a stern frown on her face as she tried to decipher what it was.

She didn't have long to analyse it before a hard kick suddenly smacked itself into her stomach causing her to lurch backwards.

She held her stomach in shock and choked, but within a millisecond, a second smack came to the back of her head, forcing her to fall into the room face down on the concrete floor.

Pain flooded her body from all directions. She was still trying to catch her breath from being winded as she looked up, a groan escaping her lips.

Her eyes filled with salty water and her face throbbed. Blood began to pour from her nostrils. She could taste the tell-tale metallic taste coming from a busted lip. She looked straight in front of her on the floor, to what she'd seen before.

She froze as she was met with the vacant eyes of Leo. His head had been placed on the floor, waiting for her. She didn't really care for Leo. But his death meant Kit's death was more probable.

She clenched her eyes shut but opened them quickly when she heard the door slam shut behind her, trapping her and whoever attacked her in close proximity. She spat blood to the floor and turned over as the large candle by the door was lit by a black-haired lady with ivory skin.

She had this huge grin on her face, it sickened Asha to her core. She hated those monsters with a deep burning passion. The way they thought they were so superior, how they acted like they were owed human sacrifices.

Asha watched lowly as the Hunter waved out the match she was holding before her gaze landed on her. She wondered if she had seen the gun she had hidden in her belt yet. Asha guessed she hadn't because if she had, she wouldn't be standing there right now chuckling like she was.

"God, you Pures are so predictable," she laughed. Her voice was sharp, and it scratched at Asha's ears. "Silly little Pure, silly little girl, poor little thing!" She sang.

Asha stayed on the ground waiting for the perfect moment to blow the Hunter's brains out. She felt smug, but she didn't show it, she had to hide it. She needed the woman to think she could take her no problems, that way she could strike successfully.

She had to play the game.

False fear filled her face; she felt like she was back in secondary school drama.

"Please!" Asha cried, blood trickled from her nose and mouth down her chin. She must have looked a state. "I-I want to live, please don't kill me!" She willed tears to spill from her eyes.

"Oh *my*! And pathetic," the Hunter scoffed, pulling out a ten-inch kitchen knife. "Now, what's going to happen, little girl, is that I'm going to let you join your lovely friend over there," she motioned to Leo's head. "In a wonderful place called heaven. Trust me, it's better than here, and besides, it's win-win. You get to live in a white castle on a cloud and I get a full belly."

"No, no, no!" Asha screamed, scrambling to her feet.

"Whoa, no, you stay exactly where you are little girl! Or I'll do it right now!" The Hunter threatened, her knife wiggling in the air towards Asha. "Plus," she almost sounded nervous, "my friends are out there, taking care of the others you were with. There's no escape, sweetheart," she grinned.

"But, but, I don't want to die, please! I'll join you," Asha begged; her mind alight with anticipation of how it was going to play out. This Hunter seemed weaker than others she'd come across; she shouldn't be a problem.

The Hunter started laughing hard now, the candlelight made her seem even more manic. "Oh yes, a wonderful idea! Another mouth to feed," she rolled her eyes and scowled.

Asha was losing her. "Then I could be a Reaper?" She suggested, remembering to make her voice waver and her eyes widen.

The woman thought for a slight moment and Asha almost took it as her chance, but instead she stayed still, trying to judge what she would do next.

"I don't really trust Reapers. Others do, but I prefer to gather my own food," she slimed. "And you look like exactly my cup of tea."

She was going to be a bit more difficult than Asha had first anticipated. "Well, just look at me!" Asha cried, pulling at the little fat around her stomach. "There's not much of me. Surely, you'd want my friends more. They're boys, they've got more meat!" She yelled.

"Anything will do at this point," the woman sighed, the scowl still prominent on her pretty face. "You know, the human race is just an infestation. We need to secure *our* existence on this Earth. *We* should be the ones in charge. Just face it little girl, the world has been taken from you. Stop trying to reclaim it. There's no point, we'll get you eventually. By my count there are far more of us left than there are you. So I say, give up. Just give up now and save yourself the inevitable," she took a breath. "We are the *Prime* race. And we will bring this world to its knees."

Asha's façade dropped.

She couldn't help it; the monster was getting too full of herself. There was about a six-foot distance between them and even though she knew the Hunter could easily throw her knife with fatal precision at her, Asha pulled out her gun, pointed it at her head and cocked it. The ivory woman froze, her face dropping like a plane out of the sky.

They'd traded places.

"You call yourselves '*Primes*'?" Asha laughed out loud, making it over-exaggerated. "That is the funniest joke I've heard in months. *Hunter scum*," she spat, ignoring the intense pain that still consumed her body. "And you're wrong," she growled. "We're taking it back. We've found a cure and we're going to kill every, last, fucking one of you."

The Hunter stared at Asha with fury before gripping her knife hard and charging towards her. She let out a high-pitched grunt as she swung her knife in the freckled girl's direction.

But Asha darted past her attack and jumped to the candle, the only source of light, and blew it out before dropping to the floor and aiming her gun at the Hunter's ankle.

She pulled the trigger and the woman screamed in agony as she fell to the floor writhing. Asha got to her feet and clicked open the door, early morning daylight flooded the room and she looked at her on the floor, clutching delicately at her ankle, her face wrangled in pain. She edged further away from the light of the sun. Asha could see that the skin that was exposed was already turning blisteringly red.

"The house is all yours," Asha said blankly as she slammed the door shut. She shoved a piece of wood under too, just to make sure she never escaped.

Her lungs pulled in deep breaths to calm herself before she placed the gun back into her belt. Her next thought was of Max and Finn. *Where the hell had they gotten to?*

She started back up the stairs on full alert. The ivory lady said something about her friends being outside and that only made her worry for Finn. Not for Max, he could take care of himself. She also thought about the others. Why had Leo been the only one to fall? Did the others make it out and leave him? Or had they been taken already and the Hunters just decided to leave Leo's head? Her mind raced and raced until she finally came up with a solution.

If they were still alive, Kit would be leading them, and if he was leading them, he would take them somewhere where they both knew, knowing that she would come looking.

The only logical place would be the tree house in the woods where they'd played when they were kids. It was safe and secluded there - they'd kitted it out as a 'just in case' place.

She had her plan. Now she had to find the others and make them resemble some sort of functional attack force. She searched the house; there wasn't even the scuttling of mice making a sound. Wiping the fresh blood from her face with the back of her sleeve, she took the risk to call out.

"Max!" She yelled, her voice echoing loudly around the barren infrastructure. "Max?"

"Asha!" He replied from somewhere outside. She quickly made her way out the back door and searched for him. Eventually, she spotted him propped up against a tree trunk down the hill, he looked injured. She ran to him and knelt by his side.

"What happened? Are you okay?" She asked, her voice more calculated than empathetic.

"I'm fine, now," he grimaced. "You okay, doll?" He was eyeing up her bloodied face with his large chocolate-coloured eyes.

"Of course," she smiled softly despite the dull pain running throughout her body.

"Knew you would be," he said, wincing.

"Where's Finn?" She asked, finding herself aware of his absence and suddenly concerned for his safety.

"He took on the Hunters that came after us. First one came outta nowhere, got me right in the head. I don't really know what happened. They jumped us when you ran in, then after that, I was out."

"You were right; it was a trap. Sorry," Asha said, remorseful.

"One thing you'll realise, Miss Flores, is that I'm always right," he smiled cockily and Asha shoved his arm, immediately regretting it as he made a pained grunt. "Did you find 'em? The others?" He asked through clenched teeth.

"Leo was there, dead," she explained, Max looked saddened, a frown gracing his face. "No other heads though. I have an idea of where the others might be hiding," she reassured him.

But wait, where exactly was that golden-eyed boy? She sucked in a panicked breath. "Is Finn dead?"

"No. He put up a bloody good fight. Didn't know he had it in 'im," Max sniffed roughly before licking his large lips. "The boy's over there chucking up," he pointed to the side of Asha and laughed lowly but stopped quickly from the pain.

She glanced over to where Max was gesturing and saw two bodies lying near each other, she couldn't make out their faces, not anymore. She clenched her jaw at the sight and looked to the bushes nearby. Sure enough, there was Finn crouched over, throwing up.

For some strange reason, it made her smile. He was learning to kill. He was good at it too, judging by the mangled bodies that were strewn side by side on the frosted grass. She cleared her throat and stood herself up.

"You need help?" She asked, offering Max her hand.

He shook his head and instead pulled himself up with help from the tree. "I'll be fine in a bit, promise," he smiled. "Where we off to?" He asked, rubbing at his side.

"Not far from here, it's a place me and Kit used to hang out in the woods," she said. She thought about how possible it was they actually did go there, considering Daisy's probable incapacitation. But she still felt it was the first place they should check anyway.

"Lead the way then," he said.

"Right."

They made the short walk to Finn; Asha couldn't help but look at the bodies as they walked past them. He must have gone completely crazy on them. She spotted the crowbar Max had given him earlier, it was coated in red and had who-knew-what lodged in it.

Finn had finished throwing up and just sat there with his head resting on his wrists, breathing deeply.

"Hey," Asha spoke calmly as she knelt next to him. She placed a hand on his shaking shoulder. He jumped at her touch and looked up to her with a pale face and frightened eyes. "Shh, it's okay," she soothed. She could be kind sometimes, and for some reason she felt somewhat protective over him. "You did good, alright?" She rubbed his shoulder. "Look, the others aren't here, so we need to go. Get yourself together," she urged before standing herself up.

"Thanks, Thorne. You saved my ass," Max said before yanking the boy to his feet.

Finn shook where he stood, his glance darted from Max to her, fear exploding behind his eyes.

"H-how are you guys so okay?" He shivered. "Your face…" he continued, staring at Asha, horrified. "But you seem so fine, how are you fine?" He was getting more agitated. "I just, I ripped them to shreds, how can I be fine?!" He yelled, his eyes welling with tears.

"You did exactly what you had to do, Finn," Asha shushed him. The last thing they needed was another attack, she wasn't sure how much energy she had left.

"Shit!" He cried, holding his blood coated hands out in front him, like he didn't want them attached to him anymore.

"Look, Thorne, we're grateful, okay? And you'll be fine. You just need some sleep. This life is over now anyway; we're going to a better place. But we ain't gonna get there if we don't move, alright?" Max bellowed.

Finn took a few deep breaths and before long he gave them a short nod. He didn't really have a choice in the matter, he had to go with them whether he liked it or not. Asha had seen something in him now, and it gave her a small hope that maybe he wasn't a lost cause. He had something of value and it was important that they all remained alive, for humanity's sake.

She kept her eye on him, gauging how well he was recovering. He had a soft soul; it was a shame he would have to break it. His face suddenly shot up in surprise, looking directly at her. She furrowed her eyebrows at him, an unspoken question in her eyes.

"Here," he said quickly before reaching into his pocket and pulling out her mother's ring. He held it out to her. "I saw it fall off when you ran up to the house."

She gasped and quickly looked at her finger. Sure enough, it was bare. *How did I not notice?* She felt like she'd betrayed her mother somehow and it wasn't a nice feeling.

She gave Finn a thankful look and hurriedly took the ring from his palm and shoved it back onto her thin finger. She gave it a small kiss and closed her eyes for a second. *I can't lose you Mamá, I won't.*

They gathered themselves and made their way to the woods. It was just a ten-minute run away, but those minutes seemed like days.

Asha led the boys past the lake where she and Kit had been inconvenienced earlier; the bodies of the Hunters they'd killed were now gone. No doubt their friends came and took them ready for dinner – they could eat their own kind, though she doubted it tasted as good as a *Pure*.

They ran through the following woods and up an off-beat trail which led to an old Park Ranger's shed. The tree house was just to the left through the trees. She had walked that same route countless times ever since she was a little girl, each time she felt excited. Now, her heart was filled with concrete and her mind was a mess.

She pushed quickly past the jutting branches of the woodland and burst out into the clearing. And there, at the base of the tree house pacing in worry was her best friend, Kit Bell.

Chapter Eight

Asha closed her eyes for a brief second, thanking a higher power for keeping him safe. She knew he was perfectly capable of protecting himself, but she also liked to think that he needed her; and visa-versa. Seeing him flooded her with an intense sense of safety; it was overwhelming.

Kit turned to the noise from the trees and as soon as he saw her, his face burst into relief and he started to sprint to her.

"*Kit*," she breathed, running to him at full speed.

She felt completely at war with herself. On the one hand, she felt like a fearless, cold hearted killer who didn't need anyone, and on the other she was a little girl running to any means of comfort.

He stalked his way towards her, his arms outstretched and his eyes stricken with gratefulness. When they collided, he almost crushed her in a deep hug. She lay her temple against his heaving chest.

There was nothing like a meaningful hug at the end of a long day, or in this case, after a horrendous morning.

She thought back to a time when her Dad wasn't trying to kill and eat her, when he used to hug her and bring her *elotes* to bed when things weren't okay. She felt her eyes well up and she clung to Kit harder. She couldn't stop herself from letting a few tears go.

But there were other people there, and she couldn't show her feelings, especially not when they looked to her for a cure. She sniffed away her emotions, bottling them up for another day and lifted her head to properly look at Kit.

"I knew you'd find us," he smiled, though his voice faltered, like he didn't fully believe it. His eyes turned a shade darker as he assessed her face. "You okay? Looks like your nose is broken," he said, poking it lightly with his thumb.

Asha winced away from his touch; it was sore, but it wasn't broken. "I'll live," she said, giving him a small smile to satisfy his worry.

He narrowed his stare before glancing behind her. "Who's the guy?"

"Finn, the Hospital Hermit."

"He looks *green*," Kit noted.

Asha turned to look, Max and Finn were nearing them. He was right, Finn did have a greenish hue to his skin.

"He's not used to killing, apparently," she shrugged.

"Seriously?"

"*Hermit*," she reiterated before letting go of him and straightening herself out.

"Daisy?" asked Max as soon as he got to them, his grave stare on Kit for an answer.

"Nice to see you too!... Somehow, she's still alive," he replied. "But getting her here took its toll. She's sort of on the brink."

Asha couldn't imagine how hard it was escaping with her in tow and then having to hoist her up into the high wooden structure. But they'd done it.

"Max?" a lavender-like voice came from above.

Asha looked up to the rustic window of the treehouse to see a flash of fiery hair paired with a pleased yet harrowed looking Piper. Blood spotted her wrinkled face and coated her hands.

"Pipes, we got everything!" He replied, holding up his backpack and racing to the uneven wooden holds up to the tree house.

Piper retreated back into the darkness and Asha stood still, revelling in the woodland sanctuary.

Finn held his arms around his chest unsure of what to do, his eyes looking from Asha to Kit with an uncomfortable stare.

She broke the awkwardness. "Finn, this is Kit. Kit, this is Finn. He kindly gave us the medicine, and almost killed us in the process," she said, giving them both a joking smile.

They did not look amused.

"Hi," Finn said, tightening the grip around himself.

"Hi," Kit replied, his tone far from friendly.

"*Christ,* I can sense the dick-measuring from here," Asha groaned quietly.

"Sorry. Nice to meet you *Finn*… almost killed them, *did you*?" Kit asked sternly, staring down the outcast with arms folded against his puffed chest.

"It's not like I meant to," Finn grunted, his eyes hardening slightly in annoyance.

She had a feeling Kit would greet him with hostility just like he did with the others, but this time she'd specifically told him that Finn was the reason for her trouble out there.

Not one of her finer moments.

Kit walked towards Finn with quick strides and Asha's breathing halted for a brief moment; she knew what he was capable of. Luckily for Finn, he stopped short of him by a foot.

"You *ever* put her in danger again; you won't like what happens to you," he warned, a finger pointed in Finn's face.

"Kit, that's *enough*," Asha moaned, pulling him away from the poor newbie who was probably shitting his pants now. "Listen, I'm fine, okay?" She said as they started to walk arm-in-arm to the trunk of the tree. "We're bringing him with us so just be nice. He's not too bad, just a twat, that's all."

Kit was quiet for a second, his jaw clenching as he thought. "Fine, but you know I-"

"I know. You want to protect me."

He nodded and rubbed the back of his head with a strong hand.

"And you can," Asha sighed, her hand soothing his arm. "Now, are you okay? What happened at the house?"

He took a deep breath, letting out a long sigh. "…I waited up at the door when you left with Max. I didn't want to go back down there. About half an hour in I heard people coming. I went down and got everyone out the back, except Leo, he got left behind. They grabbed him. I pointed to the trees and the others went there. I stayed on the other side of the door and listened, thinking maybe I could help. But there were too many voices. I knew I couldn't do anything. Anyway, that long-haired fucker ratted us out, he told them there were more of us after they threatened him. They told him they were going to kill him because he was disloyal. As if those things have any morals left… Then I ran."

"He was weak. You are strong. Remember that," Asha said as she held the back of her hand to his cheek.

He looked as white as a sheet, like stress was eating away at him from the inside. He needed a good rest, just like she did. Asha hadn't slept since the night before and all that had happened since then was enough to make an army collapse. All of a sudden, the last day and a half caught up to her and she felt faint. She steadied herself on the tree, her hand grasping at the rough bark.

"You sure you're alright?" Kit asked, holding her up.

"I just need sleep," Asha breathed quietly.

It was around six in the morning but even the bright light of daybreak couldn't stop her drowsiness.

"There's no room in the tree house, not with those three up there," Kit said.

"It's fine; they need the space for Daisy," Asha said, though a little insincerely.

She really needed to lie down because standing was becoming a problem.

"You can sleep in the log?" Kit suggested.

It would do. It was just the other side of the tree. It was a mossy, hollow thing, it was big enough for two.

She nodded her head slowly before glancing over to Finn; he was still standing where they had just been, looking at the ground. She wouldn't be surprised if he was gone by the time she woke up. After all, he wasn't being welcomed much and who knew if he believed them about a safe place. Time would tell.

Asha trudged over to the log with Kit by her side. She gave him a nod letting him know she would be alright; he returned the gesture before turning away towards the steps of the tree house.

93

She got to her knees and burrowed her way into the log which was surprisingly warm and cosy, despite it being slightly damp and barren. The smell of earth was so strong it was almost nauseating but she didn't care enough to move. As soon as she got comfy, her eyelids couldn't close fast enough; they ached with the anticipation of finally resting.

Her dreams were fast, dizzying and dense. She felt like she couldn't escape them, like the darkness was eating her. She could feel black tar running down her throat and her lungs filled with a hot grey sand that threatened to consume her. Arrows stuck themselves in her from all different angles as she was suspended in the air. She screamed wretched screams. A final arrow flew straight into her seeping heart.

Her eyes shot open and she let out a stunted gasp. She was in the log and it was impossibly dark. *How long have I been asleep?* Her fingers rubbed at her eyes and she blinked a few times making sure she was really awake. She took a moment to breathe; to recover.

A nightmare like that hadn't invaded her brain in so long; it made her feel even more exhausted than she was before she went to sleep. No sound came from outside the log apart from the natural hum of the forest.

After a minute, she deemed it safe enough to move, and crawled her way out. She got to her feet and looked around, taking in a deep breath of cool night air; it was refreshing to be out of the claustrophobic log. Her eyes instantly gazed to the moon.

She always found something so beautiful and serene about the moon. There was a certain draw that it had with her, it was something she could always count on.

—

94

She heard faint breathing and glanced down to see Kit asleep by the log, he looked peaceful, it was nice to see. From the change of his clothes and the brisk air, Asha guessed it was very early morning, which meant that she'd been asleep for an entire twenty-four hours. She wondered what she'd missed since she'd closed her eyes, so she made her way to the tree house to check on Daisy.

Asha was sure to take careful steps up the makeshift ladder. Once at the top, she poked her head up into the wooden, musty room. She saw Daisy curled up under the tartan blanket that Asha had bought for the treehouse at a charity shop a year ago. Daisy was breathing steadily and looked like she'd got some colour back in her skin, a good sign. Piper was propped up near her, her head lolled onto her arm as she snored quietly. Max was laid flat on his back with his hands placed on his chest, his breathing was almost silent which confused Asha; for such a large man, she expected something louder.

She felt a smile grace her face and made her way back down the ladder; happy that things seemed to be in order.

As she stepped down, she noticed Finn sitting down by the tree line, his back towards her and his head looking up towards the sky. A breath caught in her throat but that feeling of relief was also paired with a roll of her eyes.

A conflicted affair.

Her footsteps didn't stir him, which they should have considering anyone could be walking around, but instead he just kept his stare up. She sat herself next to him, and even then, he didn't move. After a second, she looked at him, his eyes were sunken, deep dark circles surrounded them.

"Couldn't sleep?" She asked, her husky voice cutting through the serene air.

"Doubt I ever will," he sighed, training his narrowed eyes to hers.

She could have laid into him about being braver, but she refrained, feeling that he deserved a little break from her angst. "It'll get easier to bear."

"I hope you're right. I mean, I'm guessing you're an expert. The way you took out those Hunters was... cold."

"Yeah," was all she could manage.

She looked to the mossy, leaf-trodden ground and sat for a moment, her mind glossing over the pack of Hunters she and Max had taken out. All the killing was just something so normal now that she found its existence uneventful. Yet when she allowed herself the time to dwell on it, she itched all over from the horror. To Finn however, it was new and harrowing.

"Shit, sorry, I didn't mean to offend you or anything."

"Just shut up. You don't understand, you're not like me."

"Good," he huffed quickly, biting the inside of his cheek after realising what he had said.

She swallowed thickly, letting silence fall over them for a second. The air hardened, the proximity between them felt almost unbearable. *I didn't used to be like this, this isn't me, not really.*

"Sorry, again. I'm not good at talking to girls," he turned his view from her and looked to the moon again.

"I can see that."

"Sorry," he whispered, lowering his head. His cheeks turned a light shade of pink.

"Do you ever stop apologising?"

He looked like he was about to say sorry again, but instead he sighed, defeated.

"Look, we're headed to a safe place. Maybe you won't have to do what you did to those Hunters again, at least not after we get there."

"Yeah, I know. Harbour, right?"

She nodded.

"Because you're immune, but not like we are."

"Right," Asha nodded her head slowly again.

"C-can I see?"

"What?"

"The scratch," he said sheepishly, already looking to her chest.

"You do take fucking liberties, don't you?" She gasped, mocking her shock.

He returned with a shy shrug, his stare staying curious. She rolled her eyes and unbuttoned her coat before shrugging it off. She then pulled down the front of her top to reveal the long, thin black scar that cut through her skin, marking her for life.

His eyes darkened when he saw it and he looked away quickly, like it was something repulsive. His reaction forced her to look down at it, but it was just as it always was. She hurriedly pulled up her top and hoisted her coat back onto her now shivering shoulders.

"I can't imagine what it was like," he finally said, looking to her with wide eyes.

"I don't suggest trying to," she muttered, remembering the week of torture the scratch had brought her.

97

"I um, I saw what it did to the patients at the hospital... the ones who died from it." He took in a sharp breath. "My mum wasn't the only person I tried to save. Somehow, she got through the sickness just like I did, and a few of the other patients did too. I thought we were the lucky ones when we got better," he smiled briefly before his face fell once again. "Like I said, other patients weren't so lucky. I watched their blood boil and their insides come out like rivers. I tried to help, but I didn't understand it. I couldn't help them. And the ones I could, the ones who weren't infected. Well, I uh, I realised I couldn't keep my mum alive as long if they were still switched on too..."

"So, you turned them off?"

He nodded sharply; his face wrangled in disgust. "One of them woke up as I was going along the hallway. He'd come out of a coma but still needed the machine to live. I had to turn him off. But, you know what the worst part was? He forgave me. He *actually* forgave me," he whispered as he held his arms around his pulled-up knees.

So, he did have a survival mode.

Asha let her hand rub his back slightly, wanting to give some comfort but also not wanting to let him wallow in his regrets. "You had to do what you did. Family is everything. *Mi familia* were amazing. I..." She stopped herself suddenly. Her lips hadn't uttered many words out loud about them since that fateful night. Thoughts of them were constant in her mind, but actually talking about them? She found she couldn't do it, her tongue felt heavy in her mouth, a burden.

Finn glanced up at her, noticing her turmoil. "I bet they were."

Chapter Nine

Before long, the pair found themselves asleep on the grass, exhaustion taking its toll on them. Despite Asha having slept so much already, she found it easy to slip back into another world. But when the birds started performing, they woke up groggily.

Asha wiped the sleep from her bleary eyes and peered around them; no-one was up yet still.

"I slept," Finn remarked thankfully, stretching his arms to the sky.

"See," Asha began, clearing her throat, "The horror gets easier to bear."

Finn started chuckling then.

"What's so funny?" She asked impatiently, sitting up, annoyed.

"I just realised how ironic it is."

"How ironic what is?" Asha spat, getting irritated at him once again, and he was doing so well too.

"You reassuring me while your face is caked in blood."

Asha opened her mouth slightly to come back with a witty remark, but she was cut short by the realisation that she hadn't washed her face yet; he was right. She lifted a cautious hand to her face and brushed her skin. Sure enough there was a certain roughness to it, the culprit; day old blood.

She was surprised she hadn't noticed the odd feeling on her skin, or the smell. She was more used to it than she'd first thought.

A smile tickled its way across her lips, she didn't want it to come, but her lips quivered until she couldn't hold it anymore.

"If you say, 'I told you so', I *will* hit you," she grinned.

He held his hands up in defense and returned her bright smile. Her own cheeks ached as her muscles remembered how to show happiness.

The sun began to rise behind the soft swaying fir trees; it's light casting a much-appreciated glow on the forest. Asha watched it as closely as she could, trying to savour it.

She looked away when the sun became too bright, burning her eyes. That was one thing she'd learnt. Beauty doesn't last forever; it leaves you and it does it either gracefully or painfully; there is no inbetween.

She blinked at the earthy ground, letting her eyes adjust back to normal vision.

"Maybe I should go find a stream or something," she finally said, shrugging.

She was sure there was a small creek nearby, if not, there was always the lake that she'd become acquainted with the other morning. She stood up, swaying slightly, and patted herself down.

"I'm coming with you. Can't let you go al-" Finn stopped his sentence short once Asha glared at him. "-I need a wash too," he swiftly said, saving himself from an impending beating.

"You know, there *are* other people in the group. You could hang with them?" She said as she started them on the woodland trail.

"Yeah. I don't think they like me," he said quietly.

"And you think *I* do?" Asha laughed lightly, her eyes concentrating on the rough bushy path.

He bowed his head and kept silent; she could feel the air thicken between them once again.

"I'm kidding, *kind of*. Look, you're new, okay? And you didn't exactly make a great impression," she said, a slight smile on her face.

"Even the half-dead girl gave me a dirty look," he sighed and Asha's mind went to Daisy.

"Well, that's just how she looks normally. I'm pretty sure she hates everyone."

"I get it. They don't like me because I'm a fucking coward," he sounded deflated.

"Finn, we're all '*fucking cowards*' until we're thrown into the deep end. You just haven't had so much experience yet," she replied, trying to keep him on track.

"I wonder how long it'll take for them to accept me."

"Would you stop already? I don't know why you're moaning about who likes you or not. It doesn't *matter*."

"Well, it matters to me," he said in all seriousness.

She stopped suddenly in the green masses and stared at him sharply. "*Enough!*" She shouted and a bird flew from a tree nearby. She resumed her voice to a whisper quickly thereafter. "I don't want to hear any more of it, I mean it, and if I do, you'll regret it. You understand?" She spat, pointing a finger his way.

He nodded and wrapped his arms around his chest. She rolled her eyes, took a quick breath and steadied herself before continuing through the trees and brush. Finn wallowed quietly behind her; his steps lighter than hers, like he was tiptoeing.

Fifteen minutes of silent trekking went by when out of nowhere, Asha spotted a house, smack bang in the middle of the woods.
She stopped and stared at it in a brief second of confusion before
treading lightly towards it.

It was strange to see such a man-made item surrounded by the
throws of nature. It looked distorted; like it didn't belong. She looked
to Finn who shrugged as he studied its presence. She'd never seen it
before, which was weird considering how much time she and Kit spent
in the woods.

The air around them was quiet, aside from the ever-buzzing
sounds of life from the woods brought to earshot by the gentle breeze.
The house itself seemed to have been plucked from the posh part of
town and placed there without reason. Its paintwork was clean and
untouched, which was unusual considering that trees brushed against it
from almost every angle.

Her breathing began to pick up. She wasn't sure why the house
was there but what concerned her the most was who might live there.
Even though the fear of the unknown was dominant, she knew they
needed to check inside for supplies. After all, the Hunters had taken
everything she'd cultivated. She was starving.

"*We're going in,*" she whispered.

"What? No. I-I think we should go back to the others; they're
probably wondering where we are," he spoke back quietly.

"Well, they'll be happier to see us with our hands full of
supplies, won't they?" Asha said as she walked carefully around the
side of the house.

Her footsteps made crunching sounds as sticks and twigs broke
beneath her. Finn followed her reluctantly and caught up to her side.

"This place is giving me the creeps," he shuddered.

"Suck it up. We have more people to think about than ourselves."

Asha pushed open the door and immediately a mischief of rats scuttled out past their feet. She jumped back and stifled a scream. Finn wasn't so quiet and let out a shout, looking terrified.

"I *hate* rats," he breathed out as he watched them disappear into the greenery. He grimaced and then recoiled from the smell of rot that suddenly filled the air.

Asha choked on the stench too and covered her mouth and nose. "Well," she coughed. "At least we know no-one's going to hurt us in there."

Finn nodded his head quickly and pulled up his shirt sleeve to cover his mouth. "We need to be quick," he said, struggling to get the words out.

"You can stay here if you need to, *wimp.* I won't be long. Keep guard."

He still had the weapons from earlier, but she gave him her gun just in case. She had her two trusty knives hooked in her belt, and her fists; that was all she needed.

"Okay," he sighed, relieved. "But hurry."

Asha didn't need him to stand guard, she knew that if trouble arose, she would be able to handle it. But in any case, she knew Finn had it in him to do what had to be done. That was clear from the way he handled the Hunters at the house earlier. Truth be told she did feel safer knowing that he was out there.

Inside, the house was bleak, completely the opposite to the beauty of its exterior. The horrible smell was overpowering but she held on, concentrating on the possible supplies that were there for the taking.

The morning light oozed through the windows of the house, and the light blue curtains billowed ever so slightly in the small draught. Dust particles flew around, it felt so peaceful that she had to stand for a moment to take the serenity in.

Walking through to the kitchen, she spotted a meal in mid-preparation sitting rotten on the counter. It stung slightly to think of the lives that roamed the house so normally before the destruction of Nox. It looked like whoever had lived there had spaghetti bolognese on the menu for dinner that night.

Her stomach grumbled at the thought of a cooked meal and her heart lurched at the idea of home.

She forced the thoughts of familiarity from her mind and focused solely on opening the cupboards. The search seemed fruitless, with inedible masses of food decaying away.

Up until the last cabinet.

When she opened it, her eyes lit up and a wide smile took over her face. There was chocolate, and lots of it. She was completely shaken by the amount; surely they would have been the first thing to go. Either way, she didn't hesitate in grabbing a bin bag from under the sink and filling it up with the bars of goodness. There were a few unopened water bottles too which she hurriedly shoved into the bag too.

It was too good to be true, so Asha knew they had to get out of there quick before they found themselves in the middle of a trap.

As she was making her way back through the house at speed, she was suddenly halted in her tracks. Not by Hunters, not by a stranger, but by something that caught her eye on the wall.

It was one of those footprint moulds for a new baby. It had tiny, podgy little toes. But what threw her over the edge of her already teetering position on her emotional well-being cliff was the name that was painted on it.

Ella.

Steel gripped her heart and memories of her sister invaded her reality. Sneaking out to the all night McDonalds when their insomnia hit, giving puppy eyes to their dad for extra money for clothes every month, having sleepovers in each other's rooms where they ate shit and binged Netflix. Everything shot through her and it forced her to stop breathing.

But just as quick as it came, she shut it all down.

She trudged out of the house, speeding past Finn who she didn't pay any attention to.

Her mind was hardened. All she wanted to do was get back to the others and get out of there. She needed to remove herself from the town quickly; she couldn't stand it anymore. She didn't want to be around the remnants of her old life, she needed to move on because nothing was ever going to be like it was. Her heart had finally given up. Her cheeks suddenly felt wet.

"Asha, *wait up*. What's in the bag? Food?" Finn called curiously, his footsteps hot on her tail.

When he caught up, he must have noticed her face because he immediately shot his hands out onto her shoulders and stopped her from walking, looking concerned.

She tried to shove him off, but it was no use, and she was tired of fighting.

"You're crying," he stated before taking the bag from her and without hesitation, encased her in a hard hug.

She kept her hands to her sides for a moment, recoiling from his touch, until she felt an uneasy flood of comfort from the action. Her arms then snuck up his back and she clung onto him limply, letting him hug her harder. The tears then came in a storm.

It felt good to be held by him. She breathed heavily trying to still her tears; desperately trying not to show her weakness in front of Finn, especially not since she'd been harassing him about being a wimp. She felt stupid and conflicted, it was getting too much. Her legs barely kept her standing, and she shuddered where she stood, not seeming to be able to hold herself up. Luckily for her, Finn's hearty arms were still wrapped around her.

She cried for another minute, with the honey-eyed boy soothing her, then it was time to get over it.

"I'm-I'm fine," Asha eventually said, pushing him away weakly.

She wiped her face with her sleeves and managed to use her tears to clean away most of the dried blood. Even though she hated the fact that she'd cried in front of Finn, it did relieve a certain pressure which had been building since she could remember.

"Besides, they are tears of happiness," she lied unconvincingly, faking a smile. "I found chocolate."

Finn's face beamed like Asha had just told him they'd won the lottery, which they kind of had. She knelt to the ground and rummaged through the bin bag to find the most decadent bar. She settled on a double caramel milk chocolate one and sat herself down on the forest floor, patting the space beside her for Finn. He readily sat next to her and practically jigged where he sat in excitement.

It was endearing to say the least.

"This one will be our secret," Asha smiled lightly, holding the bar out to him.

Finn nodded and grabbed it hungrily, ripping it open and breaking off half before passing it to her. Not a millisecond later he began devouring his part.

"Shit. Calm down, try and taste it at least!" Asha said before taking a small bite.

Its sweetness hit her taste buds in an explosion. She could feel her eyes widen and her mood inflate. She needed it, she needed all of it. Before she knew it, she was wolfing it down without a care, so fast she had to remind herself to breathe. She craved the sweetness, its smooth, creamy texture was a welcoming sensation. After about a minute, they had finished the chocolate.

Asha sat still just savouring the taste that coated her mouth. She burst into laughter as she looked to Finn who had chocolate all around his mouth. She wiped her own lips and licked around the roof of her mouth for any extra chocolate hiding away.

"I want more…" Finn said, it sounded like he was out of breath.

"No," Asha said reluctantly. "We should save the rest for the others," she explained as she rubbed her stomach. It was beginning to hurt; it wasn't used to being filled.

She picked up one of the bottles of water and downed a few large gulps. It took away most of the chocolate flavour but that was good, it meant she was less likely to crack open another bar. She then passed the bottle to Finn who sucked down a quarter of it.

A sudden sound of rustling peppered through the trees around them.

Asha sat perfectly still and motioned with a look for Finn to do the same. Her fingers very carefully gripped themselves around both her knives and she pulled them out of their holding place, ready to attack. Her ears picked up the direction of the sound and she watched the thick trees carefully for a moment until she saw a small head of a deer pop through the trunks. She let out a breath of relief, her eyes fluttering shut.

"*A doe,*" Finn spoke quietly. He was right, and she was beautiful.

The doe didn't seem to notice the pair as she peacefully munched on the stray leaves and grass around it. They stayed still as stone, not wanting to disturb her. All Asha could do was watch how she gracefully and silently ate her way through the greenery. It was such a different sight, and it was the first time Asha had seen a deer in real life. She embraced the moment and let her mind go blank, trying to not to think of what herself and the world had become. Here, everything was perfect, natural; the way it should be. And there she sat, blood covering her clothes and her hands clasped around deadly weapons.

She stared at the doe's markings, the white circles on her head; she was a wonder. She was thankful for the fact that the virus didn't affect animals.

She didn't know how she would cope with killer cats and dogs on top of the Hunters.

Although, it was only a matter of time before the strays became desperate. Much like humans, they'd lost their source of food, what with their owners being dead or losing their minds. Over the past six months, she'd seen various packs of dogs running around the streets, ravenous. She didn't like to think about the thousands of pets who'd been left to die in houses or couldn't fend for themselves after their dependency on humans was challenged.

She refused to think about the babies who were left behind.

Once the doe had had her fill, she wandered off past the house and into a probably more succulent part of the forest. Asha let out the breath that she'd been holding and felt happy for a brief second.

A gust of wind ticked her face and she shivered. Despite the new sunlight, the air was still biting cold. It was typical mid-November weather, but this time around they had no heating, no hot chocolate with melted marshmallows and no warm stews for comfort. It was bitter and threatening and Asha didn't want to think about how they'd make it through the next few months.

Sure, they had a small hope with Harbour but what if they didn't have all the resources to keep them warm? What if going there just meant seclusion and little else. Her body began to shiver more, desperate for a cosy blanket and a comfy bed. Things like that were fruitless and unrealistic, which in itself was strange; normality had become a dream out of reach.

"I wonder if anyone else is awake," Finn pondered, talking almost to himself.

However, as if to answer his question, a sudden sound of quick running from the trees brought with it a puffy eyed, yet excited looking Kit. He was heaving from the run; Asha could feel the heat from him as he recovered in front of them.

"Jesus fucking Christ! I've been looking everywhere for you two!" He cried, out of breath, his hands on his knees. He then looked up to Asha and pointed towards her mouth "…Is that chocolate?"

Chapter Ten

The three of them made their way back through the woods quickly; it was time to go. Apparently, during the day, the group had made the discovery of a people carrier not far from the tree house. Asha hadn't missed too much aside from that, and Daisy's steady recovery. Kit still seemed cold towards Finn, but Asha knew it would take him time to warm to him.

They reached the car in no time with Kit leading the way. When they got there, only Max stood by it. Piper and Daisy hadn't arrived yet. Asha smiled at him and held out the bin bag full of goodies for him to inspect.

Max took it and peered inside with an eyebrow raised. "Good job. We'll need this until we find something more... *nutritious*," he said before finding a place for it in the car.

"You guys have any luck finding our stolen supplies?" Asha asked openly to the three of them.

"No," Kit said flatly. "They knew how to hide it so we'd never find it again."

"Let's hope there's some supermarkets on the way that haven't been ransacked," Asha said, folding her arms across her chest.

"We'll figure somethin' out," Max offered as he joined them again. He then looked behind them. "Ah, there they are. Let's get a move on. Asha, ride in front with me?" He asked. He didn't wait for an answer and just strolled over to the driver's side and hopped in.

Asha nodded her answer, and then turned to see Piper trying to help Daisy walk. Daisy looked as disgruntled as she usually did, but that wasn't a bad sign. Piper looked ever more worried, trying her best to control the fragile girl.

"I'll get in the back," Kit said. "Leave these girls to ride in the middle, more room," he shrugged, looking to Finn to join him.

Neither of them looked happy about it, but it was true, Piper and Daisy needed the most room, they were the priority. Well, Asha was the priority, especially to Max. But he had her where he needed her, right by his side.

Asha clicked open the door to the passenger side and jumped in; she buckled in but turned in her seat to observe the others, and to keep an eye out. Piper gave Asha a small, tired smile as she climbed into the middle seat. Kit clambered in next, jumping over into the furthest seats. Finn and Daisy were next. Finn tried to help the blonde up into the car, but she proved her returning strength by literally pushing him off her to the ground and then throwing herself into her seat with Piper pandering around her, yelling about being careful with her stitches.

Daisy's attitude seemed to have fully returned, which to Asha was a relief; she was going to be okay. Finn picked himself off the ground and bumbled over the two girls into his allocated seat next to Kit, his cheeks bright red.

Everything the group owned had been piled up in and amongst everyone. She still had her bag, which really only had enough to sustain her and her alone. There was the medicine from Finn, plus the stuff from the tree house that included: the tartan blanket that Daisy was permanently wrapped in, and a few books. They also had the loot from the house in the woods which was what they had to rely on to get them through the drive. That would be easy enough considering the lengths of starvation they'd all been through in recent times; even so, Asha's stomach still rumbled.

"We'll make our way north, hopefully find a radio. If not, then we find a place to camp out until the boat comes," Max said as he started the car with a steady twist of the key, the engine roared to life and shook them briefly before dying down to a pleasant hum.

"Can I just say," Kit started, Asha rolled her eyes immediately. "Why don't we just find another boat at the docks and just go across in that? Why do we have to wait for some special boat?"

Asha raised her eyebrow. It was a legitimate question that she now wondered the answer to. She glanced to Max whose brow had creased.

"We destroyed all of 'em," he replied, his response was followed by a short but heavy silence.

"What?" Finn said quietly.

"What the fuck? Why?" Kit retorted angrily, dulling out Finn's words.

Asha closed her eyes and sighed. The idea of waiting around for a week while knowing a safe place lay just across the water filled her with a horrible feeling that something was going to stop them making it.

Max turned the wheel and they steadily crawled along the road before picking up some speed, swerving past abandoned cars and decomposed heads. "We couldn't risk Hunters gettin' themselves across to us. We had no other choice. All the boats on land were just beggin' to be used, so we ripped out their engines and used 'em for other things, like keeping things running at Harbour. You gotta do what you gotta do."

"Like killing your family, right?" Daisy muttered unexpectedly.

"...Like that," Max replied lowly, keeping his eyes on the road.

Asha swallowed hard and leant her head against the window, closing her eyes for a brief moment. She curdled in the now poisonous silence of the car. Daisy's comment burrowed itself in her brain and her heart, niggling away, trying to make her react. Nothing. She just felt numb. She was constantly reminded of that day thanks to her black scar, its memory was now just sort of there, not doing any more damage because it had already killed her.

She felt a nudge on her side and she jumped slightly before spinning her head to face Max.

"You alright?" He asked gruffly, his eyes sympathetic.

"Yeah," she replied blankly. "I just need to sleep," she lied.

"After sleepin' for what, a day?" He chuckled.

She shrugged and turned her back to him, she wasn't in the mood for chatting now, and her anxiety was beginning to take over. She thought about how the journey might go, if the car would make it all the way, if all of them would survive. All these thoughts spun around her head making her feel dizzy and sick.

Her heart sped at an alarming rate, and she had to work with her mind to help bring it down to normal speed. She hadn't felt like this in a long time, and she knew it was because there was a group of them now, not just she and Kit.

The group posed a threat to the pair; more bodies meant more of a chance of failing. She wondered for a moment why she cared so much about the people in the car. They'd just met. Why did she place their safety alongside hers? Alongside her partners? Maybe it was something to do with the fact that people were rare and sticking together was instinct.

Either way, she cursed the instant attachment.

Ten minutes passed by of her silent panic before she slowly reached into her bag and got a good grip on her trusty knives. Knowing that she had everything she needed calmed her, at least a little.

After a moment, she let them go and clicked open the glove compartment to distract herself. She rifled through the contents as quiet murmurs came from behind her. There were a lot of papers, all of which had the name 'Alan Parker' on them. Guess she now knew who used to own the car, and it seemed he had debts up to his eyeballs, judging by the countless bills and final notices.

Under all of the rejected post, Asha came across a small, fat, black folder. She pulled it out and opened the zip, revealing a stash of CDs. She felt a smile cross her lips as she flicked through the familiar names of artists.

"Queen, The Beatles or Disney Classics?" She announced to the car nonchalantly.

"There's music?" called Finn cheerfully.

She turned around to face the others and waved the black wallet up. She caught sight of Piper who had a broad smile on her face, telling Asha she hadn't heard music for a while. Kit raised his eyebrows, but he was still smiling.

"Disney," Daisy grunted, and as Asha looked to her, she stared back with a stoic face.

"Disney it is," Asha sighed lightly, pulling the bright pink CD out and shoving it into the system.

Before long, the car began to fill with the nostalgic songs of her childhood; timeless classics that gave her an invaluable escape. She felt a warmth start from her stomach and seep into her limbs enveloping her in happiness. However, that was soon overtaken by a feeling of longing and loss. The songs reminded her of a time when everything was good and being a child was full of wonder and freedom.

Any child born into this would never have what she had. Her children (God forbid she brought any into the fucked-up world) would never experience that joy. All they would know was survival. Fun would be a strange concept that wouldn't come naturally to them. She dreaded the thought of the next generation; that was, if they ever made it to a new generation.

Twenty minutes went by uneventfully aside from varying levels of moaning from Daisy who seemed to be getting in more pain. Her meds were wearing off. Piper rummaged through the medicine bag, pulled out a couple of paracetamols and prepared a bottle of water for her.

"Didn't you bring any fucking morphine or something?" She complained to Finn behind her before she swallowed down the pills.

"There was none left," he replied quietly. "It ran out in the first few weeks. I guess people wanted a…" he paused for a moment. "…a nice way out," he breathed out slowly.

Asha swivelled in her seat to look at him, he had turned his face to the window beside him and she watched as his eyebrows knitted together and a look of anguish flooded him.

What's going on in there?

Without warning he turned abruptly to her, his wide eyes catching her looking right at him. She took in a quick breath and turned from him hastily, not enjoying the fact he'd caught her staring.

"Can we make a stop?" He asked, suddenly full of panic.

"We ain't got time, Thorne," Max bellowed, his voice carried loudly around the car. "Use one of the empty bottles if you need a piss."

"I know people we can save," he said, choking on his words.

"*Carry on…*" Max pushed, though he kept his understanding tone.

"My older brother lives about half an hour north of here with his family, we're heading in the right direction. Please, he might, he might still be there," Finn pleaded shakily.

"Oh, me next, me next!" Kit cried mockingly, sticking his hand up in the air. Asha glared at him. He really could be a fucking child sometimes. "No, seriously, why don't we find every single family member we have left? I mean, it's only fucking fair, right?" He smiled over-dramatically before his face fell flat.

"Well, do you have anyone left?" Finn asked innocently enough, but he instantly regretted it as Kit shot him a dark look.

"I don't know!" He shouted. Asha became nervous about their proximity; they'd cause an accident if they actually fought in the back there.

"Get over it, Kit. They're gone." Daisy said grumpily, staring out the window.

"How the hell do you know that? Hmm? They weren't even home when it happened. They could be anywhere."

"Yeah, anywhere… in the ground, in a Hunter's stomach… But most likely dead."

"Well, aren't you just a little ray of pitch black!" He screamed, hitting the headrest of Daisy's seat hard. Asha's heart pinched and her stomach jumped. *Stop, please.*

"Hey! FUCK YOU!" She yelled, turning rapidly in her chair and swinging an open palm at him which he quickly batted away.

"*Please!*" Piper yelled, taking everyone aback, even Max stiffened slightly. "Stop this stupid bickering! It's not good for us. We work together, *or we die apart*," she spoke her last words in whisper so they'd listen.

"Right, I'm putting a ban on talking," Max ordered roughly.

Everyone settled into their seats and hushed themselves, though Asha could sense Finn fidgeting after not being given a definitive answer.

After five minutes, Max spoke again. "Give me the signal when we're near, Thorne. Every life matters now."

"*Fuck all of you*," Kit muttered under his breath and Asha whipped her head around once again.

He huffed his face towards the window and closed his eyes, his eyebrows turned up and his lips grimaced. Asha refrained from shouting at him. He was hurting, like all of them. He missed his mother and sister, and not knowing what had happened to them, not knowing if they were still alive or not must press heavily on his mind. At least she could move on from her loss, she knew *exactly* what had happened to her family. Sometimes she wished she didn't, but in the end, she knew that that was how it was supposed to go.

The stars were cruel, but they had a plan.

It was just under twenty-five minutes later when Finn began to give Max directions. Surprisingly everyone had followed the 'silence' rule that had been set down. Which was a good thing because they were all on track to kill each other before they reached Harbour. Asha was more shocked that Daisy didn't even emit a sound, despite her probable pain.

The town Finn led them through was something of an idyllic English wonderland. It was fit to burst with little shops with bunting in pastel colours, all along cobblestone streets. The pretty picture didn't last long though, and soon enough they were confronted by the violence that had ripped through each and every place since Nox.

The quaint buildings and houses had been sent into a state of disarray, leaving scorched and smashed holes where life should have been brimming. Broken skeletons littered the streets. The initial look wasn't something to give them any hope that Finn's brother was still alive. However, their own town had been ruined and they had been surviving there, so there was no way to tell.

"Up here and turn right," Finn spoke sternly from behind. Asha could tell he was preparing for the worst.

Max followed his words and soon enough they were pulling up in front of a big, detached house with white walls and blue trimming. Asha quickly scanned the place; it looked untouched, but in the driveway stood a car; not a good sign.

Finn hurriedly unbuckled his seatbelt and launched himself over the seat between Piper and Daisy, both ladies voiced their annoyance at his haste. Within seconds he'd climbed over and had shot out of the car. There was no point in calling his name to calm him down because he was already at the front door.

A heavy feeling consumed the car; no-one spoke a word as Finn kicked the door open. They all knew it was a lost cause.

Asha felt like she needed to go with him, just in case someone unwanted was in there. She looked to Max and he nodded his head like he knew what she was going to ask. She clicked off her seatbelt and calmly got out of the car, taking just her knives.

She didn't hear anything as she approached the house - also a bad sign. If Finn had found his brother, there would have been chatter. Instead, there was an unsettling silence that just made her feel like she wasn't going to like what she found in there.

"Finn?" She called, keeping her voice as low and as clear as possible.

The inside of the house was just as beautiful as the outside, not a thing was out of place. Asha looked around and let out a long breath through her nose. It was the perfect family home.

Toys were stacked happily on their shelves, tiny shoes were lined up at the door, and family portraits hung grandly. Finn looked a lot like his brother, only younger and less stocky, Asha noted.

Eventually she clenched her jaw and tore her eyes away from the preserved everyday life of before. Instead, she focused on reaching Finn, which meant stalking from room to room until she happened upon him.

The house was still silent and she found herself impossibly wondering if he'd even entered the house to begin with. That was until she heard a small noise from upstairs, like a whimper. She immediately ran to the bottom of the stairs before charging up them two steps at a time.

She only just got to the landing as Finn stormed out of one of the rooms with his head down and his hand clutching something. He barely acknowledged her as he passed by to walk back down the stairs. She could almost feel the iciness that he bestowed. It sent a shiver down her spine and she found herself not being able to move.

"*Finn?*" She said, though it was barely audible.

What had he seen? Something was telling her to leave, to follow him and go back to the others. But another part of her, a stronger part, was being overwhelmed with curiosity.

Her feet moved forward towards the open door he'd just come from. She could smell the now familiar smell of decay as soon as she got close. *Okay, now I should leave.* She knew she should have gone, but she still wanted to see. It wasn't like she'd been deprived of seeing horror, so why did she want to see more? It was the same feeling you get when you pass a road accident, you know you shouldn't look but you just had to.

She trod carefully and slowly as she approached the ajar door to the room. Once she reached it, she pushed it open more.

Her eyes struggled to adjust to the dark room within, but seconds later her vision revealed a truly horrifying sight.

Skeletons. Three of them were under the covers but one was sitting above them. The body mounds under the blanket had large dark red patches where their heads would have been and the skeleton above them was holding a pistol in its bony hand.

Asha held her hand over her mouth as her eyes rested on its skull; or what used to be a skull. The wall behind it was splattered with a torrent of dark red mass, along with black gun residue. *Oh God.*

Looking at the mounds under the sheets it was clear that two of them were children.

Asha felt sick; she had to get out of there. She turned quickly to leave; her motion caused her to feel off balance. She grabbed the wall, closed her eyes and took a few breaths; resisting the urge to throw up. With everything that she'd seen so far, that was up there on the most traumatic scale.

She felt herself begin to shake. A man would rather kill his family and take his own life than try to survive. She couldn't decide if she was horrified by it or if she was horrified by the thought that maybe it was a good idea. Either way she felt sick to her stomach, she couldn't imagine what Finn was feeling, seeing his family members like that.

Asha couldn't get out of the house fast enough, tripping at the front door. She must have looked pale as a ghost because everyone looked at her, worried. She took in a few deep breaths as she jumped into her seat and pulled the door shut a little too loudly.

The car was engulfed in a heavy, suspended silence and Asha could feel all eyes on her, like the group were waiting for her to talk.

She sighed and spoke through laboured breath. "We're not looking for anyone else." And that was final.

Chapter Eleven

Half an hour went by. Finn was deathly quiet as they continued their journey. He just stared out the window and sat motionless; his eyes looked like they'd lost their spark.

Asha wanted to ask him how he was, but that was a pointless question. She distracted herself momentarily by looking around and checking on the others. Daisy had fallen asleep, Piper was trying her best to get a peek at her arm to make sure it was all okay. Kit had picked out one of the books from their stash and was reading it, though she could tell he was merely doing it for show; his eyes weren't concentrating on anything in particular. She turned back around and stared at the road ahead.

The music continued softly around them, but it didn't serve as a distraction anymore, not in Asha's case anyway. What she'd seen in that house was a horror. It ranked closely to the first night, but her family's murder would always come out on top.

She just couldn't shake the image of Finn's brother's final moments out of her head.

She thought about how he must have poured over every possible scenario, how he decided what he did. She imagined him pulling his wife aside as she watched the news intently. She saw his wife's look of defeat as she knew what he was going to suggest. She could see his kids' faces and how they lit up when Mummy and Daddy had a 'surprise' for them upstairs. She thought about how his wife bundled the kids up onto the bed with tears streaming down her face while her husband grabbed the gun from the wardrobe.

How they told the kids to wiggle under the sheets for a game, their excited squeals filling up the safe room. She heard the deep breaths he took as he thought, *can I really do this*? And when he decided yes, she saw him give a nod to his wife who mouthed 'I love you' before descending under the covers too. She could see his veins bulging as fear began to be broken down by a need to protect. She imagined how the first shot shuddered the entire room. She heard the other child screaming only to be comforted for a second by their mother before their time came. Another shot and the wife was gone. He was left alone, a sudden flash crossed his eyes, *maybe I can go it alone,* he thought before cursing himself for thinking such a thing. Then he pointed it in his mouth and pulled the trigger.

BANG.

"So, this Harbour," Asha started with a quick intake of air. "What exactly is it?" She asked curiously, turning to Max.

She realised she hadn't really delved much into where they were headed; she just went along knowing it was somewhere safe. She heard Kit put the book down; she knew he was as curious as she was.

Max cleared his throat and kept his eyes on the road. "We have a research facility on the island which specializes in bio warfare. Handy, huh?" He paused for a moment. "Y'know, considering that Nox was an attack. No thanks to the Global Peace Corporation...I mean, they did a smashin' job, didn't they?" He groaned slightly. "We were lucky enough that some of the scientific team didn't turn. Luck is a strong word because some 'em did and most of 'em didn't survive the Sickness," he clenched his jaw. "But now, six months down the road, we're fully set up. Wind and solar power keeps Harbour goin' and with everyone on the island having jobs, it works well."

"Sounds like a dream community." Asha smiled. It all sounded so quaint and perfect.

"Basically," Max shrugged. "One that's trying to save the world," he grinned.

"About that…" Kit piped up from behind. "How is that you've already made some magical thing to keep the infection from fully turning you… in six months. Doesn't that stuff take years?"

"Well, we already knew of something of its kind being in development, that's the kind of government know-how we were privy to. We just weren't sure how it was goin' to be released, or when… And when there's nothin' else to do apart from work on that, it gets done pretty quickly," Max stated.

It *was* a little odd that Harbour had a temporary cure so quickly after it had happened, but Asha supposed that being bored, and having the right facilities and specimens to examine, it could be possible. Also, without the distractions of daily life and with the impending doom of the human race, free time and procrastination would take a back seat.

She shuffled in her chair, getting comfortable as she realised she'd been sitting rigid listening to Max. What he was talking about was a dream. She just wanted to get there and feel safe for once. The idea of everyone having these jobs and becoming part of a community where everyone knew each other was something so alien, but she wanted it so badly.

Since being with the group, she'd forgotten how much she liked being around people and not just Kit. Sure, there were conflicts but that was what turned the mundane exciting.

More personalities made for a far more interesting life. With the added bonus of her being extra immune she thought of how much she could help, and how lucky it was that Max of all people was the one to find her.

"Time for a pit stop," Max announced as he pulled over under some low bearing trees.

The light was getting brighter as the midday sun approached. It was surprisingly clear in the sky, not a cloud in sight. Despite the sun though, it was still a bitter cold. Asha pulled her hood down over her face and exited the car, stretching out her body and letting out a satisfied sigh.

She rotated her neck until it clicked and then sucked in a long breath of cool air. It was refreshing compared to the cramped space in the car. She looked to the gathering of trees before them and carefully surveyed the area. She couldn't hear anything, but she was still cautious.

"I'm dying for a wee." Daisy said sleepily as she approached her side.

"Let's go together then." Asha smiled, and held out her arm for her to hold, she looked reluctant but hooked herself to it anyway.

"Careful, girls," called Max.

Asha turned to give him a curt nod and then began the walk through the trees.

Daisy was slow on her feet; navigating over the tangled branches and unpredictable leaf-trodden ground was a challenge. They quickly found a relatively sheltered area and Asha was quick to help Daisy out of her trousers, but she pushed her away when it came to her underwear, which Asha could understand.

127

Most dignity had been lost, but the last few shreds still remained.

Asha got herself sorted and went behind a tree; she still had an eye out, who knew when an attack might come. It would be typical to happen mid-flow. Luck was on their side though, and before long Asha was clothed and helping Daisy with her unnecessarily tight jeans.

They wandered back and thankfully came across a small creek with a pool of clear water at its base. Asha stepped close to it and then sank to her knees before dipping her hands in. The water was almost freezing to the touch, but she needed to clean herself, after all, she'd had a rough couple of days where unbelievable amounts of grime had coated her body. She collected the water in her hands and rubbed her face of the dirt and blood. She had to stop her rough hands quickly though because her nose was still sore along with her cut lip. She winced slightly but carried on carefully making sure to get every inch of her face and neck. Daisy followed suit and within minutes they were clean.

"How're you feeling?" Asha asked Daisy while dabbing herself dry with her coat.

"As good as I *can* feel." Daisy sighed, glancing to the water. "This is just the icing on top of the fucking cake." she said motioning towards her injured arm.

"Yeah, I can imagine." Asha sympathised. "And losing those people back in town. It's not been a good few days for you."

"Yeah… I'm not too hung up on that." Daisy spoke quietly, her eyes darting from the water to the trees.

"What, those people?" Asha questioned.

She knew Daisy was close to at least one of them, judging by the way Piper and Max tried to console her after she delivered the news of their deaths.

"*Yeah*," she practically whispered.

"Were you close?"

"He was my dad," Daisy said bluntly.

"I-" Asha began to apologise but she stopped herself because Daisy seemed annoyed at her beginning of a response.

She thought about how Daisy reacted when she found out they didn't make it. She seemed almost *relieved.*

Asha hardly had time to think about how strange that was because in the next second, high pitched shouting travelled through the trees.

The hair on her arms stood on end and she hurriedly grabbed Daisy. They ran full force through the woods until they reached the others.

When they got there, Finn and Kit were circling each other. Kit was already bleeding from his nose and Finn was rubbing his fist. They were fighting. She ran to put herself between them, but Max grabbed her arm and yanked her back, taking care to not pull too hard. She shoved him off her, but he held her shoulders in place.

"*Get the fuck off me*," Asha warned him lowly.

"Let them fight," he said matter-of-factly and looked on at the boys with hardly a hint of concern.

"Boys, stop!" Piper cried from the side-lines. She was useless, as if they were going to listen to her.

"Oh, *Jesus!*" Daisy moaned loudly before walking straight through the middle of the sparring boys to the car.

"What the *hell* is going on?" Asha demanded.

"*Finnegan* here has some deep-seated anger management issues," Kit spat.

It all happened so quickly, Asha didn't even have a chance to breathe let alone step in to help, not that she would have been able to with Max holding her back for some reason.

Finn's fist connected with Kit's jaw with a cringe-worthy crunch. Kit's head swung back from the force and he instantly spat blood to the ground below. It took him less than a second to regain composure though and sport a wicked, blood-filled grin. Asha knew that face well; Finn was about to be in a world of trouble.

Kit stalked fast to him. When he reached him, he literally grabbed his throat, yanked him high into the air by it and drove his entire body to the ground.

The wind was blown from Finn instantly in a pained grunt; he tried his best to scramble up from where he'd been shoved, but Kit was fast to jump on top of him, pinning him right where he needed him.

That was when Kit decided to start pummelling his head with fists seemingly made of steel. Which was the exact moment Max finally let go of Asha and she leaped onto Kit's back, hands jutting out to his arms to stop them mid-air.

"Stop!" She managed to yell before he shoved her off with force.

Anger and worry broiled in her, creating a nasty concoction in her stomach.

Kit delivered one final blow to Finn's temple before feeling satisfied enough to get up and wander off, leaving everyone else to deal with the repercussions of his violence.

Finn was awake, barely. He writhed where he lay, reeling from the onslaught. Quite rightly too because his lip was busted, his nose was bucketing blood and his temple had a hefty cut across it.

Asha found herself by his side in an instant.

"Why?" She asked, helping him to prop himself up on his elbows.

He took in a few breaths and pinched his nose before tugging it; it snapped right back into place and his eyes swiftly began to water. "He said my watch was shit."

Asha looked at him with a puzzled expression before noticing the large silver watch that hung too loosely on his wrist. He didn't have that on before. Her brain quickly put two and two together; it was his brother's. That's what he was holding when he came out of the room, he must have swiped it the second he saw it.

She fished out a tissue from her pocket and dabbed it to his cheek before leaving him to hold it himself. She gave him a reassuring look before standing herself up and going to find her *pendejo* of a best friend.

He was sitting in the middle of the road cross-legged with his head up to the sky. She sat herself beside him and rested her head on his shoulder for a brief moment. He raised one of his strong arms to wrap around her, and she leant into him further.

"You know, you're making this all very difficult," she said.

His grip on her loosened slightly and she raised her head to look at him. He trained his hazel eyes to hers and pursed his lips before sighing.

"He's just an annoying prick," he said.

"Why? He's done nothing to you."

Kit pulled away from Asha completely. "He's put you in danger, and I can't stand that," he huffed, his freckles were more noticeable in the sunshine.

Asha lifted her hand to the back of his head and ruffled his curled hair. "You know you don't have to worry about me, right?" She laughed.

He fell silent and stared at the ground. "You're all I have left," he said solemnly.

His comment took her aback. Him caring for her wasn't a surprise, but it was the way he said it. She'd never heard him be so honest.

"Look at me... *Look at me*," she urged, pulling his chin to face her. "You're all I have left too. But you know you don't have to worry about me, you know that deep down. So, what is it? What's bothering you? Because you're never this fucking annoying."

"Nothing," he said before taking a deep breath of defeat. "I just... What if Mum and Scarlett are there? What if they're there and we have to wait a week to get to them? It's just frustrating, y'know? Like, I could be there earlier if we had another fucking boat, and then I could see them again."

Asha listened and patted his leg. It was all well and good imagining an ideal outcome, but she couldn't help but think of the worst-case scenario.

In her mind's eye, they were gone, and she was happier believing that; because if she didn't, she'd be holding onto a hope that would eventually eat her down to nothing. They were her family too, she loved them too.

"Maybe," she simply said.

She wasn't about to give him any ideas. There was a one in a million chance that a) they were both still alive, and b) they had found Harbour. The odds were not in their favour, but he could hold onto his positivity if it helped him.

"Come on, let's go. Try not beat anyone else up," she said before hauling herself up and patting herself down.

Everyone else had already gotten into the car and with a small rumble it came to life. Time to go. She opened the door to where Piper sat and she scooted over to let Asha climb into the back seat with Finn. Kit jumped in front and closed the door behind him before buckling in.

No one spoke for a few minutes while Max pulled out onto the road and started them on their journey once again. The atmosphere in the car was more than heavy; Asha could barely breathe, especially as she was tucked away at the very back. She felt slightly claustrophobic.

She took a glance at Finn; he was nursing his wounds, but he didn't look as pathetic as he did earlier. He actually looked a lot tougher now that he was covered in blood and bruises.

"At least you're going get a *badass* scar," Asha said, attempting a joke.

"Yeah," Finn replied unenthusiastically before facing away from her. *And failing.*

That was her cue to not talk so she just turned to the window and stared out of it, glossing over the countryside they had now entered. She watched how the fields rolled over and under each other. She liked how they'd gone into disarray; even the grass didn't look like grass anymore, more like wheat blowing in the wind. It was sort of fascinating how nature had started to reclaim the earth for its own. It made her feel bad for how they treated it, cutting it back constantly, not letting it roam free. Now, it was beautiful. She preferred it.

Before she knew it, she'd fallen asleep. It most likely had something to do with the stressful morning, the silence, and the inherent need to sleep when in a moving vehicle.

Her sleep must have only been about half an hour when all of a sudden, a loud bang shot her back to consciousness. She gasped as her heart felt like it flew out of her chest and she quickly looked around the car, assessing the situation.

"*No!*" Max exclaimed. She noticed a large plume of black smoke coming from the hood of the car. The car ground to a halt. "We need to get out. Now."

Asha scanned the surrounding countryside quickly, there wasn't anywhere to run; they were in the middle of nowhere. Not even a house was in sight; they were completely open to an attack.

They were screwed.

Chapter Twelve

This wasn't part of the plan.

Mierde.

They speedily exited the car and grabbed all that they could carry. Asha was lugging the loot from the house in the woods along with her own bag; even that was a struggle considering the weight of the water. She found a balance between them though and forced her legs to run fast towards the tree line nearby. Once there, she crouched down and settled the things on the ground. Seconds later, the group joined her and they sat breathless for a second looking around, no doubt trying to figure just exactly how they were meant to continue from here.

The surrounding areas were sparse of life. Deep in the countryside you were lucky enough to run into a cow let alone a house or shelter. The roads were surprisingly bare; Asha would have expected at least some abandoned cars from the last six months of terror but no. Not a single vehicle lay in their wake, aside from the one they'd just run from which looked like it would explode any second. It had oil cascading to the ground with a fire now growing strong from the hood of the car. When it did explode -which it most certainly would- it would create a huge noise, which would give away their open position. Exposing them to whatever threat roamed nearby. They needed to think fast.

They were in the daylight and that meant danger.

Max knelt up to get a further look around, but his brow furrowed and his eyes became narrow. It was like they were all waiting for his orders, like he was the one who should know what to do. But he looked *scared*.

"What are we going to do?" Piper cried, pushing back her long red locks with both hands while cradling her face in worry.

"We're not going to panic," Max stated, despite his obvious disgruntled look. "There was a town about half an hour drive back. But on foot it'll be too long."

Finn sat still staring at the ground in front of him; he looked like he'd given up on the whole thing, like it didn't bother him that they were on the verge of a not so happy ending. He stayed away from Kit though, which was a good idea. Kit was searching the plains with Max but both of them looked defeated.

Asha shook her head and urged herself to think her way out. What could they do? They had nothing to travel in, they were faced with an open road enveloped by countless fields, and most of them had injuries that at least slightly hindered them. She closed her eyes shut tight for a moment before opening them and looking to the horizon. She couldn't see much but what she did see was the fact that the road ahead was raised and that it sloped downwards to somewhere they couldn't see. There had to be something over the hill, there *had* to be.

"Over there," Asha said, pointing to the direction of the continuing road. "We make our way there and see what's after it. It's our best shot, there might be something, a farm for all I care."

"And if there isn't? We just let ourselves be picked off by Hunters?" Daisy questioned, a scowl on her face.

"If it comes to that we can fight them off," Asha said. "But let's keep our hopes up, for once," she glowered at Daisy.

The blonde girl sighed and tucked her face behind her raised knees.

"It's the only idea we got," Max said, standing himself up. "Be on the look-out, those buggers could be anywhere."

Asha nodded firmly and gathered her things before standing up and adjusting the bags until they felt comfortable.

"We walk. If we run into any problems, we duck into the tree line," Asha tried to sound like she knew what she was doing, but she was shaking.

"They'd best pray they don't run into us," Kit said, bearing his axe. He looked fearless. Grime and blood coated him, and his determined scowl matched his words.

Asha gave him a quick smile and then began the walk.

She would be lying if she said she was calm. Her heart was beating harder than ever, mostly through the fear of being found, but also because the sun had started to beat down and she was covered head to toe in dark clothing. Her cape coat was a small miracle though, letting some air shoot up and around her body.

Her eyes were constantly scanning the area around them. She kept her ears on high alert, making sure she could hear the constant walking of her fellow survivors and to catch out any unusual sounds. The road seemed longer than she'd first thought, even with the end in sight, she still felt like they were walking miles.

"I hope you're right about this," Finn said, catching up to her side.

"If I'm not, then I'm not. But we gotta keep going, 'cause we're not weak," Asha glanced to him, her eyes meeting his.

His lips twisted up into a brief smile before returning to their flat state.

"I felt safe at the hospital," he said with a sigh.

"Well, you're more than welcome to go back," Daisy chimed in, securing her place on Asha's other side.

"Like that's an option," he answered, his head hanging low.

"You really felt safe there?" Asha asked, ignoring Daisy's jibe.

He nodded his head in return. "It's all I've known since Nox broke out. It was comfortable."

Asha could kind of understand where he was coming from. She felt somewhat safe in the house on the hill, but that was because they were practically hidden from everyone, and she had Kit there to help her if she got into trouble. In Finn's case, he was where everyone wanted to go, and he only had his mum and the other patients to 'protect' him. Asha would have hated it there. Fending off other survivors, Reapers and Hunters by herself on a regular basis.

It would have been hell; but he found peace.

BANG.

The car behind them blew its hood and it landed off in the trees, the blast sent her ducking as she caught her breath.

They needed to find that shelter now, or they were done for.

The others gathered themselves after the blast and they continued to walk, a little faster now.

They finally approached the top of the hill and Asha couldn't help but run a little to truly see over it. She smiled broadly when she spotted a small collection of buildings, a village, about a mile down the road. It looked decidedly abandoned, which was to be expected, but it was a place they could settle for the night, or until they found another suitable car to take them north. Either way, getting out of the sun was highest on the priority list.

"Immune *and* smart. We've got a winner here," Max chuckled as he ruffled the top of her head with his palm.

Asha swatted him off and worked her hood back into place so that it covered her face enough to shield the sun. She was smiling though; knowing they had somewhere to go was always a relief. She felt a small bounce in her step as they descended the road towards the village.

"Let's just hope there's a car big enough for all of us. It's riskier in two cars," she said.

"We'll find something," Max replied.

They made it about two minutes down the road when the sound of a speeding car began to emerge from back up and over the hill.

Asha stopped in her tracks and turned to face the direction they'd just come. The wheels were coming closer and closer, she could even hear the tread they were making on the road. The car was going fast, too fast. Any survivor would be taking more care than that. Which could only mean one thing.

"Hunters," she said under her breath. "Hunters!" She yelled now, pulling Finn and Daisy with her to the side of the road towards the hedges. The others followed suit but it was too late.

A huge, all black, Range Rover careened over the top of the hill and hurtled along the road towards them. Its passengers were decked out in skin-tight clothes and balaclavas. They waved their arms out of the windows with classical music blaring full blast.

Asha counted five Hunters, and they'd seen them.

The car drove straight past them before swerving and blocking the road. They pulled the breaks and sat staring at them. Asha felt her breathing become erratic as the Hunters were still. The group stood, not knowing whether to run into the forest or to confront them. Either way it seemed they were going to fight. Asha swallowed hard and glanced to Kit who looked from her to the car before mouthing 'I got you.' She nodded her head and turned back to their enemies.

Her suspicions were proven right when the Hunters started to exit the car. She noticed that they didn't have any loot on them, or in the car. They didn't need anything. They were Hunters; all they needed was meat, their meat. Not a slither of skin was showing on them, another sign.

Max strode towards the front of their group standing his ground as he took out his bloodied cricket bat. Asha dropped what she was carrying and held her breath.

There were three guys and two women; they were all adult and skinny. They were hungry.

She fished out her knives and gave Finn a look. He took out the gun she'd given him earlier and he passed it over before pulling out the crowbar and knife Max had given him before. Daisy pulled out a screwdriver, Piper a hammer and Kit, his axe.

Asha shoved the gun into her back pocket and grasped her knives tighter as she tried to assess the situation.

The Hunters were standing in a row so perfectly still and silent that it sent shivers down her spine. They stared at each other for what felt like an hour, but really it must have been seconds until one of them spoke.

"Big Daddy in front," The main Hunter simply said, pointing to Max. The other four nodded their heads without saying a word.

"I'm no-one's Daddy," Max retorted, passing the cricket bat from hand to hand.

"The flesh on him, it's enough to feed all of us. And with the rest of them, we're set. It's perfect," his voice was horribly smooth, it made Asha's skin crawl. "Buttery, succulent," he chuckled lowly. "Oh, how we deserve this!" He sang. The others nodded again.

Everything about this particular group turned her stomach. They were different, more obscure. The less human a person, the scarier they were. The main Hunter clicked his fingers and suddenly the others revealed their weapons; twelve-inch machetes.

Not a second later they charged in sync like robots towards them.

It was all too quick, but the group jumped into action as soon as they did, pushing them back with everything they had. Max was the first to attack, his bat knocking one of them to the ground.

One of the women went after Finn who struggled to apprehend her. Kit was closest to him, but he did nothing, leaving Asha to fend for him.

She ran to Finn and pushed him backwards away from the Hunter and stuck her knife deep into her side, causing her to fall down.

She followed through with a blow to her head and swivelled quickly on her heels to counter block an incoming attack from the main Hunter.

Kit was now busy fighting off one of the men, and Piper was tackling the last two Hunters with Max.

Daisy tried to use her weapon, but her stitches seemed to have come loose because her hands were full of fresh blood.

Finn quickly herded her to the forest to hide her.

Thankful that Finn and Daisy were out of the way and safe, Asha focused on the fight at hand. She shoved the main Hunter away from her with a shout, but he swung his machete towards her, it barely missed as she contorted her body to avoid it. She kicked him in the back of the knee and slashed his forearm, which faltered him for a moment as he buckled, but he quickly got himself back up.

Her wide eyes searched for a weakness. She decided to run from the commotion, to drag him away from her friends.

She could take him on better if they were alone.

He caught up with her though, and when she turned to face him, he swerved the machete towards her in quick succession; she had to be light on her feet to avoid his constant swings.

She ducked down to avoid his onslaught but when she jumped back up, his fist connected with her jaw with a sickening crunch, and she fell helplessly to the ground.

She forced herself to stand up through gritted teeth; her efforts however were only met with a kick to the abdomen. She spat blood and practically choked as the wind got knocked out of her for the second time in the last few days.

Her glance went to the others and assessed how they were faring; blood and pain rocked them. This wasn't good.

"There's not much on you, but it'll be enough. How do you feel about becoming dinner?" He spoke, circling her as she struggled to stand up, grunts of exasperation escaped her. "Perhaps we'll mix you in with a light tomato sauce, or maybe we'll just fillet you, sear you rare. Like a fine steak." She could hear him lick his lips under his balaclava. She felt her insides twist and nausea set in.

He lunged at her again with his blade but with what little energy she had left she dodged his attack and instead, grabbed his balaclava and ripped it straight off his head.

His bare face came into view, and she was pleased to finally put a vile face to a vile person.

His eyes widened tenfold, and his hands shot up to his now burning skin. She watched as the sun's effect engulfed his skin into welting, raw blisters almost immediately.

He stumbled forward while letting out a croaked cry and she took that opportunity to toss her knife up in the air, grab it and stick it deep into his neck. He stilled fairly quickly and as she yanked out the knife, a warm jet of unrelenting, dark blood splattered her face and neck.

She coughed and spat out the infected blood that had flown into her mouth before collapsing to the ground, heaving. She wiped the blood from her eyes and once her body stopped rejecting the blow, she turned her attention to the others.

Max was putting the finishing touches on the last Hunter standing. He worked well with Piper who was stamping out their kneecaps with her hammer.

Kit spotted her on the ground then and ran full force -with a limp- to her side.

"Fuck, is that yours?" He asked hurriedly, swiping away at the blood with his hands, trying to find a wound to blame.

"No," she coughed; her whole body ached from the onslaught. "I'm fine," she lied, and instead scanned him. "What happened to your leg?" She asked, noting the way he ran.

"Nothing much. Sprained my ankle," he shrugged as he lifted her up to her feet with ease.

"Ow!" She protested, the strain on her body bearing too much pain. She steadied herself on his arm. "Let's get to the houses."

"Looks like we're using their car," Kit said, and as Asha looked up to it, she could see Max hurrying the others with all their stuff into the Hunter's car.

It was a Range Rover, hardly able to fit four people let alone six, but it was safer than walking the rest of the way, especially in their current condition. She caught a stare from Finn as she and Kit made their way over. He was shaking like a leaf, but it did look like he'd used his weapon.

"There's not much room. Kit, me and you have to sit with the girls on us," he said shyly.

"First time you had a girl on your lap, huh?" Kit joked, jabbing him with his elbow. Finn backed away and kept his eyes elsewhere. Kit huffed. "Whatever," he said before sitting himself down in the back. Finn quickly joined him; next it was Daisy who climbed her way onto his lap, and lastly Asha, who jumped onto Kit's.

Once they were all in, Max started the car and quickly turned off the blaring music that filled the car in an instant.

"*Why classical music?*" He muttered to himself as he manoeuvred them round to the direction of the houses. "Everyone alright?" He asked behind him.

They all gave varying grunts of reassurance.

Getting to the village took less than two minutes; it was more modern than the last place they were in, with its terraced unformed houses and brand-new roads. But it was empty just the same.

However, there *was* something different about it that stirred Asha's curiosity. On a few of the buildings there was a yellow sun drawn on the bricks, it looked like it was in spray paint. The drawing was the same each time. A circle with a spiky rim, like a lion's mane. It was strange, and the further they headed into the village the more prevalent they became.

"This looks safe. We'll stay for tonight." Max said as they pulled up in front of a dainty detached house with pink shutters. The house was older than the rest; it seemed homelier which made Asha smile. It had a sun too, but this one had a green spot in the middle of it. She found herself wondering what the suns were all about and who put them there.

"Looks like my house," Piper said, a wash of sadness taking over her.

Asha could just imagine Piper in a house like that, with her herbs growing in little plant pots and the smell of home baked, apple crumble wafting through the shutters.

She stopped mid-thought. She didn't want to think of a time gone by; it was over.

"Okay guys, unpack the stuff, we'll lay low for tonight," Max ordered.

They trundled out of the car ungracefully as all four teenagers entangled themselves from one another. They held what they could carry and made sure that the coast was clear before gathering around the front door. Max was trying to open the lock with a small knife, but it wasn't working. Asha put her stuff down and pulled out the trusty hairpins from her bra.

"Let me," she said as she gently tapped Max's shoulder and showed him the hairpins.

"Be my guest," he said in his gruff voice as he moved out of the way.

She gave him a slight smile and knelt down by the lock. She worked the pins in and wiggled them around, pushing them through the various lock mechanisms until finally that satisfying click came and the door opened. Standing up proudly, she folded the pins back to her bra - always handy.

"Thank you," Max said bowing his head.

"Ugh, please. Anyone knows how to do that," Daisy moaned.

"Like *you* have been any help at all," Asha spat.

She felt bad for saying it straight away, but if Daisy was going to serve it up, she would have to eat it too.

Asha pushed open the door and was pleasantly surprised when a smell of damp hit her; it made a change to rotten decay.

They shuffled in one by one and dumped all the stuff in the nicely kept living room. Asha took in a deep breath and let out a relived sigh. They were in shelter and no feeling was better than that. She and Max worked on shutting the curtains and the rest of them rooted through their stuff for water and food.

Piper walked past Asha's eye line towards the door to the living room, and she looked to Finn who she noticed was a lot more relaxed now that they weren't out in the open.

A sudden scream filled the room however, and Asha quickly spun around to see Piper bent over with her hands clasping her thigh. Blood dripped between her fingers from the ice pick that stuck up from it.

Holding it there was a little girl who was doused in blood with a scowl on her face.

"Where is she?!" She shouted, anger bubbling out of her tiny body.

Chapter Thirteen

Piper whimpered and kept her hands tight around the weapon in her leg, but she made no move to get it out of her or to apprehend the girl responsible for it.

Asha stared at the girl who seemed to be frantically looking from the group to somewhere behind them. What was she talking about? Or rather *who* was she talking about, and why did she stab Piper?

The group were so taken aback and in shock that none of them moved, even though Piper's stunted cries filled the room.

Asha's face twisted into confusion and horror as reality set in. This girl was only around eight years old and there she was stabbing someone viciously with blood dripping from her hair. This was what the world had become. The silver lining was that she wasn't infected, but she sure acted like one of them.

"Who are you looking for? We can help you," Max said as he cautiously walked towards the situation, his hands up.

The girl wasn't having any of it. With Max's advance, she yanked the pick from Piper's thigh and motioned to throw it at him. Piper fell to the floor but kept pressure on her wound.

"Whoa, whoa, whoa," Max said, promptly stopping in his tracks. "We're not gonna touch you."

A tense, silent moment passed until all attention suddenly focused on the tiny pattering of feet that came from down the hall.

Immediately, the little girl's eyes widened; she almost looked guilty about what she'd just done.

In the next second, an even younger girl came into the room. She was clutching what looked like a fat, cat toy, and she went and wrapped herself around the older girl. The girl grasped the littler girl and shook her shoulders roughly.

"Look what you made me do! Don't ever do that again. When I say stay, I mean stay!" She shouted at the child.

"But I heard something, I was scared!" She spluttered, her eyes watering. The cat toy dropped from her grasp.

Asha stood transfixed on the girls who weren't even interested in the group anymore; the others went to Piper who was giving them reassurance. She was a nurse; she knew what to do with herself.

The girl was protecting the other girl. Asha understood now.

The older girl was slightly tanned and had mousey brown hair that was tucked up in a messy ponytail. She was quite lanky for her age, with long, thin legs and gangly arms. Her ears were large compared to her head and she had harsh dark circles under her pretty eyes.

The smaller girl was pale as anything with short, dark hair. She had one half of it up in a pigtail and had a long, unkempt fringe that covered her eyes. Her cheeks were rosy, and her overall body was plump and healthy; Asha wasn't sure how.

"It doesn't matter if you're scared. You have to do as I say, you have to!" the older girl cried.

Asha could tell she was genuinely terrified for the safety of this girl who couldn't have been more than four years old. It didn't look like they were related but she couldn't say for sure; they might have been cousins.

"I'm sorry, I'm sorry, I'm sorry," The littler girl whined. Her tiny hands holding on to the other girl's arms as she still shook her.

"Next time, you stay in the cupboard. No matter what," The older girl ordered firmly.

She acted far more mature than her age; it came with the territory. She then turned her attention to the group again and pulled out another weapon from her trousers, a dagger. She pushed the smaller girl behind her –who promptly picked up her toy and hugged it- and held out both weapons towards the group.

"Why are you here?" The girl practically growled.

"We're just looking for a place to stay the night," Asha said. "We can leave. There are other houses," she offered, unsure how to negotiate with the girl who she couldn't predict.

"No, we're not goin' anywhere, and neither are you two," Max said.

Asha turned to shoot him a glare, but he was looking to the girls sympathetically. She glanced back to the older girl who had a deep frown on her face.

"You need to leave," she scowled.

"Listen," Max said. "We're going to a place called Harbour, it's safe there, no Hunters, no-one there to hurt you, I promise. It's somewhere you can live without fear. No more hidin', no more *killin'*. We're on our way there and you can come with us, we have food and drink. You'll be safer with us."

"You think we haven't been told that before?" the girl said, her hand was unwavering as she held her weapons out.

"We're not here to hurt you," Max pressed.

"Prove it," she spat. "Put all your weapons in a bag and give them to me."

"What? No," Kit spluttered.

"Fine," said Max.

"*What?*" Kit said, now with more concern.

Asha found herself wondering what exactly Max was doing but she trusted him. His judgment seemed to have gotten the group this far; surely it was logical to trust his actions despite how illogical they were. But Kit's persistence forced her to rethink her thoughts.

She pulled at Max's arm slightly and drew him to her. "*What are you planning?*" She asked discreetly. The girl was distracted by Piper's whines, she looked guiltily to her.

"*Just trust me,*" he brushed her off and grabbed one of the cushions off the sofa before dragging the cover from it and filling it with his guns, knives and the cricket bat.

Asha took out both her knives - her most prized possessions aside from her mother's ring - and placed them into the cushion case. She suddenly remembered the gun in her jeans and obediently slung that in too. She felt naked and anxious without her protection.

Her sharp glare shot to Kit. He was wary at first, his dark brows creased tightly, but he eventually gave in and handed over his axe and various other deadly possessions. With his willingness, the rest of the group followed suit and soon enough there was a pile of mismatched bags each containing everything they needed to survive.

And they'd let them enter the grip of an eight-year-old girl.

The mousey girl struggled to carry the bags, so much so that she had to get the smaller girl to carry some of them.

The sight was unbelievable, it was completely unnatural and utterly bizarre; a pair of little girls with the power of ten men in their tiny hands. Despite the odd image, Asha had a feeling they were capable of wielding such strength.

"Do you need any of our food?" Max asked.

"We don't need your help," The girl replied bitterly. "Be gone by tomorrow," she ordered before she pushed the littler girl ahead and marched out the front door into the ever-coming night.

As soon as the door shut, the group jumped into action. Asha found herself being drawn to Piper who was politely shooing both herself and Finn away from her. Daisy and Kit had other concerns and began to argue with Max who was standing his ground; he was a calm, overbearing force to be reckoned with. Daisy and Kit's combined dominance was double Max's, but they were erratic and juvenile, they didn't stand a chance.

"...I thought you'd have realized by now, but I guess you're too ignorant, huh?" Max laughed.

"Realised what? That you just gave all of our weapons to those little girls. I mean *shit*!" Kit exclaimed, his arms flailing as he ranted. "What do we do now, hmm? I don't know if *you've* noticed yet but it's getting dark and this place isn't exactly a fortress, is it? We need our weapons!"

"You can run out there and get them back if you like, Kit. I mean, they're only little girls like you said. I'm sure you could take them on, so what's the big deal?" Max said, his eyebrow rising.

Kit stalled for a second, stumped by the question and hit with a scenario. "I'm not going to fight children," he finally said.

"You won't have to… they'll be back," Max announced, folding his arms and widening his stance.

"How do you know that? The little brats are probably running around all excited now they have all the weapons Daddy could give them," Daisy moaned, holding her still bleeding arm gently.

Asha stood up and placed a hand on Finn's shoulder motioning for him to stay with the Piper. He nodded and kept his attention on the redhead as she gathered the things she needed from the medical bag.

She joined in the discussion by standing herself next to Max.

"Because two children lost in this world will always, *always* follow an adult," he answered the blonde girl.

"But you heard what she said. They've trusted adults, *like us*, before and I don't think they experienced sunshine and rainbows," Kit seethed.

"Come on, Kit," Asha started. "Think about if you were a kid right now. You'd do anything to find adults, some kind of security. They will miss their parents, that's what'll draw them to us. Right?" She questioned, looking at Max hoping she was on his track.

"Exactly. But more importantly, we showed them trust. Which I'm sure their previous encounters didn't. That's the difference, young Kit," Max grinned as he ruffled Kit's hair.

"Fuck off!" Kit growled, moving from him, eyes warning, arms in front of him.

Daisy groaned and slumped onto the sofa, crumpling into a ball and burying her face in her knees, letting out a long sigh.

"That still doesn't mean it'll work. You saw how feral that little girl was. She's probably halfway across the town massacring a defenceless dog for dinner or something," Kit protested.

"You need to have a little faith, Kit. But for now, it's a waiting game. We might as well set up here, make sure it's secure. Asha, Kit you take upstairs, Finn and I will do downstairs. Daisy, see that you stay with Pipe, it looks like both of you are in need of medical attention," he ordered, his fingers pointing to her bloodied arm.

They all followed orders like obedient soldiers under their faithful leader's command.

"This whole 'securing' thing is a little pointless if we find someone and don't have any weapons to defend ourselves with," Kit groaned quietly as they walked up the stairs.

Asha sighed, but a small smile took over her lips. "I don't know why, but I trust him - a lot. He seems to know everything there is to know about surviving out here. I think he was in the army, he's definitely tactical enough," she theorised as she peered into the first room; a quaint bedroom in perfect order with untouched photos and trophies lining the shelves. Nothing of threat there.

"I *do* trust him, I let you go off with him, didn't I? I just don't like this situation. But you're right, I think he was in the army before all this. And if he's alone, it kind of tells me that there is no army left, so we can tick them off the short fucking list of people who could save us."

"Even if there's no army left we're still being saved. I've got a good feeling about Harbour, even though it seems impossible."

Next room clear.

"I guess sometimes the most impossible thing in the world just so happens to be the only possible thing left," he said under his breath.

"How very profound, Kit. Don't go talking like that down there, you'll lose your tough guy reputation," she winked.

He shoved her and she shoved him back playfully before entering the bathroom. Her eyebrows almost shot up into the atmosphere. "Oh my god!" She exclaimed, staring at the giant insulated water butt that took up most of the room.

Kit's eyes lit up. "Dibs first on a bath!" He chuckled. She just grinned, too happy at the concept of a bath to bother about him going first.

They had to tell the others. No wonder the girls had a protective claw on this place.

After trailing through the rest of the house excitedly they found that it was fully equipped with everything they could need. It had generators for electricity, a heated water system and an abundance of clothes and sleeping things. Another wonder they found was a fully stocked larder of food. Asha felt bad about taking any of it, but they only had mere snacks, and they were in need of a good meal.

The realisation of the sanctuary they had found themselves in boosted the mood of the straggling group.

Before long, Daisy and Piper were all patched up and playing a game of snap, which truthfully Daisy didn't seem too pleased about, but she let a smile slip sometimes when she won. Finn was curled up on the sofa with a book in his hands and Kit was upstairs enjoying his miracle bath.

Asha joined Max in the kitchen and couldn't help but get excited at all the options of food at their disposal.

"Those girls haven't always been alone here," he said as he pulled out a couple of cans of tinned tomatoes and a big packet of spaghetti.

Asha hadn't seen such well-kept food for a long time; it almost looked fake.

"What makes you say that?" She questioned, her hand reaching for a sealed packet of pistachios. Saliva filled her mouth so fast that her cheeks ached.

"They couldn't have done all of this without the help of adults. I mean, this place is more advanced than some of the houses in Harbour. A lot of work went into it and I'm betting the other houses around here just the same, or at least similar."

"Because they wouldn't have gone so easily if they weren't," Asha said.

"Bang on," Max said, winking.

"And they must have lost their people recently because there's too much food."

"Nice deduction. That's an important skill out here, makes it easier to suss people out, help 'em, or get what you need," he said before he started up the hob and placed a frying pan and saucepan on it for the cooked meal they were going to have.

"Well, I'll keep that in mind," Asha said, turning away towards the living room.

"Look out for the girls," Max called after her. "They'll be back before it gets really dark."

Asha didn't answer but she stuck out a thumb through the door as she left to the other room. She was in a good mood and she hadn't been in such a mood for at least three weeks; it took some getting used to.

Despite that, she couldn't deny the overwhelming ache that consumed her body from the events of the day, and though the injuries to her face still throbbed, she was only thinking about the bath that would soothe her.

Finn noticed her smiling face as she walked in the room; he looked scared somehow.

"What are you reading?" She asked as she sat herself next to him. He edged away slightly and cleared his throat; a look of confusion still held his face. "What?" She urged.

"Nothing," he shrugged. "It's just, I've never seen you so happy."

"Yeah... appreciate it while it lasts," Asha agreed, because he was right.

It was moments like this when she was reminded of who she was before, and the severe contrast to who she was now.

He took a breath and a moment passed before he spoke again. "It's a first edition of George Orwell's '1984'. I can't believe they had it," he said, admiring the book and flicking through the pages with care, a little sparkle in his eye.

"Can I see it?" She asked and he gave it to her without hesitation.

It was a treasure. It would probably fetch around £2000 at auction on a good day. But it had no financial value anymore, which in some ways made it even more precious.

She passed it back and sat cross-legged, getting comfortable. "You like books?"

"That's like asking if I like food or something," he said, blushing lightly.

She nodded her head and smiled. "Don't get me wrong, I was a party girl for sure but my secret was that I had a huge bookshelf in my bedroom, it filled a whole wall. *Mi mamá* was always telling me to stop buying books, but I couldn't help myself. I only ever read a third of them. I think I just liked having them around."

She had always loved the comfort of imaginary worlds.

"I get that... I always felt at home in a bookshop," Finn said looking off into the room, jaw clenching, that sparkle gone.

He was longing for something; she'd seen it in him ever since they'd left the hospital.

"Things are different now. We have to get used to it, or we'll get lost in a world that isn't ours anymore," she said, pulling herself out of reminiscing too.

It was too much to bear, but in time she knew she would be able to happily look back at what once was and smile, instead of mourn.

"*Yeah,*" Finn said under his breath as he brought the book back up to read.

Asha watched him for a few seconds, noting the way his eyebrows pulled up slightly when he concentrated, how his lips pursed, and his dimples poked through.

She then took the cue to leave and hauled herself off the sofa only to be met by a wet, tousled Kit coming through the door. He looked cleaner than he'd been for around three years.

"Who'd of thought such a handsome man could be hiding under all that dirt!" She exclaimed in mock joy.

"Oh ha, ha, ha. Wait till *you* have a bath, it'll unveil your true self; an evil bitch," he joked, that familiar gleam in his eyes.

"She only comes out on special occasions," Asha smiled, taking the towel from around his neck. She gave one last look to the living room and made sure everyone was okay before she retreated upstairs to the well overdue bath, grabbing her bag on the way.

The water was already filthy from Kit's use, but she didn't mind, she'd only be making it dirtier anyway. She stripped off her clothes but left her underwear on because that needed washing too, and dipped a toe in to test the water. It wasn't exactly warm, but it wasn't cold either and by that point anything would do; she was almost entirely made of blood and dirt.

She slunk down into the water and sighed with relief; there was something really comforting about being in water. After about ten minutes, she slowly descended under the water, letting it completely cover her. She kept her eyes closed and lay there suspended in the watery embrace for a few moments, feeling herself relax.

Eventually though, she had to come up for air, but when she did, she was confronted by the murderous, haunting eyes of a Hunter.

"Nice bath?" He cackled.

She barely had time to scream or move because as soon as she saw him, his rough hands grabbed onto her temples and he smacked her head hard against the back of the tub. Her hands and legs thrashed around trying to get out of his grip, but it was no use, he was too strong and any sudden movements on her part would probably end in her snapping her own neck in his hands.

He delivered the second blow with muster.

She heard a crack when her head made contact with the bath again. The last thing she saw was his arrogant face snickering before she tumbled into darkness, her body slipping under the water.

Chapter Fourteen

She was suddenly above herself. Floating, watching, waiting. *Oh, this can't be fucking good.*

As she looked down on herself, she noticed a small cloud of blood dispersing in the water around her head. Her entire body was submerged and she wasn't awake. Her body started convulsing as bubbles escaped her mouth and popped on the surface of the water.

She was drowning.

"Wake up! Wake up!" She yelled, attempting to talk to herself but it was no use, it was like she didn't exist anymore, her cries were lost in the world.

The Hunter who had attacked her was still in the room, he had hidden himself behind the door. After what seemed like a lifetime, she heard someone burst in through the bathroom door.

"Oh shit!" Kit blurted, seeing her in the bath.

Asha was desperate to shout for him but no words came out. She wanted to warn him of the Hunter in the room, she wanted to call to him, she wanted to come back to herself, but she couldn't. She was stuck in a halfway world. Seeing her body was only a clue to what was going to happen. She was going to die.

It was her time.

The Hunter pounced on Kit before he could get to her and they struggled with one another. Kit was trying his hardest to swing the Hunter off of him and he was shouting to the group for help.

Asha watched on like it was a film, helpless and slowly slipping away.

She wondered if there were more Hunters downstairs, a full-on ambush. As if to answer her thoughts, she heard frightened yells and screams coming from downstairs, her hope faded.

Kit quickly gathered himself and flipped the Hunter over his shoulder causing him to fall onto the side of the bath; a crunch sounded through the air as his spine snapped against the ceramic. The Hunter screeched in pain as he fell to the floor at a shuddering angle. Kit grabbed the nearest thing to him- a large glass candle - and didn't hesitate in smashing it into the Hunter's head until he stopped moving.

He then hurriedly bent over the bath and wrapped his arms around Asha's limp body, pulling her out with an exasperated grunt. Water sloshed over the side of the bath, flooding the floor.

She wasn't breathing, her skin was pale and her lips looked like they were turning blue. He placed her gently down on the floor and started to give her CPR and mouth-to-mouth resuscitation. His part-time lifeguarding job coming in handy for the first time since Nox began.

Thirty chest compressions followed by two resuscitation breaths, over and over.

Two minutes went by.

"Come on Asha, not now. Fuck, not now!" He yelled between his laboured attempts to bring her back.

It's okay, she thought, *don't exhaust yourself to death, pendejo.* Her condition didn't look promising, and she didn't feel any closer to her physical body, which could only mean one thing; he was too late.

Finn suddenly rushed into the room; his unsteady footing on the wet floor landed him flat on his face next to hers. He had a fresh cut across his cheek, blood dropped onto her face as he pushed himself up to absorb the situation. She swore she could feel the warm droplets as they raced down her cheek.

"*What the-*?" He managed to say, his eyes widening at the sight of her, and the Hunter who was beaten to death on his left.

"I can't, she's not," Kit spluttered. "I can't get her to breathe," his hands were still working on pumping her chest in hopes her heart would kick in again. His arms were shaking; he was losing strength.

"Let me try," Finn said pushing Kit aside.

Kit didn't protest, and instead sat back against the wall. He held his head in his hands and stared solemnly at her. Tears tracked his cheeks.

Finn placed his hands one over the other, right under where her ribs met, making sure to copy Kit. He then started furiously pounding on her chest with his palms, keeping somewhat of a tempo.

A strange, guttural breath escaped her physical throat.

"She's breathing!" Finn cried, stopping his onslaught.

No, I'm not.

"She's not. That's an agonal breath. It means she's about to die," Kit said flatly, unable to move or react. His eyes dulled as they watched her death play out.

"No, no. Come on Asha, come on!" Finn grunted as he continued his work. His breathing matched the rhythm of his actions.

Suddenly, as he pushed down on her, she began to feel more alive. She could feel warmth seep into her limbs, she felt a little lost in the air, like she was disappearing.

Back to reality.

"Come on, come on, come on," Finn gasped, his breaths short. He was getting desperate.

"Stop! You'll break her ribs!" Kit suddenly shouted, his hands grabbing for Finn's shoulders.

Finn shrugged him off, but he did stop giving her chest compressions; instead, he opened her mouth and pressed his lips on hers, starting to blow air into her lungs.

Asha could actually feel the air flowing through her body. He breathed in a few times before stopping and checking her chest for movement. He then tilted her chin up and repeated the procedure, over and over again.

Keep going, keep going, I'm almost there.

Before all hope was lost, Asha's eyes shot open and a fountain of water escaped her mouth as she fully came back into the real world. She coughed and sputtered as Finn turned her onto her side, allowing all the water to exit her lungs without the risk of her choking on it.

Her eyes were as wide as the moon as she sucked in huge gulps of air once all the water was gone; her throat felt raw. She shook where she lay, she couldn't believe she was still alive.

Finn then turned her onto her back and lifted her shoulders up onto his kneeling lap. She caught her breath and looked around the room in awe.

She was alive.

"Ash! Are you okay?" Kit asked, he sat by her side, his hand wrapped around hers like a clamp. His hazel eyes bore into her, relief flooded them.

After catching her breath, she finally croaked. "A bit thirsty actually," she joked, a small, exhausted smile on her lips.

"Shit, you're definitely okay," he laughed, wiping his eyes. He reached for a towel and passed it her way.

"Thanks," she said sheepishly, suddenly realising her underwear was on show, and that two teenage boys were there. She took the towel and draped it over her body before sitting up with Finn's help. "*Fuck*," she moaned through scattered breaths as her hand went to the back of her head. "That's not pleasant." It wasn't a huge cut, but the bump would take a few days to go down.

"I hope Piper's in good enough shape to stitch that up," Finn said, quietly.

"What happened?" Asha asked as she stood up with the help from both boys. She steadied herself on Finn's arm, dizziness overtaking her.

"Six of them came in right after Kit went upstairs, I don't know how, we'd already made sure it was safe, but they came and tried to get Max first. Then, those girls came back. Well, the older one did, and she started taking them out..." he stopped talking and took a breath. "*She's crazy,*" he whispered.

"She'll fit right in then," Asha said through gritted teeth as she rubbed her aching chest. "I feel like I've been hit by a truck."

"That would be my fault," Finn admitted, raising his hand, his eyes were wide and apologetic.

"Hey, I'd rather have a bruised chest than not be here at all. So, thank you," she let her hand rub his shoulder before turning to Kit, "to both of you," she smiled.

Kit smiled back and took her into a hard hug, she grimaced and gasped, the pain in her ribs amplifying as he held her.

"Oh, shit, sorry," he said, quickly removing himself from the embrace.

Asha knew he meant well, so she just dismissed his apology with a limp hand and looked to the door. She could hear quiet chatting coming from downstairs, it seemed things had gone in their favour.

"How's about you two let me get dressed? I'll meet you downstairs," Asha said.

The boys nodded their heads, and after fussing around her for a final time, they left.

She listened to them as they walked down the stairs.

"Thank you," Kit said firmly.

"You don't have to thank me," Finn replied.

"No, I do. You saved her," his voice trailed off until she couldn't hear them anymore. She found herself smiling; it was progress.

Asha looked down, stretched out her fingers and noticed her ring had fallen off, for the third time in the past two days. She rolled her eyes, reached into the bloodied water and fished it out before placing it back onto her finger with ease. She admired it for a moment and closed her eyes. *Mamá, I could've joined you just then.*

Her eyes focused past her fingers and to the tub she'd just been in. She realised then that it wasn't her head she'd heard crack, it was the bath.

She dried herself off and picked up her clothes, which was a struggle in itself. She was going to need at least a few hours of recovery time before she was fit and well again.

Her relaxing bath hadn't exactly gone to plan.

She laughed quietly to herself; she was stupid to think that she would get such a luxury.

After a painful wriggle into her black jeans and top, she made her way downstairs at a slow pace.

There, in the middle of the living room, were the bags of weapons they had handed over hours before, and next to them were the two girls. The older one was clutching at her side and her teeth were clenched, thick blood coating her once again. The younger one was looking around, her mouth wide open like she'd never seen bodies before, tears stained her cheeks, her chubby arms roughly held her fat cat toy.

The amount of bodies was a little shocking to say the least. There were four in the living room. Finn said there had been six Hunters, meaning they were elsewhere in the house too. Blood seeped into the carpet and the whole house smelt of its metallic flavour. Asha swallowed the lump in her throat and stumbled to the nearest armchair before collapsing into it with a strained breath.

Piper was checking her head almost immediately; The boys had clearly filled her in on her injury. She tutted in the way a mum would when discovering a graze on a child's knee and went to fetch her medical bag.

"It's not your day is it, Asha?" Max said.

"It's not my year," she replied.

Kit stood with his arms crossed against his chest; he was studying the girls, watching their every movement. He was curious and so was Asha. They'd come back, and by the sounds of it, the older girl had helped greatly in the attack.

Asha wondered how it was possible that such a young girl could take on multiple adults successfully. But then she thought about how small the girl was, and how she could be quick on her feet and get through tight spaces without an issue. As much as she hated to admit it, and she really did, Asha thought that maybe children made ideal killers.

Piper began to clean and stitch her head wound which made her grip onto the arms of the chair tightly.

"We've been really careful. The Horsemen were spotted around here, we didn't see them, but our people did. So, that's why I didn't want you here. You might have been working for them," The older girl explained quite articulately to Max who was nodding his head with a surprised look on his face.

"Who are 'The Horsemen'?" Asha asked, wincing as Piper applied antiseptic to her head.

"Even *I* know who The Horsemen are," Finn laughed lightly but stopped when Kit glared at him.

"You really don't know?" Daisy scoffed, not being covert about her disbelief.

Asha felt like she and Kit were somehow the least popular members of the group because of their lack of knowledge. She frowned and looked to Max, urging him to explain it to her.

"They are a group of four Hunters who didn't turn quite like the others. We at Harbour have been itching to get our hands on at least one of 'em, but they're such a highly intelligent and ghost-like force, I've not seen them myself. They are like Hunters 'cept that they can go in the sunlight, which have made the regular Hunters worship them."

"Their key features, at least according to eyewitnesses and rumours, are black eyes, black blood, and the penchant for eating people raw," Max revealed, he talked about them like they were celebrities.

"They are made up of two men and two women. Apparently, they're all hot," Daisy shrugged, injecting her know-how.

"How did we not know about them?" Asha asked Kit who just shook his head.

"I heard Reapers talking about them whenever they came to the hospital for drugs. They look up to them too. They want to be the ones to provide The Horsemen with food," Finn added.

"I doubt we'll run into them. England's a pretty big place," Kit said a little nervously, like he didn't believe his own words.

"*Yeah...*" Asha breathed. She was slightly concerned about the existence of a 'super race' of Hunters. But at the same time, Kit was right, they would likely never meet.

"Tell us more about your people," Max asked the older girl, changing the subject. He sat down now, bringing himself to her level.

She looked hesitant but finally spoke. "They were nice people. The only nice people we've met," she held the other girl close to her. "They helped protect us both. I lived in the town over that way," she said pointing to the left. "We only joined them two months ago. They showed us this village. It was nice, so we stayed."

Asha noticed the girl's fingers were not only red from blood, but they were also tinted yellow, like she'd dipped some of them in paint.

It clicked.

"Are you the one who drew all the suns on the houses?" Asha asked. The others looked at her in confusion, she thought everyone had noticed them, maybe she was wrong.

The girl nodded. "It means a house is safe."

"This one had a green circle in the middle instead of a yellow one, what does that mean?" Asha questioned.

"That it's the main headquarters. I saw it in a game once," The girl shrugged.

"That's smart," Max complimented the girl. She bit the inside of her cheek and stared at him. If she was putting up a front, it was unbreakable. "If you're plannin' on comin' with us, which I hope you are, we could use some help from a girl like you. What're your names?"

"No," she simply replied, like it was a preposterous question.

"It'll make things easier to communicate. Look, my name is Max, and the others are Piper, Finn, Kit, Daisy and Asha," he explained, pointing to the group accordingly.

They all gave small waves and weathered smiles when his finger pointed to them, but the girl was not interested.

"What's the big deal about your names?" Daisy complained with a scowl on her hardened face. She was a natural with children it seemed.

"Daisy, it's fine," Max mediated the exchange with a calming voice.

"We could give them names?" Kit suggested, shrugging.

The girl frowned but didn't oppose it.

"Sunny?" Asha suggested, the others looked at her with confused eyes. "She draws suns, so, Sunny," she explained.

"Okay," said Max. "and what about the little one?"

"My name is Boe!" She shouted almost in annoyance, looking upset that they would think to call her anything else but her real name.

Sunny rolled her eyes and looked down to her. "I told you to keep your mouth shut, Boe."

"Sorry," Boe said softly.

"Is she related to you?" Piper asked Sunny.

"No, I found her after my mum and dad died. She was hungry and her parents were gone too. I've kept her safe ever since. No-one has touched her, mostly," she warned, holding Boe closer to her.

"Don't worry, we won't touch her. But we will feed her, and yourself. I think I can salvage some of the pasta from the floor." Max said before excusing himself to the kitchen where Asha saw another body sprawled across the tiles.

*

After disposing of the corpses in the next-door neighbour's garden, the group reconvened for the feast Max had prepared. Having dinner around a dining table was certainly enough to bring back a tidal wave of nostalgia and Asha hated it.

She found herself wolfing down the tomato pasta and it wasn't just to do with the fact that she was starving, it was because she wanted to escape the room as soon as she could. The food was exceptional though, and that was saying something seeing as Max had to scrape most of it off the counter and the walls; but it was a hot, home-cooked dinner nonetheless.

Everyone finished their food apart from Daisy who claimed she wasn't hungry. They learnt a little more about the girls. Sunny was nine years old and Boe was four; they'd been surviving together since the beginning and they were now interested in coming with them.

Max decided that they would stay in the village for a couple of days just to get their bearings and hopefully find a radio transmitter to contact Harbour with. Sunny also mentioned that they needed to go to the next village to collect petrol for the generators in the morning because it was almost out.

They had their plan for the following day. Next, they formed two groups, one to sleep and the other to keep watch. Luckily, they had all their weapons back which made safeguarding much easier.

Asha and Kit retired to the main bedroom of the house after their goodnights. It was cosy even though it was double the size of the other bedrooms. All four walls were covered in tapestries depicting different intricate tribal patterns, the ceiling was littered with fairy lights and most of the floor was covered in a white shaggy rug; it was comforting.

Asha didn't bother taking off her clothes, it was too cold to sleep in underwear, so she just dove into the bed and squirreled under the thick duvet; it was heaven.

"You don't waste any time, do you?" Kit joked as he whipped his shirt off, revealing his tanned, toned chest and joined her under the covers.

"I'm so tired I think I could sleep for both of us for a thousand years."

"Not one to exaggerate either," he said, jabbing her in the side with a pointed finger.

"Ouch!" She groaned, turning to face him. "Victim of drowning here."

His face fell from a joking smile to a grave stare. "Yeah, I'm trying to forget that happened," he spoke lowly. "So, let's sleep," he said turning over onto his back and staring at the ceiling.

Asha shuffled up closer to him and placed a palm on his warm chest, she could feel his heart beating fast against her fingertips. "I might have nightmares about The Horsemen."

His arm wrapped around her shoulder pulling her into his side. "The Horsemen can kiss my arse…I just hope that we're making the right decision by going to Harbour. If you get hurt again, I'm gonna question whether this is worth it or not."

"I could say the same for you."

"Yeah, but I'm not immune like you. You're important to me, and to everyone else now. Which is why I'm not gonna let you out of my sight *ever* again," he said flashing her a mischievous smile.

"Alright, stalker."

"Fuck off," Kit chuckled before settling into the pillows and closing his eyes.

Asha smiled and laid her head on his chest, the slow yet steady rises and falls sent her to a much needed sleep.

Chapter Fifteen

The next morning was an unusual one for Asha; she hadn't woken up in a warm bed for months, nor had she woken to breakfast being presented to her by a child before.

"Here, it's getting soggy," Sunny said as she placed the sloshing bowl of cornflakes on the bedside table.

Asha propped herself up on her elbows, her eyes barely open, and stared at the bowl. It wasn't made with milk, but with water instead, which didn't bother her too much. She was just happy to have a meal without worrying about where it would next come from. Her head still pounded which was to be expected, but it was feeling better than it did the night before.

"Thanks," Asha said, her voice a little gravely from sleep. She gave the girl a tired smile.

"Max wants you both downstairs quick," Sunny said before placing a bowl of cereal by Kit's still snoozing head and heading out the door.

The warm sun of the morning billowed through after her and made Asha smile even wider. She felt safe in the company of others, something she didn't think she could feel.

She turned around in the bed and focused her attention on Kit; she needed to wake him up, which was a challenge. He was one of those lucky people who could sleep through an earthquake, Asha on the other hand only needed to hear a whisper from down the street and she was wide awake.

She started by poking his back, which then turned into light punches, which then turned into hard punches, which finally ended on a slap to the face.

"What the fuck!" He moaned groggily, cupping his freckled cheek and turning around to face his attacker.

"We've been summoned. Eat up," Asha grinned pointing at the bowl next to him.

He groaned and let out a big yawn before sitting himself up in the bed and grabbing the bowl. He wasted no time digging in and Asha joined suit. They ate without speaking for a few minutes before Kit broke the silence.

"How's the head?" He asked, though his speech was mumbled through half eaten cornflakes. He looked doughy in the mornings, his eyes puffy, cheeks begging to be pinched and curly hair waiting to be played with.

"Fine. It'll heal soon enough," she said as she spooned another mouthful in.

"This makes a change, doesn't it?" Kit remarked, his hazel eyes admiring the room, the food and then Asha.

"It's so weird, and warm," Asha smiled, putting the now empty bowl down on the bedside table.

She snuggled down into the covers revelling in the heat for a moment before throwing them off her. Reluctantly, she swung her legs over the side of the bed and nestled her toes in the shaggy carpet before hauling herself into a stand. "But, we have to get going," she started, though her mind quickly realised something. "Hey, we didn't do a watch."

"Oh yeah," Kit replied, his face turning to confusion. "Maybe we did, but we blocked it out of our memory," he joked as he got out of bed. He reached for his clothes and dressed quickly.

"I doubt that," she said. Though she was a little annoyed that Max didn't ask them to do a watch, she was grateful for a full night of sleep.

When they arrived downstairs, Asha saw Daisy and Finn quietly debating, dramatically waving respective books in the air on one of the sofas, Sunny putting Boe's hair into a ponytail, Piper redressing her thigh wound, and Max hunched over a large map with an inquisitive look on his face; he glanced up when they came in.

"Mornin'" he grinned; his deep voice resonated around the spacious room. "I hope you slept well 'cause we've got a long day ahead of us."

"Yeah, about that. Why didn't you wake us to keep watch?" Asha asked, sitting herself down next to him and peering at the map. Max had highlighted certain areas in different colours; it looked like a plan.

"Thought you deserved to sleep, and we wanted to give you two some time together," he shrugged, focusing back on the map.

"What? Time together?" Kit questioned, a baffled look on his face.

"Yeah. We've been with you guys a lot. Thought you'd want some alone time."

"Oh, no, we're not..." Asha started to say, a blush hitting her cheeks. "It's not like that."

"Me and Ash?" Kit laughed, a bit too animatedly. "No," he calmed himself and looked to Max. "We're just friends."

"You hear that, Finn?" Max called over to him with a wide grin on his face.

Asha shot a glance to the sofa area, Finn's skin drained to a deathly white and he gave Max a shocked stare before his face blossomed like a rose. His argument with Daisy was quickly forgotten and he made his way into the kitchen to presumably escape. As she watched him, her heart thumped. Did she enjoy the fact that he had admitted to liking her?

Apparently. Shit.

"*Max,*" Piper said, disappointment ringing high.

Daisy was left by herself on the sofa. She looked over to Max, annoyed.

"Thanks, old man, that was the first proper conversation I've had with an actual literate person in forever," she huffed, throwing the book she was holding onto the floor. She then pulled her hood over her head and folded her arms across her chest, sinking into the cushions.

Max shook his head in amusement. "Teenagers, ey?" He smirked, looking at Asha.

She returned the smile in agreement. It was true, she and everyone else her age were a force to be reckoned with. "So, what's the plan?" She asked, changing the subject. Kit stood over her and looked down to the map, eyebrows pinched in concentration.

"The village Sunny was talking about is over here," he said, pointing to a small collection of roads and lanes not far from where they were. "I want you, Finn, and Daisy to go there, find any supplies and gather fuel from any cars left there."

"What about me?" Kit asked, concerned he was left out of the rota.

"You're gonna come with me and Piper. You see this?" He said, marking a large field area with a substantial building in the centre of it. Kit nodded his head, but he seemed confused. "This is one of Global Peace Corporation's big bases. They usually had their employees on site which means there'll be supplies and maybe even a radio transmitter. I'm hoping we'll find one, so I can contact Harbour quickly. But I don't know what might be waiting for us there, so just a heads up about that."

"Brilliant," Kit said sarcastically. He placed a hand on Asha's shoulder and gave it a slight squeeze. "What about the kids?"

"Oh, they're staying here, guarding," Max answered. He looked over to the girls and smiled.

They seemed so innocent, playing with each other's hair. They looked far different from the night before when Sunny was covered in blood and Boe's cheeks were sticky with tears.

"We're off in ten, get yourselves ready."

*

Asha packed her trusty bag with the essentials; two bottles of water, a squeezy bottle of honey, her pistol and her two knives. Once she'd gotten her bag ready, she turned her attention to her clothing. They were going out in the day, which meant covering up, and covering up well. She kept on most of the clothes she'd worn the day before but paired them with her handkerchief and grabbed sunglasses to fully cover her face once her hood was down.

She stood in front of the full-length mirror in the bedroom and studied her ragged reflection. She hardly recognised herself. Her current vibe would work well for a low budget action film with her all-black attire, hooded cloak and the handkerchief over her mouth. She had to stop herself from laughing. Although, she suddenly didn't feel like laughing because her eyes caught her off guard. They were heavily sunken and the bags under them were almost grey in colour. It was a shock for her to see someone who looked so sickly compared to who she was just six months before; a healthy young girl. Now she looked like a gaunt zombie.

A long sigh left her lips. She slung the backpack onto her shoulder before giving herself one last look. "*Eres fuerte,*" she said to her reflection. Staying positive was getting harder and harder.

As soon as she left the room, she collided painfully with someone. Her breath escaped her, but she was held steady by a pair of strong arms.

"Sorry," said Finn, their chests were practically touching from the impact.

She looked up to see his apologetic face, her heart skipped a beat as her gaze rested on his lips. He loosened his grip on her arms and took a step backwards, creating some space between them. She felt the heat lessen and shook herself back into focus.

"It's okay," she said, pulling on her cape in a nervous tick.

"I've got my gasmask, but I need to find some better clothes for going out in the sunlight," he admitted, his mouth turning up in a side smile.

"Right, well there's loads of stuff in the dresser in there. It's up for the taking," she offered, pointing into the room; her heart finally simmered down to a normal beat. "Hurry," she said before heading down the stairs, leaving him to dress himself accordingly.

Everyone was gathered and ready for the day ahead. It was odd to see all of them in their very own 'camouflage' outfits. She couldn't help but think that they looked like some sort of military faction in uniform, preparing for their mission. In effect, they *were* a pack of soldiers doing their duty, which in this case was procuring supplies for the needy and ensuring their future.

"We're being split up again, try not to cry," she poked Kit in the chest, he recoiled in his usual manner.

"I'll be happy to get away from you and your bony finger," he frowned but his face softened a second later. "Be careful out there. *Don't risk your life for them, okay?*" He whispered now.

"Kit, I don't know if you've realised this or not, but we have to protect these people. They'd do the same for us."

"It's not how we do things."

"It is. We looked after each other when it was just you and me. Well now, we've got more bodies, more people to care for. Besides, you can't tell me you won't do anything if say, Piper gets hurt and needs your help. Even if it puts you in danger?" She stared at him deeply.

"I guess I would," Kit admitted, though he looked unsure about it. "But I'm talking about *him* upstairs. I see you simping for him. That's fucking dangerous."

"Oh, come on. The day I simp for Finn, you can punch me. Right on the nose," she laughed lightly, but a tiny thought in the back of mind told her to prepare for that punch. "You be careful too. I want to see you at dinner tonight, preferably in one piece, okay?"

"You have my word," Kit replied, bringing her into a brief hug and kissing the top of her head.

Finn came down five minutes later. He wore a dark pair of jeans, a grey t-shirt with a black leather jacket draped over it. He also had a pair of black leather gloves on and a pair of black boots. To cover his face, he had his gasmask from back in the hospital.

"That is freaky as fuck," Daisy remarked flatly, seemingly not impressed with his get up.

Asha could barely see Daisy's facial expressions through her black veil - which she was happy to find in one of the cupboards - but she could tell she was pulling her natural disgusted face.

"Good work, Finn," Max grinned as he adjusted his own outfit. He wore an ensemble of dark clothing, which included his black Shearling jacket, his grey worn jeans, and tucked under his arm was a spine-tingling ballistic face shield.

Finn shrugged coyly and leant against the doorframe.

"Wait a minute..." Sunny said almost accusingly as she walked towards Finn.

Asha watched as the girl folded her arms across her chest and stared at the boy in the mask.

"Did you use to live in a hospital?" Sunny asked him. Asha's eyebrows shot up; how did she know that?

"Uh," Finn stuttered, his voice was disrupted by the mask. "I did," he said, straightening himself up off the wall, standing tall.

Sunny's face burst into an uncharacteristically broad smile, she almost looked in awe at him. Asha's confusion grew, as did the groups' it seemed because all of them stood listening to the conversation at hand, all wanting more information.

"You're 'The Apothecary', aren't you?" Sunny exclaimed, her hand going to her mouth in shock.

"'The Apothecary'?" Daisy spluttered, not able to hide her amusement.

Finn folded his arms across his chest and took a deep breath. "I was. But I'm not anymore, so…" he said, and shrugged as if to shift the attention from him.

"You helped our group. Our people went to see you and you gave them the medicine and things we needed. You were a hero to us. You're famous around here, everyone knows you. The gasmask gave it away. They said you wore one, *just* like that," Sunny beamed.

"It's no big deal," Finn muttered, shrugging.

"Thank you," Sunny said, enveloping him in a tight hug. Finn returned the favour and held her until she pulled away.

"Full of secrets aren't we, Thorne?" Max asked with a wicked smile on his face. He looked proud of the hospital hermit.

There wasn't much time to dwell on the fact that Sunny knew who Finn was, or rather, who his alter ego, 'The Apothecary' was. It was a huge coincidence which really only furthered the idea that the world was much smaller than Asha had once thought. However, she did feel like she needed to find out more information, so she pushed her time a little.

"Wait... What were you?" Asha managed to blurt out. Her confusion spilled into her words.

"I just did what I did with you and Max. Guarded the medicine, that's it."

"No, not just that! Everyone we've met has talked about The Apothecary. He's a legend. People are scared of him because he's ruthless. You needed a good reason for him to help or you didn't come out. At least that's what the stories were! Even our group were scared to go to the hospital because they didn't know what would happen in there," Sunny grinned.

"Your gun…" Asha started, remembering how she mocked him the day they met.

"…I didn't use it to tranquilize people," Finn said simply.

"Guys, can we just focus on the fact that Finn named himself the fucking 'Apothecary'?" Daisy laughed a harsh laugh.

"It fit," Finn shrugged. Asha could almost feel the heat coming from his probable blushing cheeks.

"Don't listen, Finn. You did what you had to," Piper chimed in.

"Well, that's *super* interesting but we need to get on with the day," Kit interrupted, Asha swore she could hear a hint of jealousy in her best friend's voice.

He was right though, it was time to go, which meant the group would be split up once again. Asha, although she joked with him, was still worried about leaving Kit. But they needed to make the day as productive as they could, and that meant sending everyone in different directions.

"Right, soldiers. You all got your instructions. Thorne, you just shot up in my expectations, don't let me down. Keep these girls safe," Max said, clapping his hands.

"Like we need him for that," Daisy said, gagging.

Asha ignored the comment and just looked around the room, taking in the faces of her new group and smiled. She could see the strength in every one of them and she knew they would get through this day and be reunited at the end of it. She found herself thinking about what they'd have for dinner, something that she could actually be excited about.

The full pantry made her mouth water, but they needed more than just food. If they wanted to keep the power on at the house they needed to scavenge for petrol and if they wanted to make contact with Harbour, they had to find a radio transmitter.

"See you on the other side," Asha said as she pulled Kit into a quick hug.

With that, she let out a determined breath and headed out the door into the blinding light of the crisp autumn morning.

Let us survive this, she thought nervously, glancing up to the sky and donning her sunglasses.

Chapter Sixteen

Asha, Finn and Daisy walked for twenty minutes, although it felt longer because the three teens couldn't stop bickering, and the sun was heating up the air, making it stuffy in their outfits. Luckily the wind was biting cold, which offered ample relief to the threesome.

Asha gripped the map Max had given her, she'd taken charge, and under her guidance, they were on the right track. The next village wasn't far, but anxiety still pulled at her heart like a relentless violinist. Sunny had given them all the equipment they needed to syphon petrol from cars and a roll of bin bags in case they got lucky with finding supplies. All they needed to do was get to the village in one piece. A tough obstacle to say the least.

"I'm gonna be so fucked off if I die with you two," Daisy moaned out loud as she marched between Asha and Finn. She had a heavy step, not one bit graceful.

"Why do you have to think so negatively all the time?" Asha questioned, shooting a glare her way, not that she could see it.

"I expect the worst, then nothing can disappoint me," Daisy shrugged.

"Seems like you're disappointed all the time," Finn joined in.

"Whatever, you should be too. Have you taken a look around lately, Finnegan? It's kind of the end of the world."

"My name's not Finnegan. Why do people keep fucking calling me that?" Finn complained, quickening his step to walk ahead of the girls.

"And he calls *me* moody," Daisy mumbled, letting out a sigh of exasperation.

"I mean, shit, he's not had it easy these past couple of days," Asha said, thinking about all the grief he had encountered since they found him. "Besides, it's not the end of the world. We're going to get out of this. You heard Max. Harbour is real and we're gonna get there."

"I don't trust all that," Daisy huffed.

"What are you talking about?" Asha questioned.

"It's pretty convenient that Max's walkies got trashed by a Hunter. You'd think he'd carry an extra spare if it was so important," she paused. "He has *guns*, I mean, who the fuck has guns? It's England. And don't even get me started on the fact that there's 'no boats' to get to Harbour. We just *have* to wait for this particular one... I'm just saying, he could be a Reaper. King of the Reapers or something. He's got the talk, the weapons and the look. Just think about it. He could be working for The Horsemen. He acts like he's the boss of us and we do exactly what he says. We're out here on his orders, aren't we?"

"That's ridiculous. Why would he come all this way, and go through this much effort to save us if he was just another Reaper? And his guns have helped us and probably will carry on helping us, so I don't care how he got them...And I believe the boat. You'd do everything you could to make that island inaccessible," Asha ranted. "And if you really think that, then why are you even here?"

"Because I have nowhere else to go... and I don't care if I die," Daisy muttered under her breath.

Asha didn't know how to respond to the last comment, but she understood why Daisy would stick around. She had no-one left. The fact that she would rather follow someone who she didn't trust and someone who she thought would lead her to her death meant that she was truly desperate to be around people, at any cost.

"I'm not giving up on this, and if Max is right, and I can be used for a cure, then I'm sure as hell gonna get to that island, with you and everyone else too," Asha said with certain determination.

"I'm not *giving up*," Daisy grunted, her hands flew to her head before she flung them to her sides angrily. "God! Why am I always the bad guy, huh? Everyone is on my back all the time. I can't deal with it on top of all of this '*Apocalypse Now'* shit!" She cried and walked away from Asha.

The dark-haired girl rolled her eyes and looked down at the map again. She wasn't in the mood to deal with two petulant teenagers, so she put her effort into something more valuable and strode ahead of both of her sulking companions, leading the way to the ever-nearing village.

Even though she was a similar age to both Finn and Daisy, she felt like she was at least ten years older; but she knew that was down to what she'd been through the past six months. She was certain of it.

If she had been coddled by a group of adults or even by her parents during the 'apocalypse' she wouldn't be who she was today. In a way, she was happier for it.

It had allowed her to survive as long as she had. But in another way, she hated how it happened; she mourned her youth.

She assumed Finn and Daisy were babied on the basis of their stories and the way they behaved when confronted, flying off the handlebars over tiny altercations. But truth be told, all it was was an assumption.

She didn't know anything about Daisy and how she'd been surviving. All she knew was that she was with her dad and that Max found them both; that was it.

Finn was a different story altogether. His newly revealed role as The Apothecary brought a whole new dimension to him. He had been alone with his sickly mother, and he killed for their protection. He should be like Asha; he should be hardened and less worried about things that didn't matter, like people calling him the wrong name. But he wasn't different, he was as soft as the day he came into the world, and he didn't see a problem with it. Asha put it down to the fact that he killed with medicine, so he didn't fully grasp the concept of being a killer; it wasn't real to him because his victims died cleanly, like they were falling asleep.

She was lost in her thoughts of Finn when the first signs of the village came into view. As they entered it, she surveyed the area of cobblestone lanes and uniformed cottages, and after a second, she deemed it safe enough. She motioned for the others to keep quiet still, who knew what could be lurking in the silence.

They walked without a sound until they reached the first abandoned car, a red Mini. Daisy got to work on it and Finn moved on to the next car down the road, a dark green people carrier. Asha stood herself between the two of them clutching her gun; someone had to stay on guard.

They followed the routine all the way down the main road of the village until it branched off to the woods, quickly filling the petrol cans until the amber liquid spilled messily from the spouts. They were lucky that no one seemed to have scavenged the vehicles.

Asha kept her eye on Finn who was fumbling with his many cans as he placed them on the road ready to start on the new car, which was hopefully full of petrol.

She stood with her feet wide apart, ready for action if it arose. She craned her neck from side to side, releasing the tension that was building there. Finn ripped his gasmask off, he was sweating and it was no surprise, working the cars took effort.

Asha too was beginning to get a little hot under the heat of her hooded cape, so she pulled her handkerchief down and took her sunglasses off. It gave her a little more ventilation and she breathed out a sigh of relief.

It was then that the sound of trodden tarmac came from behind her.

She spun quickly on her heel to face the woods, and that's when her eyes locked onto the gut-wrenching sight of a snarling, grey wolf.

Panic shot through her like a bullet and she struggled to breathe.

She watched on helplessly as it took slow, threatening steps towards her. Its teeth shone in a deadly smirk and its tongue flit like a snake, sending droplets of saliva into the air. A deep guttural growling resonated from the beast through to Asha's chest. Her mind ran with questions; where had it come from? Was there a zoo nearby? Why was it here? But ultimately her mind went blank and instead she let fear consume her.

Her hand quickly lost grip of the gun and it clattered to the ground, her body went numb. The wolf looked startled at the gun for a second, but then returned its icy stare fixed on Asha's frozen figure. She tried to speak to warn the others but the words got caught in her panicked throat.

"*Oh my god*," Finn whimpered from behind her. The noise of the gun must have made him turn around.

Asha could do nothing but stay where she was, her eyes transfixed on all the shades of blue in the irises of the animal before her.

"*Daisy! Where the hell are you going?*" Finn practically hissed from behind Asha. She could hear Daisy's frantic footsteps as she escaped. *One down.*

Asha thought she could handle anything that came her way. But this, this was out of her control.

A wild animal with an empty stomach was a death wish that you had no choice but to sign. In animal kingdom rules, Asha was the prey, and the wolf was the king, sitting happily at the top of the triangle munching on a thighbone. She forgot everything from every wildlife show she'd ever seen, except for the fact that you should never stare at a wolf because they take it as a threat.

Even though that thought was running around her head, she couldn't move or take her eyes away from it. She felt like if she stared at it, she could control it, tap into a deep cosmic connection and force it to leave her alone. But that wasn't going to work, and deep down she knew that.

She shook hard where she stood. *Move, move, move.*

Finn's hands slowly wrapped around her waist, and he dragged her as calmly as he could away from the approaching beast. Her feet barely worked but they went along awkwardly with his movements.

All of a sudden, the wolf lunged forward with a resonating growl that sparked the voice that had been hiding in her. She screamed, falling backwards as she attempted to back away quickly. She landed painfully on her coccyx, pulling Finn down with her. They scooted back until their shoulders hit the parked car behind them. Asha's heart burst out of her ribcage and she took in breath after breath in hurried panic.

The fall, though painful, had sent a much-needed jolt of adrenaline through her. She hurriedly shuffled her backpack off and swung it round to her lap. She then grabbed one of her knives and passed it to Finn who took it without averting his stare from the wolf. Next, she took out a knife for herself and held it out shakily in front of her. The wolf was mere feet away and its snarls made her shudder every time they ripped across its wide, bubbling smile.

She tore her eyes from it to look at Finn, his eyes were clamped shut and his bottom lip was trembling as he breathed heavily. He held out the knife in front of him, but his arm could barely keep itself up.

That very sight clawed at her heart. She returned her attention to the problem at hand and grimaced at how close the wolf was getting. Clouds of breath erupted from its vicious mouth. Her plan was to attack it with the knife if it came at them, but really, she was being unreasonably optimistic.

Her breathing hitched up and she squeezed her eyes shut just as it was about to pounce once more, assuring their deaths, but instead of the feeling of teeth around her throat, a loud banging noise assaulted her ears.

Her eyes sprung open and she saw the wolf turning to the side, its attention peaked by the battering of steel on steel.

"Come here you little prick!" shouted Daisy from somewhere up the road.

The wolf growled once and gave Asha and Finn a final look before racing over to where the noise was coming from. Asha blew out a steady breath and quickly gathered herself.

Thank you, you crazy girl.

Asha crawled quickly along the tarmac to grab the gun she'd dropped and that's when she saw Daisy. She was standing in the middle of the road with two saucepans in her hands and she was clanging them together in rhythm. The wolf was intrigued by her and Daisy looked like stone in the face of it; in fact, she was smiling wildly.

"A little closer, don't be shy!" She yelled, still banging the pots.

Asha stood herself up and helped Finn to stand and keep his balance. They stumbled behind the wolf and Asha pulled up the gun to shoot, but she was shaking too hard, she couldn't get a good shot and she ran the risk of shooting Daisy. Her frown was prominent. She wasn't sure what to do next, she didn't know what the spindly girl had planned.

In the next second, when the wolf got closer to her, Daisy threw the saucepans to the ground and took out a lighter from her back pocket. She lit it and chucked it on the ground towards the wolf.

A sudden burst of flame erupted from the road and a huge spiral of fire whipped around the beast in seconds. Asha could hear it whimpering from within its fiery cage. Daisy practically jumped for joy and laughed loudly. Asha noticed the cans of petrol nearby and then it clicked; Daisy had made a trap using the flammable liquid, she'd saved them.

The skinny girl was punching the air in victory when the wolf leapt through the flames back onto the safe part of the road.

Breath caught in Asha's throat for a millisecond before the wolf thankfully ran straight back into the woods, its head hanging low, whining.

"That was the coolest thing I've ever seen!" Finn applauded as the pair made their way over to Daisy who was pulling out a cigarette and lighting it.

"Calm your cotton socks, Finny," Daisy grumbled before taking a long drag on her cigarette and blowing it out in a stale flurry. *Where had she found those?*

"I knew there was a reason to keep you around," Asha smiled, feeling her body relax.

"I stay with you because I want to," Daisy said forcefully, but then shrugged. "...But that *was* pretty cool," she said, smiling mischievously.

"It was," Asha agreed, finding herself smiling too. "But we need to leave, right now. I don't wanna risk it coming back, with friends."

"Right, right, but before we do. The house I got the pans from is untouched, I saw a corset in there that I want. We should search it and then go," Daisy offered.

"Why do you need a corset?" Finn questioned.

"I don't have to explain myself to you," she spat and stubbed out her cigarette before hauling her petrol containers towards the house in question.

"Okay, we'll look around for a minute and then go," Asha announced, even though it was obvious Daisy was calling the shots. She frowned slightly and picked up her backpack, gathering the knives as she went.

*

The house's exterior was prim and proper just like the rest of the cottages on the street, but the interior was like a jumble sale, with mismatched furniture, contrasting artwork and piles of old books thrown everywhere. Daisy was right though; there was a lot of stuff for the taking. Asha liked how the house felt; it reminded her of family life, a whirlwind of comforting items showing her that this place was lived in and loved.

They scavenged and rustled around for fifteen minutes. Daisy took the corset she'd seen in the living room, along with a small book, Asha didn't quite catch its title.

Asha took some new knives to add to her collection, some warm clothes, a pair of Doc Martens and a classic version of 'The Great Gatsby'. Finn was upstairs, no doubt finding things to his fancy.

Once the girls had finished rummaging for things they *wanted*, they then concentrated on the things they *needed*. They made work on filling the black bags with food from the kitchen, making sure not to over pack; after all, they had to carry it back, including the petrol.

"Asha, you'll like this!" Finn yelled from upstairs.

The dark-haired girl rolled her eyes but a slight smile crossed her lips. "Thanks for making the whole street aware of your thoughts!" She accidentally shouted louder than him. Her hand covered her mouth almost immediately.

"*Funny that*," she heard him mutter.

"Oh, go see what he wants for fucks sake," Daisy groaned as she threw a bag of pasta into their horde.

"Fine," Asha huffed before hauling herself up the stairs at speed.

She walked across the hallway searching for him. "I'd better actually like this or I'll be-" she warned but was cut short when Finn jumped out of a doorway with a creepy china doll in front of his face.

Asha shouted from the shock of it and jumped back slightly, clutching her heart.

He let out a breathy chuckle and set the doll on a nearby shelf, his dimples showing, his eyes playful.

"You guys alright up there?" Daisy asked nonchalantly.

Asha didn't answer her, instead she took her annoyance out on the practical child in front of her. She furrowed her eyebrows and pushed at his chest, he moved with it.

"Don't *ever* do that again!" She yelled and pushed him again with more force this time.

But her push was harder than expected, and it sent Finn stumbling backwards causing him to trip over a discarded wooden toy box with his heel.

As he fell, he grabbed onto whatever he could to steady himself, but the only thing he could reach for was Asha.

Air whistled past her ears as she fell; her wide eyes cemented on his.

They landed in a tangled mess of limbs; Asha on top of him catching her breath and Finn underneath her letting out a pained grunt after his body took the brunt of their weight.

Their faces were mere *centimetres* from each other.

Asha could feel his body heat on her lips, their breathing quickened simultaneously; she found herself beginning to shake.

All of a sudden, she felt lost to her present self, with all the thoughts and memories of the past months fading to nothing. All that mattered was how fast her heart was racing at the closeness to Finn.

He stayed still for a second, gauging her reaction. But then his hands roamed slowly up the sides of her thighs, feather-light, making her shiver. She looked down at him, her cheeks burned and her breath slowed to almost nothing. His honey eyes captured her, trapping her right there in that overwhelming moment.

It was then that she realised how lonely she'd been.

Sure, she'd had Kit with her, but it wasn't the same. She'd never had a boyfriend or girlfriend before, but that wasn't the point, the point was that she liked feeling wanted; she was only human.

And Finn wanted her in a way Kit never could.

She moved her hands to the floor either side of his head to prop herself steadily above him. She blushed, she couldn't keep her stare from his and neither could he to her. Blood pumped wildly around her body; she could feel the heat between them rising. It felt like a lifetime, but in reality, it had only been seconds.

She found herself moving herself ever-so-slightly against him; his fingers gripped her thighs hard in response as he raised his hips to move with her.

Holy shit.

They hadn't even kissed, yet she felt herself bursting at the anticipation of it.

Just as the heat became unbearable, and the stare became too much, Finn sat up hurriedly to meet her swelling lips with his, but before he could get there, Daisy suddenly appeared at the door.

Asha pulled away from him with a quick intake of air and looked quickly to the begrudged girl staring at them.

"Gross," Daisy remarked flatly before heading downstairs.

Asha shook herself out of her apparent trance and jumped off of the boy beneath her at lightning speed. She willed the feeling deep within her to go, but it was there, and it had only just begun to build for him. She longed for what would have been.

"You okay?" Finn asked as he awkwardly hauled himself off the floor and pulled his t-shirt down from where it had ridden up.

Asha caught sight of his toned abdomen and had to look quickly to the floor, jaw clenching, but she nodded at his question. She felt completely off guard and she didn't like the feeling, not one bit.

There was only one thing on her mind, and it wasn't being created by her brain, it was coming from far below.

Not now, not now.

She was all of a sudden aware of the weightlessness on her middle finger. Her ring had fallen off once again, she didn't hear where it went. She let out an exasperated grunt and began scouring the wooden floor for the silver heirloom. Anything to distract herself from herself.

"There," Finn said, pointing to the ring which had parked itself just next to the door. His own cheeks were flushed in a slight pink colour.

After noting where he had pointed, she watched as he adjusted his now-bursting jeans bashfully before turning from her, clearing his throat and looking out of the dusty window.

"Thanks," she said, flustered, and bent to pick up the ring before catapulting out of the room where things could have taken a very, very big turn.

Chapter Seventeen

Kit watched as Asha left, and a deep sense of dread filled his stomach, the same one that seemed to engulf him every day.

It was a hazardous thing being the best friend and sole companion of Asha Flores. She was fiery, stubborn, and challenging. Everything she did, she did for a reason, but that didn't mean Kit always agreed with her. A lot of the time he found himself thinking about what might happen to her if one of her plans went wrong. What if she died? What would he do? He didn't like to think about it, but it was a way of coping. Practising strategies for coping was becoming more necessary, especially with the arrival and integration of a new group of people.

The more he prepared himself for it, the better he would deal with it.

He knew full well Asha could handle herself, he knew that from their childhood. She would be the one to stand up to dickheads in the pub, she would be the one to drive across town for anyone in a crisis, she would be the independent one of the two of them.

She was nice once too, but Nox put an abrupt end to that part of her.

Kit knew he had changed too. He had tried his hardest to stay who he used to be, but it was impossible. All he thought about now was surviving. That was who he was, a survivor.

Gone was the cheeky lifeguard, gone was the fuck boy eyeing the girls playing at Asha's tennis club, gone was the boy who'd score hat-tricks with the boys on a Sunday afternoon.

He'd lost his soul to the virus. But he was going to get it back, all of it.

"Kit, come out back with me for a minute?" Max asked, he didn't wait for an answer, only made his way through to the garden instead.

"Have fun out there," Piper sang and gave Kit's shoulder a small squeeze before joining the two girls in the living room.

Kit removed his motorbike helmet and his jaw clenched as he set it down. He then threw his bag to the floor and followed the burly man out to the large garden.

There was a trampoline on one side and a stagnant pond on the other; but there was something odd in the centre. Max had set up what looked like a firing range, a table with a few tin cans set out in a perfect line. Kit looked from the table and then to Max with a frown on his face.

"What the fuck is this?" He asked.

"If you're gonna come with us, then you're gonna have to be able to shoot a gun, *well*," Max explained.

Max had a semi-permanent hunched stance, it was like he was trying to lower himself to normal sized people, although, if he did straighten up, he'd rise above Kit and that wouldn't be liked by the freckled boy. He pulled out a pistol and attached a silencer to its nozzle before he strode slowly to where Kit was standing.

"I know how to shoot," Kit moaned. "I've been paintballing at least six times," he frowned as he grabbed for the gun.

"Ah, ah, not yet," Max toyed, pulling the gun from his reach.

Kit audibly groaned and crossed his arms. "Are you serious? Look, why do we even need to do this? I have my axe. I've been using it for the past six months, why isn't that good enough now?"

"Would you just listen to an adult for once in your life? I'm doing it to prepare you, just in case," Max said, his voice was deep and threatening. He narrowed his stare at Kit and then back to the gun at hand. "This is a real gun, not like them toys you've been shootin' at your mates with. This is the real deal; you *will* kill with this."

Kit rolled his eyes and chewed the inside of his cheek. He knew it was different to anything he'd held in his hand before, but who was Max to act like the boss of him?

Kit was his own boss.

"Look, just give it here," he said and yanked the gun out of Max's hand.

Before the hulking man could take it back, Kit took aim at his first target, an empty can of baked beans. He closed his left eye and aimed it right at the centre before squeezing on the trigger. The bullet struck the tin and it pinged into the air before landing on the soft grass. He turned to look at Max with a smirk on his face.

"Beginner's luck," Max muttered.

They spent half an hour going over the basics of the gun, making sure Kit knew the ins and outs of arming, disarming, putting on the safety, reloading, and everything else to make sure he didn't hurt himself or one of the others. He could make a hit which was the most important thing, and Max seemed to be happy enough with that.

Kit holstered the gun and assembled his outfit for the day once again, he began to feel slightly anxious at the persistence Max had with teaching him how to use a gun.

He wasn't sure why it mattered, and still didn't know why his melee weapon skills weren't enough for the mission.

"You ready, Wolf?" Piper asked Kit as she emerged from the living room.

She was wearing a long grey skirt that just missed the floor; a long-sleeved top, a velour waistcoat and a witch-hunter hat to cover her head. A floral sheer scarf covered most of her face, but her kind eyes shone brightly still.

"Wolf?" Kit questioned; his voice was barely audible through the thick helmet on his head.

"Yes, Wolf. Your aura is very telling of the animal. You're very much a leader, Kit. You have the charisma too, I can imagine girls have been throwing themselves at you all your life," she paused slightly to let out a light laugh. "Courage drives you. Your heart... It's big and warm. Not that you'd admit that, but I see it," she said softly, meeting his eyes with a certain nurturing care.

Kit had to break away from looking at her. She reminded him too much of his mother and the thought of not knowing what happened to her or his sister constantly battered him.

"Do you do that to everyone?" He asked, clearing his throat.

"I sense everyone's animal self, yes... Max, he's a Grizzly Bear. Asha, she's a Lioness, no doubt there. Daisy is a Fox, Finn a Panther. And the two girls... Sunny is a beautiful Owl, and little Boe, she's a clingy Koala," Piper said with an air of pride.

"And what about you?" Kit asked, even though he didn't really care. He thought the whole 'aura' thing was a load of shit. But his auntie was from Brighton, he was used to having hippie, earth-loving conversations.

"Well, my mother -God rest her soul- always thought of me as a Doe," she said simply and walked out the front door into the day.

"Let's go," Max ordered as he bustled past Kit.

He did as he was told despite feeling constantly annoyed by it. As he stepped outside, he looked up to the sky and wished that it was a clearer day because that meant less chance of running into some of the braver Hunters. Unluckily for him, many clouds scattered the horizon.

The majority of the journey to the Global Peace Corporation site was done in silence. Kit didn't feel like speaking to either of his teammates because he was too busy worrying about Asha. He had a funny feeling brewing within him and he knew it wasn't just his stomach reacting to a rare full dinner and breakfast. However, he had to push that feeling aside when they reached the exterior fencing that surrounded the main group of buildings of GPC.

It was time to get to work.

It looked fairly desolate, no signs of life; that was a good start. With the assumption that everything was ready for them to infiltrate, the threesome got to work on climbing the fence. Kit found it easy enough, what with being generally fit from his past hobbies. He did have to help Piper over the last hurdle, which took a little bit of energy, but once he'd hoisted her over the top, they both landed strong on the other side.

Max had already jumped over and was looking around, securing the perimeter. He had pulled out his gun, a semi-automatic pistol, and was holding it in front of him, ready to shoot.

"Now, I don't know what's gonna be in there to greet us, so be on your highest guard," he ordered, his brow furrowed and his eyes wide. He looked nervous.

Kit nodded in response and tucked his shirt in to make his gun easier to reach; he then gripped his axe with both hands and walked alongside Max as they approached one of the main buildings. The large green door at the entrance had been left wide open; it was both a blessing and a curse.

Max did a little run and flattened himself on the wall beside the door frame. He quickly peered his head inside and took a step in with his gun outstretched. Kit and Piper stood outside until he motioned for them to come in, it was clear.

There was nothing much in it, just a few benches and chairs; it looked like it could have been used as a place to eat for the employees on site. There were vending machines dotted along one of the walls, but they were of course, empty. Kit sighed as he strolled around the spacious hall. Max marched around looking under the tables and Piper checked all the hidden spots for anything of use.

A sound of something metal hitting the floor came from the direction of the door they'd just come through. When Kit turned to look, the door was suddenly slammed shut and he clocked what had flown in. His heart jumped into his mouth. It was a smoke canister, and it was beginning to spiral out with a nauseous gas.

They were not alone.

Another can crashed through the window near to Max and it blew straight away sending an explosion of thick, billowing smoke around the room. Kit could hear Piper yelling and some scuffling coming from whom he presumed was Max, but he couldn't see anything.

The whole space had filled with the toxic smoke, which was seeping dangerously through his motorbike helmet.

Another can flew in and hit him on the arm. He shot down to the floor and started to crawl in the direction of the door. His breathing was quick, he was starting to suck in the smoke, it tasted bitter. He was terrified. Whoever was out there was hell bent on getting them out of their place, and they weren't messing around. But he couldn't stay in the room, he had to get out into the fresh air, even if there were people out there, he could take them. He *would* take them.

He finally reached the door and stood up, but whoever was attacking them had locked it. He yelled out an exasperated shout and swung his axe hard into the handle over and over, desperation rang high in his grunts of exertion. On the fifth hit, the handle came off the door and Kit pulled the thing open, tumbling into the fresh air.

He felt like he was suffocating, so he quickly opened his eye piece, he could see again, but when he looked around, he barely had time to register the man aiming a gun straight at him just a few metres away. His eyes widened and he took to the ground just as the man pulled the trigger. The bullet hit the building behind him, but the man seemed to be having trouble with his gun, perhaps a lodged bullet. Kit had to take this guy down, now. He jumped to his feet, drew his own gun and cocked it. His fingers were trembling, but he had to do this, he had to.

He squeezed the trigger and the bullet hit the man in the thigh sending him to the grass in agony. He couldn't leave him like that; he still had use of his arms and that was a problem. Kit ran to him, pointed the barrel of the gun at his forehead and looked him straight in his eyes. The man looked petrified and held his arms up in surrender. Kit clenched his jaw and breathed steadily as his finger squeezed at the trigger.

"Sorry mate," he muttered as the gun shot vibrated in the air.

Just as he did so, something hard and fast hit his helmet. It rocked his head and as he turned to face the direction it came from; he clocked his attacker. There was another, much larger man, stalking towards him with his smoking gun pointed right at him.

Realisation set in…*He shot me in the head.*

This man was having no problems with his gun and he looked full of rage with his veins practically bursting from his reddened face.

He was coming in hot. Kit didn't have time to prepare his gun to shoot again. Instead, he sidestepped, dodging the close-range bullet flying towards him and swung his axe into play. He ran in a zigzag pattern straight at the guy who was now having trouble getting a good shot at him. Kit's plan exactly.

The man panicked when Kit got to him, which gave him ample time to swing the axe deep in his side. He could hear the ribs crunching as the metal hit them. The man fell down backwards with a pained grunt, bringing Kit with him. The axe was stubborn at coming out and he still had a strong grip on it.

Kit clenched his teeth as he struggled to pull the axe free of the man's body to deliver the last, deathly blow but he couldn't, and before he knew it, the man had his gun shoved up under his chin, Kit closed his eyes and held his breath. *This is it.*

Two things happened in the next second.

First, a burning singeing came from the hot barrel of the gun being pressed against his skin, and secondly, a deafening gunshot sounded in the air.

Once he realised he was still alive, Kit looked down to see the hollow eyes of the guy beneath him.

A spray of blood and brain spilled from his temple onto the grass; he'd been shot in the head. Kit took in staggered breaths and looked to his right. There was Piper lying on the ground with her gun still smoking. She gave him a sweet smile before standing herself up.

"Come on. Max went into that building," she said, pointing at a tall brick building where the company logo was displayed for all to see.

"Coming," Kit said shakily.

He stood up awkwardly and his fingers roamed to his newly inflicted wound. It was raw to touch but he figured he had a circular burn under his jaw. Another scar to add to the collection.

He caught up to Piper and passed her his axe as he prepared his gun for another onslaught.

Once he'd finished, he holstered it and took his favourite weapon back. He held it tightly and kept his attention peaked in every direction; Piper led the way to the building and Kit covered her.

"That was a close one, huh?" She chuckled as she opened the door.

"Yeah," was all Kit could reply with.

He was concentrating more on the fact that they were now entering another possible death trap. They had no idea how many people were around, and no idea where Max could be.

"Was he alone?" Kit asked.

"Yes," Piper said softly.

"Right. Because leaving us for dead and exploring the place himself is such a great idea," Kit moaned.

He thought about why Max would leave them there outside. Maybe it was because he knew where a radio transmitter was, and maybe he was planning on coming back to them. But still, Kit was puzzled by it.

It was when they reached the stairwell of the building that they saw the first body. They followed the string of throat slit men and women all the way up and through to the top floor. They weren't Hunters, they were people, like them. Pures.

Max had been quiet in his little escapade, not using a bullet in any of the victims he'd left in his wake. There was a thick blood trail that started at the bottom of the final set of stairs. Kit assumed Max had been hurt by one of the people. It gave them a crude map to where he was.

They crept along the spilt blood down a winding hallway. When they turned the corner, they saw Max hauling himself into a room, a deep grimace on his face and his gun pointed out.

Kit was convinced he heard someone in the room exclaim '*Max Bennett!*' and not a moment later, a loud gunshot burst from the room.

The pair ran to join Max and found him propping himself up on a desk, a large gash spitting out fresh blood from his side. He looked exhausted and out of breath, but he looked a hundred times better than the guy who was now lying crumpled on the floor with half his head missing.

He said his name, I'm sure he said Max's name.

"Max!" Piper cried and scurried to him, inspecting his wound.

"It's okay, trust me, I'll survive it," he said calmly. "Now that them Reapers are gone, we can get on with things. There's a radio right there. What's say we give Harbour a call, hmm?" He grinned widely.

"How do you know they were Reapers?" Kit asked sternly, eyes cold and burrowing.

If they were Reapers, they wouldn't have been trying to kill them, they would have been trying to capture them for future bargaining.

"I don't know, but they were trying to hurt us, so we took care of 'em. Simple as," Max stated before turning his attention to the radio transmitter on the desk.

Kit surrendered his conflict and sighed. Instead, he watched as Max fiddled around with the knobs and turned them to specific channels. His gaze kept going to the half-headed man. He felt sick just looking at him, so he forced himself to keep his eye on the door behind them, making sure they really were alone.

The sound of static suddenly filled the room and with a few more turns of the transmitter, the static went and a silent but clear line was found.

"Get in!" Max celebrated quietly and then cleared his throat, he pressed a button and spoke into the microphone. "Hello Harbour, this is Max."

A moment of quiet tension passed, Kit gave Piper a concerned, anxious glance, when suddenly a crackle came from the speakers.

"Bonjour, Maxwell."

Chapter Eighteen

Asha walked fast back to their headquarters. She wasn't going to risk being outside any longer than she had to, especially after what had just happened. She was at war with herself over the almost kiss between herself and The Apothecary. She was utterly conflicted. Her heart and other organs were telling her go, but her mind was screaming no. Plus, she still couldn't get over the fact that a wolf had almost mauled her to death.

It was naïve of her to think that animals would stand by and let humans thrive once again. *Of course,* they'd be more inclined to explore what was once urban ground, where people roamed in their inconsiderate masses. Humans were to blame for the rotting world, and it was the animals' right to want to preserve the new beginning that Nox gave them. Nature would prevail and take what was once theirs in the end.

Before long, Asha began to see their village with houses marked with Sunny's branding. It meant they weren't far from what they called home, at least for the next night.

Asha tried her hardest to push what happened with Finn away from her mind because it threatened to stay there; it threatened to dig and dig until she'd have no choice but to accept her feelings. She couldn't let that happen. If she began to really like him, she knew he would just cloud her judgment.

Also, she knew that if Kit caught wind of it, he wouldn't be happy.

He would look at her differently; he would think she'd gone soft. She couldn't let him think that because *she* was the one to keep them going, *she* was the one to lead them; *she* was the one to save them.

"This bag is splitting," Daisy groaned through a strained breath. They were all carrying far too much, but it would be worth it once they got back and produced their bounty to the others.

"Hold it like a baby?" Finn suggested. He looked like he was struggling to carry his six cans of petrol, but he continued on with a slight grimace on his face.

"Oh, thanks a bunch Bob the Builder, that's something I would never have thought of myself," Daisy mocked him as she scooped the large bag into her cradled arms with a clench of her jaw.

"You're the one that asked," Finn retorted quietly.

"Stop it, both of you," Asha instructed, keeping her gravelly voice low. "We're almost there."

Five minutes later, they arrived. The main house seemed to glow with the warmth of safety and welcoming. The big painted sun on its front door shone brightly; they'd made it home. They hustled up the walkway and Asha tapped on the door briskly.

"It's Asha, and co," she said through the wood firmly.

Eventually, a small but strong voice came from inside. "That's not the password."

"Open the fucking door!" Daisy yelled harshly, her face sporting a scowl.

"*Daisy,*" Asha said, looking at the girl in annoyance.

Nothing.

"Alright Sunny, it's *'Pearl of the Ice Sea'*," Finn said as he bent down to the letterbox to try and peer through.

"What the hell?" Daisy muttered.

"It's some book she likes," Finn shrugged and adjusted the petrol cans in his hands.

With his answer, the door clicked open and there stood Sunny, the rat-like girl, with half a hot dog in her mouth. She looked them up and down and then turned back into the living room, munching away.

"No, yeah, thanks, we've got this!" Daisy called after the girl as she shuffled down the hallway with her heavy bags. "*Little brat,*" she then whispered.

"I heard that!" Sunny shouted back.

"I like her," Finn chuckled and made his way through the house to the generator to fill.

Asha found herself smiling at the mismatched, occasionally hostile, group of people she'd somehow become a part of. She liked the conflicts of it all; it reminded her of what a real family was like, something that they'd all lost.

Asha joined Daisy in the kitchen and lugged a black bag of food through with her. She knew Daisy wouldn't be pleased about being left to unpack all the goods they'd found, so she helped her unload. Half the time was spent looking in wonder at all the bits and pieces she hadn't seen yet. She could be easily distracted, especially if there wasn't an imminent threat.

Once Asha had finished helping the blonde girl, she made her way to the living room where the two little girls were.

Boe was digging into a bowl of cold spaghetti hoops and simultaneously drawing a picture, which seemed to have a lot of tomato sauce on it. Her fat cat toy was accompanying her as per usual. Sunny was chewing on her hot dog sausage as she sat reading on the sofa above the smaller girl.

They were never more than a foot away from each other; it was slightly heart-warming to Asha. They both looked so normal, like there was nothing going on outside those four walls. It looked like it was a Saturday morning, their parents hadn't woken up yet, and they'd helped themselves to an interesting choice for breakfast while watching cartoons on TV.

"Why are you staring at me?" Sunny asked, startling Asha out of her partial blackout.

"I wasn't. I was wondering what you were reading," she said confidently as she strode over to sit next to the young girl.

"I've read it ten times now. It's about a girl who is half robot and when the world ends, she's left there alone because she's the only one that can survive, and then she meets another half robot person and then they live happily ever after," Sunny beamed. "I wonder if there's a half robot in real life. Maybe we'll meet them. This is the end of the world, right?" She questioned, swallowing down the last of her snack.

"It's not ending; it's just sort of having a sick day. It'll be better soon," Asha said softly.

"I'm not Boe's age. I know something's wrong and it's not the world '*having a cold*'," Sunny replied, closing the book and looking up to meet Asha's stare.

Asha chewed on the inside of her cheek and furrowed her brow; she didn't know what to say. She realised now that she couldn't say anything to make the girl feel better or more sheltered from the truth. Sunny was much smarter and more in the loop than any other nine-year-old she'd ever met. But she could have guessed that from the way she was able to kill with seemingly no regrets.

Sunny filled the space where Asha's response should have gone.

"My mum tried to kill me, and my dad tried to stop her. But then she bit him and then both of them came after me. I locked myself in the attic... my brother was still in his room; they killed him, he was screaming and crying. I was in the attic for three days and then I got too hungry and thirsty... I had to go downstairs. I saw blood everywhere, but my parents were gone. Then a man came into the house, and he looked like my parents did, with that horrible cloudy skin. I killed him with a knife, and after that, I went outside and everything was different and wrong. People were screaming and everyone was hurting each other. People were shouting that the world was ending. So yeah, I know it's ended, you don't need to hide that from me, or her," Sunny said, motioning to Boe with her foot. "She knows it too," Sunny finished, her eyes stone cold and her face flat.

"My family are dead! Sunny is my mummy now!" Boe sang happily as she continued to colour in her drawing.

Asha was consumed by a sickening feeling; innocence had been lost. She couldn't sit with the girls any longer; it was all too real.

She made her way upstairs to the bathroom and sat on the edge of the tub she'd almost lost her life in, her head in her hands and her mind coming apart.

The girls were proof of the generations that were going to grow up in the new world. Even if they defeated the Hunters and rid the ground of Reapers, the people who were left, people like Asha and the rest of her group, they would be the new horror show. The things that they'd been through just to survive would shape them into cold, ruthless psychopaths. And sooner or later, they'd bring life into the world and pass down the same tendencies to be able to survive. It was a vicious circle.

After ten minutes, the crushing thoughts dispersed, and Asha took in a few deep breaths to calm herself. She was stronger than this. She knew deep down that the world would never be normal again, at least, not in her lifetime. Maybe she would survive better now, knowing now that there was no point in working towards a repeat of life, instead she had to work towards a reboot.

She left the bathroom and wandered down the hallway towards the bedroom she and Kit were sharing. She felt like she needed to lie down and do something other than worry about everything. Maybe she would read a book, or nap.

When she got there, however, she was met with the sight of Finn pushing something underneath her pillow.

As soon as he saw her, he snatched his hands away from the bed and shoved them behind his back. His cheeks flourished and his lips pressed together; he looked like a child being caught with his hand in the cookie jar.

"Can I help you?" Asha asked, stepping further into the room and removing her coat. She flung it onto the armchair and sat herself on the bed before beginning to take her shoes off. She looked to Finn the whole time, waiting for a response.

"Actually," he began to say, his demeanour relaxing. "I was going to leave this as a surprise but since you're here and you've seen me... here you go," he smiled, holding out a small parcel made of newspaper and string.

"What's this?" She asked as she took it from his grasp and pressed on it, trying to figure out what it was.

"Just open it," he beamed and sat himself next to her on the bed. He looked expectantly from the package to Asha.

She scanned his face for a moment, noting the cuts and bruises that littered it. Sighing lightly, she unravelled the string carefully. She ripped away at the newspaper, sending a scrap of it onto the floor. Once she'd made an opening, she tipped its contents into her open palm.

A silver necklace pooled in the centre of her hand and attached to it was a light-filled gemstone encased in a delicate, silver design. It was a thing of beauty. She picked it up and dangled in front of her face, admiring it.

"Finn, I-" she was speechless.

"It's a moonstone. At least that's what I think it is. My mum was really into her gemstones, and if it *is* a moonstone then it represents strength and intuition," he smiled, his dimples shining. "I found it in the house we were in. Your ring keeps falling off, so I thought you could put it on here. The chain's not very long, so it won't get caught on anything."

Damn you.

Asha still couldn't find the words to say.

Looking down at the ring on her thin finger, she thought about how happy her mum had been when she gave it to her, much like how happy Finn was right then. It was more than enough to make her heart soar and her smile broaden. The feeling she was experiencing was overwhelming. She slipped the ring off her finger with ease and looped it onto the chain to sit with the gemstone hanging in the centre.

"Can you?" She asked Finn, holding out the necklace to him and turning her head to face away from him.

"'Course," he said, taking the necklace and gently draping it around her neck. He fumbled a little with the delicate clasp, but he eventually fastened it properly.

Asha reached up to touch the gem and the ring when it was in place. It fit almost like a choker, leaving no room for someone to yank it off her, or for her to get it hooked around something accidently. She turned back to face him, her smile refusing to leave her.

"You really didn't have to do this," she said bashfully.

"I know. I just wanted to," Finn smiled softly.

After everything that she'd said to him, after every piercing glare and every physical and mental blow, there he was, looking at her with his heart on his sleeve and the stars in his eyes. He didn't care how she'd treated him, he wanted her to be happy, he wanted to see her smile.

Asha couldn't comprehend the boy. Why would he go out of his way to give her something so thoughtful and precious? *Her*, the one who constantly made him feel as useful as gum on the bottom of a shoe.

He was everything that she didn't believe existed in the world anymore.

Despite all the death and pain, Finn managed to keep the sun shining. He found the time to wrap a present, and that spoke mountains to the dark-haired girl.

She took in a breath and caressed his cheek with her fingertips before shuffling closer to him on the bed. He cleared his throat as she placed her other hand on his other cheek, gently pulling him towards her. She licked her bottom lip slightly and looked to him. She could feel him trembling and realised she was too. Her eyelashes fluttered as her eyes traced over every part of his face before stopping at his lips.

He cupped her face in return, his fingers tangling in her hair as he quickly closed the gap between them. The room seemed to disappear and all that mattered was the two of them, together.

Their lips touched for a millisecond when frantic knocking came from the front door.

They broke apart immediately.

Asha looked to Finn with wide eyes before sprinting out of the room and down the stairs where Daisy was opening the door. Piper and Max stumbled in first. Piper was holding the hulking Max up; he was bleeding from his side. Kit followed close behind so the worry that had been in her since the morning diminished. She quickly pushed past the bumbling threesome and stalked into the living room.

"Kids, away from the sofa, now!" She ordered the two girls who rocketed out of the way just before Piper laid Max down; he sunk into the cushions and moaned deeply.

His injury looked like it had been initially sown up, but the loose stitches had opened, revealing a large gash in his side. The others seemed fine. Piper busied herself with attending to him and the girls watched in awe.

Daisy and Finn offered their help, which gave Asha the chance to check on Kit.

He was standing in the doorway of the room, a look of anguish on his face. Asha walked fast towards him and threw her arms around his chest, encasing him in a deep hug. He returned the favour, but he felt rigid and that stirred curiosity in her. She pulled away from the hug and looked up to him, he gave her a wary side smile and her gaze trailed down to his motorbike helmet.

"Is that a bullet hole?" She asked, her voice shrill and her mouth open.

"I need to talk to you, *alone*," he replied sternly.

Chapter Nineteen

Asha didn't get a chance to answer Kit before he grabbed her arm and roughly pulled her down the hallway into the dining room. She protested silently to his forcefulness with a frown on her face but went along with his movement. He closed the door behind them and set his helmet down on the table.

"What the hell is going on? What happened to you guys?" Asha demanded, something wasn't right, and she needed to know. She noticed a weird ring of red skin under his chin.

"We went to GPC," he said, his eyes on the floor.

"Yeah, I know that much. What happened there?" Asha asked, annoyed.

"We got ambushed straight away and Max left us," he said, looking down to her.

"What?"

"Someone tried to gas us. I got out and killed a man, and then another one came, and he shot me in the head, well, helmet. Piper killed him, and she said she saw Max go off on his own," he paused for breath. "We followed him. He'd killed everyone in his path; *Pures*. When we found him, he was going into an office, and I know I heard someone shout 'Max Bennett'. Then Max shot them in the face and pretended they were just some Reaper. But they *knew* him, they said his name. I'm not crazy," he said in a hushed voice, like he was scared someone might hear him.

"Are you sure they said that? Maybe you misheard them," Asha offered, her brain trying everything to defend Max.

"Max never told me his full name. But the way you just looked at me when I said it, tells me that you know it. Now, how would I mishear a name if I never fucking knew it in the first place?" He stared at her intently, his breathing quick. "Something's off, Ash. I don't know what, and I don't know if we're in danger, but something isn't right," he looked around the room wildly, eventually resting his gaze on her. "...I guess one good thing came out of this... We made contact with Harbour. They're real and now they know we're coming. More importantly, they know you're coming, and they sounded excited."

"It's real? *It's real.*" Asha couldn't help but smile, and all the talk of Max emptied from her head. There was hope.

"Yeah, they sounded nice," Kit seemed to force a smile.

"What aren't you telling me?"

Kit was silent for a moment and then sighed. "After the call, Max made me and Piper gather supplies, but I kept sneaking a look at him in the office. He was searching for something and in the end, he grabbed a blue folder and put it in his bag. I don't know if it's important, but this whole day has put me on edge," he shrugged, and though his face was like steel, he wasn't okay.

"I see... I can't believe you got shot in the head and lived to tell the tale," Asha remarked, reaching up to give his hair a ruffle.

Kit snatched her hand mid-air, holding her wrist tightly. "Stop! Will you just listen to me? This is important," he spat.

"Ow!" Asha complained, yanking her hand from Kit's clutch and narrowing her stare at him. "Look, it sounds bad, it really does, and I *do* believe you. But listen to yourself; you're too hot right now. You can't confront him the way you are. This isn't a time to be making enemies, not when there are guns, lives and futures at hand. I promise we'll talk to him the next time we settle somewhere. But tonight, I think we all need a rest. Now... we're gonna go out there and pretend you didn't tell me all of this. I don't want anyone thinking we're against them, not yet... Are you with me?" She asked, jabbing a finger to his chest.

"Yeah, always," he sighed, defeated. "...What's this?" He asked, toying with the new piece of jewellery around her neck.

"It's nothing," she shrugged as she opened the door and made her way back to the main part of the house.

They joined the others in the living room. Max was still laid out on the sofa; his shirt was now off and Piper was dealing with the harsh wound. Finn hovered around holding a bowl of water filled with clean rags. The girls were still watching what was happening and Daisy was doing something in the kitchen. Max didn't seem to be fussed by his injury, but he did respond to the stitches with varying grunts.

"Who managed to hurt *you,* Max?" Asha asked lightly, a smile on her lips.

She looked over his form; he seemed even more muscular than she'd first thought. The fact that he was so big gave her an insight into the conditions at Harbour. He didn't look all withered like them; he was well sustained.

"I didn't see their knife, but they didn't see mine either," he grinned before wincing at Piper's handiwork.

"So, what happened?" Asha asked, standing herself opposite the injured man.

"We managed to make contact with my friend at Harbour," Max announced. The room sang with anticipation and excitement. Asha beamed, hearing it from Max only made it more real.

"What did they say?" Finn asked, his words tumbling out fast.

"He said they're going to send a boat in two days, giving us enough time to make it up there. I also informed him about Asha and her unique immunity. He is very excited to meet you." He smiled, looking at Asha. "They know about all of you, they're getting your residences prepared for your arrival."

"Residences?" Daisy questioned from the kitchen, her voice echoing.

"Everyone at Harbour gets assigned a house. It's a way of keeping order and track of the people there. We've occupied the town centre, it's where the main buildings are, like the hospital, and the labs," Max explained.

Piper finished up his wound with a quick clean. She smoothed over a bandage and gave him a gentle pat. He grimaced slightly as he manoeuvred his shirt back on and sat himself up straight. Piper went to clean up in the kitchen.

"Wow, houses for everyone. Who would have thought our generation would ever own a house, to ourselves?" Kit joked flatly. Even though he sounded sarcastic, Asha knew he was excited deep down.

"Do I get a house?" Boe asked Max happily, as she crawled across the floor and clambered up onto his lap.

Max groaned slightly as she knocked his newly bandaged wound, but he quickly softened and slipped his arm around her. "Not yet little one," he smiled, pinching her chubby cheek, the sight of it made Asha smile, Boe was tiny in the cradled arm of his. "You and Sunny will live with Piper."

"Yay!" Boe squealed and hopped off to find Piper.

"What if I want to live with Finn?" Sunny asked.

"I'd be honoured," Finn grinned over at Sunny, a hand on his heart, his face joyful.

"We'll sort it out when we get there," Max said, bringing the attention back to him. "We'll leave in the morning, make our way up north. No harm in gettin' there early," he said.

*

Later, Daisy served up a vegetable pie with packet mac and cheese. It surprised Asha that she'd bothered to take dinner duty, but she appreciated it highly. Macaroni and cheese was one of her all-time favourite meals, it was just so comforting and deliciously bad for her. Even though the one on her plate wasn't homemade, it definitely made a worthy substitute.

"A wolf?" Piper questioned, her face in complete shock.

"Yeah, Daisy basically set it on fire," Finn said before stuffing his face with a mouthful of pasta.

"Good to hear you guys put your skills to the test," Max noted, he looked almost proud of the trio.

"Looks like we've all had a day from hell then," Kit said flatly, his stare was down as he toyed with his food.

"That wasn't even the scariest part," Daisy began, she hadn't touched her pasta. "I had to witness Asha and Finn hooking up," she mocked throwing up.

Asha froze mid-bite and threw daggers at the blonde girl.

"Huh?" Sunny asked. She looked bewildered at the reactions from around the table.

"No, we weren't!" Finn protested; he looked worriedly to Kit whose eyes were bulging slightly.

"What?" Kit asked through his teeth.

"Nothing happened, I swear," Finn finished; he swallowed the lump in his throat.

"That's not what it looked like..." Daisy snickered.

"Ash?" Kit pushed.

Asha could feel his eyes boring into her, she looked up to meet his deathly stare. "I fell on him, that's it," she said with conviction, but her body betrayed her, she was blushing wildly. She couldn't help but think of how close they'd gotten to kissing just hours ago.

"Oh *shit,*" Kit spat, disgusted. "That necklace came from *you,* didn't it?" He asked, directing his glare at the nervous boy next to her.

"I thought she could use it for her ring," Finn replied, he was trying not to look Kit in the eye.

"Great, that's just great," Kit laughed exaggeratedly. "Do I get left with Daisy? Wadda you say, Blondie? Looks like love's in the air, you fancy it?" He asked, a giant smirk on his face.

"Hate to break it to you... Actually, I'll enjoy this. I bat for the *other* team, so there's no way in hell, this," she pointed between them, "is ever going to happen."

"Great! Hear that, Ash? You could go for Daisy too if you wanted," Kit yelled before devouring his food.

Asha had never seen someone eat as angrily as Kit was; she was worried he'd choke. At the same time, she wished he would; he was being a *puta madre*.

"I ain't saying anything about it. Just be careful kids, alright?" Max said.

"Young love is so lovely," Piper chimed. She looked radiant despite the day she'd been through.

"I'm full," Asha announced as she pushed herself out of her chair abruptly and left the room without a second glance.

She wasn't in the mood to be accused of feeling something as terrible as love.

She stormed upstairs leaving a silent dinner table behind her, she didn't care that her actions made her look guilty of what they were thinking; she just wanted to be alone.

Once in the bedroom, she stripped down and searched the various drawers for some form of nightwear. She thought she deserved to feel comfortable instead of sleeping in her dirty clothes like she had done the last few nights. She eventually found a thin jumper and a pair of cotton shorts; she put them on and topped the ensemble off with a pair of woolly socks.

In the old world, when she needed a break from being a wild teenager, she loved shoving on some pyjamas and cuddling up in bed with a hot tea and a good book. She'd have to do without the tea because she wasn't going downstairs again, so she rummaged through her backpack and pulled out the book she'd found earlier and then nestled into bed, pulling the covers up to her chin.

She read for what felt like an hour, tossing and turning into different comfortable positions in the bed. But when the door clicked open her eyes shot to the clock on the wall, it had been three hours since she'd left the table; the book was almost finished. Kit stepped cautiously into the room, his head low, his stance guilty.

Asha rolled her eyes and put her book down before diving under the covers and staying there. She heard Kit groan as she descended into the warmth and then listened to him walking over to his side of the bed.

"Don't even think about getting in!" She yelled.

He just sat on the edge of the bed and sighed. "I'm sorry," he said, he sounded somewhat sincere.

"What for?" She asked moodily; her face ached from frowning.

"For being such a massive, *Broccoli Head*."

Asha felt hugely nostalgic at the sound of their childhood dig. She found herself both crying and stifling a laugh. They'd been at each other's throats the past few days, not that that wasn't normal, but most of the time they were at least half joking about it. She felt like Kit was really angry at her for various reasons. Maybe it was the decisions she'd made, or maybe it was Finn, she didn't know.

All she did know was that she missed him and how they usually were together; anyone looking at them from the outside would wonder if they really were best friends.

"You *are* a fucking Broccoli Head," she huffed as she threw the covers from her face and sat up in the bed. She wiped at the tears that had involuntarily fallen.

He met her eyes with a crooked grin. "I know," he sighed once again. "I'm just trying to protect us."

227

"I know you are, and you're doing a good enough job. We're still here, aren't we?" She said, her voice threatening to crack.

"Barely," he murmured and sat for a moment in silence, his face twisting with the thoughts that clearly plagued his worried mind.

"Look, Kit," her voice broke and her cheeks were stricken with tears again. "I have no idea what to do, I don't have a fucking clue. I'm trying my hardest with all this information and these promises, but I don't know if I'm making the right choices, I don't know anything about this. I wish I wasn't immune like I am, then I wouldn't have to worry about the entire world being on my shoulders. And I know you don't agree with what I'm saying or what I'm doing with this group. But if you can think of another way to deal with everything then please, enlighten me. I'm tired of trying!" She cried, she tried to keep her voice quiet, she didn't want the others to hear her. She didn't even want Kit to see her like this, but he was the only one she could really trust; and he'd pulled her through her blips time and time again; visa-versa.

He hung his head and closed his eyes before moving himself across the bed to sit next to her. He then pulled her into his side and held her there tightly. She wrapped her arms around him and laid her head on his chest; she caught her breath as she silently cried.

"I didn't really think about all that," he said, his voice grim. "You're doing great, Ash. I probably would have led us in a different direction, but that's me, and it would probably be the worst path. You're usually the one with your head on straight; I was never the smart one."

"Going to Harbour is your decision and I'll follow you, protect you, and carry you if you fall. Not that you will. I'm just saying," he let out a deep breath and tightened his grip on her. "Whatever you think is best to do, we'll do it together. Don't be tired of trying, 'cause I need you."

*

They went to sleep around 10pm, which was early for them. Kit told Asha he would cover her watch; she protested, but the tiredness from the day had consumed her and just as her eyes began to close, she agreed.

She must have been asleep around five hours because when she was woken by the sound of hard rain, she felt groggy and disoriented, like she felt when waking from an unintentionally long nap. Her hand flopped onto the empty side of the bed where Kit should have been had he not taken her shift.

She smiled briefly and nestled back to drift off to sleep once again, but a muffled sound coming from next door made her eyes shoot open and her throat close.

She heard people, and they were laughing.

Chapter Twenty

Asha lay like a statue for a moment, listening to the hysterical chatter coming from the other side of the wall. Fear entombed her. She could make out around five separate voices muffled by the concrete wall, and that was only who she could hear.

"*No-one in this place,*" One voice oozed.

"*Onto the next house then,*" Another replied.

They were coming.

She tossed the covers from her body and grabbed her backpack, which was thankfully already packed with everything she needed. She swiped her coat and shoved it on, and then retrieved her knives from the chair. She left the gun in her bag; she didn't want to make any unnecessary noise. She then lugged the backpack onto her shoulders and bore her weapons as she stepped feather-light out of the room.

There wasn't a sound throughout the house. Everyone - including those on guard- must have been asleep. It was the only logical reason as to why no-one else was trying to get out of the house to safety.

The talking from the mystery people became clearer; they were out on the street now, their harsh voices and incoherent babbling seeped through the walls around her. She shuddered; she had to get everyone up and out, now.

She glided down the hallway, her feet barely making a sound as they padded bare along the wooden boards.

She cornered the stairs and made her way down to find both Kit and Daisy fast asleep where they should have been alert and on guard. Their weapons were slumped in their limp hands and soft snores escaped their lips. Surprisingly, another person was sleeping on the sofa beside them; it was dark, but Finn's features came to light quickly enough.

Her heart leapt.

She rushed towards them and shook their shoulders with the backs of her hands, making sure the knives didn't touch them. Kit awoke with a start, spit catching in his throat.

He coughed loudly and Asha quickly shushed him with panic running through her stare. He immediately quietened and looked at her with confusion before realisation set in.

Daisy perked up clumsily, holding her gun tighter to her chest, her cautious eyes never leaving Asha.

Finn shot up like a bolt at the commotion.

"*There are people going house to house. Probably Hunters. We need to get out, now,*" she whispered, her eyes darted wildly around as the sounds of speaking got louder from outside.

Kit's eyes widened and a look of guilt took over him; he was supposed to be on guard, he was meant to be protecting them.

"Shouldn't we hide instead of going out there?" Daisy questioned. And she did bring up somewhat of a point.

"If we hide, there's more chance of a fight. We are so close to Harbour; I'm not risking losing anyone. Finn, you filled the car out back with petrol, right?" Asha asked, her worried eyes burned on his.

"Yeah, it's full," Finn said quietly, nodding his head wearily.

"So that's where we go. We need to be as quiet as possible. Finn, Daisy you go to the car and make sure it's ready. Kit, wake Max and Piper. I'll get the girls. No guns, no noise. We don't want them to find us, we don't want anyone to get hurt. *Go,*" Asha ordered. Her skin burst into goosebumps as the cool air in the house took effect on her bare legs.

The others nodded their heads in agreement, and they all shuffled out of the room, taking care of how loudly they trod.

Asha and Kit tiptoed up the stairs. At the landing, they gave each other a final look before he went right and she, left.

She passed the bathroom, her room, and finally she reached the door to the room the girls were sleeping in. She held her ear to the frame for a brief second to check for any noise before twisting the knob and entering the room.

Breath escaped her as she was suddenly faced with the sight of a towering, lanky figure crouching over the dozing body of Boe.

In the next millisecond, Asha noticed the open window, the snarl on the Hunter's lips, and the empty bed where Sunny should have been. She grasped her knives even tighter and didn't take her hardened stare from him.

His skin practically glowed in the moonlight that flooded the room, he looked like a creature of nightmares, with bony, hungry fingers, about to delve into the poor child in his reach. He was drenched in rainwater, which somehow made him even more grotesque. He didn't look too phased by Asha's intrusion, in fact, he smiled, and a goofy set of teeth filled his mouth.

"The more the merrier," he finally whispered, his words cutting through the taught silence in the room.

"Don't *touch* her," Asha growled gripping her knives even harder, indents forming in her palms.

"*Please!*" He laughed and his head knocked back in response before his gaze fell to the small girl once again. "No-one gets in the way of my meals. And she is rare, I need her," he breathed out, licking his lips. His sickly fingers pulled out a small blade from his sleeve and he toyed with it in the air around Boe.

Asha stalked forward but as she did so, he quickly held the blade just above Boe's tiny jugular vein. Asha stopped in her tracks and stared in fear at him. She willed herself to think of a way out of this without attracting the attention of the other Hunters. *Think, think, think!*

"Any closer and her blood is on your hands," he smirked and then threw his head back in another manic laugh.

But he didn't finish.

A shadow from behind the man suddenly jumped onto his back. A little hand grabbed his hair and yanked his head back even further while another little hand sliced a knife across his pasty neck.

A torrent of dark blood spilled from the fatal wound. His hands reached up to touch his throat and gurgled yelps came from him until he buckled to the floor in silence.

Sunny hopped off him before he hit the ground and wiped her knife on the back of his shirt.

Soft shuffling came from behind Asha, and in the next second, Kit, Max and Piper appeared at the doorway. She turned to face them, her eyes scanning their concerned faces before jumping into action.

"To the car, now," she said calmly and motioned for Sunny to go with the others.

Boe was, unbelievably, still sleeping despite the fact that she was almost Hunter food. Asha walked over to the bed, her bare feet treading in the blood-pool forming around the Hunter's open neck; it didn't bother her.

Piper beckoned Sunny with open arms and she grabbed her backpack –which was larger than the girl herself- and went to her before turning to look to Asha with a frown.

"I've got her," Asha reassured the mousey girl.

With that, Sunny nodded –though her frown didn't falter-and left, followed closely by the redhead. Max and Kit surveyed the room and the two girls who remained once more before retreating too.

"Hurry," Kit said as he left, and Asha smiled in response.

She smoothed the hair around Boe's forehead. She looked so peaceful and innocent. Her delicate snores filled the room as Asha worked out a blanket sling to hold her in.

Once Boe was secured tightly against her chest, Asha tested the strength of her handiwork by jumping and twisting on the spot. Boe was still in dreamland. Asha was envious of her ability to deeply sleep, but she guessed being four years old had something to do with it.

After the age of sixteen, feeling tired seemed to be a constant state.

She slung her backpack on once again, feeling very weighed down with the addition of a small human. She sheathed both her knives within the folds of the sling, ready to grab if need be.

She hadn't heard any commotion happening from outside, which was a good sign. It meant that the others hadn't run into trouble, yet.

The car was around the back of the house on the opposing road. It was a large people carrier with just about enough room for the eight of them. It was the car that the girls used when their group were still alive. So, all Asha had to do was get there without being seen.

Simple enough.

She trod lightly down the stairs and through the living room. She wanted to go to the kitchen so badly; just thinking about all the food they'd be leaving behind made her heart sink. They would find more, they had to. She stepped towards the back door, which was open; presumably the others left it like that when they escaped. She turned to look into the house for a moment and realised she'd been leaving crimson footprints in her path; she had to get outside to muddle her tracks.

The rain was coming down hard and fast; the sound was deafening as the world drowned in the storm's glory. A rumble of thunder shuddered the ground, it was closely followed by a crack of lightning slicing through the gloomy sky. Asha was instantly soaked and sure enough, the shower of cold water woke the sleeping beauty wrapped around her.

Boe squirmed but Asha held a hand over her head to protect her as best she could from the rain as she ran through the garden towards the back gate.

"Tally!" Boe demanded, her high voice cutting through the rain in a shrill fierceness.

"Shh!" Asha urged, she wasn't sure who or what Tally was, but Boe needed to be quiet.

Mud filled the gaps between her toes as she ran.

Once through the gate, Asha found herself in a dark alleyway with tangled shrubbery looming overhead, blocking whatever moonlight trying to break through to guide the way. However, what she *could* see was Kit's tall silhouette at the end of the alley to the right. He was beckoning her frantically.

She made to move towards him but as she started to run, her feet were suddenly bound together, and she was pulled from under herself.

She threw her arms out to break her fall, but she still landed on Boe with a smack to the sodden ground below. Before she could even react, she was dragged back towards the house by whatever was binding her ankles. She struggled against the force, and in the process turned herself onto her back, giving some relief to Boe who was now screaming her head off.

Asha could now see the perpetrator, a hardy, muscular woman with a broad smile on her face. In her hands was a huge black whip, her arm muscles practically throbbed as she pulled Asha further and further towards her reach. She only needed to pull her a few more metres before she could claim her prize.

Unluckily for her, her prize was armed.

Asha plucked out the knives from within the sling and struck the ground either side of her. The blades sunk in just enough to give her some stillness, which she used to yank her legs towards her, bringing the Hunter careering face-first to the muddy grass.

Asha then quickly worked the whip from around her ankles and jumped to her feet before turning to sprint back to the alley.

When she turned, she instantly bumped into Kit who steadied her with his hands on her shoulders. He gave her a quick look over before glancing over her head to the Hunter who was now getting herself up. Instead of trying to get them again though, she gave them a sickeningly curved smirk and then walked slowly towards the house.

"Run, little mice, we're after you now," she shouted over her shoulder before disappearing into the darkness of the house.

How many of them were there? There was no way to tell. All Asha knew was that they had to get out of there and fast. She soothed Boe and ran to the car with Kit right by her side.

The alleyway offered temporary protection from the storm, but once they were out of it and onto the road again, the sheets of rain buried her. She felt her bones shiver.

The lights from their car buzzed through the watery cloak of the storm and the comforting rumble of the engine vibrated through the bustling wind.

She ran fast towards their escape vehicle, but Kit ran faster and opened the door for her to jump through. Just as she ducked into the car, she caught a glimpse of a couple of Hunters. They were running towards them, but when they saw the car, they stopped and ran back to where they'd come from. She just about heard them say something through the rough winds.

Get the car.

"They have a car; we need to go now! Hurry!" Asha shouted to Max who was in the driver's seat.

Kit hauled himself into the people carrier and closed the door with a slam before Max swerved them around and drove at full speed down the wet road. Asha sat with her arms held tightly around Boe's shivering body. She finally caught her breath and glanced around the car briefly, noting everyone's attendance. They all looked concerned and very much soaking wet. But they were all there and that was all that mattered.

The headlights lit the way along the tarmac, which was a necessary evil. It showed the Hunters where they were, but without the lights, they would most likely crash. Luckily, the Hunters had to use them too, which showed the group how far oncoming danger was from them.

"There," Asha said pointing to the rear-view mirror as a clear set of lights appeared behind them.

"We'll lose them," Max said, his voice was grave and low. He was concentrating hard on the less than safe terrain.

Asha sat back in her seat, not wanting to panic herself too much. She needed to stay strong, positive, if not for herself, but for the others.

Kit put a reassuring hand on her shoulder, and she turned to give him a short nod.

The car trundled along the road. Suffocating silence and anticipation filled the interior. The Hunters were still behind them; it didn't look like they were going to give up any time soon, which meant they had a night of fleeing ahead of them. It sent Asha's stomach into disarray.

They had been so close to losing Boe. Asha didn't want to think about losing any one of them, but especially not her. The Hunter was right, children were rare, and children as young as Boe were almost unheard of. The children who had survived the sickness would be the new generation, the fit, invincible generation. They had to be protected at all costs.

"I want to go home now," Boe moaned in her little voice.

Asha stroked her back and thought to herself crushingly, *so do I.*

Just then, Max took a hard right and the group were thrown to one side of the car in the abrupt force.

"Jesus!" Daisy cried from behind Asha.

"Sorry, bear with me guys. I think we can lose them across the river that's comin' up," Max grunted.

Asha looked ahead and watched the route through the windshield. Dark twisting lanes melted into each other, and she wondered how Max could navigate them through it all so easily. They drove hurriedly past a sign saying that a bridge was close by. Asha turned around to look at Finn. She hadn't fully checked on him yet, and she felt she should have.

"Everyone okay?" She asked towards the group, but her stare was on him, on his golden, squinted eyes.

His face was almost white; he probably hadn't had much sleep. The various cuts and bruises that littered his skin practically glowed red and purple in the moonlight. He looked like a rejected canvas of an artist who'd given up. He wasn't a blank portrait anymore; he'd fought, and he'd lived.

"Yeah," he answered her, a slight glint in his eyes as he caught her stare.

Asha found her heart beating a little faster, she quickly turned back in her seat and peeked at Kit who was giving her an all-knowing look. She rolled her eyes and flung the back of her hand at his shoulder.

"Shut u-" Asha began to say, but she was cut off by a sudden cry causing her heart to halt.

"MAX! Stop!" Piper screamed murder.

Max slammed on the brakes, sending everyone flying forward, screams and yells came with the jolt. Asha barely had time to register what had happened but when she looked out front, she could see what the problem was.

The bridge had collapsed.

They were trapped.

Chapter Twenty-One

All eyes went to Max for instruction. The situation: they were trapped between the ruined bridge and the oncoming Hunters from the woods behind them. The solution: they needed a way across. Asha could feel the exasperation bubbling around the group. Could they not catch a break? Heavy breathing and chattering teeth filled the space in the car.

"*What the fuck do we do now?*" Asha whispered, shooting a glance at the burly man in front.

He was frozen, thoughts probably running wild through his mind.

"Max!" Piper shouted, her fiery locks flew out as she turned to him, pulling him out of his ice-like state.

"Right, everyone out. We're jumping the gap and driving this thing into the river," Max ordered.

He clicked off his seatbelt and practically flew out of the car, immediately opening the doors on the vehicle as he ran full force making sure to get it done quickly. The rest of the group gathered their things and piled out of the car, exposed to the stormy elements.

The rain still fell like a blanket over them, making Asha shudder uncontrollably. Daisy moaned and groaned, trying her best to rub her arms into some state of warmth, it was a futile attempt. Finn wiped the rain from his eyes and glanced to the road they'd been on, no doubt searching for the oncoming lights of their possible attackers.

Kit was crouched down helping Sunny who was struggling to put her huge backpack on. Piper was by Max's side, they both stood at the edge of the crumbling concrete, studying where the bridge had fallen into disarray.

Asha held Boe's head against her chest still, shielding her from the rain as she made her way to the edge too. She peered at the gap, it was substantial, but it was jumpable if they took a good run up. She couldn't help but look to the raging river below. It swirled angrily, tempting her into the abyss. She pulled herself from the hypnotising sight and looked to Max.

"They'll be on our arse any minute," he said, noticing her stare. "We have to do this, now."

The rest of the group gathered around, trying their best to hear Max over the sleeting sounds of the storm.

"We jump over one by one. I'll stay behind and throw the young'uns over, then I'll set this thing to drive into the river. If they catch up to us, we have to make 'em think we went in. Shit, if we're lucky they might go in themselves. We almost did if it hadn't been for Piper's eagle eyes," he said sternly, giving Piper a soft touch on her shivering shoulder.

"I'll go first," Kit stated, adjusting his backpack, preparing for the run up.

"Okay, Kit first, Ash next, Daisy, Finn, Piper. Then I'll throw the girls over. Let's go," Max ordered with a spinning hand, and everyone backed up and formed a line ready to go.

Asha motioned for Daisy to undo the knots of Boe's wrap around her. As she did so, Asha held Boe's weight until she could place her steady on the ground.

Once down, the wonky fringed girl toddled over to Max who had a sullen looking Sunny to his side. It was a dangerous task, but it was the only option they had.

They could hide on their side of the river, but they ran a risk of bumping into the Hunters, and who really knew how many there were. Also, Max was right, if they thought the group had crashed into the river then they would at least gain themselves some time.

Kit took in a few deep breaths, the rain started to dispel, and the early sun began to peep up from the stormy sky. Asha watched him closely as he began his run, her heart was in her throat, and her eyes were wide in anticipation. But he ran well and when he reached the edge, he catapulted himself across with ease. He landed roughly, his knees buckling as his feet hit the concrete on the other side. However, he recovered quickly and straightened himself up before turning to face the others and giving them a thumbs up.

Kit's no-fuss jump sparked a touch more confidence in Asha which was much needed because she had been a little nervous about making the leap. She glanced behind her briefly to see the various faces of fear and impatience.

She then looked down to her bare toes and was suddenly aware of the uncomfortable feeling of gritty tarmac under her skin. Even so, she planted her feet firmly on the ground and stared ahead to Kit who was waiting patiently for her to join him.

She manoeuvred her body into a running pose and waited just a moment more to psyche herself up before throttling forward towards the gaping crevice in front of her.

Her bare feet kicked up gravel as she ran, and her stare hardened as she approached the gap. Cold, biting wind assaulted her face and the remaining spits of rain flew into her vision. But she had no time to wipe her eyes, it was now or never.

Her speed was constant and as her toes curled on the edge of the fallen concrete, she hauled her body through the air, cape coat catching slightly in the breeze. Everything felt like it was in slow motion, suspended. She flew gracefully and her legs shot out in front of her to land…but she wasn't going to make it, not quite.

She grimaced as her toes scraped down the opposing, crooked edge of the bridge and her body fell down the gap. Her eyes widened in panic when her feet found no safety, but she couldn't do anything apart from try her best to grapple onto the bridge and stop herself from falling completely.

Luckily Kit was there in an instant; he caught her and his strong hands hooked under her arms to yank her up from her almost watery grave. She couldn't help but look down at her dangling feet over the raging river before she got pulled over and onto the welcoming concrete.

She caught her breath as she sat propped up on the bridge. *I should have taken a bigger run up.* As she looked back, she saw Max moving everyone back a little, learning quickly from her mistake.

"Don't fucking scare me like that," Kit practically hissed as he helped her to stand.

"*Piss off,*" she whined as she peeked at her toes which were nicely scratched and bleeding from the impact.

She grunted as she stood up and composed herself by taking deep, calming breaths. Her entire body shivered; she had spare clothes in her backpack, but she knew she had to save them for when she truly couldn't handle the cold anymore.

It was Daisy's turn next and the pair on the safe side of the bridge watched as she made the jump painlessly.

Finn came after, a look of anguish filled his face as he jumped, but he made it safe and sound. Asha went to him as he landed steadily and rubbed his back gently. They stood together and watched Piper run up and leap carefully over the exposed plummet. They had only taken a minute to jump across, which meant they only had a few more minutes left until the Hunters found them, which meant getting through the next part swiftly.

Max geared up and picked up Boe before striding fast towards the edge. He couldn't make the run up because it was too risky throwing her over with too much movement, so he just had to stand at the edge and throw her static. Kit moved right to the edge and held his arms out ready to catch her.

If she felt stressed before, she didn't know what this feeling was now.

Max looked to Kit who nodded in return as he widened his stance. Max then whispered something to Boe who shook her head fearfully and started to cry. There wasn't time for crying and Max knew that, so in the next second he wrapped her back up in her sling and threw her precisely into Kit's waiting grasp.

She screamed as she flew through the air, but as soon as she was cradled in Kit's arms she quietened down and actually giggled.

It must have been a fun feeling for her. Asha would be lying if she said she'd breathed in those moments because she didn't, not one breath.

Finn moved to the edge then in preparation for Sunny's turn. Max tossed over Sunny's bag first of all, which probably weighed more than the girl herself. He also threw as much of their stuff over as he could. Then, he picked Sunny up, cradled her like a baby and got himself ready to throw her. She was much longer and heavier than Boe, despite her skinny frame. Asha watched as Finn gave Max the signal to throw and she found herself holding her breath once again.

Max turned in the motion to throw Sunny but just as he let her go, he crumpled.

It all happened like a muffled, broken video tape.

Max yelled, holding his side, and Sunny dropped like a brick straight down the gap.

At the same time, Finn jumped.

Asha sank to the edge speechless as she watched Finn grab Sunny mid-air and cocoon her before they both hit the freezing water with a sickening pop.

Screams, yells and shouts surrounded Asha, but her head felt like cotton wool, she was having trouble processing what had just happened. She looked up wearily to Max who groaned as he grimaced at the sight below. His side was bleeding; he must have ruptured his stitches.

The pair had popped up on the surface, but Finn wasn't awake. Sunny was desperately trying to keep his head above water as her feet trod the blisteringly cold and rough rapids.

Sunny was going to die if she kept trying to keep him from drowning. They were both dead in the water. Asha was frozen, she couldn't think of what to do except for stare with a gaped mouth and uncontrollable tears flooding her vision.

"No, Kit stop!" Piper suddenly screamed from behind her.

Kit? Asha turned but she didn't turn quick enough to stop him from jumping too.

"No!" Asha screamed as her hand jutted out to grab him, even though there was no way she'd ever have touched him.

All she could do was watch him hit the water. She knew he would make the fall, but it was the water, it was the pneumonia. It was having more bodies to warm up, it was lowering their chances; it was the possibility of losing all three of them.

Asha's world was a blur. She was barely aware of her shoulder being shaken into submission by bony fingers. It was only when Daisy yanked her head around to look at her that Asha was sucked back into a cold hard reality.

"Asha!" Daisy screamed in her face.

"I'm here, I'm here," Asha replied blinking fast, hurtling back to reality; her scattered breaths fogged in the frosty air.

"Come on, we've got to go. Grab everything," Daisy instructed, pulling the dark-haired girl to her shaky feet.

Asha shot a look over to Max who was gesturing for her to run with the others before hauling himself into the car to start it.

"Get down the river! Catch them!" He shouted over to her. His face was wracked with guilt.

Asha nodded firmly and quickly gathered what she could before following Piper, Boe and Daisy who seemed to be so far ahead she wasn't sure she'd catch up. But she did.

She was out of breath as she sprinted alongside Daisy. The blonde girl's face was coated in a cold sweat, and she looked to be in a lot of pain, more than usual for someone running. Asha didn't have much time to be concerned because in the next second there was an almighty crash. The car had been planted. It was really time to go. They had to find the others before they became no more than human popsicles.

They raced through the tangling bushes that lined the river, bumbling over rocks and dodging the exposed roots of old trees. Asha watched the river as she ran, spotting the waterlogged trio splashing together, trying to hold on to each other as the river tried relentlessly to separate them. Finn was awake now which was a blessing; their chances strengthened. Asha found it difficult to run so fast alongside them whilst trying to look both at where her feet were going, and where they were headed, but she managed.

After a moment, she decided to drop the bags she was carrying. They were slowing her down and she could always go back for them. With less weight, she was able to speed past Daisy, Boe and Piper, making it to a clearing at the river's bend. That was when she saw the fallen tree bridging the water where it wasn't supposed to be.

She assessed the situation.

The three of them were coming hard down the river and they were on their way to collision town. But that also meant they would be stopped in their tracks, and they would have a good shot at getting out of the river.

Asha ran up to the very edge of the water, wincing as her bare feet were submerged in the icy water. She waved her arms, gaining the attention of Kit who was looking to her with panicked eyes. She pointed animatedly to the tree and Kit, though he was twisting and turning in the rapids, nodded in acknowledgment.

Daisy and Piper caught up to Asha and threw their bags down to the ground before joining her along the riverbed. Boe was placed strategically on a tree stump where she wouldn't see what might happen.

"Find something to pull them in, quick!" Asha shouted to the women, never taking her eyes off the incoming trio.

The two of them followed instructions and within seconds Piper was brandishing a long branch with pointed spikes protruding from its end. It would do the trick and Asha thanked the stars that there was something so close to hand.

Despite the warning about the tree, Kit and Finn still hit it with a shuddering crunch, making Asha cringe. But what made her really shout was the fact that Sunny had somehow been pulled under the tree in the motion. She might not have gotten a good hold of the wood, or maybe the boys accidently lost their grip of her, but either way, she had slipped underneath it and she hadn't reappeared.

Kit and Finn had a secure hold on the tree trunk, but their faces were doused with anxiety.

"Where is she?!" Asha screamed to them.

She was met with a shake of heads and worry filled eyes.

"I'll go under! Finn, you go to land," Kit ordered, his breaths deep and exertive.

"What? No! I'll get her," Finn yelled back at him, twisting to face him.

"*Get the fuck over there before I knock you back under,*" Kit growled.

Asha could hardly hear them over the winds that seemed to have picked up, throwing leaves and debris up into the air swirling around her; but she could see that Finn had been told what to do, and he was shuffling along the tree towards her.

"Piper, the branch!" Asha called, turning to see the red head already ready to go.

Piper and Daisy manoeuvred the branch over in Finn's direction; all the while that was happening, Asha watched over Kit who was preparing to dive under the water.

Max suddenly appeared from the trees behind them, out of breath and brandishing the bags Asha had dropped, plus his own. She glanced over to him; she saw his shirt was soaked with blood; he wasn't in a good way. He chucked the bags to the hard ground and jogged over to her.

"What's goin' on?" Max asked as he looked around pained, his palm pressed on his side, stilling the bleeding just a touch.

"Sunny's gone under. Kit's getting her," was all Asha could blurt out.

Max grunted his concern and followed Asha's stare over to Kit who took a deep breath and dived under. Finn was being dragged onto land by the girls and the burly man moved to help with that.

Asha wanted to help Kit find Sunny, but she didn't want to put herself at risk by going into the river too.

She stared intently at the water, watching as bubbles escaped quickly to the surface and movement pushed the water in all different directions. It looked like Kit was fighting something under there. Then it hit her.

Sunny must have gotten caught under the tree itself, she hadn't gone anywhere, she was right there. Asha's breathing stopped and her hand went to her mouth. *Please, please let her be okay.*

As if to answer her pleas, a huge eruption came from the water and up came Kit spluttering, grasping onto a lifeless and positively grey, Sunny. Her head lolled onto her chest and the very sight of it forced tears to escape Asha's eyes.

"Jesus Christ!" Max bellowed, running to water with the long branch. He waded in up to his calves and beckoned Kit to move faster along the trunk.

"Oh no!" screamed Piper, falling to her knees at the sight of the little girl.

Kit was having trouble holding onto the tree and Sunny whilst trying to move, but he did it, probably out of pure adrenaline. He needed to get Sunny to shore, he needed to bring her back.

Asha didn't know what to do. She didn't want to look at the small girl; she couldn't do anything to help her. It was that helplessness that forced her to think of some other way she could be of use. Then she remembered Finn and the fact that he was slowly giving into hyperthermia.

She tore her eyes away from the little life in jeopardy and instead ran over to Finn whose lips had turned blue.

He was shaking uncontrollably but even he was more preoccupied with Sunny's fate than his own. Asha had to take charge. She needed to warm him up. She would deal with the others afterwards, after they fixed their little fighter.

She whipped off her cape coat and yanked Finn's drenched shirt off of him, exposing his bare skin to the elements for just a second before draping him with her prized possession. He shivered and melted into the fabric, taking in as much heat as he could. Asha helped sit him down and prop him up against a tree. She then ran to grab her bag. As she searched for it among the other bags, she tried to ignore what was happening, but it was hard to not hear the panicked cries of Piper, the grunts of Kit giving CPR and the desperate way Max was repeating Sunny's name.

She quickly found her bag and raced back to Finn whose eyes were fixed on the lifeless body behind her.

"*My fault,*" Finn shivered, barely getting his words out through his chattering teeth.

"Don't you *dare* say that," Asha warned him, shooting him a glare.

She shoved her hand into her bag and pulled out a big woollen jumper. She then took her coat off of Finn's practically convulsing body and instead hauled the jumper onto him. It was drier than her coat, it would do him well.

"*She…*" Finn began to say, his eyes filling with tears, he was overcoming the shock and now letting emotion in.

"Finn…*Finn!*" Asha yelled, grabbing hold of his face and turning it harshly to look at her and her only.

He looked to her with broken, honey eyes that sent her heart into overdrive.

"Whatever happens to her, you did everything you could. She would be so grateful, Finn, she would be *so happy* that you did that for her. Listen to me, and look at me," she soothed him, making sure his eyes stayed on hers. "I've never seen anything more brave," she smiled softly, stroking his cheek lightly with her thumb.

They held their stare for a fragile moment before growing sounds of panic became stronger behind them.

Finn's demeanour dropped and his stare fell, he was giving up. Asha whipped her head around to look at the others, her eyes frightened and her heart doing the river dance.

She looked upon the sight before her with a heavy heart. Her hand instinctively went to Finn's eyes, covering his view from what seemed to be happening. They were losing Sunny; she was going to die. Finn didn't even move her hand from his eyes, he just sat shaking violently, whimpering.

Sunny was somehow greyer than she had been when Kit pulled her out of the water, her eyes were slightly open, and her mouth was slack. Asha thought to herself if it was possible to hope for life to come back to an already dead body.

Kit was following procedure; a procedure he'd already had to go through with Asha only yesterday. This time however, he looked like he was fighting a losing battle. Sunny looked far worse than Asha had done, and even then, he couldn't bring her back, Finn had to help.

Max knelt by Sunny's head and said her name over and over again, demanding her to come back, as if that would help.

Piper looked defeated, hollow, about ready to die herself. Daisy was nowhere to be seen and thankfully Boe wasn't either.

She shouldn't have to see her saviour die.

Asha turned back to face the half-drowned boy in front of her, her hand was still covering his eyes, shielding him from any more trauma. He wouldn't stop shaking. She wanted so badly to make him feel warm, to bring some sort of relief to him. She wanted to take all the pain away. She wanted him to smile, to bare his dimples, to have a sparkle in his eye. She wanted him to be happy. But more than anything, she wanted to hold him, to comfort him and tell him it was going to be okay.

She took her hand away from his face, his eyes quickly locked on hers, tear-filled and threatening to spill. It was then that she realised, she shouldn't ever scold him for getting upset, or for being scared; she should praise him. He *felt*. He embraced his emotions; he didn't care that the world constantly told him not to. She had let the world take her emotions from her; she'd listened to it when it told her to stiffen up her upper lip.

She'd obeyed her surroundings and betrayed her heart.

The oddest feeling suddenly washed over her. It was like a humming warmth, a foreign sensation, something she hadn't felt for a while. She was overcome with her emotions. Emotions of fear, sadness and the strangest of all…love. Or at least a sense of it. Her hard exterior crumbled down like the bridge they'd just jumped, and all of a sudden, she felt like she used to be. Human.

It was him; it was always going to be him.

The noise from behind them continued in a panicked dance between life and death, but to Asha, the world had just become full of colour, bright and coursing. She wasn't happy, she was drenched in heartache, but she felt it, she felt all of it. She let the tears roll down her cheeks and a cry escaped her lips. They were losing their little sun; she knew it and she had to face it right away. There was no suppressing her feelings, she was in charge of them, and she would take them on as they came, never to save them for another day again.

Without warning, Finn pulled her hard against him, holding her tightly in his arms. Her head found solace in the crook of his neck, and even though he was soaking her with icy water, she only wanted to be closer to him. His body still rocked from the cold, but he kept a steady hand soothing her back. Her heart felt full.

That's it, she thought, *I've fallen.*

Chapter Twenty-Two

A sudden, choked spluttering came from behind them, followed by sighs and shouts of relief. Asha jolted up from her mourning and closed her eyes for a brief moment, letting out a happy breath.

Finn sat up straight and peered over her shoulder; his smile told her everything she needed to know before she turned around herself.

Sunny was alive.

Kit was helping her to sit up, getting rid of all the water that had invaded her lungs. Piper was quietly praying to the sky with her hands together, and a thankful Max was rubbing his creased forehead with a heavy hand.

Asha's happiness was almost too much for her to handle. She needed to express it somehow and the first thing she looked to was Finn. She grinned widely and wiped away her tears before encasing him in a hard hug. When she pulled away, he smiled softly at her, his dimples coming out. *At last,* she thought, and her heart relaxed.

Now that all was somewhat clear, she could lend a helping hand. She jumped off Finn, grabbed her bag and ran over to the rest of the group, fishing out the remainder of her dry clothing, ready for the pair that needed them the most.

"Here, take these clothes," she instructed Max, taking more care in the future problems rather than embracing the beautiful moment of the problem they'd just solved.

Max took the random assortment of clothing from Asha and also searched his bag for extra things to wear. Piper was cradling Sunny who was now fully awake and sobbing, quite rightly. Daisy had reappeared with Boe balancing on her hip, she looked dark but relieved, and Boe just sat there staring, legs swinging lazily. Kit was sat there next to Sunny, his eyes wide, shaking hard. Asha went to him and helped him shrug off his shirt and his trousers, hurriedly replacing the swamped clothes with relatively dry ones.

"You did it!" Asha beamed at him.

He seemed in a daze. "I-I," he started to say but his shivering took control. He stared at Sunny, his eyes grateful and relieved. "I didn't think I'd be able to bring her back. I couldn't with you," he said sadly.

"You've done so much for us, Kit. Just shut up and get warm, okay?" Asha said lightly, pinching his cheek.

He frowned and pushed her off, but he looked to her again and smiled. "Thank you."

"No worries. I knew keeping spares would come in handy," she grinned, tugging at the jumper she'd thrown on him.

When Asha turned around, Sunny was completely covered in various layers of clothing and Piper was still holding her in a vice-like grip; like she was never going to let her go. Asha couldn't blame her of course; Sunny was one of them. She had colour to her face once again and she was breathing heavily, making up for lost oxygen.

Asha found herself smiling at the sight of the clearly distressed and injured child.

Only because she was happy that she didn't have to prepare a pint-sized grave for her, not because she enjoyed her pain.

The screeching of tires fighting tarmac suddenly hooted through the trees, followed by an ear shattering crash, that was closely joined by the sound of something big and heavy dropping into water. Asha's sight shot to Max who was already staring at her. The Hunters had gone in just like they'd hoped. But that hope, Asha realised, was not something they should have banked on, because now the Hunters were on a direct route to them. They had to get away, quickly.

It was a matter of getting under the cover of the trees, which wasn't too much trouble seeing as though they were already at the tree line. Asha led the group to a secluded area of woods, where the air felt somehow warmer and sheltered. A good place to stay while they found a proper hideout, which the dark-haired girl already had her mind on.

Once everyone was settled in, hidden by the greenery, she packed her bag with essentials.

"What are you doing?" Max questioned, eyeing her inquisitively as he approached her.

"I need to find us a place to stay. We can't be out in the open, especially not with those three. They'll give into the cold soon. I know they've got dry clothes now, but they need more, they need a building. I'll scout the area. I'll be quick," Asha explained calmly and quietly, not wanting Kit to hear. But much to her dismay, he did.

"What?" came a chattering voice from behind her.

Asha rolled her eyes and finished packing her bag before she went over to Kit who was being warmed up by Piper. His skin was reddened from the cold water and the biting wind. She knelt by him, feeling his stress.

"I have to go. I'll be back soon," she reassured him, giving Piper a thankful smile.

"No, you can't go alone," he shivered, his eyes pleading her not to leave.

"I'm going. Get warm, I'm going to find us somewhere to stay the night. You won't survive the cold; not like you are," Asha explained as best she could, trying to get him on her side.

She had to go alone. It was down to her and she was happy to do it. Her skin prickled into bumps as the wind began to pick up; a run would do her some good. She saluted Max, who was looking after Sunny, from across the clearing.

She then wandered over to Finn who was being tended to by Daisy, much to her apparent annoyance, judging by the look on her face.

"I'm off. I'll come back for you guys when I've found somewhere to stay. How are you feeling?" She asked Finn, noting the blue hue still shining on his lips.

"What? Where?" he asked, panic blowing his eyes wide at her.

The way he looked at her, it threw her. She felt overwhelmed by the amount of care he seemed to have about her. Her heart inflated to twice its size.

Fucking hell.

"Don't die," Daisy helpfully added.

"I just have to find somewhere for us," Asha explained, her stare not once leaving Finn.

"Be careful." He said gravely. "I don't think I could face you not coming back."

"First, I'll find you guys somewhere warm… then I'll disappear," Asha teased, but when Finn showed no sense of humour, she stopped her smile and looked down thoughtfully to the ground before glancing up to meet his unwavering gaze. "I'll come back; I promise."

"Don't break it," he added once again, looking to her with a warmth and need that Asha could hardly deal with. Her cheeks burst into flames.

"Shit, you really, really need to get a room because I'm starting to feel fucking sick listening to you two," Daisy groaned, still unwillingly rubbing Finn's arms into life.

"You didn't think I was just finding a place for us to stay warm, did you?" Asha smirked at her.

Finn's cheeks reddened further, and it wasn't from the cold.

"Just go, Jesus Christ," Daisy breathed out, exasperated.

Asha couldn't help the smile that took over her. She took a certain pleasure in disgusting the blonde girl.

Once she was happy enough with the group slowly recovering, she worked on finding something to leave a trail with. She was never going to find her way back to them using just her instinct. Luckily for her, she found a whole load of brightly coloured mushrooms growing in their hundreds at the base of a large oak tree. They may have been poisonous, but as long as she didn't put them near her mouth, she would be fine.

She picked as many as she could and shoved them into her bag. As quickly as she could, she ran, desperate to find somewhere safe. After five minutes of running and dropping mushrooms, she finally started to feel warm.

Despite that, she had a constant cold feeling in her stomach, the feeling of dread.

She wasn't seeing any buildings or forest outposts. She desperately needed to find somewhere, or else her friends' lives might be in jeopardy. She ran and ran, scooting under branches and jumping over fallen logs, covered with tangled vines. She became out of breath and took a quick break, looking back at the trail of colourful fungi behind her. She wiped her brow of sweat and carried on her journey with a new sense of urgency.

Time was running out.

Two minutes later, her pounding feet brought her to a civilised area, if you could define a church and a bus stop as 'civilised'. Her face burst into a bright smile and she felt relief wash over her. She slowed her walk down to a stroll as she neared the church, taking in it's beautiful exterior and its promise of safety.

Asha had never been a religious person. But even so, she always found a certain comfort when in a church. She couldn't explain it; all she knew was that she felt warm, guarded and accepted when she was surrounded by the stained-glass windows and cosy stone walls. It could have something to do with the feeling of love, hope and praise that fills a church, but she would never truly know. Either way, she was happy that she'd found somewhere to settle for the night.

She tentatively placed her palms on the thick wooden doors and pushed her way slowly into the damp building. It was quiet, the creaking hinges echoed loudly throughout the vast space. She winced slightly at the noise and slowly closed the doors behind her, taking extreme care not to make even further noise. She stood for a second with her back against the wood, admiring the beauty of the church.

Neat rows of pews filled most of the floor, with prayer cushions tucked delicately underneath them. Early morning light cascaded through the stained-glass windows, creating sparkling patterns which twinkled in Asha's eyes. The musty smell filled her lungs and she breathed in deeply, enjoying the soothing feeling of the rustic smell. The air was warm and she knew straight away that this could be the place to rest.

She wanted to go back and bring the others, but she needed to do a quick search of the place to make sure it was completely safe, and to look for any clothing they could all change into.

She dropped her bag on a pew and walked down the central aisle, her bare feet hardly making a noise as she padded along the wooden planks. She wrapped her cape coat around her harder, folding her arms across her chest, keeping her warmth to herself.

The church seemed relatively untouched, which was a good sign. There was no nod to life, or anyone having lived in it, apart from the bundled-up pile of blankets that sat right next to the altar.

Asha curiously, quietly, walked towards it, eyebrows furrowed and a falter in her breath. She hoped and prayed that someone wasn't under all of them, waiting to ambush her.

She stood by it and watched it for a second, checking for breathing before kicking it hard. The lightness of the impact flooded her with relief. It was just blankets. She smirked and picked up a couple to put in her bag right away.

Before she could turn around, however, a wooden stick struck the back of her knees.

A scream caught in her throat as she helplessly buckled backwards, knocking her elbows and head on the stone floor. The fall on her back winded her and the hit to her head confused her. Her eyes struggled to stay open, but she wasn't unconscious. Everything went fuzzy, dream-like. She forced herself to blink fast to try and wake herself up to full alertness, but it was no use. Hot liquid pooled under her hair. She must have ruptured the stitches Piper had put in.

Small moans escaped her lips, her fingers moved slightly as she writhed slowly on the floor. She had no strength; everything was a mixture of reality and blackness. She dipped in and out of a state of awareness, and her thoughts buzzed lazily around her skull.

I have to get those blankets… get to the others… Awake, Asha, awake!

A few seconds later, crusty, dry hands wrapped around her wrists and she was dragged across the floor. Her toes curled and scraped painfully along the stone as she tried desperately to stop herself. As she blinked, she watched the ceiling of the church, the stone arches, the hanging chandeliers. All of which made her that much sleepier.

She was then vaguely aware of being lifted up and into something. Her moans became more vocal, her head pounded and her right elbow felt severely bruised.

She was still slipping between worlds, but she could feel herself coming back, inching back in control. Her recovery wasn't fast enough though and before she knew it, she was strapped into some sort of seat, her hands behind her back, waist clinched, ankles bound and a gag in her mouth.

She was unable to do anything. Her head lolled onto her chest, until something was placed under her face. The smell of it was so potent and poisonous that it brought her all the way back to consciousness in an abrupt instant.

Her head flung up and her eyes blew wide open as she gasped loudly, recovering from her partial blackout. Straight in front of her crouched a skeletal, middle-aged man, his long greasy hair fell down his sharp face and his crooked teeth shone as he smiled hauntingly at her.

In his hands was a small pot of liquid; its smell still coursed through Asha's nose. He was Pure. But the fact that he'd knocked her out and tied her up led Asha to a blaringly obvious conclusion.

He was a Reaper.

Panic engulfed her as she pulled against her restraints. The gag in her mouth pushed hard against her tongue and she felt like she was going to throw up. Her eyes practically bulged out of her head as she muffed a scream of help. Who she was shouting to was another question, but she felt it was the only thing she could do. She was trapped. The others didn't know where she was, and she couldn't get out of her bind.

This was not good.

"I haven't had a catch for a while. Everyone reaches for their 'blankie' in times of need," The man croaked, his smirk everlasting.

He put the pot down on a thick mahogany chest behind him, which gave Asha time to look properly at where she was. She was in a darkened enclosed cubicle, which she quickly realised was a confessional.

She very briefly thought of all the things she could confess, like constantly lying through her teeth to her parents, being lustful, and -not forgetting- the murdering spree in the last six months. *How ironic,* she thought, that she'd ended up right where her sinful-self belonged.

"You're a little on the small side, but my Hunter group don't mind that. Anything pleases them," he continued, twiddling his stick fingers in front of his face. "So, girl, what do you have to confess? This is your last chance, before death. Speak to the Lord and he will cleanse you," he smiled, motioning his hand to the wooden partition to the side of her head.

Asha turned to see what he was gesturing at, which was when he disappeared and opened the grated gap of the confessional to look to the other cubicle. Asha peered through and there sat a skeleton fully adorned in holy clothing. A priest to hear her pleas.

The white neck piece hung loosely around the spine, bits of faded hair still stuck to the top of the skull, and the black robe sank into the wooden chair, framed only by bones. Its vacant eye sockets were staring directly at her, speaking pain and sorrow to the dark-haired girl.

Asha just sighed, defeated, before turning to look ahead of her, out of the box.

Tears filled her eyes and her whole body deflated, relaxing into her handcuffs. She was all out of ideas, all out of hope. But she couldn't wallow; she had to fight, whatever way she could.

"Come on. You must have something to say," the Reaper moaned, coming back into view. He stalked to her and Asha filched as he pulled out her gag. "Go on! Speak to him! Confess!"

"...*Fuck you,*" she choked.

His hand jutted out to her throat and his stick fingers clasped tightly around her neck, closing her airway. She felt her veins pulsing deeply against his cold fingers, her eyes widened and her hands vigorously tried to escape their metal casing to get him off her.

She panicked for a few more seconds until he let go of her suddenly and returned to just standing in front of her. She sucked in breath and coughed away the trauma to her throat. Her whole body squirmed as she regained herself after the attack.

"Now, let's try that again," he said, a little out of breath.

"...How many are you?" Asha eventually asked sternly, creasing her brows.

"Of me? Only one of course. The Lord only needs one to carry out his work. That's me," he said softly before bowing, like he was something special.

"Good," Asha said simply. She would figure out a way to kill him.

"Now, what is your confession?"

Asha was silent for a moment, a thousand thoughts of how to escape filling her mind, she let out a deep breath.

"Come, speak now, then I'll put you to sleep. The Lord wouldn't want you to be in pain for the journey to the afterlife," he said, eyes sparkling.

"...I'd like to confess," Asha finally said, her eyes narrowing.

"Go on child, we're listening," he reassured her as he pointed to the sky.

"...*Impure thoughts,*" she smirked with a dark stare.

"Of what? The Lord needs specificity, or he can't grant you forgiveness."

"Men…women. And right now, *you*," she practically whispered. It was time to play bad, it was time to elicit his sickly desires.

She was young, he was alone, surely he'd be longing for some kind of human connection. A physical connection. If he was going to believe that she *wanted* him, she needed to make it believable, she needed to make herself blush, to prove to him she wasn't lying.

Her thoughts instantly went to the honey-eyed boy who'd stumbled so clumsily into her life. The image of his lips danced in her vision, his fingers gripping her hips, his closed eyes, his pink cheeks, his heavy breathing. *How he would call her a good girl as he…* Her heartbeat rocketed tenfold and she began to feel her cheeks heat.

She kept her stare on the Reaper, looking deep into his eyes, making sure he felt what she was feeling. He was locked on her stare for a moment, looking a little lost before snapping himself out of it and frowning so deeply it looked like his face might stay that way.

"You disgusting sinner! You don't deserve retribution!" He growled before grabbing her gag and shoving it back in, not caring how rough he was with her.

Oh no.

He stepped back and looked at the broken girl once more before slamming the confessional door shut. He left the little window on the door open, presumably so he could look in on her when he pleased. Asha thought about how much time she might have left. She assumed he'd gone to prepare whatever he was going to use to put her to 'sleep' with.

*

A long time later, she jolted awake. She wasn't dead yet, in fact, she was still in the same position as before, she ached.

Maybe he's forgotten about me? The thought flickered into her mind, but it was immediately met with confusion and doubt. There was no way he would have just left her there. Something was wrong. She glanced down at her constraints, wriggling to determine the room she had between them and her. There was very little leeway. Her waist already felt sore from the practical metal corset holding her awkwardly in place.

She'd have very little luck getting out of it, not to mention the fact that her hands were handcuffed behind her back, and her ankles were bound with coarse, thin rope, doubled and tied in a knot three times over. A sudden worry crossed her mind. If something happened to the Reaper, then she would be left where she was, and no-one would know she was there. She'd meet a similar fate to the priest beside her, rotting in confession.

Bile rose in her throat. She needed to get out of there, she had to find a way out. Her mind buzzed for a minute, then she had a sudden idea. She yanked her wrists hard against the cuffs. Even if she broke one of her hands, at least she would have a better chance on getting herself out.

She breathed in a few deep breaths through her nose, her eyebrows turned up and she gave herself one last moment of determined thought before she pulled up her wrist hard, crushing it through the small metal clasp.

Asha screamed unapologetically past her gag, yelping at the pain that flew from her wrist up to her brain; tears streamed down her hot cheeks as she returned her wrist back into the handcuff.

268

She hadn't broken her hand, not even close, but the pain was still enough to make her stop trying, at least for the moment. Her body began to shake with adrenaline.

Pain is temporary, death is permanent. Don't be a fucking wimp. Pull your hand through, you stupid girl. The others are waiting. Pull it, pull it, pull it!

Her thoughts built and built. Filling her with strength, with courage. She didn't have to do it for her, she had to do it for them.

She had to do it.

"GOD!" She screamed as loud as she could against the gag, before going to pull her hand out of the handcuff.

"You called?" A weedy voice swam through the confessional window.

Asha halted her attempt to escape in an instant and looked up to see her old Reaper friend staring in at her, a small smile on his face.

Her chest heaved and her tears stung her eyes as she resigned herself to being put to sleep for Hunter meat.

"Oh, don't pout like that, child. You won't feel anything," he grinned at her as he held up an injection full of a clear liquid to the window.

He was taunting her.

Something shone in her eye. He was wearing something metal around his neck, something silver; something of *hers*. Her necklace and ring looked completely out of place around the dirty neck of the Reaper; everything in her boiled. How dare he take something like that from her.

"Oh this?" He questioned lightly, looking down to the precious stolen goods. "Consider it a small donation to the church," he smirked before holding up the injection and squirting it a touch, preparing it for insertion.

Asha glared at him with hell fury and a scream began to erupt from her throat, but her anger stopped quickly when the axe head flew into the Reaper's cheek, straight through his sickly smile.

Chapter Twenty-Three

Asha watched horrified as the axe was pulled roughly from the Reaper's head. She caught glimpse of the life leaving his eyes just before he fell out of her sight. A second of worried panic shot through her about who was on the other side of the door. What if they wanted to hurt her too?

But her thoughts were quickly put to rest when the flimsy wooden door flew open and there stood her brother, her partner, her saviour, Kit. Her body relaxed and her mind quietened to nothing but happiness at seeing him. And there in his hand was her necklace, now spotted with blood, making it look sinister; tainted.

"This seems pretty important to you, thought you'd like it back," he grinned cheekily, but a hidden sense of overwhelming relief flooded his face.

Asha let out a choked laugh through her gag, her tears still curling down her cheeks. Tears of happiness now, however.

Kit grinned and went to give it to her, realising pretty quickly that she was incapable of moving, let alone taking back what was hers. His eyebrows shot together and he stood for a second thinking.

"Huh," he said before looking to her. "Did you see where he put the keys?"

Asha shook her head and was then aware of the fact that she still had a gag in her mouth and Kit was there to easily take it out. She grunted at him and stared down to her mouth, silently requesting his services.

"Right!" He said with a jump in his step.

He carefully pulled the fabric out of her mouth and let it hang loose around her neck. Its wetness sent a shiver down her spine. She was thankful she didn't have to taste it anymore.

"How the hell did you find me?" She asked him, exasperated, relishing the relatively clean air in her lungs.

"You were gone for too long, so I followed your trail. At least what I assumed was your trail. Mushrooms, yeah?" He shot her a questioning look.

"Bingo," she grinned wearily.

"But the trail stopped about fifteen minutes from here… the wind's been getting stronger, must have sent the mushrooms haywire. Anyways, I wandered around for a while, not really knowing what the fuck to do. I was getting worried. I know the others would be wondering where I was and if I'd gotten lost, but whatever, I just had to find you. I'd never leave your arse behind, you know that."

She smiled a soft smile, just happy to have him talking to her.

"So yeah. I ran around the woods... I'm fucking sick of trees. I did leave my own trail though. Unravelled one of your jumpers. You've been gone for three hours; did you know that?"

"What?" She instantly thought of all those minutes in the freezing cold for the group. "How are the others?" She asked, panicked.

"Fine. Me, Finn and Sunny were running around in circles for a while to warm up. Sunny's still in pain though, from, well, everything."

"And Finn?"

Kit rolled his eyes. "He's his normal annoying self. Insisted he come with me, but I convinced him to stay and look after the girls. Besides, how could I do my knight in shining armour act with a snivelling lovesick sidekick?"

Lovesick, the word made her ears turn red and her mind fill with him once again.

"Okay, but you still haven't told me how you found me," she insisted, needing to put facts in the place where an apparent miracle had taken place.

"Oh, right. I saw this guy out gathering berries. I was actually gonna ask him if he'd seen anyone around, but that was until I saw your necklace on him. He didn't have blood on him, and he looked pretty calm, so I guessed he hadn't done anything to you yet, so I followed him until now. And then, bam. Dead thief on the church floor," he shrugged, glancing down at the chopped face resting in a hot, bubbling puddle of blood.

"Thanks, you truly are my knight in shining armour. I thought I'd spend eternity trapped in here," Asha groaned, shuffling in her metal constrictions.

"Well, until I find the keys, you're gonna have to stay there," Kit said before bending down and checking the body of the Reaper. No luck.

"*Hurry,*" Asha whined, not enjoying the fact she was inconveniently stuck and the only person who knew where the keys were was lying bleeding at her feet.

"I'm gonna shut the door while I go look, okay? Just in case someone comes in," Kit said without waiting for a response.

Asha obeyed, not that she could rebel against his orders in her state. It was a good idea anyway, seeing as she couldn't fight and the box would hide her well enough. She listened to the noises Kit was making as he strode around the spacious building, hearing furniture being searched, things falling off counters and him bumping into things making him curse. She sat perfectly still and quiet, aching to hear some sort of victory yell from him, but it didn't happen, not for ten minutes at least.

Eventually, the door to the confessional flew open and Kit waved a chunky set of clanging keys in the air, a bright smile on his cheeky face. Asha's whole body soared, finally, a way out. Kit worked quickly to locate the right keys to each part of her intricate casing. He then used one of her knives to cut through the rope around her ankles, which had rubbed into her skin deeply, binding her with red shackles of soreness.

She bent down to soothe them with her hands for a moment before standing herself up. As she reached out for Kit, her senses betrayed her, making her feel light-headed and weak. He caught her and she gripped onto his slightly damp shirt. Her eyes set upon her hand which had flourished in all shades of purple from where she'd attempted her escape. A groan escaped her throat as she studied it and the rest of her body. She was a walking punching bag, a rag doll, a collection of scars, bloodied and broken.

Kit held her up for a moment, grazing his eyes over every part of her. His brow furrowed and he shook his head, closing his eyes.

"Sorry I didn't come earlier. I hate seeing you like this," he moaned quietly.

"It's my fault, not yours," she reassured him, but the uncomfortable pain made her wince as she said it.

"Right, I'm gonna get the others. Do you wanna come?" He asked her once he was sure she could stand by herself.

"I'll stay, get things ready for us," Asha said, looking around the place, wondering where she could set up camp.

She'd rather stay behind and be a little domestic instead of going for a long run. She was in no fit state, and besides, she was looking forward to seeing the others' faces when they arrived at the little sanctuary.

"Okay, here, take these though," he said as he passed her her trusted knives along with his favourite axe.

"What do you have?" She quizzed him as she took the arsenal anyway.

"I have enough to protect me, don't worry. I'll see you soon," he said accompanied with a hard hug which made Asha whimper slightly. "Ah, I did it again. Sorry, see you!" He grinned and gave her one last look before running out the towering church doors.

Asha watched as he went, her hand up in a limp goodbye for a few moments even after he left. Finally, she blinked a couple of times and dropped her arm, bringing her back into focus. She darted her sight around the room, wrapping herself in her arms, shuddering. *Time to get to work.*

She knew she had to get rid of the body first. If there was one thing that brought the mood down at a housewarming party, it was a recently deceased person.

She shoved her knives into her bag which she then slung around her chest, leaving her arms ready to be utilised fully. Then, she gingerly tucked her growing hair behind her ears and walked over to the Reaper's body. She quickly realised that moving him would pour blood all through the church, so she decided to take one of the blankets from his infamous trap and use it to stem the blood.

Once his head was wrapped, she hooked her arms under his and dragged his heavy weight towards the church doors. She moaned and groaned the whole time, struggling to move his corpse out of the building, but she managed, just about.

She backed out into the now bright sunshine and found a bit of momentum to haul his body off into the nearby bushes. Kit was right, the wind had picked up, and despite the sun blazing down, she shivered. Once she hid him well enough, she fell to her knees from the exertion on her wounds. She sat catching her breath and stilling the pain that scraped its way around her.

A few moments passed before she felt okay enough to stand up and carry on. Her mind was on a sleeping area now, and she knew just where to get what she needed for it. She trudged back to the church and bee-lined to the altar where the blankets lay.

Before long, Asha had found two spacious rooms up in the rafters of the church. They made perfect secluded places to rest for the night. She had adorned them with all the bedding they could want, clothes which she had found tucked away -presumably donations-, and enough candles to see them through the night.

She was just about to delve into a rather large wooden cabinet, which was hidden away in the back of the now empty storage cupboard, when she heard chatter coming from outside.

She recognised one of the voices as Kit's, followed by Piper's light laugh. A smile crept onto her freckled face, and she found herself feeling excited to show her group what she'd found for them. She half-ran to the main body of the church and just reached the entrance when Kit opened the door, letting the sunlight streak in. She took in the sight of her haggard group, smiles on all their faces.

Asha clocked Finn quickly which made her grin wider than she thought possible. How could someone have such an effect on her? This wasn't the movies where people fell in love the instant they saw each other, this was real life, but somehow, he made her feel just like that.

He moved past Max who was surveying the area and walked fast to Asha who was more than ready to accept the hug he gave her. He held her close to him and even lifted her up off the ground, enough to make her squeal.

"You almost didn't keep that promise," he said softly, looking at her so directly that she felt vulnerable.

"A Latina never goes against their word," she smiled, guiding him to place her back down to the floor.

He closed his eyes and smiled to the side, his dimples baring.

Fuck.

"Alright, happy reunions aside, let's get warm and eat something," Kit announced to everyone, which pulled Asha out of her practical trance.

"Everyone, follow those stairs and you'll find some rooms, make yourselves at home," Asha instructed, pointing to the back of the church.

Finn gave her shoulder a slight pinch and excused himself to join the others.

"I want the softest bed!" Boe said happily, jumping up and down on the spot.

"Come on little one, we'll find you something," Piper soothed, resting a hand on her little back and easing her along.

Asha smiled, and then looked to Sunny who gave her a nod. The girl was looking far better now that she was up and walking around, instead of waterlogged and down. Asha did notice a large red mark across her forehead, something she hadn't seen before. She must have bumped her head in the river; explaining why she couldn't escape the log. She'd been knocked out. Asha forced herself to focus on the present and tore her eyes away from the mousey girl to look at the burly man coming towards her.

"Well done Miss Flores," Max congratulated her, holding out a hand to shake.

Asha's eyebrows furrowed slightly, unsure of the gesture, but she honoured it. As she did so, he gently turned her hand in his and looked from her to the purple bruises, his face darkened.

"Let's try not to hurt yourself anymore, hmm? I need you in one piece... we all do," he said solemnly, staring at her with his almost black eyes.

"I'm sorry," she instinctively said, finding herself blushing from something, guilt maybe.

"Don't apologise, just, take note," Max finished before setting off to the stairs.

Asha watched as Daisy shuffled into the church, she looked unbelievably pale, like what little pigment she had had been sucked from her skin. She was also breathing unnaturally heavily. Asha was confused. The others weren't out of breath, which meant they probably walked at least the last part of the journey. So why was Daisy struggling so much?

The rest of the group had made their way up the stairs, so Asha took the opportunity to probe the weathered girl. She walked towards Daisy, who was crouched down and seemed hell-bent on not making eye contact. She was taking too long to take off the bags she was holding, making sure to fuss over nothing to distract from Asha's imminent questioning. But Asha wasn't easily swayed, and she ignored the stone wall that Daisy was so desperately trying to build in her face.

"Hey, you feeling okay?" Asha asked, resting a hand on Daisy's stick-like arm. She was freezing cold, clammy.

The blonde girl pulled away with a grunt. "I'm fucking fine," she breathed out, but her voice was so weak, she barely had the strength to say the words.

"Okay, stop lying," Asha said sternly, folding her arms across her chest and staring at the girl who still hadn't turned to look at her.

Daisy was still for a moment; her fingers went to her injured arm and touched the bandage nervously.

"Is it your wound? Is it getting worse? Let me see. Have you told Piper?" Asha bombarded the girl with questions as she bent down to her level, reaching for her arm.

"NO!" Daisy shouted then, shooting a glare at Asha and revealing her grey, sunken eyes.

279

The dark-haired girl pulled away but kept her stare on Daisy, taking in her appearance completely. Her once ice-blue eyes had turned into a dull colour, making her seem like she was slipping away, turning into a character from a black and white movie. She looked exhausted, damaged and all together dead. How could she have deteriorated this rapidly without any plausible cause?

"Just...leave, me, alone," Daisy huffed, standing herself up quickly. But as soon as she did so, she fell, holding her head.

Asha was quick to catch the girl before she hit the floor. "Shit!" She gawked, shifting her knees so that she could rest the slender girl comfortably on her.

"*God...*" Daisy moaned, her face scrunched up and her eyes closed.

Asha watched as tears slipped probably unintentionally from the girl in her arms and she held Daisy as she started to shudder from crying. This wasn't about her arm.

Daisy was the kind of girl to hide from the world, to put up a steel front in the face of warmth. The problem was that one day, everything would come out, all at once, painfully.

Asha didn't ask her anything, she didn't want to make it worse, plus she didn't want to attract any attention from the others; Daisy would hardly appreciate that.

A few moments past and the girl's crying quietened.

"I-I have problems," Daisy said between teared breaths.

"It's okay," Asha soothed quietly, her heart squeezing from seeing her in such unwanted turmoil.

"No, it's not..." Daisy groaned, sitting herself up from Asha and wiping her eyes.

The girls sat there on the floor in silence for a moment. Asha knew Daisy wanted to tell her more, to get whatever it was off her chest, so she would sit there not saying anything until she did. Daisy breathed out a couple of times and closed her eyes before opening them to Asha, a look of somewhat relief in them.

"I have problems with eating. Especially when something bad happens," she admitted, looking a little embarrassed, but happy to say it out loud, like it had been burrowing in her for a while.

"Oh," was all Asha could say, which wasn't helpful at all; she cursed herself immediately for it.

"...Yeah...I haven't eaten...since my dad..." she trailed off, looking to the stone floor.

"Since I met you," Asha affirmed, remembering all the times she'd noticed the girl not touching her food.

It all made sense now.

It answered the questions about Daisy's health, how she seemed to be in pain most of the time, how her moods swung violently from one to the other, how she took her anger out on others, how her body seemed more like a skeleton than a person. She had clearly been battling for a while; she was a dishevelled and beaten soldier in the war against herself.

Asha felt like she'd only scraped the surface of Daisy and her seemingly troubled life, but at least it was a start. She felt determined to be there for the girl, to help her through anything and everything.

She was her friend now.

Asha dove into her backpack and pulled out a bottle of water and a small bag of nuts. She held them out to Daisy who looked at them like they were going to kill her. Asha's face softened.

"I know," she started. "But you know you need at least something to keep you going. You haven't eaten anything in four days," Asha explained, still holding the stuff out to her.

"I can't," Daisy sighed, but she looked like she wanted to.

Asha thought for a second. "You're struggling right now. This will tide you over, make you feel better, and you'll still be okay. You'll still look the same tomorrow. You can pick however many nuts you want to eat and stick to it. But you have to have this whole bottle of water," she lightly ordered, trying to make Daisy see sense in the moment. Her issues would take longer to defeat, but if she didn't eat now, there wouldn't be a chance to save herself because she would die before that could happen.

Daisy frowned and shook her head.

"Please, please try," Asha begged.

"But..." Daisy said, trying to think of an excuse to not eat it.

"Is it your dad? Is this because of him, not just now but before, in the real world?" Asha asked, her voice hushed.

Daisy nodded her head slowly.

"...Did he hurt you?" Asha questioned, feeling like she was being a little intrusive, but she could feel it working.

Daisy didn't even have to voice her answer, it was evident in her face in how it twisted, wrangled in the memories. Asha felt anger. She hated the fact that a father could hurt his little girl, make her feel so horrible and unworthy, enough to cause her doubt and anxiety. She found herself glad that he was dead.

More horrifyingly, she was glad she'd watched him die.

"Don't give him that power. Don't you dare give him the power to make your life a misery. Live and live *proudly*. You deserve to breathe and eat and love! Fuck him. Why should he have a hold on you still? He's gone, he's dead and gone. You're free Daisy. You can rest easy; you don't have to worry anymore. You have your life back, the way you want to live it. So please, eat the damn nuts!" Asha preached, holding a hard stare at the girl.

Daisy pondered for a moment, her eyes flitting from side to side as her mind whirred. She finally looked straight up at Asha with hope in her eyes and a small smile on her face.

She shot her hand out and took four nuts from the bag. It was a tiny amount, but even the smallest of a start could lead to the beginning of a big change.

Chapter Twenty-Four

What happened on the church floor stayed on the church floor, and once the girls joined the others upstairs, their lips were completely sealed. It was their secret and Asha felt a certain sense of pride and accomplishment for both herself and Daisy. It was nice to see her smile, at least a little.

The group had split themselves up between the two rooms that Asha had set up. Max, Piper and the little girls seemed to have claimed one, and the boys had claimed the other. One room for the adults and children, and the other for the teenagers; surely a good plan. Daisy went straight to their designated room, but Asha went into the one with Max, wanting to talk to him.

He was unpacking some clothes and helping Piper prepare some snacks for the girls when Asha wandered into the room. He looked up and smiled at her.

"Nice job with all the blankets," he remarked.

"You have no idea how much trouble I went through to get them," Asha laughed lightly. She could laugh now.

"I can see that. Thank you though, this is pretty sweet," Max replied, his smile ever prominent.

"You think it will be a good place to stay until we head to Harbour?" She questioned, propping herself against a dark mahogany chest of drawers near him.

"Seems fine to me, we'll have to leave early tomorrow anyway. Make sure we leave with enough time," he said, handing a packet of crisps to Boe before turning his full attention to Asha.

284

"Even if we *were* late, they'd wait for us, right? I mean, they know we're coming..." Asha said, a hint of worry in her voice.

Max kissed his teeth and looked to the ceiling. "In theory yeah," he said returning his gaze to her. "If we were a few hours, or even a day late, they'd probably wait... But if we were later, they'd know somethin' happened. They wouldn't be able to wait forever. They wouldn't know where we were, we've got no means of communication. So really, we should be gettin' there early to avoid being left behind."

"Won't there be another boat? To pick up the other Finders?" Asha asked, piecing together all the possibilities, just in case.

"Yeah, you're right. That boat should come in two days after we get picked up. So, I guess that gives us extra days if we need it. But, shit, I wanna get there as soon as possible, don't you?" Max asked with a cocky grin.

Asha smiled her agreement and took that as her cue to leave. She felt unusually relaxed after seeing her group settling down and doing normal things like smiling and having snacks.

She turned the corner into the 'teen room' and filled with warmth when she saw Daisy sitting on one of the blanket beds, munching on the nuts she'd given her. Asha found herself feeling quite hungry too, so she quickly located the pile of food that had accumulated in the centre of the room and gazed over all the options. There were a couple of bags of crisps, a cereal bar, two bars of chocolate and a few bottles of different drinks.

"Oh my god, I'm spoilt for choice," Asha remarked, looking sarcastically to the food and then to the two boys who were sat surprisingly close to each other on neighbouring beds.

"Welcome to the Michelin star restaurant, 'The End of the Fucking World'. It's been getting pretty popular these past months," Kit smirked before chomping on a peanut bar.

"I can see why. Such a posh selection of food!" Asha laughed before reaching for a cereal bar and sitting herself in between them.

"How you feeling?" Finn asked her, his mouth was cradled in crumbs from the biscuits he was eating.

Asha motioned on her mouth for him to wipe his own. "I'm good, better now that I'm eating," she smiled before opening her cereal bar and biting it.

"We seem pretty secluded here. We might actually get a good night's sleep," Kit said, finishing up his bar.

"As long as we all stick to our guard postings... and stay awake for them," Asha said slightly accusingly.

"Shut it," Kit retorted.

"We tried!" Daisy shouted from where she was sat.

"I know, I know. It was just a little joke, a little *'we almost died because of you'* joke," she said sticking her tongue out at both Kit and Daisy.

"Not funny," Kit groaned, lying himself down on his 'bed'.

Asha didn't even have time to apologize or come back with a smart remark before the sounds of a screaming toddler burst in through the open door. She had never seen four teenagers jump to attention and run so fast in her life.

Once they reached the other room, Asha was relieved to see Boe crying, but not for any kind of sinister reason. She was sat bawling on the floor, Piper next to her trying to console her.

Sunny was frantically searching for something in her enormous bag and Max was standing there with his arms folded, not looking too worried.

"Tally!" Boe yelled, her cheeks red and wet with tears. Her wonky fringe stuck up in every which way.

There was that name again, the same name she was shouting when Asha held her in the rain. Could it be Sunny's real name? She looked over to the mouse-like girl, but she wasn't reacting to it like it *was* her name.

"Who's Tally?" Daisy questioned, but no-one answered.

"I can't find it!" Sunny said, annoyance lacing her tone. "She was playing with it in the woods and I put it back in the bag, but now it's gone," she sighed, surrounded by all the contents of her now empty backpack.

"It's okay we can find you another one?" Piper suggested to the inconsolable little girl.

Boe responded by screaming louder. Asha winced and looked to Max who shrugged his shoulders.

"Who the fuck is Tally?" Kit pushed, getting agitated by the screaming child.

"It's her toy cat!" Sunny shouted back, her face in a deep frown that extenuated the dark, prominent bags under her eyes.

A lost, obese, soft toy cat called Tally was now the biggest of their problems - ironic.

"I saw it sticking out of the bag when we were walking, I should have said something... It's probably fallen out on the way here," Finn said, the look of guilt plagued his face.

A collective roll of the eyes shot around the room.

"Sorry," Finn shrugged and Asha could feel the heat from his now cherry cheeks. "I'll go and get it."

Asha's face shot wide. "Not on your own you won't."

"Wanna join me?" He asked her, knowing the answer.

"Sure. We'll follow Kit's jumper trail back until we see it. It's not like there's anyone around that would have picked it up. We'll find it," Asha said confidently, glancing around the room to gage everyone's response.

"I should come," Sunny offered.

"No, you stay here and comfort Boe, you know how to do it better than any of us," Asha said, raising her eyebrow.

Sunny nodded her head and joined her 'little sister' and began to work her magic, stroking her dark brown hair and pinching her chubby cheeks until she giggled. Asha peered at Max, he gave her an approving look.

"Go, be safe and get back quick, I hate hearing children scream," he chuckled a low chuckle, but he was being serious.

"Will do," Asha said with a nod of her head.

She turned out of the room followed by Finn, Kit and Daisy.

"Well, I'm obviously coming too," Kit snapped, giving Asha hardened stare.

"No, we won't be long. You need to rest," Asha assured, telling him with her eyes that she'd rather have at least some time alone with Finn.

He certainly noticed her plea, but anger broiled across him because of it. "Fine," he eventually concluded, much to his dismay. "You two have a *splendid* time," he said before knocking Asha's shoulder with a light punch.

"We will. See you soon," Asha grinned, finding herself happy from annoying Kit, and from the idea of actually spending some time with the boy who made her feel everything.

"I'll just have fun with the undefeated champion of Miss Happy over here," Kit remarked slyly, gesturing a thumb to behind him.

Daisy scoffed her obvious feeling of offence. "I'll have you know that I'm not just a grumpy face, you limp-dick, jock-ass looking, shit-breath, fuck face!" She huffed, pushing her way past him and into their bedroom.

Asha couldn't help but laugh as Kit pulled a look of sarcastic worry. He really brought it upon himself most of the time.

"Wish me luck," he grinned at the pair before following the blonde girl and closing the door. Asha could hear Daisy's protests almost immediately and it made her laugh again.

"Shall we?" Finn said, breathing a sigh of relief now that the drama had subsided.

"Let's," Asha smiled.

*

They had the most important objective in the world. Reunite a little girl with her favourite toy. It felt so far from the challenges that they'd all faced for the past six months, but it was a welcoming change. Asha and Finn walked the woods for half an hour, making sure to follow Kit's trail of wool so that they would happen upon the cat toy, which was hopefully still in one piece.

They talked about nothing for a while, enjoying the positive company that they had now created for themselves. Pushing through trees and hopping over holes in the ground, they found themselves lost to the world, but still on track to find Tally.

"Really? Never?" Asha asked, her shock coming out.

"Nope," Finn replied curtly, ducking under a low hanging branch and twiddling the blue thread that hung from it.

"That's surprising," Asha said, scanning the trees for the next thread.

"It is?" Finn asked, thrown.

"Yeah," Asha started, pointing at the next blue string about ten meters ahead of them. "I put you down as a romantic."

"I am!" Finn almost yelled, clearly offended by Asha's thoughts.

"So, how come you've never been on a date before?" She asked, flashing her bright eyes.

There was a moment of pause from the boy and the only sound that came was the crunching of twigs and crispy leaves being trodden on.

"I dunno," he finally sighed. "I had one girlfriend when I was sixteen. I was too poor to do anything other than watch movies at home with her... I put out fairy lights and snacks though," he smiled softly, reminiscing.

"Then that's a date!" Asha exclaimed, letting out a breathy laugh.

"Oh..," he replied, touching the next waypoint.

"...At least it is to me," Asha shrugged, following his long stride.

"Then I've been on hundreds," he grinned back at her, his dimples baring.

"Thought so," Asha smiled back before pulling her stare from him and looking to the ground instead.

"What about you?" He asked.

"What *about* me?" Asha quizzed, looking up to meet his gaze as they walked.

He scrunched his face up lightly. "Don't make me say it," he moaned, smiling still.

"What?" She groaned sarcastically back, raising her eyebrows.

"How was your love life?" He asked, and soon as he did, his face burnt like hell-fire and he closed his eyes from sheer embarrassment.

"Ew," she replied, physically recoiling from the question.

"I know, shit, I feel disgusting just hearing myself ask that," he said in the most endearing way.

"Well, since you asked so awkwardly..." Asha laughed shifting her bag around to rest on her back, her hand held tightly to the strap. "I had a sort of girlfriend when I was younger."

"*Right...*" he said quietly. He was either expecting her to continue her story, or he was mulling over what she'd said.

"I... I don't have a preference, you know, boys or girls. You don't think that's weird, do you?' she asked, slightly worried about his response.

Even though she was proud of who she was and never hid it from anyone, she was still aware of the amount of hate and prejudice set upon anyone different.

She knew deep down that Finn wasn't the kind of person to judge her for who she happened to love, but you never truly knew who was capable of being closed-minded and let's face it, inhuman.

"Not at all!" He smiled, flooding her with relief.

Asha's mind flew straight to her, to the girl who'd changed her life for the better and worse. Her long, mousey hair, her almond eyes, her sad expression. She never got over her, not once. But she was lost.

"It was love. *I was sure of it*," she said almost in a whisper, unsure of why she was saying it out loud to the boy who she believed she liked.

"I don't doubt you. I always found it annoying when adults told me I was 'too young' to feel love. I call bull shit," he grinned, clocking the next thread to follow.

"I'm happy you think that way too," Asha replied, a smile creeping back onto her face.

"Mhmm, so, after her?"

Asha took a deep breath and sighed. "After her I never committed to anyone. Not that she scarred me for relationships. I don't let people ruin important things like that for me. I mean, she did scar me, but you know... I just never felt like that again so I never...I um..." she was going to say it, she couldn't help herself, "I think I feel that way n-OW!" a piercing pain suddenly rushed through her as her foot twisted in a sunken hole in the sodden dirt.

She limped back immediately and stood hopping on one leg as the pain grew, spreading through her foot. Finn was quick to hold her up by her side.

"Ow, fuck," she seethed, sucking in air to deal with the pain. "That serves me right for talking about my feelings."

Finn suddenly left her side and bent down so that he was low enough for her to climb on his back.

"Here," he simply instructed, pointing to behind him.

"What? No, no way!" Asha protested. She wasn't about to let him carry her, not for the long journey they had ahead of them.

"Oh, come on," he rolled his eyes, but his face was still soft and light.

"I'll break your back," she argued, though the fact that she was struggling to stand, and her face was filled with pain didn't help her case.

"Worth it," he said, glancing up at her with a side smile and a dimple which made her whole being soar.

She slowly resigned herself to recreating much of her childhood. "Okay, well, you asked for it," she warned as she cackhandedly climbed onto his back.

Eventually, her arms wrapped around his neck, and she got into a comfortable spot on his back before resting her legs around his waist. He stood up with ease and adjusted her accordingly. Memories of playing in the park with her family assaulted her brain; she could see Ella's face as she manically laughed while perched on their mum's back while Asha clutched onto their dad's, racing in the sunshine.

"You weigh nothing," he remarked as he began their adventure once again, making sure to account for her head height and the low branches. Memories slipped away, thankfully.

"That's because I'm holding my weight," she said through a strained voice.

"Well stop. It'll only get painful for you, and I can handle it. I'm quite strong," he said, she could hear the grin on his face.

Asha rolled her eyes. "If you do say so yourself."

"Come on!" He practically demanded her.

"UGH!" She huffed before letting her dead weight go.

"See, I'm fine," Finn assured her.

"*He says through gritted teeth*," she replied lowly, tightening herself around him, not wanting to slip down with the movement.

"Shh," he hushed her, his quaint lips pursing.

They were almost back at the river when they finally saw Tally. It was covered in mud and they were close to missing it. But its obese, roundness stood out in the worn path. Asha pointed at it and jumped against Finn's back causing him to hold her tighter.

Once they reached it, Finn carefully put her down – her foot felt ten times better- and she immediately grabbed the soaking wet toy and held it up proudly.

"Teamwork," she smiled at Finn who was red-faced and out of breath from carrying her for so long – without complaint.

"Yeah, we make a pretty good one," he said.

Asha looked over the toy in her hand as Finn sorted himself out. She squished it slightly and water dripped down her hand. She was still amazed by how fat it was and wondered to herself why they would sell such a toy. But she had to admit it was pretty cute.

"...You might hit me but... what were you going to say before you twisted your ankle?" Finn asked, his eyebrows raised, his eyes kind.

Asha frowned. *How was that of all things on his mind?* "You're right, I do want to hit you."

"Sorry," he murmured, cracking his back from side to side.

"Why do you want to delve into my feelings? Can't you see I'm keeping them close for a reason?" She said jokingly.

"Because I feel like you want to, but you're too scared," he simply said, standing with his hands in his pockets; he saw through her mask.

For some reason unbeknownst to Asha, her eyes started to well up and she found that she had no voice. *How can he do that? How can he just open my ribs and see right inside?* It was unfair. How could someone rip your secrets from you without you even realizing they existed? She wasn't sure how, but she knew that he could. She stood there, her pooling eyes never leaving his.

"It's okay," he said softly. "You don't have to say it."

How do you know?

"I feel the same," he admitted, and Asha's eyebrows turned up as he unintentionally tore her apart. "I knew I felt it the moment I saw you, and honestly you threw me. Shit, I told you my real name. Why would I do that? The front, the character that I had, crumbled; I had no control. You instantly made me lose my logic."

"*But, how...?*" she managed to say so quietly it was almost a whisper.

How does know that I like him?

He began to answer her question without it finishing on her lips. "When I said I wasn't coming with you…" he began, glancing to the ground before looking back up to meet her gaze slowly, "your whole body deflated and your face dropped like something poisonous had shot through you."

"You acted angry, but I could see what you were feeling deep down. You didn't want to leave me... and I didn't want to let you go either, but I was torn," he sighed heavily. "When you left, I had this horrible feeling in my stomach. I knew I had to follow you; I was getting ready when the Hunters came. I was coming to find you," he finished, stepping closer to her.

Asha didn't know what to do or say. So, she decided to be sarcastic, her normal defense mechanism.

"...Well...now you know my big secret. I need to know yours!" She grinned too widely, trying to cover the fact that she couldn't deal with the tsunami of emotions that threatened to drown her. The tears fell, instantly betraying her.

In the next second, she noticed his face suddenly go a little stern and his eyes go to the side of her before coming back to look her in the eyes. Maybe sarcasm wasn't the right response for right now.

"I'm sorry for what I did to you," he replied bluntly.

Those very words burnt a hole in her heart as she tried to think about what he'd done to her. Was he lying about how he felt? Was he making fun of her? Was he breaking her already? She had to know.

"What did you do?" She asked quickly, her voice wavering and her face begging him not to hurt her.

"*This,*" he whispered as he pushed her shoulders so hard that she fell backwards through the bushes behind her.

She landed with a thump as her tailbone hit the ground below her and she watched as the greenery quickly obstructed her mostly from his view. She stared up at him with wide eyes, tears tracking her cheeks, her face contorted in both pain and confusion.

That was until she heard the voices.

He tapped on her feet which she realized were still sticking out onto the path.

He was hiding her.

Without hesitation or defiance, she hauled her feet towards her so that she was completely covered by the shrubbery. Her eyes locked onto his as her whole body froze solid.

In that tiny moment, everything the pair had to say to each other was said.

His eyes told her that he was sorry, they told her that he was doing this for her. They told her that he loved her, and he would die for her.

Her eyes told him that she was sorry for everything, sorry that he got caught up with her, that he would die for her, and that she'd let him.

She held her breath as he broke their stare and ran. She sat like stone, not breathing, barely existing.

"There's the guy who was leaving the tracks!" one voice said.

"He doesn't look heavy enough to leave those tracks," another voice exclaimed, getting closer.

"The fuck does it matter? Let's get him. We need another good hunt," A girl's voice now rang loudly.

Asha watched frozen as not three, but six people sprinted just inches from where she sat hiding.

Six against one didn't seem like a fair way to go.

She was still in shock. Tears relentlessly clawed down her face, reminders of what had just happened.

As she stared into the green around her, everything became blurry; she found herself trapped in an invisible static. Even though she wished she could, she knew in herself that she couldn't risk going after him. She would die for him if she could. But she couldn't. She wasn't allowed to be selfish. She had to stay alive for the sake of mankind. She couldn't be a romantic, not like him.

Fifteen minutes passed and although Asha had started breathing, she still wasn't sure she was actually alive, what with her heart being broken and all.

To think that such a pure and comforting soul would sacrifice themselves for a girl like her. She was nothing compared to him.

A sudden, familiar, gut-wrenching scream screeched its way into Asha's ears from afar. She felt the leaves around her shudder from its sound and it was the final nail in the coffin of the boy who not only made her feel human again, but who showed her that there were still good people in the decaying world.

She let out a wrangled sob to match the yells of his pain that peppered her with invisible bullet wounds.

It was the first sound she'd made since being encased by the leaves, and that very fact made her gasp and jump up before sprinting back in the direction they had first come from.

As she ran, she pulled down the blue strands from the branches she passed. She needed to distance herself from the lethal group who may come back for her when they finally realized that their deductions were right, and that they were in fact following two people, not one.

Chapter Twenty-Five

Asha's chest burnt from the running, and from the heartache that consumed her. The dull pain in her ankle had started to flare up once again and she wished that she still had her ride.

But he was gone.

As she approached the church, her run slowed down to a limping hobble, eager to get some sort of comfort, but also, struggling to get to where she'd have to relive what happened to Finn.

She dragged her foot behind her, one hand clasping Tally and the other holding the pendant and ring around her neck, her only reminder of him. She was sweating and her ragged breaths blew out clouds into the cold air. Her cheeks felt like they were on fire from her tears drying into a freezing wrap around her face. She needed to get inside, quickly.

She stood at the door breathing rapidly, recovering from the run as her free fingers fumbled to grip onto the handle. They felt numb all of a sudden and she couldn't hold anything other than the toy. She cried out her frustration and barged the door with her shoulder, hard. She hit it three times before it got pulled open and she fell in, landing into Max's chest.

"Whoa, what happened?" He asked, holding her out so he could look at her.

Asha didn't want to say anything, so she instead turned to face Boe who had already spotted her toy and was waddling over with a huge grin on her face.

Asha struggled to walk towards her, so she ended up just holding out Tally until it was taken from her.

Once that was back in Boe's possession, Asha felt like she could collapse. The whole group seemed to be in the main part of the church and by then they had gathered around her, waiting for answers. Why was she alone? Why did she look like a traumatized child?

She stood shaking, threatening to tip over.

"Ash!" Kit was immediately by her side, helping her to stand.

She could feel everyone's eyes boring into her, demanding an explanation, but it just made it harder to get the words out. She felt so weak, like she could break into a thousand pieces right there and then.

"Where's Finnegan?" Daisy asked cautiously, forcing Asha to answer.

In between her increasingly scattered breaths, she managed to answer. "...He pushed me."

"Is that why you're limping? I'll fucking kill him," Kit barked.
Too late for that.

The fire burst in her. "PUSHED ME OUT OF THE WAY, YOU PRICK!" She screamed in his face. Tears cascaded down her cheeks once more.

"Asha, Asha, compose yourself," Max calmed her, taking her from the view of a hurt looking Kit and leading her –with help from Piper- to a pew.

The dark-haired girl sat where she was put, feeling fragile enough to be moved without a care. She stared ahead of her to the stained-glass window depicting a scene full of colour. She didn't want to look at her group, not when Finn wasn't in it anymore.

"Where is he? Where's Finn?" Sunny asked, parking herself on the pew in front of Asha, leaning over to her.

"...He's gone," Asha said, going completely numb.

"What?" Max bellowed a little too loudly in the echoing church.

Asha closed her eyes and sighed sadly, taking more care of her breathing. "There were Hunters... six of them. They followed our trail... but he was carrying me... they thought there was only him. He knew it and he hid me from them. He heard them coming before I did... he saved me," she breathed deeply, controlling herself in the wake of panic.

"How do you know he's gone?" Max demanded, standing in her view now, arms crossed, face frowning.

"He was screaming..."

"Oh no," Piper whimpered, covering her mouth as her face twisted.

"No!" Sunny shouted and promptly jumped up and kicked the wooden pew.

"...I was just starting to like him," Kit muttered, clearly feeling guilty for how he treated the boy who'd thrown himself to the flames for Asha.

"*Shit*," Max grimaced rubbing the top of his shaven head. He had failed to protect one of his survivors.

"Where's that boy?" Boe asked innocently, squishing Tally until it seeped water to the floor.

Sunny went to her and bent down. "He's gone. He's where our parents are now."

Boe scrunched up her face. "NO! That's not good! Bad!" She yelled before storming off.

"We don't know that he's dead. We should go out and look," Max said, his voice low and gravely.

Asha shook her head. "I heard him. He's not coming back," she said quietly, remembering how harsh his screams were, how he sounded like he was choking on his own blood.

"What about the Hunters? Shouldn't we go and kill them?" Kit questioned.

"Finn led them away. When I heard him, he was far. He wouldn't have given us up."

"But there are still Hunters at large," Max added.

"We're safest here, aren't we? Why go out there and put ourselves at risk of getting killed when we could just stay inside?" Daisy huffed, hand on her hip, blonde hair falling in front of her face.

"...She makes a good point, *I guess,*" Kit turned and pulled a face at the disgruntled girl who glared back.

"She does. We'll just have to be on extra alert," Max sighed heavily. "I don't want to lose another one of you."

"I'd like to say a few words, and light a candle," Piper announced and went off to presumably find the candles and matches.

Everyone waited in an uncomfortable silence, none of them really wanting to say goodbye to one of their own.

When Piper came back, she handed out a thin white candle to everyone except for Boe who was going to share Sunny's. Slowly, they all made their way to the metal structure where old candles had melted down to the small pillars which held them.

The ceremony of it all was almost too much for Asha to bear and she could feel her panic rising again.

It made it real.

Piper lit her candle first and placed it. "Finn had a good soul, and it was that very thing that took him from us. He didn't deserve it, and I just hope that God will welcome him with open arms and take him to a better, and more peaceful place."

Max followed. "I'm sorry," he simply said, lighting his candle.

Kit rolled his eyes but managed to light his candle without any trouble. "Finnegan, thank you for saving Asha, more than once. I'll never be able to really thank your arse, but hey," he shrugged and moved away.

Sunny and Boe rather cutely lit their candle and placed it in the lowest stand, they didn't say anything, only looked saddened and then shuffled away, looking to the grown-ups for action.

Daisy sighed and obediently followed the routine. "Even though you annoyed me a little, you never really did anything bad I guess... Actually, you didn't do *anything* wrong. Bad people seem to live, and the good seem to die for us. Fuck the world, fuck fate, and fuck this," she moaned and blew out her candle before storming off.

Asha felt a heaviness descend on her that she could hardly hold. It was her turn, and everyone knew she wanted to say so much more than she actually could.

She kept her eyes down, looking only at the candle. She stuck it in its place and struck the match before lighting it, finalizing her grief.

Her hand instinctively went to her necklace.

"I didn't think I'd have to do this. I didn't think I'd feel this way..." Asha started, but she couldn't continue, she couldn't make a speech, her heart wouldn't let her.

Kit's hand was suddenly on her back, rubbing it in big circles. It was time to say good-bye.

"...I won't forget you and what you did to me."

*

The atmosphere in the church kept dropping as the afternoon went on. The loss of Finn had had much more of an impact than any of them could have imagined. The cruel joke of it all was that they were so close to getting to Harbour. It really put all of their mortality into perspective. No matter how close to safety they were, they could be taken at any time, just like him.

Asha busied herself by going through the bags of clothing that had been left in the church as donations, sorting them into piles for each member of the group.

It was a laborious, organizational and monotonous task that perfectly filled the void she had in her. She needed to put her mind to something and being around the group just wasn't good for her, not yet.

Once she'd finished that, she just laid herself down among the piles and drifted in and out of a sleep which she really needed but didn't want.

She had little control over her dreams which meant that whatever had happened to her in the real world would most definitely crop up in 'la la land'. Something that she didn't need to be reminded of.

Her fingers clasped her necklace, and her mother's ring; the weight of the grief was almost suffocating, but at the same time, she felt a sense of calm and comfort from them.

It was early evening when Max came into the room explaining that he, Piper, Sunny and Boe would take the first sleep, meaning she, Kit and Daisy would be on guard until early morning. Asha nodded her acknowledgment and hauled herself up, finally feeling at least a little readier to face her friends.

She watched as Max retreated into his 'bedroom' and she then wandered down the stairs, found her bag with her weapons and joined the other two outside.

"Hey," was approximately all that Asha said to Kit and Daisy for the five hours that they were out guarding.

She had been taken over by a sadness that made her feel like a stranger to herself. She couldn't even join in with the jokes that her friends were making, nor could she utter any other words; she didn't have the strength or will. Her eyes stayed on the tree line, hoping, aching for him to return somehow, but she knew that was a fruitless and damaging train of thought. She needed to get over him and get over him quickly.

Before long, Max came down to relieve the teenagers from their posts. Asha gathered her stuff and followed Kit and Daisy to their room where she was dreading having to actually sleep.

She threw her bag to the floor and started to take off her coat when she noticed Kit had a huge grin on his face. She watched as he rummaged under his blanket bed before pulling out three, clinking bottles of dark liquid. Asha's eyebrows shot up and she stared at him questioningly.

"Look who found the communion wine!" He chuckled as he handed them a bottle each. "I thought it would put us in a better mood, give us something fun to do."

Asha took the bottle from him, its contents sloshing enticingly around. She felt a smile creep across her face.

"Aha! It worked, I'm a genius," he smiled at her, but the smile was filled with empathy. He knew it wasn't going to fix her, but it would help.

"Finally, you're good for something!" Daisy exclaimed, eagerly taking her bottle and opening it with a satisfying pop. "Bottoms up," she said before raising it to her lips and gulping the red wine down.

Asha looked to Kit who shrugged and did the same. She sighed, gripping the cork. *Hell, this is for you, you God damn, honey-eyed gift.* The bottle was opened in milliseconds and lifted it to her mouth; redness spilled down the corner of her lips as she did so.

The teens looked to each other and laughed simultaneously as they began their sleeping shift like they used to start every Saturday before a night out.

*

"Yeah well, it's not like I'm not good looking, is it?" Kit beamed, slurring his words.

It had been less than an hour since they'd opened the wine, but it was almost gone, along with their sobriety. Mixing a mostly empty stomach with grief and alcohol was never going to be a good idea.

"Oh my fucking god you are so up yourself. It's actually embarrassing," Daisy said, disgusted.

Asha looked over to her, blurry eyed. Daisy was actually quite a pretty girl despite the faces she tended to pull. She had striking sky eyes which Asha hadn't really paid attention to before. Her blonde hair contrasted heavily with her thick dark brown eyebrows; it made her even more distinct and beautiful.

"Deny it then," Kit smirked.

"Oh, shut up you egomaniac," Asha told him off with a roll of her eyes, but she was still smiling.

"Come on, Ash, you can vouch for me. All I had to do was walk in a room and the girls would be creaming," he bragged, his lips stained red.

Asha shook her head laughing. "You really are something else," she raised an eyebrow at him and took the last gulp of her wine. "I tell you, you are fucking lucky to have even had a girlfriend before. She put up with so much from your arrogant arse," Asha tutted, rolling her now empty bottle across the floor.

"Don't be so *cruel*! I'm a great boyfriend!" He mocked his anger, knowing full well what he was like.

"What is it? Opposite day?" Asha laughed, settling herself in the blankets. Her head had begun to swim.

"Oh, *ha ha*. Good one," Kit moaned sarcastically.

"I think we hit a nerve," Daisy giggled, looking at Asha.

"Seems like it," The dark-haired girl winked back.

"Don't start flirting using my pain," Kit demanded, sitting up straight now. staring at them, his gaze hazy.

"Lesbians don't fancy every girl they see. We can control ourselves, unlike some people," Daisy remarked, shooting him a disapproving look.

Kit shrugged animatedly, his face matching his action. He then picked up his bottle and sucked down the last of the alcoholic liquid. The girls sat quietly, giving each other amused looks.

"Daisy?" Kit suddenly asked.

"What?" She spat back.

"Have you ever kissed a boy?"

Daisy's face grew wide but then quickly fell with a blush, her brow tightened. "No."

"Then how do you know you're gay?" Kit asked, crossing his arms, assuring his stupid question.

"Kit, that logic is ridiculous! How do you know you're *not* gay? You've never kissed a *boy!*" Asha protested.

"I'm *joking!*" He said, holding his hands up innocently. "...But how about we try it, just so you can be sure, hm?" He said so charismatically that even Asha got pulled in, only slightly. He was certainly a good-looking guy; he was once described as a Greek God by one her friends, even though he was only half Greek. His tall, broad nature mixed with his boyish freckles and warm eyes made for a deadly combination; one which most girls couldn't resist.

"Daisy, don't listen to him. Don't validate yourself for his perversions," Asha shook her head, staying strong for the spindly girl.

"Come on Blondie. What harm would it do? We're in a hell of a world right now, literally. Plus, I've been cooped up with Asha's ass for six *long* months. I need something," he sighed, pleading his case.

Asha scoffed. "You forget that *I've* also been trapped with *you!*"

"That's beside the point," Kit blew her off, his stare never leaving Daisy.

"Oh my god! If it will stop you talking for even a second, I'll take one for the fucking team," Daisy caved, her blue eyes narrowing at him.

"Daisy you really don't have to," Asha reminded her, a more serious tone to her speech.

"It's fine. I'm drunk. He's being annoying. I'll end it," she hiccupped, crawling over to Kit who was sitting on his knees.

"You heard the lady," Kit winked over at Asha who scowled half-heartedly at her best friend.

"Just get it over with so I don't have to watch this actual assault for too long," she huffed, folding her arms hard across her chest. The world blurred slightly.

Daisy propped herself on her knees just in front of Kit who dwarfed her with his frame. She glanced up at him with what seemed like a confused but inviting stare. Asha looked on, despite the uncomfortableness that started to grow in her. Kit's tongue graced his bottom lip lightly as his large palm cupped Daisy's fair jaw softly.

The blonde girl took in a quick breath, a prominent blush spreading across her cheeks. Kit's other hand traced under chin, pulling her towards him. Daisy closed the gap uncertainly, he held her face with both hands now.

What a day, Asha thought to herself bitterly.

They kissed. Daisy was nervous at first while Kit was full of confidence, guiding her with gentle pecks. But the pecks became longer, and in an instant, Daisy raked her fingers through his hair, and he yanked her closer. Their bodies moved achingly on each other. The heat was building at an alarming intensity and Asha had to look away, a frown on her face.

Suddenly Daisy let out a breathy gasp which caused Asha to finally put her foot down, but when she whipped her head around to tell them to stop, Daisy had already moved away from Kit.

In fact, she was halfway out the door holding one hand over her mouth and the other on her stomach. She ran full force out of the room, wide eyed, and Kit was left there looking torn and suffering from a bruised ego.

Asha burst out laughing, the feeling of unease gone. "I didn't realize you were that bad a kisser!"

"Must have been the wine," he muttered as he reached for Daisy's discarded bottle and drank from it. Drowning his sorrows.

Asha chuckled a little more, loving seeing Kit fall flat on his face. She then got herself up to check on Daisy, grabbing a bottle of sports drink as she went. She followed the draught that came from the now wide-open front doors of the church.

She shivered slightly, but she handled the cold without having to put her coat on. The freckled girl scanned the outside area, giving Max a nod. He cocked his head to the left of him where Asha noticed a small figure hunched over, shaking.

"Here, drink this," she said, offering Daisy the bottle of drink when she approached her.

Daisy stood herself up straight, one hand pressed against her forehead and the other reaching out to take the bottle. She took the lid off with her teeth and drank half of it down, pulling away finally with a deep breath. Asha watched on, making sure she was okay.

"Ugh. Well, I feel great," Daisy said sarcastically, but giving Asha a weak smile.

"That's what you get from hooking up with Kit," she taunted the girl, but gestured to the bottle. "Drink it all, it'll help."

"Thanks. I guess I'd better go back and restore his sense of lady-killer-ness," Daisy shrugged.

So, she wasn't disgusted by him. *Strange.*

Asha was lost in her train of thought when the sounds of heavy treads came rustling through the treeline. A breath caught in her throat, she had no weapons on her, neither did Daisy. The alcohol in her body practically disappeared as adrenaline took its place. Max held his gun up to his eye line, stalking forward slightly, one hand gesturing for the girls to get behind him. Asha could feel his tension from where she was standing, and it only instilled fear in her more.

When Max was nervous, you knew something really bad was happening.

The three of them watched the dark trees with precision, waiting for whoever it was to reveal themselves. They didn't have to wait long before a voice seeped through the tangled masses of woodland.

"Don't shoot," A tired, *familiar,* voice begged.

From the darkness, about twenty feet from where they stood, a bloodied and beaten Finn ducked through the tree trunks into the glowing moonlight.

Asha's hairs stood on end and she instantly pinched herself to check she wasn't dreaming.

She wasn't.

Chapter Twenty-Six

"Thorne?" Max questioned, lowering his weapon immediately.

You see him too, Asha thought. There he was, and he was smiling, though very weakly.

Everything flooded back, every thought and feeling blew up inside her; she knew what she had to do. She had wasted her time with him before, now she was getting a second chance, and she wasn't going to ignore it.

Her feet took to the ground and she shot straight into his barely open arms, knocking him backwards a few steps. She encased him in a tight hug, wanting to feel how real he was, and he was real. He was alive and he was in her arms, right where she wanted him to be.

She realized then that she was crying because a sob came uncontrollably from deep within her, a happy sob, but a sob all the same. His strong arms held her against him for a moment before they both came apart, arms interlocked, taking in relieved breaths.

Asha burst into a smile and her hands shot up to hold his face, tiptoeing up to his level. She looked him straight in the eyes for a brief moment and her heart soared out of her body.

Their gold shade shone beautifully in the moonlight; they looked yearning, grateful.

Asha closed her eyes and pulled him towards her. She pressed her lips against his deeply, tears rolling down her cheeks.

His hand ran up the side of her face and tangled into her hair, holding her against him.

His kiss was warm and gentle, yet ferocious and demanding. *Finally.*

They eventually drew apart slowly, their hot, heavy breath mingling in the small space between them. Asha held her eyes closed as she lived fully in the wake of the kiss. Finn had both his hands around her face now and he kissed her forehead gently before resting her head against his heaving chest. She melted into his embrace becoming oblivious to the world around them.

She was thrust abruptly into reality however when he suddenly collapsed right from her hold. He didn't reach the ground though, because she instantly grabbed him and held him up as best she could. He was awake but he was struggling under his own weight, whatever he'd just been through must have taken it all out of him.

"Max!" Asha cried.

Max and Daisy promptly ran over and joined Asha, making it much easier to lift the battered boy. Asha let Max take most of his weight and instead ran alongside, studying the injuries that he had sustained.

Under the eerie glow of the moonlight, Finn's skin burst in a thousand different bloody tones. His clothes were coated in thick mud and grass, they were ripped in all different directions.

There was also something that Asha somehow missed before. There was a huge, dark red bloodstain on his chest. His shirt wasn't ripped there which could only mean one thing.

He'd fought to the death, and he'd won.

The foursome careened into the church, not taking enough care of the noise, but also not really minding because they were all too preoccupied with getting Finn inside and safe.

"*I'm okay,*" he reassured with a quiet, breathy voice.

"Clearly," Asha replied, pointing for Max to take Finn upstairs.

"Finn!" Piper was now on their tail, her face bright at the sight of the boy they thought they'd lost. "I'll go and get the medical bag!" She added before she disappeared her room.

Asha ran ahead of everyone to the door to their bedroom. She flung it open and clocked Kit downing the rest of Daisy's wine. His eyes widened and he quickly got himself up when he realized who they had with them. He jumped out of the way so they could put Finn down on the mess of blankets.

"What the fuck?" Kit exclaimed, his hands rubbing the back of his head. "We thought you were dead!" His voice carried in the small room. His lips were stained red.

"You can't get rid of me that easily," Finn half joked, half warned.

"Right, give him some room… Pipe will be here in a sec, alright, Thorne?" Max said, squeezing Finn's shoulder lightly with a big hand.

Finn gave him a thankful nod.

"Wait you didn't lead anyone here, did you?" Kit asked accusingly.

The question made Asha feel a pang of unease. She knew Finn had a habit of doing that. She had been so blinded by her emotions that she completely forgot about the real dangers out there.

"No," he replied, wincing as he adjusted how he lay.

"I'm going out anyway. Gotta keep guard," Max said giving Finn a look over before leaving.

It was quiet in the room once the burly man left. Daisy made her way over to Kit who was still in a certain shock at the sight of Finn. Asha stroked the resurrected boy's cheek and pulled out a couple of twigs from his tufty brown hair. He smiled softly at her and she returned the gesture, her eyes feeling doughy and heart shaped.

"So, is this a thing now?" Kit annoyingly questioned from behind them.

Asha rolled her eyes, sighing and turned to face him. "Okay, let's get this over with," she sighed, pointing to her nose; the promise she'd made not long ago rearing its ugly, painful head.

'The day I simp for Finn, you can punch me. Right on the nose.'

It took a hot second for Kit to remember what she was referencing, but when it clicked, his eyes brightened, and a wicked smile graced his lips. "Oh, this is gonna be good."

Finn and Daisy exchanged the most confused of glances before setting their stare back on the pair who were now standing a foot apart from each other.

"I'd rather not have to break my nose back into place after this, so bear that in mind," Asha instructed, narrowing her eyes at Kit who seemed far too excited about what he was about to do.

"I won't make promises I can't keep," he grinned, flexing his fingers in and out of a fist.

Asha kissed her teeth while looking him up and down. She should have known better than to make a deal with the boy who seemed to get a high from inflicting pain. "Just get on with it."

"To what degree do you think you're guilty of, just so I can base the force on that."

Asha thought for a moment before clenching her jaw. "Just fuck me up."

He didn't need telling twice, and with her words came an instant punch to the nose, just as agreed upon. Though Asha did feel like he held back a bit, it still left her with watering eyes and a throbbing appendage. He chuckled while smoothing out his knuckles.

"You two are literally insane," Daisy remarked, sharing a nod with Finn.

"It was well-deserved," Asha admitted. *And totally worth it.*

"Well," Kit breathed out before stretching his arms up high, "We'll leave you two lovebirds alone. Fuck knows I don't wanna be in here very soon," he said, a smirk on his face. "Take it easy though, Finn. You don't want any more injuries, y'know?"

"Why did I even kiss your annoying arse?" Daisy groaned, linking her arm with his and dragging him towards the door. She gave Asha a look to say, 'you're welcome' and the dark-haired girl smiled thankfully back.

"Because you love you it, obviously," Kit chuckled, scooping up some blankets as he followed Daisy's pull out the door.

Finn and Asha were alone for about thirty happy seconds before Piper, Sunny and Boe ran in brandishing seemingly every medical thing they could carry.

When she saw him, Boe threw everything she was holding onto the floor and dive-bombed herself straight onto his stomach. He crumpled up, the pain evident in his shocked choke. Asha gasped and quickly picked Boe up and off the now writhing boy and set her down next to the fire-haired nurse they were lucky to have.

"Boe, darling, you have to be careful of our Finn. He's very hurt right now, and you might have hurt him more," Piper very calmly spoke to the plump girl who now looked very guilty.

"I'm sorry, nice boy," she said, her lips quivering, ready to cry.

Asha gave the littler girl an empathetic look, she was just excited to see him, she could understand that. Her focus then went to digging through the medical stuff, looking primarily for antiseptic wipes, anything to stop infection. Sunny knelt next to Finn and placed her palm on his clammy forehead, stilling him.

"You made me really sad," The mouse-like girl said in a whisper.

"I-I'm sorry," Finn answered, wincing.

"It's okay, you're back now. I blew out all the candles."

*

Once Finn was cleaned and dressed up in his assortment of bandages, Piper gave him a couple of paracetamols before shooing the girls out the door with her.

"We have to go back on guard. It's our shift. Please sleep, Finn. Your body needs to rest and recover," Piper smiled before closing the door behind her.

Asha had been sat patiently crossed legged, letting the girls coo and fuss over Finn, but now it was her turn.

She felt like she'd been waiting for an eternity, every second pulling by like tar. Now that she was certain that no-one else would disturb them, she slowly crawled her way across the wooden floor to him.

He was propped up in a cosy concoction of soft blankets, woollen jumpers and rugs. He looked happier than she'd ever seen him, despite the fact that he had to have stitches in his arm, and his face was covered in countless bruises.

He watched her intently as she crawled to him, never breaking the stare, which ignited something in Asha. She carefully draped herself over his right side, laying her head on his chest and hugging him with her arm, while her right leg entwined with his. His arm snaked underneath her and held her close, tracing shapes with his fingertips on her stomach. She shivered.

Before they got to what they both clearly wanted, Asha needed to know the answers to his survival. She needed to understand it, she needed to know if there really were such things as miracles, or if people were just grossly underestimated.

"How did you do it?" She asked quietly, circling her finger on his chest.

"Do what?" He questioned with a heavy breath.

"You know…survive?"

"Oh," he paused for a moment before letting out a deep sigh. "All I knew was that I had to lead them away from you. So, I ran fast, really fast. Once I was far enough away, I hid and then used the oldest trick in the book," Asha peeked up at him, a quizzical look on her face. He glanced down, smiling. "I threw stones to distract them," he said, and looked back up to the ceiling; Asha tucked herself more into him.

"Honestly I didn't think it would work. Hunters are supposed to be super intelligent, that's one of their perks, right? I did that following them all the way down the woods, picking them off one by one after luring them to me, splitting them up from each other. The last one was the worst. He'd finally realized that all of his friends were gone and that they'd been beaten. He was so *angry*. I thought about running and leaving him, but I wanted to finish it so I could come back to you, knowing that I'd made it safe." Asha's heart hurt.

"We had the biggest struggle; I almost didn't think I'd win. It was all a blur, but I got him to the ground, knife out on his chest. He tried to push me off but he couldn't. Then he went to grab for something. I felt a hard knock on my head and everything went black... When I woke up he was underneath me, the sun had gone and I was covered in his blood. When I passed out, the knife must have turned sunk into his heart. I was lucky," he finished, holding her tighter to him.

Asha was so happy to hear him tell his story of victory, knowing that every moment of it brought him to her, under her.

Her mind suddenly filled with what would happen next. She let out a breath, feeling a warmth spread from below.

As his fingers lightly pressed against her hips where she lay, her breathing rocketed.

Her instinct kicked in; she couldn't stop herself. She knew he was injured, but she couldn't hold out anymore. It had been too long; she was only human.

Before he could do or say anything, she was out of his embrace and on top of him in an instant. Her legs found their place either side of him and she leant down to kiss him, hard.

He sat himself up quickly, meeting her lips with as much force while wrapping his arms around her, pulling her closer and closer against him. Her thighs squeezed him between them, feeling *everything*.

As her lips pressed longingly against his, moans escaped her throat unwillingly. The very sounds seemed to ignite something in Finn, causing him to temporarily forget that he'd just endured an ordeal because he began rocking her against him, over and over, blind to the pain surely coursing through him. He groaned in her mouth causing her cheeks to blossom, her heart to stop and her own moan to drag out loudly as she tried to contain her pleasure.

All that coursed through Asha was pure electricity.

Pure, fucking electricity.

Her back arched as he began peppering her neck with kisses all the way down to her collar bone. She was trembling in his hold, breathless and unable to keep still on him. Her eyes rolled to the other side of her skull, and she let her head fall back, desperate breaths clouding the air above her.

She tensed momentarily however as his lips lightly grazed over her black scar. Her head whipped back up and she looked down at him, watching as he was careful to kiss her there.

His eyes drank her up as his need grew with urgency against her thighs.

"You're a fucking queen," He remarked, breathless.

She couldn't help but chuckle at him. "Be a good king and shut up," she replied lowly as her fingers worked at opening his jean button.

Chapter Twenty-Seven

The next morning was a rushed one, with everyone getting themselves ready for the final trek of their journey to the 'promised land'. It took more than the sun shining in for Asha to be woken up. She'd had the kind of deep sleep where you forgot momentarily that you're living in the real world, where you felt like the dream was your reality, and you had no desire to leave it.

Once she was nudged gently awake by Finn, however, she was reminded that there was no place she'd rather be. Sure, the world they actually lived in was one full of death, misery, disease and heartache; but there was always something or someone who made all of it worthwhile. She had opened herself to him and he hadn't hurt her, he was what she had been waiting for.

It had only taken the end of the world, but he was there.

"You..." He began, pushing a strand of her hair from her eyes.

"Me?" Asha questioned sleepily, glancing up at him as a feeling of contentment washed over her. She suddenly didn't feel like being angry at everything anymore.

Finn smiled, dimples prominent. "You're unlike anyone I've ever met."

"You mean to say you've never met a half Mexican, bisexual, potty-mouthed, murderer before?" She questioned him with fake shock.

"Well," he faltered for a second, nodding to himself, "Yeah, exactly," he laughed.

Asha knew what he meant though; she silently revelled in his compliment.

Her thoughts began to run through the events of the night, making her heart beat unnaturally fast and her cheeks hum with heat. She wasn't sure if it was because it was the end of the world, but that was one night that she would never, ever forget. Her breathing hitched up as she touched at her heavily swollen lips.

"I wonder how soundproof this room is," she mused out loud, not quite caring in the answer. She was unapologetic about pleasure.

"Kit's gonna kill me," Finn remarked.

*

By mid-morning they were all –aside from the little ones- gathered in the main body of the church, putting the finishing touches to packing up their stuff when Max came back in from outside with a huge grin on his face. He was brandishing a set of keys which swayed enticingly from his finger.

"We won't be walking," he announced to the church. "They've got a minibus out back which just so happened to have the keys in it."

"Thank God!" Piper exclaimed lightly.

"Good, 'cause I am not in the mood for walking any kind of distance," Kit said blankly, hoisting his now very full backpack over his shoulder. "I'm hungover as fuck."

Asha glanced up to him and noted how he had heavily sunken eyes and a general greyness to his skin. It looked like he hadn't slept for a week, let alone a night. She wasn't feeling a hundred percent herself, but she was sure she looked better than he did.

"Serves you right for gettin' drunk when you shoulda been sleepin'," Max tutted, a knowing smirk on his face.

"Yeah, that's *part* of why I'm tired," Kit grinned cockily before shooting a quick look to Daisy who was busy shoving her bag full of clothes and drinks.

Christ. It seemed it was an exciting night for all.

"We're all running on the bare minimum. Let's get our stuff and go," Max ordered then, snapping everyone to attention.

Sunny wandered in then with a jumping-for-joy Boe. The pair looked cuter every minute that passed where Sunny didn't have a scowl on her face and blood on her hands. Boe was clutching something excitedly and Sunny had an almost prideful look on her face as she looked at the chubby girl.

"Looky looky!" Boe giggled, holding up a CD Walkman.

"Wow, Boe! That looks great! Is it all yours?" Finn grinned, kneeling down to her as she got closer.

To Asha, he looked so kind and paternal, talking to her, but she very quickly found her mind wandering off to memories of last night again. She stood staring, stunned at the juxtaposition of the person in front of her.

Her fingers subconsciously stroked her bruised throat.

"Yup! All mine!" Boe squealed, looking at it in her hands with a huge smile on her face.

Asha snapped out of her reminiscing, back into the present moment.

"We found these too," Sunny said, holding out a few CDs and a couple of pairs of headphones.

"Good find girls," Max approved. "Now, let's get a move on. Has everyone packed all those clothes our 'muney' made for us?" He asked, winking at Asha, she half returned the gesture as she concentrated more on sucking the blush back from her cheeks.

Everyone gave an affirmative sign, but the fact that all their bags were fit to burst was all Asha needed to see.

Her piles of tailored clothing had brought a smile to everyone's face, plus it gave them their very own wardrobe for when they arrived at Harbour. The fabrics would be the first things that they truly owned. Something normal, unlike the weapons they'd grown to love. Her moment of sorrow had brought joy to others - it was all she could have asked for.

"Excellent," Max beamed, his tall bulking figure straightened out before he clapped his hands. "Let's get in the van."

*

Just like at school, the 'cool' kids sat at the back of the bus, while the 'teachers' and young ones stayed at the front. It wasn't the most spacious of vehicles but the name of it should have given that away – 'minibus'. The seats were all sorts of tatty and it smelt damp and mouldy, but it felt like their own.

Excitement grew in all of them when the bus started up and they began their drive. It was a nice day, crisp and inviting. The sun was glorious, the clouds seemed to have taken a day off.

Despite the dangers of the sun, none of them had dressed in their camouflage. It probably had something to do with the fact that they only had two hours to go before they reached the open arms of Harbour.

Asha sat herself next to Finn on the very backseat while Kit and Daisy sat opposite each other on either side of the aisle. They were turned towards Asha and Finn, with Daisy's thin legs sprawled over her two seats, and Kit's stretched out in the aisle.

"I can't believe we're actually going to be somewhere safe so soon. They're probably already waiting at the dock for us," Finn said happily, looking around the teenagers, throwing his arms round Asha's shoulders.

"About bloody time," Daisy muttered, twiddling her hair into plaits in front of her sullen face.

The sun shone in through the windows in scattered bursts as they passed tree after tree. Asha reached over and wound down the window, letting a light and cool breeze flow through, making her hair dance around her vision. She tucked it away quickly behind her ears and leant her head on Finn's shoulder.

In just a few hours she would be safe, she wouldn't have to worry about killing or hiding. She would be able to return to a somewhat normal life where her biggest problems would be miniscule compared to what she had to deal with in her current situation.

She would finally be able to breathe and not worry about whether she'd exhale it or not.

Perhaps she would find her true self once again. She smiled to herself, thoughts of relief wrapping her in a comfy state of happiness.

They journeyed on for another hour and half and with every mile that passed, the mood of the group inflated.

They were just thirty minutes away from their freedom.

Asha was feeling all kinds of nerves and butterflies, and looking around the van, so were the others.

Smiles didn't seem like they were going to go out of fashion around them any time soon.

"I wonder if they'll have the red-carpet ready for your highness," Kit joked, flashing Asha a wink. He popped a piece of chocolate in his mouth and smiled.

"Fuck off. I'd be so lucky," she laughed back, sitting up now. Finn shuffled a little and stretched his arms upwards.

"Well, you'll be a celebrity at Harbour... won't she Max?" Kit called to the front of the van, finishing his mouthful.

Max nodded his head but kept his eyes on the road. "I guess you're right. We all know each other on the island. So, everyone will *definitely* know you."

Asha grimaced slightly. The thought of everyone knowing, or worse, wanting to know her, filled her with an unsettling dread. However, the feeling of excitement far outweighed any negative thoughts so she pulled back her smile and softened against Finn once more.

"Better get practicing my autograph then," she smirked.

"Oh, you have your fans in mind already? Jumping the gun a bit, aren't you?" Kit poked fun at her, ruffling his curled hair with his hand.

"Shut up," she moaned, rolling her eyes brightly.

"You two are like an old married couple," Daisy jutted in, unravelling her plaits.

"Well, we did tie the knot once. What was it... ten years ago?" Kit grinned looking up to the dark-haired girl.

Asha's mind suddenly tumbled back to when they were eight years old. Two goofy kids with more than enough teeth missing between them, dark tousled hair and uncontrollable freckles. He proposed to her with an onion ring at lunch one day, saying that he wanted to marry her before anyone else could. She had accepted, but on the condition that they never kissed because boys were 'gross'. The ring was gone by the time the school bell rang, but their attachment hadn't died down.

"Yeah, I need to look into divorce proceedings, thanks for reminding me," Asha chuckled, poking her tongue out at him who was already pulling a face at her.

"I thought you two weren't like that," Daisy said, looking to both of them with her big ocean eyes.

"We most definitely are *not* like that," Asha scoffed.

"Why? You jealous?" Kit narrowed his hazel eyes at the spindly girl, a certain flirt to it all.

Daisy stared at Kit like he'd just called her every name under the sun. Asha wasn't sure if the blonde girl's eyebrows could furrow any further than they already were, but she managed it.

The silence between them was deafening.

"Woah. What's going on with you two?" Finn asked, Asha was confused as well and waited patiently for an answer.

"I knew it! I knew all guys were the same," Daisy smiled a mean smile. "And you wonder why I pretend I'm gay," she huffed harshly at Kit before turning herself completely to the window, blocking everyone out.

The atmosphere turned sour and thick in an instant.

328

"*What the fuck did you do*?" Asha groaned accusingly at the *pendejo* before her.

"Nothing," he rolled his eyes and shrugged his shoulders, but there was a glint in his eye and Asha knew it well. He was lying.

"HA!" Daisy barked, keeping herself faced away.

"Oh, come on you guys, we're almost there, let's have all these dramas once we touch the ground at Harbour, hmm?" Max ordered from the front, his voice low and booming.

Sunny turned in her seat to look but she and Boe were both plugged into the CD Walkman they'd found earlier. It was a blessing because they didn't need to be a part of the teenage troubles.

"We should all be happy!" Piper beamed. She turned and caught Asha's eye giving her a soft look.

Asha pulled away from all the interaction and instead stared out the window, letting the breeze smooth over her face as she watched the countryside roll past her lazily. Finn planted a kiss on the top of her head and she relaxed once again as she watched the straight, seemingly endless road ahead of them. They were so close now; she could feel her skin bursting into goose bumps and a marching zoo form in her stomach.

"*Not long now,*" The honey-eyed boy whispered in her ear.

"*I know,*" she breathed out before turning to look up to him with a small smile.

When she looked to the inside of the bus, Kit seemed to have skillfully moved over to where Daisy was sitting. He placed his hand on her thigh trying to turn her around to talk to him.

"Fuck *off,*" she warned.

"Come on, I didn't mean it. Well, I mean you probably *are* jealous considering last night..."

Daisy whipped around so fast there was no time for any one of them to step in before her palm sliced Kit's cheek, the slap resonated shrilly in the air. Asha gasped and Finn's hand went to his mouth, worry washed over the pair. Kit backed away holding his face, his eyes wide and still on Daisy who was giving him one final glare before turning back to the window.

"What the FUCK is going on back there?" Max shouted, finally looking back to them.

All eyes went to him worriedly, but no-one could utter a response because all of a sudden, the sounds of earth-shattering popping erupted around them and the van swerved out of control.

Max tried desperately to stop it, but he failed. The countryside span sickeningly as the vehicle careened without a care across the road. Screams, shouts and panicked yells ran high around the van. Finn grabbed Asha and encased her in a solid grip, keeping her guarded.

She squeezed her eyes shut and imagined it wasn't happening.

The van finally came to a shuddering halt in the ditch that ran alongside the road.

Once the initial shock of it subsided, Asha slowly opened her eyes, thankfully noting that they were still in one piece and that the van hadn't decided to flip over on its side or something disastrous like that. In fact, everyone seemed to be right where they had been, which was a miracle considering none of them hadn't been wearing seatbelts.

She took in everyone's shocked yet uninjured faces, their eyes wide and their mouths downturned. But they were okay. They were all okay. Heavy breaths filled the space around them and the first sound to explode around them were the cries of Boe.

"Everyone alright?" Max turned around, properly assessing the situation. He had a look of grim guilt on his face, but it wasn't his fault, if anything it was theirs for distracting him.

A chorus of weary replies followed his question to which he nodded his acknowledgement before throwing his door open and jumping out of the van. He bent down by the side of it and came back up with fury in his eyes. Asha watched as he stormed along the road, following their scorched tyre marks. He was looking for a reason, a cause for his loss of control. He needed to take the blame away from him. She would have done the same.

"Let's get the fuck out of this time bomb," Kit coughed, hauling himself out of his seat and navigating the aisle to the door.

"You okay?" Finn asked, releasing his vice-like grip from around Asha.

She looked up to him and smiled, nodding slowly. "I'll be fine, thanks to your armour," she laughed lightly.

"This is another shitty thing to add to list of reasons why I am the world's biggest fuck up," Daisy groaned, her hair falling in front of her face as she exited the van.

Piper was already out of the vehicle, pulling Sunny and Boe out with her. Asha sighed and grabbed her backpack before shuffling her way down the aisle of the van and to the open door. Finn followed close behind, and once they were all out, how screwed they were finally settled in.

"So, we're stuck out in the open once again. Great," Kit groaned, his hands flying into the air at his annoyance.

"Why must you punish us so much?" Piper questioned her god up above. The little girls were either side of her, being held there with her motherly arms.

"We shouldn't have expected anything less," Asha sighed, feeling downtrodden by fate and disappointed in the world.

"Come on, we'll be alright. We've just gotta get changed and walk," Finn said, his voice a little too upbeat, making everyone else collectively groan.

Max trudged back to them now, a sweat forming on his brow, he still looked angry. "Must have been bloody glass on the road. I dunno how I didn't see it," he moaned, his voice grumbling.

"There's no use pointing the finger. Can we fix the car?" Asha asked him, moving away from Finn and walking towards the burly man whose shadow engulfed her.

"All four wheels have blown. There's no way we can get her running again," he explained, his face forming a deep frown.

"Then Finn is right," Asha began, carrying her voice more as she addressed the whole group. "We get in our disguises...We walk to Harbour."

Chapter Twenty-Eight

Max estimated it would take them about two hours to reach the dock on foot. The idea of walking for that amount of time assaulted Asha with thoughts of all the things that could go wrong between then and getting there. There was so much time left to chance, so much time where anything could happen, and not for the better. But they had no choice, and according to their leader, the road that led to Harbour was a desolate one. In other words, there was little to no chance of finding another car to use.

With an air of acceptance, the group simply walked with one destination in mind, a new home.

They had taken about five minutes to rustle through their bags and produce suitable disguises for their journey; all sticking with their signature styles of post-apocalyptic fashion, branding themselves without knowing it.

Asha wore her trusty cape coat paired with skinny jeans, Doc Martens, a maroon handkerchief covering her lower face and a pair of thick sunglasses. It felt slightly odd to be back in her stealth outfit. Her mind had settled into a less paranoid frame of mind, what with her emotions being spilled and her brain finding comfort in a sort of love. But being back in her fighting clothes, she slipped straight back into the 'all-out war' mind-set she disliked so much.

Kill or be killed.

She kept herself near the front of their hurriedly moving posse, along with Max who walked with a long stride.

They had trekked for just twenty minutes, keeping on the very side of the road in case unwanted company came along, but Asha was already getting tired, hot and bothered. The sun was blaring on them, unusual for November. So much so that when she looked ahead, the horizon on the road danced and blurred in the heat.

"This must be the final test," she said to Max, her voice muffled by her handkerchief.

"Somethin' like that," he replied, his own voice distorted by his nerve bending ballistics mask. "But we're getting' there. Noah, the leader of Harbour, will hardly be able to contain himself, I'm sure."

"Is he who you spoke to?" Asha asked, her mind conjuring up an idea of Noah.

She thought it ironic that his name was that of the biblical man who harboured those in a freak, worldwide collapse. She also found it comforting in a strange way. The image of a tall man with broad shoulders, and a knowledgeable, weathered face came to her mind.

"Yeah. He would not stop talkin' about you. He's a scientist, the main guy working on the cure, so you can imagine how exci-" Max began but he stopped sharply and lifted his arm to her chest, causing Asha to look quickly to him.

The freckled girl followed his eye-line. Her stare widened. Right ahead of them, a person had run out into the road from the trees. He wasn't facing them which meant that he somehow hadn't seen the gang of frighteningly dressed people coming up behind him.

He was also not wearing any camouflage which meant he was immune. He seemed to be concentrating on something just in front of him, he had a catapult in his hands and he was pulling it back. Asha looked quickly to the road ahead and noticed a huge rat scurrying away from the man.

The man let the catapult go and something small and hard flew through the air with a whistle before smacking the rat into submission. The man grabbed the air with one hand in celebration and started to run towards his catch when Max began his walk once again.

The rest of the group followed cautiously as Max led them up onto the road. The shuffling and movement of them caused the man to finally turn around and notice the company he was in. He looked like he was Korean, tall and lanky with limbs far too long for him, his oversized coat drowned him and his scruffy beard made him look much older than he probably was (perhaps late twenties). What was more noticeable about him was the look of utter terror on his face. That was when Asha realized who they looked like.

"No!" He cried before going to run, his chubby rat bleeding down his hand.

"Wait, wait!" Max yelled, stripping off his mask.

Asha quickly whipped off her hood and handkerchief, the rest of the group followed suit and uncovered their faces too, showing the man that they were not Hunters. He stood shaking a little as his face turned from fear to acceptance and then straight back to fear.

"W-Well, even if you're not infected i-it doesn't mean that you're not Reapers!" He stuttered, backing away.

"Do you *really* think that *we're* Reapers?" Max questioned jokingly, trying to make the man feel at ease.

"H-how would I know?" The man asked, he had deep green eyes that seemed to glint in the sunshine.

"Look at us, twat," Daisy jumped in. "We've got no car, we're carrying everything we own and we're in the middle of the bloody countryside. We are not fucking Reapers."

"We have *children* with us," Piper added in her soft voice.

"We're actually on our way to the docks. We've got a safe place to go called Harbour. You should come with us. You won't have to tuck into rat for dinner anymore," Max grinned, gesturing towards the rodent still clung limply in the man's grip.

"I don't believe you," he said, his face dropping, his voice wavering.

"She's immune to the scratches and bites. We're taking her to Harbour so they can make a cure. It's real, you have to come with us," Kit chimed in, pointing to Asha who gave the man a small smile.

He looked at her with disbelief. Something quickly flashed across his face but Asha wasn't quite sure what it was. Whatever he was thinking though seemed to quickly disappear as his face turned back into a distrustful stare.

"I-Immune?" He managed to stutter.

Asha rolled her eyes - to be believed meant to be seen. She worked her coat off and pulled down her top just enough for him to see the extent of her black scar. The scar that started it all, the thin line that cut her down the middle, the black mark that reminded her everyday who she really was, a damaged beacon of hope.

"Oh my god," he gasped, dropping the rat to the road below.

"What's your name?" Max asked the thin man.

"Uh-um it's Harry, I'm Harry," he answered, without taking his eyes off Asha's scar.

"Well, Harry. You comin' with us or not?" Max said, laying out an ultimatum.

Harry looked over the group, really picking them apart. He was being cautious which Asha could understand. After all, they *were* asking him to put his life in their hands, he had to be sure that he was making the right decision. He didn't take too long to come to a conclusion.

"Okay, I believe you. But we have to go and get my brother, Jude. We live in a house not far from here," Harry explained, gesturing with his head behind him, to the forest.

"Okay," Max agreed, a grin on his face. "You guys got anything to drink?"

Harry looked up to him with a broad smile and nodded his head firmly.

*

The house wasn't far, just like Harry had said. It was only a matter of ten minutes before they ducked through the greenery and into an open area of land, where a dominating country house stood proudly. It was mostly white in colour, with dark brown trimmings and grand windows. Ivy clung to its walls, clawing its way up to the thick thatched roof, and moss coated every boarded-up window. It was magnificent in its homely grandeur.

"We found it a few months ago. It's really something, isn't it?" Harry beamed as he hopped up the front steps to the hefty oak door.

"It sure is," Max replied, his eyes taking in the beautiful home.

Harry pushed open the door, it creaked loudly on its rusted hinges and a waft of cooked potatoes shot through from the darkness. Asha's stomach groaned and ached. The smell was mouth-watering and she found herself following in quickly after Harry, wanting to get her hands on whatever was being served.

The rest of the group trundled in, walking slowly within the dim light of inside, keeping close to Harry who was leading them expertly through the winding, crooked corridors of the vast house.

"Jude must have started some lunch," he smiled back to them before clicking open a door towards the back of the house, revealing a brightly candle-lit kitchen with a man cooking by the oven.

Asha's breath caught in her throat as she was suddenly reminded of the last time she walked into a dark house that felt like home, to the kitchen where a man stood cooking with his back to her, to the moment he turned around and everything stopped. But this wasn't six months ago, this was now. And the person who turned around wasn't her father, it was a man who stood with a plate of food and a puzzled look on his face.

He's not him.

"Woah, Harry. What's going on? Who are these people?" He asked, frozen with the plate in his hands.

He looked around ten years older than Harry did, placing him in his late thirties or so. His ethnicity was also different, which intrigued Asha immediately – he was Caucasian.

Height wise, he was similar if not slightly taller than his younger brother, but his form was the opposite. He was broad and muscular under his fitted, white, cable jumper, unlike his lanky sibling. His hair was much shorter than Harry's and it was lighter in colour. He also had a rosiness to his cheekbones which made him seem safe somehow. His blue eyes, they glimmered with a sparkle of power.

"They're new friends," Harry revealed, throwing his bag to the corner of the room. "They're going to take us to a safe place. We have to go by a boat which is waiting for them right now."

"Is that so?" Jude pondered, placing the plate of sliced steaming potatoes on the wooden counter. He looked inquisitively at the group, they all stayed silent as he did so, feeling a little vulnerable in another man's home. Asha's mouth stung with the temptation of the hot food within her reach.

"You can trust us. Name's Max." The burly man stepped towards Jude and stuck his hand out.

Jude clenched his jaw, his hard eyebrows turning in. "My brother might have fallen into your façade but I'm a little harder to please. Harry has always been a *pushover*," he threw daggers at his brother before returning them expectantly to Max.

"That may be so, but he's right to trust us. We're just tryin' to get somewhere safe. We have a ticket out of this whole thing. Nox will be over as soon as we get to the island. You and your brother are welcome to join us," Max explained, his hand still out waiting to be met.

Jude looked to the floor thinking for a moment before letting out a sigh.

"Jude, that girl's immune. She's gonna make the cure," Harry jutted in pointing at Asha, making her nervous for some reason.

Finn instinctively wrapped an arm around her waist, like he could sense her unease.

Thank you.

"Really," he stated more than asked. He was a very calm force, but still a force. Asha could see his jaw clenching; she couldn't take her eyes off him.

"Really," Max reiterated and stuck his hand out further towards him. "So, you comin'?"

Jude stared at Max for what felt like a minute, everyone else stood barely breathing waiting for a response. Apart from Harry who struggled with one of the slices of potato which was too hot for his fingers. He yelped and it landed on the floor.

"Max. Anything to get away from this hell of living with my brother," Jude smiled a wicked smile and shook his hand with muster.

"Great. So, let's get a move on then," Max said, clapping his hands. "Do you need to pack anything?"

"Hey, the boat will wait for us, right? Let's have a drink, eat something," Jude offered. "That's if Harry manages to leave some for everyone else," he moaned, glaring back at his brother who was looking to him guiltily while chewing.

"I guess so," Max started, looking back to the group who shrugged their response. "A drink and some food wouldn't be so bad," he smiled.

"Perfect. I always liked having company, people to please," Jude grinned, his pearly whites showing. "Harry, take them to the dining room won't you. Have some manners," he spoke coldly.

"As you wish, dear brother, or should I say, Oh Mighty One?" Harry replied sarcastically, but he seemed to regret it as soon as Jude shot another look at him. He sighed. "Come this way guys," he said, leading them through another door.

They followed obediently. Asha was left confused by the relationship between the brothers, but she kept her mind focused on the food she was about to eat.

The dining room was spacious with a long mahogany table right in the centre, candles were placed around barely lighting it. There were many chairs that lined the table, like a feast was about to take place. Asha could imagine the sorts of wealthy occupants who dined there once. It felt luxurious just to be there. There were two places set out for a meal, one for Harry and one for Jude. They were at the heads of the table.

"Please sit where you like. I'll be right back, I have to help his Royal Highness with the drinks," Harry practically curtsied out of the room. He was under his brother's influence, wholly.

Once the door closed behind him, the group all looked at each other with unsure expressions. After a brief moment of getting over the fact that they were in a country mansion and in the midst of a family fallout, they sat themselves down on the uncomfortable, decorative chairs.

"I don't get why we're sitting here having a drink and a snack when your friends at Harbour are waiting for us," Daisy complained, rolling her eyes and putting her feet up on the table.

Piper hissed at her to put them down immediately. The blonde girl pulled a disgusted face but complied.

"Because I don't know about you, but I'm pretty thirsty. Besides, we want to bring them with us, and they want to do this for us, so we're doing it," Max huffed, resting his elbows on the table.

"We should eat as quickly as we can and then leave," Kit said, tapping his fingers on the table, making echoes.

"I actually agree with Kit," Finn started. "It makes me nervous that we're *wasting time* making friends. We need to get to that boat."

"And we will," Asha jumped in. "It won't take long to do this. Plus, it's nice to actually be served for once, instead of going out and scavenging for scraps of a meal," she said, and as she looked around the table, the others seemed to agree with her with slight nods and small smiles.

At that moment, Harry returned, walking backwards through the door holding onto a tray with precariously clattering empty glasses. He wobbled slightly as he turned around, finding his footing, but he managed to walk the glasses safely to the top of the table where his place was set. Jude entered quickly afterwards carrying two glass pitchers of an orange drink.

As he passed her, Asha could smell that it was orange squash, the kind you got given at school for lunch. It sent some much-needed nostalgia running down her spine and her mouth suddenly felt chokingly dry.

Once Harry had set down the glasses, he waited by Jude as he began to pour the thirst-quenching, sweet drink equally into each glass.

"It's been a while since we've seen anyone around. I was beginning to think that we were the only ones left," Jude said, his concentration solely on the drinks, but his face was amused; he was happy.

"Things aren't like that at Harbour. We are about four hundred strong. It took a while to get them there but we managed. There's less people out here now. I think we're comin' to the end of savin' anyone else," Max replied, a certain sadness in his voice.

"How did you find out about it? We have a radio, but we haven't heard anything aside static and dead air for the past five months," Jude inquired, finishing up pouring the last glass.

He then sat himself down at the very head of the table, leant back in his chair and folded one leg over the other, his arms rested on the sides of the chair. It looked like that was exactly where he belonged.

Harry started to place each glass in front of everyone, making sure not to spill a drop.

No-one seemed to want to take the first drink. Everything they had been taught about strangers told them not to take a drink from someone they didn't know. So instead, they sat staring intently at the conversation being exchanged between Max and Jude. Asha felt like she was like a pawn, watching the two kings deliberate, she felt small and helpless.

"I work there. I help find survivors on the mainland and I bring 'em back to the island. I've been doing it since the beginnin'," Max explained, looking from his drink, to Jude who seemed indifferent to the new information.

"It's lucky we ran into you!" Harry beamed, sitting down and taking a big gulp of his drink.

Asha's mouth turned to sand at the sight of the cool drink being swallowed by Harry, but she still wasn't so sure.

"Luck is all we've got left," Max stated, his fingers touching his cool glass lightly.

"Well, I certainly feel lucky," Jude grinned before taking his glass and gulping it down whole. He wiped his lips with the back of his hand and sighed in relief. "Mm, the water is colder this time of year, no need for ice," he said as he poured himself another glass.

The fact that Jude and Harry weren't hesitant in drinking the drink that had been served made everyone spring into action almost in sync. Asha took tentative sips but eventually downed half her glass in one. It was so refreshing to her Sahara mouth that she couldn't help but almost finish it. The little girls emptied their drinks within a few moments, and Jude was quick to refill their glasses; he did seem to get joy out of serving people. The rest of the group had either half-finished or almost finished their drinks by the time Jude started to talk once again.

"So, what are the connections between you all? I've always been a nosey person, but since we're survival companions, I don't feel like I'm intruding," he smiled, his natural charisma seeping in.

"No secrets and all that," Max agreed with a clear of his throat.

"Exactly," Jude murmured. "You know that myself and Harry are brothers. But of-course we're not *blood brothers*. Our parents adopted me first.

They couldn't have kids of their own, but then twelve years later, Harry the miracle baby was spawned," he finished, he was unapologetic in his bitterness.

"Yeah," Harry simply said, sucking down more of his drink.

Asha felt a tension rising in her, she wasn't sure what it was, but the whole situation and the way Jude and Harry spoke to each other, made her feel like something wasn't quite right. She felt awkward and her stomach knotted in the presence of two brothers who seemed to have a long, dark hatred towards each other. The origin of their dislike was clear now, one was chosen, one was a gift. Both had a right to the top of the tower, but only one seemed to be winning.

"Well, I'm Max and I work at Harbour," he said, a hand on his chest. "This is Piper, she's our very capable nurse," he explained, gesturing to Piper who sat next to Harry.

She blushed; her wrinkled cheeks close to matching her fiery hair. "I try my best," she sang.

Jude looked at her for a little longer than he should have, making Piper peer to her glass and drink. "...I feel that you're the mother-type in the group," he said, his eyes now scanning everyone.

Piper swallowed her mouthful with a kind smile. "Oh, well, that would be an honour," she said with wide bright eyes.

"The kids, whose are they?" The persistent host asked, moving straight on from Piper who twiddled her thumbs now.

"None of ours," Max stated, giving the girls a reassuring smile. "They came as a team, and a pretty good one at that."

"Sunny is my mummy now!" Boe said harshly, her face turned into a frown. Sunny placed a hand on the top of her head, rubbing it. Boe quickly smiled and calmed.

345

"Sweet," Jude said with no emotion.

"If we're doing this bull shit 'say an interesting fact about yourself' introduction, then I'm Kit and I'm the immune girl's best friend," he said matter-of-factly, crossing his arms and leaning on the table, an unamused look on his face.

Jude nodded his head a touch and then looked to the blonde-haired girl whose scowl could cut through ice. She glanced up and caught his eye and exhaled, annoyed.

"Daisy."

"Is that it?" Jude poked, his eyebrow rising.

"Bite me, Captain America," Daisy growled, staring him down with her sapphire eyes. He did resemble him in some ways, Asha noted. Less hero-like though.

"You get used to her," Max jumped in, an apologetic smile on his face.

Jude held a hand up to Max and shook his head, a clear smile on his face before turning his attention to Asha who had been avoiding his stare since they sat down.

"Immune girl, what's your story?" He asked, and the air turned cold.

Asha took in a breath and sighed, sitting herself up, Finn's hand pinched lightly at her thigh. "I'm Asha and I was scratched by my infected dad and I didn't turn," she finished and sat back, holding her hand over Finn's.

"What makes *you* so special?" Jude asked, but his tone was accusing and dark and it caused her heart to stop.

The whole atmosphere of the room twisted, contorting to the way Jude had spoken his odd question.

No-one said a word, especially not Asha who just kept her eyes on the empty glass in front of her. Finn cleared his throat, Kit shuffled in his chair and Max sat still as stone, his eyes on Jude, cautious.

Maybe they were nervous, maybe they were never good with people, maybe this was just how they were. You can't expect everyone to act the same way as you, and if they don't, it doesn't necessarily mean that they are dangerous, it just means they're different. With that thought in mind, Asha relaxed, just a little.

"And who's the other guy?" Harry hurriedly asked, changing the subject. All eyes went to the honey-eyed boy.

"I'm Finn, um, I just want to stop running," he spoke gently and then looked to his lap.

"Am I the only one who feels like we're some sort of group therapy session?" Kit laughed out loud, out of place.

"Don't you think we all need that?" Jude questioned him, a poison to his tone. "I'm sure you've all done things, terrible things, just to live. I know *we* have. Things that are hard to bear," Jude glanced down at his watch for a moment, a flicker of anguish flashed across his face before he glanced back up to everyone. "Which is why this Harbour is such a great thing, right? So we can finally go back to normality. Rules and regulations. People in power who don't deserve it... Society in its unjust, toxic way. Back to a world where you're told when to eat, breathe, sleep... shit..." he trailed off then, letting his monologue carry heavily around the table.

Asha watched on nervously, drinking down the rest of her drink. At the same time Kit kicked her lightly under the table and Finn squeezed her thigh. She jumped a little and swallowed her drink quickly, giving both of them a stare. Kit looked back with unease, he wasn't happy with the strange questioning and calmness of their hosts. Finn just seemed to have grabbed her for some form of comfort. This wasn't a pleasant table. Asha wanted to leave.

"He's joking," Harry laughed nervously as he too checked the watch on his wrist.

"Sorry," Jude apologized suddenly, snapping himself out of the darkness he'd tumbled drastically into. "I go off on a tangent sometimes. I'm sure Harbour will be great, a fresh start for all of us," he smiled a winning smile and the whole room inflated. A shared silent sigh of relief spread.

Asha's stomach suddenly growled loudly, she pressed on it hard, embarrassed. "I don't mean to be that bitch, but are we gonna eat anytime soon?" She asked quickly, looking to Jude who took his time to meet her eye.

"Oh, yes," he said slowly, checking his watch, then shooting a glare at Harry who minutely creased his eyebrows, then looking back to her. "I have something in the oven cooking to go with the potatoes. You'll be fed soon, I promise," he said lazily.

"I'm sleepy," Boe quietly moaned, her eyes shutting.

"*But we have to go,*" Asha barely whispered, realising she was losing whatever game she was playing at that moment.

"We will, don't you worry your pretty, little head," he smiled, oddly confident.

Asha held her eyes on Jude for a minute, noting the blank look that was cast across them, one that wouldn't be there if a normal person had just been told they were being saved. He looked impatient, but not to get out, he looked impatient, like he was waiting for something to happen right there and then.

All of a sudden, Boe and Sunny collapsed off of their chairs, and in that instant the room started to blur and spin; confused voices danced in the cotton wool that was now Asha's hearing. The glasses jumped in front of her very eyes and fear gripped her heart in a chokehold.

What the fuck is happening?

She breathed quickly, panic twirling her in a tornado. She felt like she was moving rapidly but she was still sitting there in her chair. All of her eye movements slowed almost to a halt. She caught glimpse of Kit attempting to get up, his fist outstretched, but he fell on the floor unmoving. Piper's head dropped hard on the table, her hair spreading around her like a red crown. Finn had already collapsed out of sight. Daisy slumped unavoidably in her chair, her eyes meeting Asha's frightened ones briefly before drawing closed. Max let out a pained grunt, he was desperately trying to stay awake but he too succumbed, falling with a loud thump to the floor below.

Asha stayed up longer than the others, her eyes filling with tears as she watched Harry stand near his brother, head hanging low. Jude looked straight at her, a stretched, sinister grin on his face before bringing his fingers to his lips and whistling. In the next second, several doors around the room flew open and in marched a row of men, all suited and booted for a hunt. They had static, stern faces as they circled the table.

"*No, no, no,*" Asha whimpered, the act of talking feeling like she was pushing a pole through the eye of a needle.

Jude pulled a mocking regretful face. "Oops," he said, his shoulders shrugging animatedly.

He began to laugh; it seared her to her core. His cackling face was the last thing she saw before the world went black and she sank into a deep, deep sleep.

Chapter Twenty-Nine

Asha woke with a start, not being able to move properly and hardly able to breathe. She had a gag in her mouth, her hands were tied behind her back, and she was laid on a bed where her ankles were handcuffed to the metal bedposts. A cry burst from under the cloth in her mouth and her eyes immediately filled with tears. She screamed until her throat was raw, thrashing around on the bed. She wasn't wearing her coat anymore. She'd been stripped down to her jeans and vest top. Her necklace was gone, so was her ring.

NOT NOW, NOT FUCKING NOW!

The room she was in was dark, but not dark enough to mask what was in it. It was quite a large bedroom, but even the sense of space was lost on Asha whose whole world became the bed.

Trapped.

The windows in the room had been boarded up from the inside but there were cracks which let through the quiet light of dusk. The most troubling detail about the bedroom was that she was alone.

"No!" She screeched, her voice echoing around her.

Her head pounded and with every tear that rolled down her cheek, a headache began to blossom into something so painful, it knocked Asha for six. She lay there breathing as best she could through the gag and stared at the ceiling. There were glow-in-the-dark star stickers dotted around it, luminous, not comforting in the slightest. Her eyebrows drew together and she let out another, cry, defeated this time.

At that moment, the door handle clicked and a soft light shone in. Asha quickly looked to the side of her where the door was and she saw a dark figure holding a candle. His smile glowed above its flickering light, he looked like he was emerging from the depths of the underworld.

Asha stayed still, staring at him. He whistled towards the door and three men came in holding more candles, bringing her prison into full light. They left quickly after Jude gave them the order to go, shutting the door behind them.

"I hope the room is okay for you. I have to say, it's one of the more premium ones. Memory foam mattress," he grinned, placing his candle on the bedside table and sitting himself comfortably on the bed next to her.

Asha's swollen eyes remained transfixed on the man inches away from her. Relentless tears streamed down her face, diffusing any air of toughness from her. Her breathing was quick yet stifled. He frowned slightly before gently lifting her head and untying the gag from her mouth, freeing her of its constraint.

"That's better," he said so calmly, like he was a kind person helping someone in need.

Asha took in deeper breaths, giving her body the oxygen it craved.

"Eesh, I know it's a bummer," he grinned coldly, holding his hands up in defense. "But, we all have an agenda, we all have to survive. We all have to sacrifice something once in a while."

"Why?" Asha croaked; her face scrunched up in dismay. "You could have come with us! You could have been saved!"

"Where would the fun be in that? Honestly, you need to use your head. *Think!*" He spat the last word, a darkness to his stare.

"Where are my friends?" She demanded, panic raising her voice an octave.

"Perfectly fine, for now. You'll see them for dinner. In fact, I think I can hear Harry coming now to prepare you for it," Jude slimed, holding his hand to his ear, his eyebrows raised in anticipation.

"Prepare me?" Asha questioned shakily, not really wanting to know the answer.

"Yes, dinner is a *whole affair*. But I wanted to be here when you woke up," Jude grinned sickeningly, pairing it with a wink that made the dark-haired girl shudder.

She felt as helpless as a thin leaf being battered by the wind. The fragility that coursed through her made her feel like she was a ghost, barely even there. She couldn't breathe or comprehend what was going on. One thing that she did know, however, was that this was the final stop in the journey of her short life.

This is it.

"People usually look ugly when they cry," he mused softly, reaching to stroke her face.

She yanked herself away from his touch with a short shout.

"Hm, understandable," he said to himself and sighed looking to his watch.

Asha wanted to scream at him, to hit him with all her strength, but she had nothing left.

She was weak in the moment; she knew if she even tried to defend herself from him, she would end up looking more and more like a broken doll, shattered to pieces in his palms.

So, she remained silent, stoic, somewhere far away. That was the thing about silence, it made you a mystery. It left it difficult to know what you were truly feeling, making people question themselves and their perceptions. Better to make people curious than to give them control over your emotions.

Oncoming footsteps clambered into Asha's ears and a feeling of dread quickly filled her. Jude looked up and gave a quick nod to someone who came into the room.

"She's ready," he muttered before standing himself up and leaving.

Harry set down a metal tray on the bedside table, Asha turned and saw what was on it, a vial of clear liquid and a needle with a syringe attached to it. Whatever it was, it was most definitely what Jude was referring to when he said she needed 'preparing'. Asha's chest heaved and her eyes burst wide.

"It's better if you don't resist," Harry said sadly. He still hadn't looked her in the eye, which angered Asha so much.

"Look at me!" She screamed at him, piercing his skin with her glare.

He clenched his jaw and frowned before finally dragging his gaze upon her, but he quickly looked away again instead to the tray and began fiddling with its contents. Anger boiled in Asha, filling her with a rage that threatened to spill out in molten lava.

"*Pathetic,*" she spat with venom.

"You couldn't understand," he said shaking his head lowly. His fingers worked expertly as he poked the syringe into the vial and drew up the strangely thick liquid. He pulled it out and expelled a little onto the floor, making sure there were no air bubbles.

"I don't think I want to understand how a monster thinks," Asha muttered, forcing her stare away from him and to the plastic stars above her.

"Sorry," he said. "You're going to feel a small scratch."

He wasted no time in finding a patch of bare skin on Asha's arm. She didn't move a muscle, there was no point, so she just lay there waiting. She felt the sharpness as the needle penetrated her skin but didn't react.

Whatever Harry was injecting her with, it made her veins ache, like her blood was trying to push it away. She moaned in pain as it travelled through her body. Harry stood back and watched her for a few minutes as she writhed in the discomfort.

But before long, Asha could no longer feel her fingers or her toes, then she lost her legs and arms, then she lost her chest, and lastly, she lost her neck. Now she really couldn't move. She shot a concerned look at Harry who sighed apologetically.

"It's a paralytic, it'll wear off in a couple of hours. No long-lasting damage. But it makes you moveable without issue, and that's how Jude and the others need you," Harry explained, looking like every word made him twinge inside.

It was an odd sensation, even though she couldn't feel her body, her mind was telling her it was still there and that she could move. But as she strained her eyes to look down at herself, she knew there was no chance of her even shaking a finger.

At least I'm not dead. For a moment, she had thought 'dinner' meant being served to Hunters.

"I need to put this on you," Harry said, holding up a large piece of fabric, a blindfold.

Asha was completely out of control of herself. She couldn't help when the fabric was tied tightly around her head. She couldn't help when she was hauled up by two pairs of strong arms and carried away. She certainly couldn't help when she was placed in a chair with leather belts strapping her upright. And she couldn't help when her blindfold was whipped off.

She was someone else's property now, someone else's toy.

Her head was strapped so that she could look upon what was in front of her. She found herself wishing she still had something covering her eyes, because what she saw was something she wished she hadn't.

She was sat around a table, a little smaller than the one they had been sat at earlier in the day. But instead of glasses of refreshing orange squash and plates of hot potatoes, the table was bare. Lining the table were her friends, all of them tied up and stone still, just like she was. Next to everyone was an IV drip and another bundle of something that looked medicinal, with tubing and a large sac filled with an unknown substance.

Asha glanced at everyone individually. She couldn't show any emotion in her face because she was frozen, but her eyes did the talking for her. The little girls were the hardest to look at. Boe's hair stuck to her forehead with cold sweat and Sunny looked guilty, she had failed in protecting her one and only.

Kit had a fire growing behind his eyes. Daisy looked as if even her eyes had been paralyzed too. Finn was staring at Asha like if he looked away, he would never see her again. Piper's eyes were so swollen from crying that it was hard to see the colour in them. And finally, Max. His eyes were screaming.

Jude was sat at the head of the table, the glowing light of the hundreds of candles in the room flickered on his skin. Around the walls stood the men who Asha had seen earlier. They had their arms crossed in front of them and they stared ahead, not concentrating on anything. They looked like robotic soldiers, waiting for their orders. Harry stood beside Jude like his faithful servant. The room was eerily silent aside from the rasping breaths from everyone around the table.

"I do like having guests," Jude grinned, breaking the quiet. "We haven't had them in a long while have we boys?" He looked around the room; the men shook their heads in unison. "So you can imagine how excited we were to get the message that eight visitors were on their way," he chuckled and sat back in his throne-like chair. "I must say though, you are very lucky to have come to us. You are in for a more than dignified death. You've found yourself in the Reaper den for The Horsemen. Yes, that's right, The Horsemen come here looking for a feast. And they *are* mighty. One of the girls is right up my street. Brunette, no older than twenty. But, she always looks sad, plus she's got a hankering for human flesh so, I don't risk it," he winked at Max, like he would know the feeling.

"They trust our services and in the beginning, we provided them with plenty to chew on. I dare say we were one of the pioneers of Reaper culture. We help the new race to survive. We feed those who are weary and hungry. So, welcome to The Samaritans," he grinned widely, raising his arms like they should be impressed.

"We will endeavour to make your stay as painful and as long as possible. You see, there's very little to entertain a man these days, and we are all men," he took a deep breath and sighed. "But I digress. You will stay with us until The Horsemen arrive, which by my calculations is in another two weeks."

Two weeks? Asha's heart pinched, if there was any way of getting out of there, they would miss the boat, they would be stranded. Another more pressing thought invaded her mind. She couldn't let herself be killed. She had to save the world. She had to get to Harbour. Her breathing picked up as her heart beat a thousand beats a second.

"Which gives us enough time to fatten you up at least a little bit. Some of you certainly need something on your bones," he said accusingly, shooting Daisy a glare. "So, without further ado, dinner is served," Jude announced, his fingers clicking.

The men around the room began to move. There were eight of them, coincidentally one for each of the group. Asha watched ahead of her at Finn, she wanted to break out of her restraints and hold him, tell him everything was alright, but she couldn't. And she wouldn't have been able to lie like that, no matter how hard she tried.

Each man grabbed an IV drip and inserted them into the group without any hesitation. Asha couldn't feel it of course, but she *could* feel the liquid that had begun to enter her.

"Just a vitamin concoction, nothing to worry about. Like I said, we need to keep you healthy," Jude explained, clicking his fingers again.

This time the men grabbed the other contraption that was beside everyone. They moved in sync, like it was a play that they had performed countless times over. Asha's head was suddenly tilted back so that she was now staring at the ceiling. Her mouth was then forced open and a long, thick tube was pushed down her throat. She gagged and spluttered as much as she could in her paralyzed state. Tears filled her eyes from the invasion, and the sounds of her friends' suffering only made the tears come faster. She shut her eyes tight and began chanting numbers in her head, willing it to be over.

Moments later, a heaviness set in her stomach and not long after that, the tube was removed carefully. Asha's eyes still watered, and the tears fell fast when her head was tilted back to face everyone. In that second, one of the candles to the right of the room tilted over, knocking two others down with it. Jude clicked his fingers and two of the men dealt with the growing flame by stamping down hard with their steel capped boots.

"You know what? Enough with the candles. Turn on the lights," Jude ordered, disgust in his face.

One of the Samaritans trudged to the light switch that was by the door and flicked it on, bringing the room into full brightness. They had electricity. That very fact made the dark-haired girl even more fearful; with power, they were capable of anything.

"You didn't think we were really living like *that,* did you? Candle to candle? No heating?" Jude laughed animatedly, gripping his stomach.

"This place has been running to full capacity for months! Where do you think we keep the bodies? Just piled up in a room to rot? *No, no, no,*" he sighed shaking his head, his green eyes looked up to them again. "The basement is a place where you will all end up, in one way or another. Hopefully we won't have to put you in the freezers. Hunters prefer their meat fresh of course, like anyone would. Freezing the meat makes it lose its quality, its finesse... You might be thinking, why wouldn't I make it to the two weeks? Why would I be frozen? I thought you were looking after us, Jude? Well, I don't hate to break it to you, but like I said, we like to have our fun and we've each developed some form of 'frowned upon' leisure. Those who can't handle it will clock out early. Which is why we have plenty of freezer space."

Everything inside Asha crumpled. *Frowned upon leisures?* Jude's words burst around her, igniting a pure panic that forced her vision into whiteness.

"Speaking of," Jude slimed, his face bright with evil lust. "It's time to play our favourite game!" He chorused. "Harry. The hat."

Harry instantly produced a hat from behind his back. It was an old, tattered top hat with a purple ribbon tied around the base. Jude snatched it from him without a thank you and started to stir it with circular movements.

"Each of my men will take turns in picking out a name. You will be assigned to them. They will take care of you, and in return, you will participate in whatever they will," Jude explained, his voice calm, completely the opposite to the horror he was describing.

The Samaritans silently lined up beside Jude who bore the largest smirk on his face. He shook the hat towards the first man. His large, tattooed hand delved in and pulled out a piece of paper. He opened it and read the name.

"Piper," he said in a deeply gravelly voice.

Jude pointed to the red-headed woman with a wink and the man proceeded to stand right behind her, unmoving, unemotional. Piper's eyes filled with salty tears and they tracked down her face.

Oh God.

The next man, tall with caramel skin, went and pulled a name from the hat.

"Finn,"

Jude chuckled, pointing at Finn. "You aren't a lucky boy."

Asha tore her eyes away. She couldn't watch her friends being called out to slaughter. She wished she could cover her ears and block it all out, but she couldn't. She wished she could take all of the pain they were yet to endure and have it all for herself. She wished they hadn't trusted the nervous stranger on the side of the road. But there was no point in wishing, not anymore.

She imagined what each of the men were capable of, what kind of sick fantasies they each had. She didn't dare to delve; it was too much to bear. But looking at each of them, she could tell there was a new level of darkness behind their stale eyes, one that threatened to end the people around her, and the world as she knew it.

Before long, everyone had a Samaritan standing hauntingly behind them. Apart from Asha.

There was one man left who had a jagged scar down the side of his face and a look of pure hatred in his eyes.

Even though it was obvious he was going to be put with her, he still walked up to the hat and reached in, only, he didn't pick out a name, instead he looked to Jude with a confused stare.

"Sorry, Ajax, no-one for you. Better luck next time," he shrugged, not sorry at all.

Ajax nodded his head acceptingly and skulked back to the side of the room, arms in front of him, clasped together, resigned. Jude then placed the top hat on his head and stood up, stretching out towards the ceiling. He was tall, taller than any man in the room, even Max and Kit. He dwarfed everyone and everything. He started to stroll excruciatingly slowly around the table. Asha braced herself, she knew what was coming.

"Now, I don't usually want to play. I'd rather let my men have some fun because I'm a good leader and I care about how my people feel. But sometimes, I just can't help myself," he continued, inching closer to the freckled girl. "And this time, I thought I deserved a little treat," he took a few more steps until he was right behind her. "I picked my name out of the hat before we started. Written on it were the letters *A, S, H, A,*" he whispered each letter bending down to her ear, causing her to explode into goosebumps. "So," he began, standing up straight and placing his hands on her cold shoulders. "We've been assigned. Now, take everyone back to their quarters. The fun can begin," he spoke with chilling excitement.

Asha had gone into a state of shock. She couldn't react or respond to what was going on. Her mind had forced an invisible film over her, cocooning her from the barbaric situation she had found herself in.

She watched on as her friends were taken one by one out of the room, not being able to speak back to them as they screeched through their stares. Her mind, body and soul had taken a break.

Without being able to help, she just sat there, waiting for her monster to take his prize home.

Chapter Thirty

To Asha's surprise, Jude left her in her room straight away, letting her 'recover' from the injection. His reasoning didn't surprise her though. He said she was no use to him like that, which only made her dread what he would do to her when the medicine wore off. She was tied to each bed post, it made her feel incredibly vulnerable and horribly uncomfortable.

She lay staring up at the glowing stars that littered the ceiling, finding herself thinking about when she'd see real stars again, if she ever would. She thought about the hundreds of times she'd stepped out into the night and looked up to see a clear sky sparkling with fallen suns. She remembered how it filled her with a happiness that she couldn't describe.

Looking at them and finding the few constellations she knew, grounded her, filled her with wonder. Her favourite one was the Little Bear because it was the first one she'd learnt about, and it was a little harder to see than others; making it just that much better when she did spot it.

Please let me see them again, please.

True to Harry's word, the drugs started to wear off around the two-hour mark. She could feel a tingling in her fingers and her toes first. Then the feeling spread through her like wildfire, igniting her limbs into action. She breathed a heavy sigh of relief. A tiny part of her thought she'd never be able to move again, thankfully that wasn't the case.

She rocked and pulled against her restraints, hoping to make some sort of leeway, but she was tied down with little room to move.

The door handle turned and its metal squeak pierced her ears. Her heart stopped.

"Good," came the voice from behind her.

She closed her eyes and refused to open them. She didn't want to see the look in his eyes, the look that would tell her that she was his and there was nothing she could do about it. She felt his footsteps as they curved around the bed. She heard him bend over her and then felt her gag being taken out. She tore her eyes open then, staring him down.

"Why?" She seethed, her eyebrows furrowed and her lips quivering.

"Why what?" He asked nonchalantly, sitting himself by her on the bed.

"Why are you keeping us?" She pushed, a blaze in her glare.

"I thought I made myself clear."

"We aren't like anyone else you've had," she pleaded, her eyes threatening to fill.

"I know, that's what makes you so... enticing," he grinned, his blue eyes glittering.

"But we can put an end to Nox, we can make the cure. You just have to let us go!" She begged now, losing her anger.

"You forget that *you're* the one that's special. Don't lump yourself in with the rest of your group. They are nothing but mere meat to be harvested," Jude said, his words cutting her.

"...*I need them,*" she whispered, not meaning for it to come out; the urgency betrayed her.

"Rule number one. Don't show your weaknesses. Someone might use them against you. Although, it's a little late for that. You've already told me everything I need to know," he said lowly with a chuckle that sent shivers down her spine.

Asha's heart started to hammer furiously. He was right, she had trusted him, they all had. They revealed everything to him; where they were headed, what their plan was, and worst of all, who they were to each other. He had every bit of leverage he needed to mould and burn each and every one of them. And they had no choice but to give in. Asha immediately thought of Kit and how he would die for her, without question. The reality of that decision was imminent and that very fact made her blood turn cold and her hearing pulse loudly in her ears.

Jude sighed lazily, twiddling his thumbs. He shouldn't be allowed to act so calmly, he shouldn't be allowed to play God, he shouldn't be allowed to laugh. That was it, no more begging girl, no more being the victim, it was time to take charge.

"You really think they're going to spare you?" Asha asked coldly, gazing at him with ice.

"How little you know. We are the best, we serve the best, they respect us," Jude said.

"The infamous Horsemen *respect* you?" Asha smiled. "They don't *respect* you. They *use* you."

"Even so, we are their chosen provider. We will remain by their side."

"You're more *stupid* than I thought!" Asha laughed, which made Jude sit up straight and look impressed. "You're so blinded by the power you think you have. They're not going to keep you around. They can eat their own kind, but they won't do that, not until every human is gone. That includes you. You're delaying your death, but you're not stopping it. You're serving a force who won't think twice about eating you. You're nothing special. You won't join them. You need to stop the killing and betrayal of your kind. You need to let us go, you need to let us end this," Asha breathed, every word took it out of her, but she had to say something, anything to change his mind.

Jude scoffed. "Do you really think I want this to end?" He threw his head back in a deep laugh. "I'm living like a *king*. I finally have the respect I deserve from people who are less than me. If I give this up, I give up my lead. I give up what I've worked so hard for, not only in this life, but before. Do you know how much respect a defence lawyer gets? I'm sure I don't have to answer that; the implication is clear. So, why would I end it? I want Nox to continue, forever," he said with vigour. "...You being alive is a problem. A problem which I intend to keep to myself. *My dirty little secret,*" he smirked as he practically undressed her with his eyes. "Besides, maybe when the time is right, I'll use you as my own personal weapon. Or I might just kill you with the others. The future is bright," he shrugged, a grin still across his lips.

Rage bubbled in her. He looked at her more like she was property with every passing second. She would never be his. She hated the connections he was sewing to her, binding her to him like a tattoo.

"The fact that you'll be left to represent the human race makes me sick," Asha spat, not really knowing what else to say.

"Really?" Jude asked brightly. "The thought of it fills me with joy. I'll finally get the recognition I deserve."

"If you keep me away from Harbour. You will kill humanity," Asha cried.

"Say it again, *in a whisper*," Jude replied, his eyes narrowing, a smirk fresh on his lips.

"Fuck you!" Asha yelled, letting a choked cry escape her lips.

Jude shook his head. "Enough talking," he rummaged in his pocket. "I'd like to introduce you to something that is close to my heart," he smiled, pulling out a wheel of what looked like pins, all with different colours on the end.

"A pinwheel?" Asha questioned in a tiny voice. Confusion set in.

"Observant," he sighed, but perked up when he looked at it again. "Each of the colours represent a different part of the body. More specifically, a different pressure point on the body. I assume you've heard of acupuncture?"

As soon as she heard the words, she knew something very bad was going to happen to her. She could do nothing but nod her head in answer. Fear entombed her.

"This is different, it will offer no relief. Quite the opposite actually. But the same principles are in place," he grinned an evil grin.

Asha writhed in her restraints, she knew she couldn't escape, but instinct told her not to give up.

"You can squirm all you want, but really you'll just be doing yourself harm. This involves a lot of precision," he spoke with such poise, it chilled her to the bone.

"Please, don't," she breathed heavily, eyebrows turned up, face wracked with horrid anticipation.

"This is a two-way game. Otherwise it's not fun. You get to spin the wheel," he said, lowering the rainbow pinwheel down to her reach.

She let out a stunted yell as she shoved the wheel away from her, causing it to clatter onto the hardwood floor below. Regret filled her immediately.

Like a flash of lighting, he whipped out a small hammer and connected it with one of her toes. The crack of bone made her stomach flip and her dinner threatened to make another appearance.

She whined and groaned as the pain clawed its way up her foot. Her toe blew up in flames. She couldn't even scream, shock put a stop to that. He returned the hammer to his belt and tutted before picking up the pinwheel. Her entire leg shook from the impact.

"There are plenty more piggies who might not make it to the market. That's entirely your choice," he explained in an oddly soothing voice. "Now, spin the wheel," he ordered her again, placing it back in front of her now trembling fingers.

Asha's face scrunched up in dismay, but she moved her fingers until they touched the wheel. The tops of the pins were smooth, their colours bright. She let out a breath and spun it.

Jude closed his eyes and lifted the wheel to his level before stopping it with a simple touch.

He opened his eyes slowly, looking upon what pin he'd selected. He didn't seem the happiest, but excitement still danced across his eyes.

369

"*Starting off easy I see,*" he whispered, setting the wheel down and removing the chosen pin - blue. It glinted against the candlelight and Asha's panic rose.

"What does it mean?" She asked, shaking.

Jude didn't answer. He just reached for her arm, his long fingers wrapped around her wrist, stopping her from wriggling too much. Her whole body heaved, wanting so badly to pull away and run out of the room.

"Stay still, Asha," Jude smoothed. "*Be a good girl.*"

He carefully twisted her arm so that the soft fleshy side was right in his path. Then, he hovered the end of the needle just below where her arm bent in the middle. She breathed rapidly watching his eyes as they concentrated intently on where he was going to poke her skin. She began to choke on the dryness of her throat brought on by the quick breaths. She didn't move, she knew she would make it much worse for herself if she did.

She obeyed him.

With a precise and sudden movement, Jude sunk the needle straight through her flesh and it hit something wiry inside.

Asha's eyes blew wide with the pain that shot through that very point. It winded her and she screamed a stifled scream. Her face twisted and turned trying in some attempt to deal with the intensity that ran through her.

How could something so small create so much chaos?

Her fingers stretched impossibly far as the course of pain travelled through her arm. She'd never experienced a sensation like it.

It wasn't the most painful thing she'd endured, but it was the strangest. When she forced her strained stare to Jude, she saw him smiling, not widely, but he was satisfied.

It was then that Asha realised something.

Hell wasn't a place; it was a person.

Chapter Thirty-One

There are few times in life when you think to yourself, how am I supposed to move on from this? The answer is plain and simple. You move. That thought consumed Asha as she lay on the bed, numb yet tingling. It had been an hour since Jude left her, but she could still feel his pin-needles all over her body. He hadn't grown tired of the game, not for a long time. The dark-haired girl wasn't sure she had any scream left.

She shifted herself as much as she could, feeling an ache at every point of entry. The pain was instant, but the recovery was long and dull. She felt empty, defeated, broken. There was absolutely nothing she could do to help herself, and it killed her. It killed her knowing that her friends were likely suffering the same, if not more. And she couldn't help them.

The sadness and betrayal had left her body in a slow whisper. She felt nothing.

Her mind tried its best to show her a happy memory, to push some life into the damaged heart that lay under her ribs. She caught glimpses of her family, smiling and laughing. The holiday to Mexico where they roamed the orange flower covered streets munching on Gansitos. Laughing at Ella when she came home drunk for the first time and threw up over the priceless, imported rug. Her mum and dad dancing the salsa in their living room like they'd invented it. She tried to think of it all, before it was too late and she wouldn't be able to see it again.

Death was something that she'd been preparing herself for ever since Nox arrived. Even before then, she was always cautious of it, always aware that it would happen. She counted herself lucky that she'd lived this far. Being on a bed, tied up in the Samaritans' grasp simply didn't surprise her.

She felt ready for death and she refused to go out angry.

So instead, she lay quietly, staring at nothing, letting the minutes pass. Judging by the lack of light coming through the cracks in the boarded-up windows, she was alone until the deep night.

Her thoughts on death jumped around in her mind, dancing and teasing her. And she did ponder them. But after a while she started to feel like something was wrong. She didn't want to die.

She *wasn't* ready.

There was so much more to do, and the thought of not being able to do anything more filled her with panic. She had to get out. She had to fight for her survival, just like she'd been doing for the past six months. Her whole life had been catapulted into hope when she met Max, and she would be the world's biggest twat if she let that hope fizzle and die. She couldn't give up, not when the stakes were so high.

She had to find a way out.

With a new attitude fresh in her mind, she was ready when the door handle twisted open. No more doing nothing, she would take a stand and be fierce, because if she didn't, she'd lose herself and everything that came with it.

"Hey," Harry said quietly as he closed the door behind him.

"Fancy seeing you here," Asha replied coldly, lazily letting her gaze fall on him.

"Sarcasm, that's a good sign," he smiled lightly, but a deep sadness glowed in his eyes. "Jude asked me to bring you these. If you need them," he said, holding out three white pills.

"Asked or demanded?" Asha questioned. Her idea of escape forming.

"Huh?" Harry looked confused.

"Jude, he acts like your master. Not a nice one," she replied.

"It's not like that," he reassured with a shake of his head.

"Really? Because it seems to me that he intimidates you, and you cower in his presence. Don't bother lying, Harry. I can see it written all over your face. Everyone can. So, why lie? It's not like he's in here, is it? It's not like he'll punish you for admitting that he practically owns you. He'd probably love it," Asha said firmly.

"What is it? Poor adopted boy got shown up by the real baby? Couldn't handle it, so he made you feel like you were nothing, that you somehow owed him something because *he* was the first. He never let you forget it, did he? He made you feel bad for him because you were the real child and he wasn't. You've been making up for it ever since you were born, haven't you? He was chosen, you were a gift. You both deserved the love your parents gave you, but the fact that you shared blood didn't sit well with your psycho brother," Asha continued, feeling Harry crumble a little more with every word she spoke. "Has he ever done anything like this to you? Has he hurt you like he hurt me?"

"No," he replied in a hush.

"I don't believe you."

"Listen...you're right.," Harry sighed. "But it doesn't change anything. He's my brother, my family. And even if he treats me like a slave, he's all I have left. It wouldn't feel right to leave him."

"He doesn't care about you, Harry."

"Of course, he does, he's my brother."

"Would a brother force his brother to kidnap people? Would a brother make his brother kill people? No, Harry, it doesn't work like that. Why give him your love when all he gives you is an IOU which he'll never honour?" Asha whispered, suddenly worried that Jude could be listening.

Harry didn't answer, but Asha could see a million answers and thoughts forming behind his frowning face. He was her ticket. If there was any way of bringing down the Samaritans, Harry was it. Asha needed to test how weak and how ready he was to revolt against his brother. To her delight, it was clear he was cracking. Slowly but surely. He was the chink in Jude's armour and she would crack it wide open.

"You can change this; you can change your life and the lives of everyone who's left. But being stuck here, helping your brother, you will be killing the world. You have to get us out of here so we can start life again!" She cried, her unwanted desperation coming out.

"Shh!" Harry quickly shut her down. "Don't talk like that. Now, do you want these pills or not?" He looked angry but there was a glint in his eye.

The seed had been planted.

Asha didn't push it. She had a few days to work on him. "No... do you have anything for sleeping? I don't think I can on my own," she asked, reeling from everything that had happened since she stepped foot in the country mansion.

Harry nodded his head and promptly left the room. Asha was alone for five minutes before he returned, brandishing an injection.

"Don't worry. It's harmless and it will put you to sleep in seconds," he explained, concentrating on preparing it for insertion.

"You have a lot of serious medicine at your disposal," Asha commented, looking slightly worried at the injection, but ultimately feeling she could trust it.

"We have a lot of serious medical needs in this business," he replied curtly, bending down and smoothing out the veins on her arm. Flashbacks to Jude and his pins made her stomach heave.

"Wait," she interrupted suddenly. "How are the others?" Her eyebrows turned up and her question faltered at the end.

Harry took a deep breath and let out a resounding sigh before sticking her with the needle and pushing its sleep-inducing contents into her. His lack of an answer sent her spiraling into a foggy black hole as the drugs knocked her out.

She dreamt of red, screaming and darkness.

After being in a fuzzy state of unconsciousness for what seemed like an eternity, Asha was suddenly awoken by water being bucketed onto her head. She shot up from where she lay with a gasp, but she was immediately yanked back into place by her restraints. She choked the water out of her lungs.

"Good morning!" Jude chimed as he turned the light on. "Well. I should say good evening. Whatever my idiot brother gave you, put you to sleep for twenty hours, which just wasted time really. I could have had a lot of fun with you, but I will make up for that, I'm sure. Besides, you look somewhat beautiful when you're asleep, so I let you. You're welcome," he smirked, bowing slightly to her. "But now, it's dinner time."

"Please don't paralyze me," she croaked.

"Oh, I'm not. We only do that in the beginning. It's more fun to see your reactions for the second dinner," he grinned which made Asha wonder what he was talking about. "But, I do need to put this on you. And if you even *try* to run. You will regret it with everything you have," he warned with his sapphire eyes as he held up a blindfold.

Asha nodded her head slowly, she'd comply, it was better than not being able to move.

Jude had her up and blinded within a minute. He led her carefully through corridor after corridor, winding and weaving her around the large house. She noted how he touched her around the waist, his fingertips pressing carefully against her. His footsteps echoed around them, but her bare feet hardly made a sound. She could smell the dampness of some areas of the house, she could tell they weren't used much. When they neared the dining room Asha was well aware of the smells of food and the smells of a group of people. It told her she was the last to dinner. Fashionably late.

She could sense everyone in the room but no-one spoke a word.

She was sat down in a chair and buckled up just like before, except now she could feel how the leather straps clinched against her skin with a burn. She let out a breath of pain as the last strap pinched her. With that, her blindfold was removed and quickly relocated to her mouth, serving as a gag.

Her friends sat before her in their varied states of existence. She didn't manage to look at all of them before her eyes started to well up.

Daisy's skin flourished in purple, red and black. Fingerprints dug around her throat like they'd been painted on in ink; her eye was bruised and bleeding, and her lips were swollen. Kit looked dazed and confused, with thin strips of blood caked down his neck from both of his ears. Finn had lost all the colour in his skin and he shook like a leaf in a gust of wind. Max had deep cuts down both his arms, along with smaller ones scattered all around his dark skin, opening him in shades of pink. The little girls somehow looked okay, apart from the fact that Sunny looked like her life battery had been removed. Asha held back her oncoming cries, trying to remain calm, but where was...?

"Thomas, where's your lady?" Jude questioned the big man with the hand tattoos.

"She couldn't hack it, sir," he said with a grunt to clear his throat.

"Dinner?"

"No, sir. She didn't make it past the night. My bad," Thomas shrugged. "Already prepped her in the basement."

He then pulled out something long and red before gently laying it in the seat where Piper should have been sitting. It was a lock of her hair, her beautiful wavy fire-hair.

No.

"Well, it's your loss, isn't it? Had too much fun too soon, hmm?" He asked the man and he nodded firmly. "So, one down. A little sooner than expected."

Asha looked at Max who was pulling so hard on his restraints with fury in his eyes. A yell burst through his nostrils and in his next movement, one of the bands around him broke. His Samaritan was fast to put an end to his outburst, because almost as soon as it started, he stuck Max with a needle and his eyes closed.

The whole room began to blur in front of Asha as grief took hold. Piper was gone. Her death was only the start. This wasn't a joke, this was real. They were going to die, no-one was safe.

A ringing sounded in her ear, like she'd just been punched and her hearing was off balance. But no-one had touched her. She couldn't focus on anything. The only thing she could feel were the hot tears tracking her face.

After a moment, she could hear whelping and it took her a second to realise it was coming from her.

"What an awkward start to dinner. My apologies," Jude spoke with somewhat remorse as he took his seat at the head of the table.

Varying levels of crying, shouting and struggle came from around the table as each of the group settled the loss of their angelic nurse, their companion, their friend, their mother.

She was the one who was least deserving to die at the hands of monsters. Her pure soul and her calming energy kept a blanket over the group. Asha felt like it had been ripped away along with her. She felt unsafe. She'd already gone through losing her real mother, now to lose her surrogate. She didn't know how much more she could take.

She looked over to Kit with blurred eyes, he stared back, hazel eyes wide and needy. Asha hadn't seen him look so vulnerable and desperate in her life. His eyebrows were turned up and he was mouthing something under his gag.

It took her a moment, but when she realised what he was saying, she cried out.

He was saying good-bye.

Chapter Thirty-Two

The rest of dinner went by, but Asha didn't manage to retain its memory. She could only remember being carried back to her room because her legs refused to work properly. Jude took it upon himself to make her comfortable, which only added to the confusion and upset that she was feeling.

Once she was in bed and tied back up, she fell asleep surprisingly quickly. It was deep and she felt a little lost in it. She didn't dream.

When she woke up, he was there, waiting. She wasn't sure how long he'd been sat there, but the light coming from behind him told her it was morning and that she'd survived another night in the hands of the Samaritans.

"Do you remember yesterday when I said I'd make up for lost time?" Jude asked her, his voice starting her day off bitterly.

"*I remember,*" she whispered, catching her breath from her sleep.

"Good. You're a good girl," he smirked, pulling out his multi-coloured pinwheel.

She shuddered at his words. "You don't get to call me that."

"I get to do whatever I want with you. Time to play."

Dread flooded her and the memories of the last run-in she had with his special game came back with a vengeance. Her heart started to stutter, knowing what was going to happen. He moved it to her fingers and waited until she weakly spun the wheel. She closed her eyes and let out a deep breath.

"A green one!" He announced.

Green meant it was going in just above her knee cap. It was more painful than going in the arm because sometimes when he did it, it scraped the bone.

His fingers pressed firmly on her leg and she stayed deathly still, knowing that if she didn't, she'd pay for it. He was quick to shove the needle through her skin and she winced, keeping her scream in. He'd managed to make it not so bad, which she was thankful for. But he didn't seem satisfied with how much pain she was in. It didn't fuel him enough.

"Again," he ordered, holding the pinwheel in her reach.

She complied and lay there waiting for him to make his selection. When he stopped it, his face lit up and a flash of anticipation graced his face. Asha looked to his fingers and to what colour he had chosen. It was a black headed pin. She hurriedly scanned the rest of the pinwheel, there weren't any more of them, there was only one, and he was holding it.

"Unluckily for you, this one's my favourite. It's a treat and I get a little more excited because it's rare. I need to turn you on your stomach," he explained, setting down the pinwheel.

"What does the black one mean? Where are you putting it?" Asha frantically asked, shuffling away from his strong hands as they started to untie her.

"You'll find out soon enough. Why ruin the surprise?" Jude replied, his voice like caramel, sickly and suffocating.

Panic built like a rocket in her. As soon as her hand was free of her restraint, she instinctively swung it at the blue-eyed man.

Her fist connected with his chin with a pop and he threw his head back, but he was silent. Asha stilled and stared at Jude who seemed to be containing his rage. She breathed heavily, her brows turned up.

"You touch me again, little girl, and your boyfriend will die. That I can promise you," he whispered, soothing his face with his hand before glaring down at her.

Finn. She slumped back into the bed, defeated.

"I'm sorry, I'm sorry," Asha apologized, hating every moment of it. She'd become a joke.

"Now. I'm going to untie you and tie you back up, on your front. Do you understand me?" He spoke with increasing power.

"Yes!" Asha cried, feeling completely useless.

He moved her roughly, twisting her until she was face down on the bed. He then tied her back up just like he said, and pulled up her shirt, baring her back to him. Her skin broke out in goosebumps as the slight draught in the room tickled her. He walked his fingertips from the small of her back up to the base of her neck. He touched her so feather-light that her insides squirmed. His forefinger prodded a space right between her shoulder blades; even that felt wrong.

Asha turned her head so that she could look up at him, he was frowning, concentrating. She wondered what could be so special about the black pin, why it was so rare.

"You're going to need to be extremely still for this, Asha. If it moves more than a millimetre, you won't be able to walk again."

She began to shake violently, though she tried desperately to keep her body as stable as possible. *Come on, come on, be still.*

He placed a palm right on her spine, pushing down on her, causing her to gasp for breath as the air was shoved from her abruptly. Then, she felt the needle as he toyed with where he was going to place it in her. Prick, prick, prick. Every second that went by just escalated the anticipation in her.

Without warning, the pin was stuck directly into the centre point of her spine. Pure white pain blinded her and she couldn't breathe let alone scream. She had never felt anything like it. She thought she was floating, whistling away in the breeze. She couldn't see a thing. The pressure built and built from the very spot where he poked her, sending her head into fuzz and her heart into overdrive. She didn't think she was capable of feeling such pain, such shattering pain.

After a moment of suspended terror, her body finally let her scream. And she *screamed.* The red hotness surrounding the pin grew and grew. Her limbs began to spasm from the intrusion, and she tried with all her will to be still. She shoved her face into the bed and bit down on the pillow, crying out, begging for it to be over. Her whole body felt tight, so tight she wasn't sure if she would be able to relax it ever again. It ached and pulsed and pushed her further and further from sanity.

Jude then pulled the pin from her, and all at once the pain stopped and it threw Asha into desperate breaths and inconceivable exhaustion. The pain was gone as suddenly as it had come; she was left to lay in its wake. She hadn't let a tear go while it was in her, but the removal of it came with a huge release, causing her eyes to bucket, soaking the sheets beneath her.

"Sweet melody," Jude sighed happily, standing himself up from the bed and going to the door.

He turned the handle and stepped out into the corridor, letting Asha cry out loud from the assault. Through her yelps she could hear Jude talking.

"I'm going to get the shower ready for her," he muttered.

Shower?

"What? No, Jude, no." Harry's voice came into earshot, worried.

"Don't question me. You know better than to do that," he ordered, shutting the door so that Asha could now only hear muffles of their voices.

A shower? Asha could hardly believe her ears. In fact, she didn't believe them. Her mind was in such disarray, disjointed from the pain, that she could have heard anything. Even so, her thoughts began to conjure up the feeling of being in a hot shower and her mouth actually turned up into a small smile. The door suddenly flew open and it made Asha jump.

She glanced up to see Harry's dishevelled looking face. His beard seemed to be wirier than before, his eyes were bloodshot and his hands were shaking.

"Hey," he said quietly.

"Do you have anything to end the pain? Please, I don't think I can take that black one again," Asha whined.

"He'd notice if you didn't scream," Harry shook his head, a dark frown on his face.

"*Harry*," Asha whimpered. "You can stop all of this. You have everything you need to stop him. You have to be brave, please! Look at what he's doing! I'm existing just to be scared of him. Imagine what my friends are going through. The little girls! You're letting them get hurt! I can't take it anymore, Harry! Stand up to him, stand now!" She cried now, shivering.

She had to show him that she was breaking, that he was the only one who could stop her suffering, she had to show him that she was close to losing it.

He ignored her pleas and rolled her shirt back down.

"Harry!" She yelled.

"Shh! Stop, just stop!" He hushed her with a stern look.

She knew he didn't want to be doing this, but he was sick, his mind twisted by the overpowering hands of his brother and for that she could understand his actions. Although, at the same time she knew that he was capable of standing up to Jude to do the right thing, and that very fact made her angry to look at him, the weak man.

"Why don't you want me to have a shower?" She asked quietly now, intently staring at him for his reply.

He looked down for a second of what seemed like panic, before lifting his eyes to her, he looked different. He was rehearsing something in his mind. He was going to lie to her.

"I just know how the shower gets temperamental. Boiling hot to icy cold," he shrugged unconvincingly.

Asha furrowed her eyebrows. "It's not going to be a repeat of Hitler's sick trick, is it?"

"What? No," he replied, shocked. "You'll be fine. Just be careful with the controls is all," he smiled forcefully.

So, she *was* getting a shower. One part of her wanted to jump for joy, she hadn't felt water falling on her skin for a long time, she hadn't washed properly for what seemed like forever. But there was another thought, a direr one. Her suspicion of why she was allowed to have such a luxury weighed heavily on her. Either way, she had no choice but to do what Jude wanted.

Three of the Samaritans came in to join Harry and they systematically untied her and then carried her through the house. They stopped at a glass door towards the end of the upstairs hallway. Asha could already see the steam billowing from inside. The men set her down steadily, making sure she could stand by herself. Her broken toe moaned, but she managed to keep her weight off it.

Harry handed her a large pink towel, and she took it, rubbing it between her fingers, revelling its softness.

"Don't bother trying to escape. Just enjoy what you're being given," Harry ordered, but his orders felt less prominent than his brother's.

"Why am I allowed to do this?" Asha asked, looking to any of them for an answer.

"Boss says you have ten minutes," the one named Ajax stated, and with that he opened the door and roughly pushed her in.

Asha stumbled into the fog of steam and looked back to her captors just as the door was slammed shut, and locked. The heat of the room wrapped around her, swirling at her feet. It was comforting and she let out a deep breath.

The room was small, fitting only a shower and a sink. It was tiled from ceiling to floor and a wall plant hung near the window.

It was dead, but it still made the place feel a pinch homely. The window hadn't been boarded up in there, the sun lit the whole place up, bringing a real smile to Asha's worn face. She walked the short distance to the glass and wiped away the condensation, revealing the outside world.

Just looking out made her feel a deep longing. Freedom was so close; she had her hand on it. Glancing down, she noted how the jump from the window wouldn't hurt her too badly. There were thick bushes lining the house, somewhere she could land. She gripped the towel in her hand and a sudden and unstoppable thought catapulted into her mind. Hurriedly, she wrapped the fluffy towel around her right hand and pressed her other hand against the window. She drew back her delicately armoured fist and sent it full throttle to the glass.

But she stopped before she crashed through it.

She stood frozen, contemplating and compiling her contradicting thoughts. The chance to escape was *right there* She could bust through the window and jump to freedom within seconds, she could be on the boat in a few hours. She had a chance to get to Harbour and save the world. But if she did that, she'd be leaving her friends to die. As soon as Jude knew she'd escaped, he'd have them all killed just to spite her. There wouldn't be time to bring back-up, he would slit their throats and shove them in the freezers until they became useful to him once again.

If she left, she'd have their blood on her hands; if she left, she would be saying goodbye to the only thing close to family she had left.

A sudden noise from behind her startled her. She spun on her heel and saw Harry stalking his way towards her, worry on his brow.

"Don't!" He warned, hand outstretched. "I can't help your friends if you do that."

"What do you mean?" Asha questioned, unravelling the towel from her closed fist.

"You have seven minutes left. Take this. Just, trust me, it'll help you," he held out a large white pill and looked to her with such honesty that she took it from him without question. "Things will change, before it's too late," he finished and quickly left the room, trapping her in with the steam and the pill clutched in her palm.

Seven minutes. She snapped to it, running to the sink, cupping her hand and filling it with water. She then popped the pill in her mouth and drank it down with the cold water. She wasn't sure what it contained, but she had a feeling that Harry was beginning to see sense. He looked like he wanted to help her, so she trusted him.

She quickly undressed and jumped into the already running shower. She winced at the temperature, it was scalding hot, but after a moment she got used to it. The feeling of water showering her was borderline euphoric. Her eyes rolled to the back of her head and she closed her lids, letting the water completely engulf her. She hadn't been able to wash properly for six months so when she reached for the soap, she didn't stop washing until it went down to a small nub.

Next came the shampoo. Her thick, dark hair was scrubbed and clean within minutes, it licked at her neck with its dampness. She inhaled the sweet scents of the shower, enjoying every moment of the experience. She found herself silently thanking Jude for making up for the brutal black pin.

She stood unmoving, eyes closed for a few minutes, swaying in a state of absolute ease; water cascading down her body. But sure enough, time was up, and with it came a hard knocking on the door, jolting the freckled girl out of her trance.

She frowned lightly, but her mood stayed inflated from the shower and how clean she felt. Sighing happily, she opened up the door of the cubicle. She stepped out into the now cold feeling air and onto the shaggy mat.

In the movement, her head suddenly felt full of pressure and black spots started to invade her vision. She moaned and stumbled, hands out in front of her.

The last thing she remembered was hoping that she didn't hit her head when she fell to the tiled floor.

Chapter Thirty-Three

The sleep in Asha's eyes glued her eyelids together which made it difficult to fully open them. She blinked harshly a few times before finally, light came streaming into them. Her head felt fuzzy and her temples pounded with a dull headache. She looked around the room, nothing had changed and it felt almost as if she'd just closed her eyes for a few minutes.

However, the memories of the black pin and the shower suddenly came flooding back to her, making her painfully aware of what had happened before she blacked out. She had ended up in bed though, and looking down, she realised she'd been put into a set of rose-gold, satin pyjamas.

Her mind buzzed with confusion; it was then that she was aware of an intense aching that seemed to erupt from her abdomen, consuming her body all at once. She pulled against her constraints as she tried to move herself into a comfortable position to ease the aching but it was no use; instead she squirmed in pain, making no sound.

How can I ache so much without having moved?

A thought crossed her mind, it must have been the repercussions of the black pin being jabbed into her spine. It would explain the engulfing ache. Even though she had figured out why she was in pain, she still felt it, and it was horrid. As she wriggled around on the bed, pulling at the handcuffs, the door began to open.

She froze and looked up to the doorway, her heart stunned. *Please don't be Jude.* She begged to a higher power. A seemingly endless second passed by before Harry stepped through the door. His eyes were wide as he looked at her; almost like he wasn't expecting to see her awake. Immediately though, she felt at ease and her body collapsed into the bed, her wrists hanging loose against the handcuffs.

He hurriedly closed the door behind him and locked it with the brass locker. She then watched him as he walked his way over quickly to her. When he came closer to her, she noticed that one of his eyes was completely swollen shut and a painful, purple flower had blossomed over it.

"What happened to *you*?" She croaked.

"You're awake," he spoke in a hushed voice, so he couldn't be heard.

She looked to him and furrowed her eyebrows; he was avoiding the question. "Yes," she could feel a lump in her throat which she tried to cough away, "and whatever you gave me for the pain, didn't work. I feel like I'm having the worst cramps," she swallowed hard trying to coat her throat with liquid and attempted to speak again. "How long," she coughed again. "How long was I out?" She asked curiously.

"Oh. Sorry... it should have worked. Um," he hesitated for a moment, which slightly worried her. "You've been asleep for about an hour," he said under his breath as he shrugged.

"I feel like I've been asleep for days," she answered. She couldn't imagine passing out from the shower would keep her out cold for more than an hour, but her body told her something different. Plus, she realised then that her hair was completely bone-dry.

Harry swallowed thickly and cleared his throat before sitting himself down next to her on the bed. The mattress jumped a little as he sat, and she adjusted herself so she was slightly propped up on her elbows. "Well," he began. "That's usually how I feel after a nap; disorientated," he said as he reached for a bottle of water before holding it up to her dry lips.

Asha instantly forgot about what they were talking about. All she could think of was the pure, refreshing feel of the cold water racing down her throat and she sucked down as much as she could. She couldn't remember ever being this thirsty. Once she'd had her fill and her stomach couldn't hold anymore, he tilted the bottle downwards and pulled it away. He glanced down at her, his eyes brimming with sympathy.

His grass-green eyes looked over her wrists which had begun to turn raw from the constant battering of the handcuffs. She caught a glimpse of horror in his eyes and it almost made her feel happy. Maybe the more brutality he saw, the more courage he would gain to finally put a stop to all of this. It was barbaric and he was the only one who could change anything about it.

Asha's mind hurtfully jumped to thoughts of the group and she almost sprung off the bed with urgency. "The others," she asked quickly but quietly. "Are they?"

He nodded his head reassuringly and closed his eyes for a moment. "They're fine,"

"No-one else is gone?" Asha asked, her heart heavy.

"No. I told you, I'm trying to help them," he replied curtly.

She felt herself relax a little more knowing that her friends were alive, for now.

"So, what happened to your eye?" Asha asked again.

"I ran into a door," Harry answered, sarcasm ringing high.

"Ha. Ha," she groaned, rolling her eyes.

"Why even ask?"

"*He* did that... why?"

"He never needs a reason. You've met him, right?" He sighed sadly, looking to his watch, frowning.

"Are you late for something?" Asha enquired.

"*We* are," he said before starting to untie her. "Dinner time."

*

After she was partially tied into her chair, Harry lifted her blindfold, but didn't put it into her mouth like before. This time, he let her have her mouth free, and her arms. She was sat at the head of the table, opposite Jude who gestured to her with a glass of wine before taking a sip. Unease spilled from her heart. Why was she allowed to speak at dinner? Why weren't her arms tied down? Why was she getting all the special treatment?

She studied her friends who surrounded the table like silent, unmoving zombies. They were much the same as the night before, except they all seemed a little greyer and bruised. The life from their eyes had vanished, along with any motivation to even look up.

But someone was missing.

Harry had said that they were late for dinner, so why was Finn's seat empty? Fright gripped her throat with vigour.

"Where is he?" She demanded, her shaking voice calling her friends to full attention.

"Who?" Jude asked, a bright smile on his face.

"*No...*" Asha breathed, her eyebrows pinching together. "You said you wouldn't hurt him if I didn't touch you again!" She yelled now, feeling panicked that Finn wasn't where she could see him.

"I did say that, didn't I?" Jude asked nonchalantly, sipping down some more wine.

Asha sucked in a quick, hurt breath and started to slam her palms on the table over and over again. All the while, she screamed. Cutlery and glasses wobbled and clinked with her forceful hits, sending one drink to the floor. It smashed loudly on the hard wood, and the sound and shock of it brought Asha back to Earth. Breathing heavily, she brought her outburst to a slow stop.

She was angry, so angry that one person had so much control. She was fuming over the way her friends were being laid out as bait in front of her. This was all Jude's game. It was his game to mess with her, make her life as much of a hell as possible. She stood in the way of his complete dominance over the rest of the human race. He wanted to punish her, for his sick pleasure.

Asha was tired of playing.

"Where is he? Answer me, or I'll break out of here and slit your throat right where you sit!" She screamed, her throat coarse.

"Oh, *good girl*. I love it when you talk like that. Don't you love it boys?" He asked the room, keeping his icy stare on the shaking, dark-haired girl.

The Samaritans nodded their heads in unison. Asha noticed that Finn's allocated torturer wasn't present. Was he in the basement preparing him?

"Just tell me where he is," she ordered lowly.

"He's come down with something and I didn't want him infecting everyone at dinner. Simple as that," Jude answered surprisingly.

"*He's still alive*?" Asha whispered, suddenly aware of how much her heart was aching at the thought of him being gone.

"Yes, well, we don't make a habit of killing people too soon."

".... But you don't have a problem torturing them... Torturing children!" She screamed at him, her fists balling up, her fingernails cutting into her.

"How was your shower?" He asked cockily, raising his eyebrow.

Everyone around the table looked at her with a stare that told her she was the only one to be clean. She suddenly felt immeasurably guilty for having indulged in such a treat. She glanced up at the two little girls, dirt, sweat and blood clung to their skin like paint.

Her breathing picked up and she felt her eyes begin to sting. Kit stared at her with betrayal ringing loudly. She hated feeling in the wrong. She was a good person really; she didn't want others to suffer when she sat pretty.

Jude was pushing her again. She grew angry as the boring stares of her friends ripped her apart.

Payback time.

"Why did you punch your brother?" She asked calmly, looking to him with hooded eyes.

"Excuse me?" Jude asked, his face unamused.

"Well, if we're asking questions... What did he do? Must have been *bad.* Family don't hurt family," Asha spat, a twinkle in her eye.

"I *would* tell you. But it's far more fun knowing that you haven't a clue why," he smiled, his gaze dragging down her body. "How do your pyjamas feel? I picked them out specially for you."

"Oh these?" She questioned sarcastically, her finger pointing to her chest. "*Lovely.* Though I feel like they need more colour," she grinned before grabbing the wine glass in front of her and splashing it down herself, splattering the pink with deep red.

Jude's jaw clenched as he narrowed his eyes at her. "*Bad girl,*" he muttered, drinking down the rest of his wine.

He suddenly stood up and threw the glass towards the wall, it shattered into a hundred pieces, stunning the whole room for a moment. His fist then connected with the table with such force that the wood jumped. He was furious, unhinged.

Asha's blood froze in her veins. She'd pushed him too far, and she knew that she would have to pay for it. Some part of her was glad that she was going to be punished. She deserved to feel something other than special to her captor. The group needed to see that she was just like them, that she was suffering too.

He sniffed and wiped his nose with the back of his hand as a devilish grin grew across his darkened face. His fingers then crawled slowly along the table until they reached a knife, one far too sharp for cutting food.

He picked it up swiftly and launched it towards Asha.

She squeezed her eyes shut and she swore she could hear it whistling as it cut through the air. She braced herself for the inevitable, but she wasn't hit. Instead, the sound of splintering wood came, and as she opened her eyes, she saw that the knife had stuck itself 2 inches from her on the table.

Panicked muffled yells subsided from her friends. She just sat there breathing heavily, staring at the knife, thinking about taking it. But Jude was by her side in an instant with a warning in his stare.

She wriggled in her seat, trying to inch away from him. Kit shoved hard against his restraints, shouts gurgling from behind his gag, his eyes bulging wide. Asha gave him a quick look of despair before she had to look at Jude who reached for the knife once again, yanking it free from the broken wood.

"*Not in front of them...*" Asha breathed quickly, suddenly aware that he might slaughter right there and then; her friends shouldn't have to see that.

"Oh, please. I don't want to *kill* you," Jude smirked, toying with the knife near her throat as he leant over her, his immensity was dizzying. "Think of it like this. You're the anticipation of a finger on the trigger. A constant buzz. The heat before the kiss. I wouldn't want to snuff you out. But it doesn't mean I can't hurt you... Mark you as my own."

All of a sudden, his strong palm pushed her harshly down onto the table. Her hands jutted out to stop her face from smacking onto the hard wood and she gripped tightly onto the edge of the table. She clenched her teeth and breathed rapidly, spit flying. Half of her felt fear for what he was going to do to her.

The other half dared him to touch her.

He clicked his finger and someone put their hand on the back of her head, holding her face to the table. From the sounds of her friends yelping and whining, she knew that something painful was about to be inflicted on her. She caught a glimpse of metal, casting light from the ceiling.

She stayed still as Jude's fingers gently moved her hair away from the back of her neck. She stayed still when he started to cut her. She stayed still when blood rolled down her neck in beads of darkness, dropping to the table. She stayed still, because now she had everything she needed to kill him.

Once he was finished, Jude bent down to her ear, his hot breath made her shiver.

"It's some of my best work yet. I even got a perfect curve to 'J'."

Chapter Thirty-Four

Asha went willingly back to her room after dinner. She didn't utter a word, her mind was working in overdrive, noticing every detail of the route she walked back. They forgot to blindfold her this time, perhaps it was from the commotion at the dinner table. Either way, Asha used it to her advantage, picking out any possible escape route. Looking for anything she could use as a weapon somehow. She disappeared into herself. The stinging from the back of her neck reminding her every second that the only way she would truly feel happy, was if she killed Jude, in the worst way possible.

As they were walking down one of the many crooked hallways, Asha noticed one of the Samaritans slinking out of a room. She peered in through the open door to what lay behind and instantly her stomach knotted. There, lining the walls, were cages upon cages of rats. The smell of sawdust hit her and just before the door was shut quickly, she caught wind of their scurrying, nibbling sounds.

The whole thing was an act; a fatal play designed to capture the audience, literally.

Once back in her room, she lay down on the bed and flopped her limbs so that Harry had an easier job of shackling her to the posts. He looked at her, concerned, but eventually left her to sleep. And she slept, for a long time, dreaming of glistening metal, iron blood and wide smiles.

When she woke up, she was alone, which was a rarity since Jude seemed to make a habit of watching her sleep.

This morning however, he was nowhere to be seen. Asha let out a small yawn and her stomach growled at her. She frowned and looked towards the door.

"Room service!" She yelled, a huge smirk on her face.

When no-one answered her, she sighed and geared herself up.

"I SAID, ROOM SERVICE!" She screamed murder.

Not a second later, the door opened and in came Harry with a look of pleading on his face. He held his hands up and waved her to be quiet.

"What the hell are you playing at?" He asked, his voice hushed.

"Did the King not manage to wake up to be by my side today?" She asked cheerily, sending Harry's expression into a state of confusion.

"What?" He breathed. "No, he's busy with stuff."

"Did send you as his replacement? Did you not want to watch me sleep? I've grown used to it now, I sort of like it. It makes me feel *special*," she smiled, not feeling connected to herself.

"What's gotten into you?" He asked, his eyebrows pinched together.

"Oh, I don't know. It could be the fact that one of my friends is dead... or it could be the fact that the boy that I love is being hidden from me... or it could be the pins that have been creating little hells in my body... or it could be the fact that I now have a wonderful 'J' crusting with blood at the back of my neck... or... do you really need me to fucking carry on?" She growled, narrowing her eyes at the lanky, green-eyed boy.

"No."

"When is it that you're going to help us? Because, around about now would be ideal," she spat.

"I-I don't think I can," he stuttered, rubbing his arms with his now shaking palms.

"*Harry,*" Asha muttered accusingly. "You spineless little..."she paused, feeling tears spring at her eyes, her reality truly setting in. "You said if I escaped you wouldn't be able to help my friends. Well, I didn't leave, I'm right here. So, save us. Stick to your fucking word!" She cried.

"I'm sorry," he said lowly before quickly leaving the room, shutting the door loudly behind him.

Asha stared up to the stars. Tears pooled in her eyes before they spilled slowly down to her ears, making the pillow wet. He was their last hope, and he was a coward. Served her right for putting her faith in a scared little boy who couldn't stand up to his older brother.

She stayed in a state of suspended sadness for what felt like an eternity. Not feeling the energy to even move a finger, or cry. Time went by in a strange way in the Samaritans' house. Night turned into day without a warning, hours seemed to last weeks, sleep came when it wanted. Asha had lost track of how many nights she'd spent there, but she rationally estimated it to be three nights, no matter how impossible that felt.

As the sky outside turned orangey pink, its light seeped through to her. Asha wondered whether she would ever get the chance to enjoy the warmth of it on her skin ever again. The harsh truth of what lay ahead of her in life knocked her.

If she couldn't get out, she was looking at her life ending in less than two weeks. And what kind of life would she lead? Certainly not one of fullness. It would be spent in pain, in confinement and in grief.

She couldn't end her life happily.

"*Mamá*," Asha started, quietly. "I don't know if you're there, but I hope you are," she felt a little silly, speaking in the empty room, but an odd sense of comfort fell over her from it. "I think it's time. *Lo Siento, Mamá*. I tried, I tried really hard to stay alive. But I think I might actually die soon. And I'm not sure if knowing it makes me feel any better. You didn't know you were going to die. Or maybe you did, in the last few seconds, I bet you were really scared!" She cried out loud, tears flooding, wishing she still had her ring.

"I'm scared now too. I thought I could make it, *Mamá*. I thought I was brave and strong. But I can't get out. Kit's here too, somewhere. He misses you. I guess we'll die together. There's something poetic about that, huh?" She took in rapid breaths. "I think I fell in love, *Mamá*. Better late than never, right? I think you'd like him; you'd be pinching his cheeks and forcing feeding him your special *pico de gallo* with tortillas," she paused, composing her cries, her head felt hot.

"...I'm going to die as someone who isn't me. I'm not the woman you raised. I've done so many horrible things. I've killed people, I've liked killing people. I'm a monster, *Mamá*, a real-life monster. And I'm sorry for that. I hope that when I join you, you can forgive me for everything that I've done to get here."

"I hope you're proud of me. I know that even if you weren't you'd still tell me you were. You were always a good mum like that. I miss you, *Mamá*. It's not long now. I'll see you again soon, and I'm going to give you and Ella and *Papa* the biggest hug ever. We can be a family again." The hazel-eyed girl whimpered, shaking on the bed until she fell back into a rough and winding sleep.

Chapter Thirty-Five

Asha was tossing and turning from her disjointed nap when the sound of a door being kicked in catapulted her into coursing consciousness. Her eyes struggled to adjust to the dim light in the room but as she gasped for breath, she became fully aware of the scene that was playing out in front of her.

Jude was dragging Max into the room by the scruff of his jacket, the burly man struggled against him, but it was to no use. Jude was strong, and Max was most likely highly medicated with some concoction or another.

Right behind him came Harry who was pulling a defeated looking Kit through the door. He had to work hard to move him along, Harry wasn't the most capable of people to carry weight. Both of her companions had gags in their mouths and blood covered them in various speckles and colours. They both looked to her with glassy, pained eyes; her heart jumped.

"What! What's going on?!" Asha demanded, her voice unnaturally high.

The brothers propped Max and Kit up on their knees facing her. Suddenly, Jude whipped out a pistol from his jacket, cocked it and held it against Max's head.

"NO!" Asha screamed, adrenaline rushing out of her every pore.

She pulled hard against her restraints, trying to put a stop to what was happening, but she couldn't get out. She screamed out in frustration.

"Choose!" Jude shouted, his eyes looked frantic, his hair was jutting up in a mess. "Max or Kit! Choose one to die right now or I'll just kill both!" He ordered.

How could he ask her to make such a decision? She looked wide-eyed to both of them, seeing their pleas written in their pupils. Pleas for their life, or so she thought.

Harry yanked the gags from their mouths.

"Just kill me," Kit begged, Asha hadn't heard him speak for so long, she didn't realize how much she missed hearing his voice, his stupid, amazing voice.

"What?" Asha asked, exasperated, tears pooling.

"Just do it, get it over with. When you get out of here, Max will take you to where you need to go. Just-"

"Shut up, Bell! Asha, do what you want. But I've lived my life. You know the direction we're headed. You're gonna get out of here, I know you will. You take Kit with you," Max bellowed, his stare hardened.

"Tick tock, tick tock," Jude chimed, scooping his hair back with one hand while the other kept the gun prodding at Max's temple.

Was this another one of Jude's sick games, or was he serious? There was no way of telling. But what Asha did know, was that something didn't seem right with the blue-eyed devil. He was less composed than usual. He seemed crazed, and that made him unpredictable. It made him unstoppable.

If he *was* telling the truth, it meant she had an earth-shattering decision to make and she'd barely woken up.

If she chose Kit, she would lose the only thing she had left of her family, she would lose her best friend, the last person who knew who she really was. If she chose Max, she would have to say goodbye to the man who gave her hope, she would never reach Harbour, she didn't know the way, or the radio channel; she would never put an end to Nox.

Two sides of her mind battled with each other, ripping her rib cage in half, laying her guts to the floor and tearing her heart in two. She could be selfish and save the boy who she'd grown up with, or she could be selfless and give herself to the world through Max's hands.

Her lungs pulsed like a pneumatic drill, sending her breaths hard and fast in front of her. Time was running out, Jude was practically jigging on the spot, desperate to pull the trigger. If she didn't give him an answer within the next few seconds, he would grow tired of the game and just kill both of them regardless of what her final decision might have been.

She looked from Max, to Kit, and back again. A cry of anger, sadness and overwhelming pressure escaped her lips in a wrangled mess. She couldn't bear the weight of it all, she wanted to die in their place, she didn't want to choose.

"Time's up, Asha. Choose, now!" Jude shouted so hard his spit sprinkled out in front of him. "NOW!"

"Kit! I choose Kit!"

She didn't even realise she'd made that decision. But deep down she knew it was the one that made the most sense. It didn't matter how right it was though, because he was *everything* to her.

He had been right there by her side from the very first day he moved next-door when they were four, when he got his head stuck in the gap between the fence with a bright grin. She felt like she'd spent her whole life with him. They were partners in so many senses, even the end of the world wasn't enough to split them.

Until now.

"Interesting choice," Jude grinned before stepping to the back of her best friend, positioning the gun.

"*I'm sorry, I'm sorry, I'm sorry*! *I had to!*" Asha blabbered, her tears fogging the last sight of Kit being alive. Her heart broke and broke and broke, crumbling to dust within her heaving chest.

"It's okay. I would have done the same. I love you, Broccoli Head," Kit soothed, looking at her with a forgiving smile, which then turned to a determined frown. He was preparing for the final sentence of his story.

Asha cried and cried, screaming all the while. She couldn't look. She squeezed her eyes shut as far as they could, until it hurt her. Her body shook like she was sat in the middle of the Antarctic with no clothes on. She willed for it to be over, so that she wouldn't have to see what she had done.

The shot rang like a cannon in the small room and the breath was sucked straight out of her body, leaving her gasping and wheezing.

Her eyes opened slowly, bracing themselves for what they were about to see, but when the fog of guilt dispersed from her vision, she was greeted by Kit's eyes; he was very much alive.

She was flooded with relief but then with fear as she shot a look at Max, checking if he was the unlucky recipient of the bullet instead.

But he was alive too.

A slow, rumbling chuckle started to sound in the room.

"You really are the most gullible girl in the whole world," Jude chimed, tossing the gun to the floor.

Asha spaced out, reeling from everything her mind and body had just been through, all for a joke. Her breaths struggled to come from her shuddering frame.

He was a master manipulator, and she couldn't work him out. Which left her vulnerable to him, just where he wanted her.

"Get him out," Jude ordered Harry as he pointed at a relieved looking Kit.

"W-what's going on?" Asha asked, her mouth felt like cotton wool and her thoughts danced in front of her eyes in a hurricane.

"That was just a little tease," he grinned a toothy grin at the girl before looking annoyed at Harry. "Hurry up!"

The lanky brother used all of his energy to haul Kit up to his feet and guide him out of the door. Asha gave him a small smile and he returned the favour with a wink. He was going to be okay. Once the room was empty - bar Asha, Jude and Max - the King of the Samaritans started to pace.

"This is the real deal. You *will* have to make a decision, Asha. One that will change everything for you," Jude said, walking around the bed.

"How can I ever trust you?" She asked, still catching her breath.

"Oh, you can trust me. Your life depends on it."

"Surprise me," she moaned, preparing herself for the next choice she'd have to make.

"I have a proposition that involves every one of you living," he stilled, crossing his arms across his broad chest.

Asha scoffed before looking at him with squinted eyes. "What are you talking about?"

"It's very simple. You can either choose to stay here with everyone and die with them within the next few weeks. Or you can agree to come with me and the rest of the Samaritans, as our personal trophy, while I let your friends go free."

"What? Why? Why would you do that?" Asha questioned, her words tumbling out uncontrollably. She was thrown by his proposal.

"Because I like you. You're something I want to keep. And if that means I lose a few bags of meat for my clients, so be it. I'd rather keep you somewhat happy and have you with me, than to not have you at all," he shrugged, like what he was talking about wasn't insane.

"Oh, and you're welcome, Max, to take what you need from her. Blood, hair, anything you like for your 'miracle' cure. But once I let you go, you won't find us again. We have many houses around England, and we make use of them on a clockwork schedule." Jude let the news set in for about a second before he let out a sigh. "I'll give you two some privacy to come to your decision. You have a minute," he said before heavy treading out of the door and closing it.

Asha knew what she had to do.

"There is no discussion," she stated quietly. "I'm staying with them and you're going."

"No way! We're going to find a way out of this together. We have two weeks to fight this. We can make it out. I'm not leaving you behind. And good luck convincing the others to leave you too. We won't go," Max argued, standing his ground.

"You don't know that we'll survive this! They have us guarded 24/7. If even one of us tried to get out, whether we failed or not, they'd kill us all instantly. They don't have remorse, Max, we're a game to them. And they are not gracious losers."

"Even if we left and took blood, hair and skin from you, it wouldn't be enough to test and make the cure from. We need *you*. We need all of you."

"But at least you'd have a *chance*," she pleaded. "Max, you have to agree with me. The likelihood of us getting out of here on our own is a million to one. This is our chance to get you out. You can save the girls! Take as much you need from me to try and make the cure. You can still save the world, Max."

He thought for a moment, his deep brow creasing. "But you'll be with them, with *him*. They will torture you for the rest of your life."

"I know," Asha sighed, a glimpse of her dim future darting across her mind. "But at least I would be living, knowing that you're all safe, and that there's a possibility that you made the cure. That's enough for me. What use am I to the world if I'm not alive?"

"We will come and find you. Jude said clockwork, right? We'd camp out, figure out the routine. Bust you out, bring you home."

"Waste of time, Max. You know how he plays. You need to let me go. Put all your effort into the cure. *Take the deal*."

"Time's up!" Jude shouted, pushing open the door and strutting in, a smirk on his face.

"Get the equipment ready for Max to take what he needs from me," Asha replied, low and sombre.

Max swallowed thickly, but didn't he interject. Asha sighed a silent sigh of relief. There was no point in putting up a fight against her. This was what she wanted. In an ideal world, she would kill Jude and run off alongside her friends to safety. But this wasn't a picture-perfect life, it was full of bone crunching twists and turns. She had to do what was right for the family she had created, and for the rest of humanity.

"I was secretly hoping you wou-" Jude began but he didn't finish.

Asha's controlled stare watched as his face dropped to nothing and his body suddenly crumpled from the feet up, sending him to the floor like a sack of potatoes. The freckled girl looked to Max who had already started to try and free himself from his handcuffs.

Not a second later, Harry burst through the door.

Asha and Max froze for a moment, thinking perhaps Harry would think they had something to do with it. But when he looked down at his unmoving brother, a smile lit up his face and immediately Asha knew what had happened.

"What changed your mind?" She asked, a bright grin on her face.

He glanced at her with sorrow filled eyes and breathed. "Your mother."

Chapter Thirty-Six

Harry didn't waste any time in unlocking all of the restraints that held Max and Asha in the Samaritans' captivity. She could hardly believe that her dreams were coming true. They were going to get out, and there was nothing that could stop them now.

Once free of her chains, Asha jumped up and kicked Jude's lifeless body hard in the side before running to her stuff which had been thrown on a chair in the corner of the room. She shrugged her coat over her stained satin pyjamas. Her necklace and ring sat in the very centre of the chair. Her fingers snatched the homemade beauty up and quickly secured it around her neck once again – her heart felt somewhat more intact. She then fished out her knives and slung her backpack over her shoulders before hurrying out of the room, following Harry.

The first room he brought them to contained Kit, who was already geared up and ready to go. He must have been freed first. His Samaritan was lying on the floor, and his eyes were open. That's when Asha realised that he wasn't dead. His eyes were moving, and he looked terrified.

"They're alive," she said out loud as Kit took her into a deep hug. She hugged him back with force, but her stare remained on the man on the floor.

"Paralyzed. It'll last only half an hour, so we need to be quick," Harry explained, shooing everyone out of the room and closing the door before locking it with his clinking set of keys.

"Let's get the fuck out of here," Kit growled, running alongside Harry as he navigated the growing group behind him.

"Looks like we're all going to make it to Harbour," Max said to Asha as they ran.

"Don't jinx it," she replied, keeping her focus on treading the wooden corridors of their personal hell.

The next room they came to had a man lying on the floor just outside the door; it was Daisy's Samaritan. Asha pushed past Harry and kicked down the door herself. The blonde-haired girl was lying in bed, wrists red raw from the handcuffs that bound her to it. Her face was badly bruised and she somehow looked even skinnier than when she went in. Her grey, glistening eyes lifted to the noise, and as soon as she saw them, her face burst out into a dopey smile.

"Thank fuck!" She cried out joyfully, Asha had never seen her so happy before, she also noticed that she had a tooth missing.

"Harry, hurry up," Asha demanded, pointing to her friend's shackles.

Harry jumped into action and unclasped Daisy from the bed. Max and Kit helped her to stand, she was extremely weak and she had countless bruises and scrapes covering her skin from head to toe. She looked like she'd been beaten half to death, four times over. Daisy quickly shook her hair in front of her face and wrapped her bony fingers around her stick arms.

"I made a deal with them," she croaked. "That they could do whatever they were gonna do to the girls, to me instead."

Asha stalked her way to the shivering girl and wrapped her arms around her, feeling Daisy crumble as soon as the embrace took.

The dark-haired girl held the fallen angel in her arms for a few moments before tearing herself away. She moved Daisy's hair away with her fingertips and planted a kiss on her jutting cheek.

"Thank you," she murmured to her, and Daisy responded by looking at her with glistening, ocean eyes. She didn't have to say anything at all.

It was Sunny and Boe's room that they went to next. When they opened the door, they were met with the smell of urine. The group immediately freed them from the chairs they were tied to and Max carried Boe who was crying inconsolably. Asha knelt by Sunny who looked like she'd been thrown around like a toy. Daisy held Sunny tightly by her side.

"Did they...?" Asha questioned the mouse-like girl nervously.

"...They didn't touch *her*," she simply said and closed her eyes, taking in a deep breath.

Asha shot up and turned to Harry who was standing in the doorway, his stare was to the floor, looking guilty. She could feel an immense and overwhelming anger building right from her core. But there was someone else they needed to get before anything else happened.

"Let's get Finn and go!" She ordered the room.

"I know where he is." Daisy said, her eyes wide.

"You saw him?" Asha asked, her glare screaming at Daisy to talk.

"My Samaritan took me down to the basement last night – to show me the freezers. There are different rooms down there," she spoke, with no emotion, her focus going blank. "I saw him being taken to one of them. He was screaming."

"Harry, take us there now!" Asha roared, pushing him out of her way and into the corridor, he protested slightly at her violence. She was having none of it and pointed a finger accusingly at him. "Don't you dare make a fuss of that. Do you realise how much we've all been through? And you're complaining at a little *push?"* She screeched in his face, he flinched. "GET. FUCKING. MOVING!" She yelled, giving him no choice but to start walking, fast.

The rest of the group hobbled and limped along the corridors, Max stayed to the very back, making sure everyone was safe, whilst Asha stayed up front, never more than thirty centimetres from the bearded brother. He didn't speak a word to her, he was probably scared of what he had released. With every second that passed, Asha was unsure of how well she would be able to contain the rage that was growing like a storm in her chest.

Within a minute, Harry was leading them down a dingy, damp staircase, sending them further and further into darkness. When they reached the bottom, he flicked on a light switch and Jude's words suddenly became reality.

Lining two walls of the space down there were freezers upon freezers, each with padlocks on them, each big enough to hold a person. On one of the other walls was a glass door leading to a sterile medical room, and on the other wall there was a thick, steel door.

In the very centre of the room was a surgical table surrounded by medical equipment. There was a drain right underneath the table, it was stained red and amber. The smell of antiseptic and metal filled Asha's nostrils completely; it stung. As she looked to the freezers once again, a damaging thought shot through her.

"Which one is she in?" She commanded, her voice echoing the haunting words around the dim space.

Harry didn't answer, but he started to walk towards one of them. Asha felt satisfied by his advance so she turned her attention to rescuing her 'prince in distress'. Daisy was already standing next to the steel door, her head hanging low, tears dropping onto her bare toes. Asha heard a click from where Harry was, meaning he'd unlocked the freezer where Piper lay. She marched to him and yanked his arm to follow her to the next room.

"Open it, quickly," she ordered, waiting impatiently as he sifted through his many keys.

Max moved in the corner of her eye and she darted a look to him. He was opening the freezer door. His face dropped instantly and he let out a ground-shaking shout before punching the plastic door so hard it cracked. Asha wouldn't look, not yet.

Finally, Harry located the right key and clicked open the heavy-duty door, hauling it towards him.

The stink of blood hit the group with an intensity so forceful it made Daisy turn to the side and throw up. What made Asha almost lose her non-existent stomach contents, were the bodies that lay mangled around the room.

Their intestines had been pulled from their bodies like a magic cloth trick, never ending ribbons twirling around themselves. Deep lacerations opened up the muscles of the men who had been unfortunate enough to be at the sharp end of whatever had cut them.

These Samaritans were certainly more than paralyzed; they were annihilated.

What was most chilling of all, was the fact that in the very centre of the room, surrounded by the brutality, was Finn, sitting cross legged and looking to them with a tilted head and a huge smirk. His lips were smeared with blood, as were his hands.

When he grinned wickedly at them, Asha noticed the blackness of his eyes and the flesh that was stuck between his teeth.

"Welcome, to my becoming," he spoke unlike he'd ever spoken before, his voice sly and piercing.

The group stood stunned by the scene in front of them. No-one uttered a word.

Asha could have sworn that his veins showed up darker along his forehead, like he had, blackened blood.

No, no it can't be.

In that moment, she lost her faith in the world around her. *Everything* changed. She could feel it, her body and mind forming into something new, something to deal with what had happened. She'd endured just a little too much now. Her heart was no longer there.

My Finn.

My infected Finn.

"You know the story about how the Samaritans are the 'main providers' of food to The Horsemen?" Finn asked, uncrossing his legs carefully and standing himself up in one swift movement. "Well, they were right. But what they didn't tell us was that they created them," he looked up to them, licking his bloodied lips. "Infection by consumption," he explained softly.

Asha reeled at the sight of him, at the tone of his voice, at everything.

His skin wasn't pale like the others, even The Horsemen had pale skin, which could only mean the infection hadn't taken all of him just yet. Despite the fact he was chowing down on their diet, he still bore his human skin.

There might still be time.

"There's more than four, too. Each of us is less powerful than the last somehow. But they said I'm a pretty strong candidate," he grinned, shoving his hands in his pockets and rocking back and forth on his heels.

The good always fell first.

Asha stared at the boy who she had let herself fall in love with. Her body shook violently, both with horror and untethered fury.

"Max, the boat. Does it have the serum, the one that stalls the infection?" She asked through gritted teeth, keeping her stare on her now dark-eyed boy.

"It does," Max replied curtly.

"Knock him out," she said lowly, the life and spark had left her.

Without question, the hulking man strode into the room, taking care not to slip on the coagulated pools of blood in his path.

Finn looked up to Max and smiled widely.

"Max, don't come near me with all those open wounds. My mouth's wateri-" Finn chimed before Max's fist shunted into his temple, causing a blackout.

Max caught him in his arms and carried him out of the room of horrors. Asha followed close behind him, looking at how Finn's face was now relaxed, innocent, more like himself. She felt the cry come before it erupted from her. She couldn't stop it.

He was the only piece of gold left in a world full of coal.

The Samaritans had taken him from her, they'd taken the only boy she'd ever let into her frazzled and broken heart. They'd taken the last bright soul, and they were going to pay.

There was only one way her conscience could rest easy; they all had to die.

Once Max laid Finn's sleeping body at the base of the freezers, Asha hauled herself up onto the surgical table, kicking off everything that was on it, sending it all clattering loudly to the concrete floor below. The noise intrigued the little girls and they looked up at Asha, waiting. Kit's face was twisted in adrenaline-fuelled anticipation, his eyes set on her in awe and comradery. She could always count on him, always.

"Harry," she started in a flat tone. "You're not going to like what's going to happen next. But it has to be done."

"What?" The Korean man asked cautiously, darting his eyes around the group, he looked terrified. He was outnumbered.

"Pray your last prayer for your brother," she said coldly, looking down at him before turning her attention to Max. "Lock him in the steel room."

"What? No! Don't leave me in there!" He yelled as Max's grip homed in on him, dragging his writing body to the room they'd carried Finn out of.

"Just for now. So, you don't stop us," Asha said, feeling nothing.

Kit met them before they reached the steel room and he broke the keys from Harry's grasp with a cocky shrug. Harry screamed but Asha didn't care. She waited until he was locked away before she addressed the group.

"Kill them. Kill all of them," she instructed, her darkened stare gazing at each of her motley crew. They all nodded their heads with fire in their eyes. "Leave Jude... He's mine," she added, adrenaline seeping into her veins.

Payback was a bitch.

Chapter Thirty-Seven

The group dispersed around the house like assassins. Asha stormed, weapons at the ready to her room. When she reached the door, she stood for a moment, knife handles digging hard into her palms. This was it; this was what she had been fantasizing about ever since she drank that fucking orange squash. She finally had the opportunity to end Jude's existence.

She pushed open the wooden door before slipping into the room. Once in, she slowly closed it behind her, making sure to use Harry's keys to lock it. When she was alone and trapped in the room with him, she took Jude's second gun from his belt, slouched off her backpack and put it in it before throwing it to the bed. *Always handy*. She then took a deep breath and felt a smile crack open her face.

"Look where we've found ourselves," she said, delicately placing her knives on the floor.

She then knelt down to Jude's bulky body, which was face down. The position wasn't going to work for her and what she wanted to do, so she scooped her arms under his, and jerked him with all her strength until he was lying on his back. She let out grunts of exasperation, his weight was more than double hers, and it was a dead weight.

His pupils had almost fully dilated, but they turned to pin pricks when he feasted his eyes on her. Pure terror and panic rang through his frantically moving glare.

"Hello," Asha breathed smoothly. "We need to stop meeting in here," she grinned as she picked up her shorter knife, holding it in Jude's view.

A single noise came from within him. A yelp.

"You know, I thought your face would be the last thing I saw before I died," Asha gazed down at him with dead eyes. "But it looks like you'll be staring at mine instead."

Asha felt powerful, more powerful than she'd ever felt before. She was worried she would lose herself to it. But that worry was soon overtaken by the realisation that she'd already been lost. She bit her lip and stared down at him in silence for a moment, her eye twitched slightly as the pain of her group burrowed into her vision. One thought permeated her; how completely fucking unfair the world had been to Finn – it genuinely killed her.

"You are pure evil, Jude, and unfortunately for you, I think it's rubbed off on me," she spoke quietly, listening to his rampant breathing. "Maybe it was the way you lulled me with special treatment and then punished me like a dog on the street. Or maybe it was my friend being killed by your men, or perhaps it was the fact that you turned Finn, into a flesh eating PSYCHOPATH!"

He blinked fast.

"*But...I can forgive you for that,*" she now whispered, twiddling the knife in the air above his face. "If you promise to do one thing," she said lazily, looking at him. "Can you be a *good boy*?"

Jude moved his sapphire eyes up and down, indicating a 'yes' to her. She grinned and bent down to his ear, breathing her hot breath against his skin.

"*Stay still,*" she instructed softly, and his wheezing rocketed.

423

She held the knife like a pen and pulled out his arm, soft side up to her. Her finger traced lightly against his skin from his wrist, all the way up to the crook of his elbow where a large vein bulged. She prodded it with her fingertip before lowering the knife point to it and slicing it open slowly. The blood chugged out in a red river. Her smile grew. She then reached for the other arm and inflicted the same flick of her knife to his vein.

Next, she reached for her longer, thinner knife and squeezed his upper thigh. He was muscly, but she could get through to the artery, if she used all of her energy. She thought back quickly to the anatomy of the human body, something she had learnt at school, and pinpointed the exact place where she needed to puncture.

She drew her arm back and pushed on it, sinking it into his leg with determination all the way down to the handle before pulling it out quickly with a sucking sound. Her focus stuck to the place where she stabbed him for a few seconds before hot dark blood began to spurt out. Dark meant artery, artery meant death. She matched it on the other leg and sat by his head, watching as his body started to convulse against the power of the medicine in him.

After thirty seconds, he still wasn't dead. *Tut, tut, tut.*

So, Asha stuck her knife into his neck, slipping the metal into his jugular with ease. As she yanked it out, a torrent of blood coated her hands, and she found herself playing with it, letting its warmth spread across fingers.

Her vision began clouding more with a grey haze, something she couldn't shake. All she knew was that she was no longer Asha Flores. She was something new, something dangerous.

Something, not someone. Not anymore.

She held her hands up in front of her face, her vision blurry and dreamlike as she stared at the redness. The sounds of Jude's choking breaths accompanied her bizarre frame of mind.

Without a thought, she closed her eyes and trailed her fingers over her face, painting herself with him. When she opened her eyes, she suddenly felt exhausted, so she lay on her side, facing him, propping her head up with her hand. Her other hand lingered on his heaving chest, ticking him softly.

The world went grey.

"Say hello to the Devil for me. Tell him I'll be late," she said as the life behind his eyes shot out of him in a sudden instant.

Her mind went blank, and any thought of who she was disappeared and turned into a greyness which completely consumed her. She lay on her back now blankly for an unknown amount of time before she was lifted up roughly from the floor and flung straight back into reality.

"What the fuck, Ash?" Kit questioned, his eyes wide and his brow pinched. He looked like the scared little boy who got his head trapped in the fence all those years ago. Her heart shuddered.

He was holding her up to his eye line, her feet scrambling to touch the wooden flooring below. She shook her head hard, her hair falling in front of her eyes. Her legs felt like jelly and she felt guilty and frightened by the way Kit was looking at her.

The grey was gone.

He gazed down at her with genuine concern, and as she looked behind her, she remembered what she had done.

Behind Kit, the door sank limply on its hinges. She hadn't even heard him breaking in. She felt like she'd dropped off the face of the earth for a while. Now she was back, her face was sticky and all she could smell was sour blood.

"I-I don't know," she stammered, finding some steadiness in her footing as he set her down gently.

"...Let's go," Kit eventually said after making sure she could walk by herself.

*

When the pair arrived back in the basement, Asha felt more like herself. She put her partial psychotic, grey blackout down to stress and shoved it to the back of her mind, where she'd bury it forever. The image of Jude lying there convulsing in his own blood however, seemed to have been tattooed into her sight, and the feel of his blood saturating on her pyjamas and drying on her cheeks was enough of a reminder. She shivered, and it wasn't because of the cold.

Harry had already been released from his temporary holdings and he was pacing around the basement, worry humming from him. The rest of the group were slouched around waiting but jumped to attention when the pair walked through the door. Finn was still out cold on the floor, his face calm, but still bloody.

"What happened?" Max questioned, walking fast to Asha who had almost forgotten what she looked like.

"Leave it," Kit warned, standing in front of the recovering girl.

Asha didn't even really register Max's question; all she could do was look at Harry. Suddenly, something switched inside of her and she could feel her body being taken by that grey feeling once again.

"Let's get out of here, stop wasting time," she instructed, and everyone started to gather themselves, she then narrowed her stare at Harry. "Except you."

The group stopped moving and stared at both Asha and Harry. The air grew thick and all that could be heard was the rapid hearts of six confused people.

"What?" Harry asked, blushing slightly as he realised all eyes were on him and that he was being singled out.

"You're not coming with us," Asha repeated herself, feet shoulder width apart, her hardened glare concreted to him and no-one else.

"Asha, you're not thinking straight right now," Max interjected, practically whispering next to her.

"*Shut the fuck up*, Max," she spat without looking at him.

"Stop," Kit lowly warned, assumedly at Max, or maybe not.

That grey was looming in her vision again.

"Can we just leave all of this and get the fuck out of here!" Daisy cried out; Asha could see her arms cradling the two little girls from the corner of her eye.

"Oh, *we* can leave. But Harry is staying here," Asha said, crossing her arms.

"I set you free. I *betrayed my brother* for you. I'm coming with you," Harry spoke spitefully, standing his ground.

"Ash, what's going on?" Max questioned, overwhelming fear had begun to radiate from him.

There was a strange and uncomfortable feeling festering in the room. Asha could feel it and no doubt everyone else could too.

They couldn't understand why she was exiling Harry from their escape. It truly baffled Asha. It was time for her to make them see the light, to see things from her point of view.

"Do you all really think he should come with us?" Asha asked, a scowl on her face.

Looking around the room she saw uneasy nods of heads, but nods of heads nonetheless. A vein bulged in her forehead.

"Let me ask you this... Who brought us here?" She asked, glancing around, noticing the sudden frowning eyebrows and glares aimed at Harry. *Keep going.* "Who could've let us walk by? Who could've told Jude there was no catch from the day? Who could have come with us when we revealed where we were going?" With every question, the group began to collectively frown. "Why didn't you come with us, *Harry*? Why did you bring us here?" She asked, her voice ringing high and expectant.

He breathed heavily and looked to the floor, rubbing his arms. "I...uh," was all he could manage.

"This man right here let us get beaten... tortured... killed... and WORSE!" Asha shouted, making Daisy wince and cover the girls' ears. "He did *nothing* to help us the *whole* way. He gave us the drugs that put us to sleep, he kept us paralyzed, and he stood by while the Samaritans had their way with us... And look how easy it was to take them down," she seethed, getting closer to Harry who was standing tall, but he was shaking.

"Asha," Max was right behind her, following her every step. He was probably afraid of what she would do.

He was right to be afraid.

"Max, leave her," Kit said, sounding close by too.

"Shame you had to wait until we'd lived through our own personal hells before you lifted a finger!" Asha screamed, her fists balling and unballing in quick succession.

Grey, grey, grey.

"You're free now," was all Harry had to say, and blood boiled in her.

"And you think that gives you the right to a good life?" Asha scoffed harshly, through gritted teeth.

Harry clenched his jaw and darted his eyes around the room before letting out a huffed sigh and crossing his arms to match the freckled girl. "I'm not staying here, and you can't make me." He spoke like a spoilt, rotten child. "Even if you leave without me, I'll find my way to Harbour. I have time," he smirked with a one shouldered shrug.

Asha hadn't thought her plan through thoroughly enough. Harry was right. He knew the direction they were headed in; he would eventually find his way to their perfect, little, safe haven. He would taint it with his cowardly sins.

Her stare dropped to the floor momentarily and her whole face frowned. If they left, there was no guarantee that he wouldn't just follow them close behind either. As she looked down, she noticed that Max had picked up the gun that Jude was going to use on him. It was tucked within reach in his waistband.

A solution to her problem presented itself in cold metal.

"I can't let you do that," Asha said before snatching the gun from Max's jeans and looking ahead.

Grey.

The split second went by in slow motion. Harry's face flew open in shock and two pairs of hands grabbed for the gun. Screams and yells muffled in her throbbing ears. But no-one could stop her from aiming the barrel at Harry's heart. No-one could stop her finger as it squeezed the trigger. No-one could stop the bullet as it obliterated Harry's life with a deafening bang.

After he fell dead to the floor, everything came sucking back into normal speed, and Asha's fingers lost grip of the gun. It clattered noisily on the hard stone below and Asha's breathing increased tenfold.

She suddenly felt extremely hot and began to feel dizzy, sweat streamed down her face and nausea throbbed in her stomach. Something was very, very wrong with her. She lifted her hands to her view and looked on horrified as the veins along the backs of her hands pulsed with thick, *black* tar. *What is happening to me*?! She shot a frantic look at her best friend.

"*Kit*?" She stammered, but he could do nothing but look on at her in pure shock, like he no longer recognised her.

A hard knock landed against her temple, sending her instantly into blackness.

Chapter Thirty-Eight

Asha opened her eyes in a hurry as she was unexpectedly thrust off from where she was lying and onto the hard floor below, gasping.

As she looked around from where she'd landed, she realized quickly she was in the underbelly of a boat. The air around her tasted salty and fresh, and the sea breeze brought in a spray of water through the porthole.

They'd made it to the boat.

Her fingers soothed her right temple where pain flourished. She then remembered what the last thing she saw was. Hurriedly, she brought her hands to her view and made sure her veins were their normal, only slightly darkened colour, unlike the abyss that seemed to engulf her right after she killed Harry.

They seemed to be average enough for her, which filled her with much needed relief. She glanced down at herself, she'd been changed into a pair of black leggings and an oversized sweatshirt. She felt a lot cleaner too; it made sense that they got rid of her wine-stained clothes and fixed her blood-streaked face. They didn't want her to seem as insane to Harbour as she really was, not just yet.

The space below the deck was around twelve-foot by ten-foot, and it was crammed full of different boxes, most of which Asha couldn't tell what they contained. From what she could see, some of them held water bottles and others seemed packed to brim with soft materials like towels.

Asha had been lying on one of four sofas that lined the storage cabin. On the sofas opposite her, she saw all of the groups' belongings piled high. That was when her eyes caught sight of the backpack she knew to be Max's. And that was when she remembered what Kit had told her all those nights ago, when he came back with a bullet in his helmet, and a ring of red under his chin.

She glanced up to the only door leading up to the top deck and stayed silent for a moment, judging how much of a chance she had to take what was in his bag and not get caught.

Adrenaline coursed through her as she delicately crawled over to the fated bag, her eyes constantly flitting from its zip and the door up the stairs. Her fingers fumbled slightly as she heard heavy footsteps up above her. Heart jumping, she practically flew back up onto the sofa and closed her eyes.

After listening to trudging feet overlap and cross above her head for a minute, she realised no-one was coming down anytime soon. So, she set off on her covert mission once again. This time, she undid the zip with ease and immediately found the folder Kit was talking about. It was a dark blue colour and it felt thick with papers. She held it in her hands, aching to read through whatever Max was hiding, but a sudden excited squealing from above forced her to shove it into her own bag and cover her tracks as best she could.

She used the sofas to help her to stand, and once she adjusted to the motion of the ocean, she began her walk up the white stairs. Her fingers pushed against the door that opened upwards, letting the streaming light of midday shine through. She squinted in the brightness of it all and hauled herself up and out of the cabin.

Kit was just ahead of her, leaning against the riling. At the noise of the door opening, he turned around and a smile burst across his lips. "Ash!"

"Hey stranger," she smiled at him and looked around. The sea was a brilliant blue, and right ahead of them was an island with a mammoth, white flag flapping at its dock. It had a giant 'H' painted on it in light blue. "*Harbour!*" Asha breathed happily.

She stumbled to the edge of the boat with Kit, grasping onto the cold metal barriers, not taking her eyes off the promised land ahead of her. She could hardly believe that they had it in their sight. All the torment and aching to get there felt worthwhile and necessary.

Though they'd lost a few along the way, some in other ways than death, she still felt like everything had led up to this exact moment.

The happiness and relief of it all flooded her every cell, and she couldn't help the huge grin that blossomed on her tired face. Kit's strong arm pulled her into an embrace as he stood next to her, looking on at where they belonged.

"We actually made it," he said, a chuckle on his lips. "*We actually made it.*"

Asha laughed lightly and jumped where she stood, reaching up to wrap her arms around Kit's neck. He hoisted her up onto him, and she wrapped herself around his sturdy body. He held her close and she could feel his heart hammering in his chest. As she looked over his shoulder, she saw the rest of the group dotting the decking.

Daisy gave her a quick nod and busied herself with making sure the girls didn't fall overboard from the excitement. Boe was clinging onto the blonde girl's hip, balancing well. Sunny pointed to the island with a grin on her face, looking up to Daisy who smiled a gapped smile back.

Max had begun to make his way over to Asha, his stride long and direct. He looked concerned, but underneath, she could tell he was just as relieved as she was. She hopped off Kit and moved towards the burly man.

"Max, you did it," she beamed.

"*We* did it," he corrected her with a quick smile before taking out a medical torch. "Look directly in the light, I need to check that you're reacting *normally* to things," he instructed as he tilted her chin up and shone the blinding light into her eyes, causing her to wince. He repeated the procedure for both eyes and sighed.

"You seem to be doin' fine. Luckily," he paused and raised his eyebrow. "You had a bit of a blip back at the house. Seemed to me like Nox somehow became activated within you. It's somethin' we need to fully test you on before we start creating a cure," he said, putting away the torch. "We gave you the serum to try and bring you back to your usual self, which seems to have worked. You'll be happy to know that we caught Finn's infection in time too. He'll need constant medication from now on though, and he'll probably be unstable for a while," Max explained, rubbing his shaven head with a heavy hand.

"But believe it or not, we have kids your age who are going through the same thing, so he won't be alone. You have to be careful Asha. Anythin' that raises yours or his heart rate runs the risk of triggerin' a turn," he finished, giving the dark-haired girl a gentle pat on the shoulder before walking towards the cockpit where a grey-haired woman helmed the wheel.

Asha looked around for Finn, feeling Kit's stare on her. She thought quickly about what Max had said. Anything that raised their heart rate would 'trigger' a turn. Did that mean Finn would turn back into his Hunter-self? Did it mean she'd one day turn like him too? She wasn't sure, but all she did know was that things between the two of them were about to become even more complicated than before, and her heart sighed a deep sigh of longing.

"He's been sat behind the Captain's bay since we got on," Kit said, giving her a small nudge in the right direction. "Go to him," he said, giving her a side smile before turning to face the sea once again.

With his permission, Asha felt a jump in her step as she sought out Finn. It didn't take her long to find him sat with his back to the ocean and his knees held against his face. As soon as she saw him and his sorrowed demeanour, she felt her chest pinch and her eyes widen. She wanted to run and hug him so hard that he'd explode, but she knew that physical contact could set him off, so she resigned herself to sitting down next to him, just close enough to feel his body heat.

"Hey," she said softly, twiddling her thumbs. She looked behind her to see Harbour getting even closer.

"Hey," he replied weakly, his skin was paler than its usual tan self, it made her stomach flip nervously, remembering what he almost became.

They sat in silence for a moment, with the sounds of rushing water and excited chatter surrounding them. It felt like they were in a little bubble of trauma; their very own, personal world full of memories they'd rather forget. Asha suddenly realised how similar they were to each other.

They both had Nox running through their veins, they both had blood on their hands and not because they had to. She felt oddly fragile next to him, like they could both break if anyone touched them. She glanced up to see Kit with his firm biceps and general glowing-self as he gazed ahead; he looked like a God compared to the two shrivelled infected kids who sat deathly pale beside each other.

"I haven't stopped throwing up," Finn croaked, letting his stare meet hers, his eyes were brimming with tears.

"At least you're not talking like one of them anymore," Asha offered, a light shrug on her shoulders.

"That wasn't me. I didn't have control. It was like I was watching myself from inside, but everything in my vision was this off-grey colour, like I was dreaming." A couple of tears fell, but they stopped then.

"Grey?" Asha questioned. "That's what I saw," she added quietly, unclasping her hands, her fingernails left marks in her palm.

"I've felt like my body's been rotting from the inside ever since they fed me that meat. I knew something was wrong with it, but I was so hungry, I ate it anyway," he cried, Asha noticed how the space under his eyes looked like red bruises, they contrasted harshly with his skin. "They didn't even have to force me."

"But they would have," Asha soothed, placing a hand absentmindedly on his leg.

He shuffled away abruptly, looking to her with wide, fearful eyes. "You can't do that," he warned, and both sadness and panic washed over him, so much so, Asha could physically see it.

She stared at him, mouth agape, feeling a sense of shock and betrayal. Max was right, she couldn't touch him. She felt like a child having her favourite doll put behind a glass pane.

Always there, but always out of reach.

She swallowed the lump in her throat and nodded her head briskly. "I won't forget," she couldn't forget the aching agony of it.

"Right, ladies and gentlemen!" Max boomed, stepping out onto the deck again, all eyes went to him. "Arrival in T-minus two minutes! So, head down below and grab your stuff. We're home!"

*

Stepping off the boat and onto solid ground threw Asha for a moment, but she found her footing soon enough and kept up with Max's stride.

The pier was long and thin, used for the unloading and loading of boats. All along the wooden structure were flowers of various different shapes and colours.

They filled the blowing air with a sweet scent; it brought a smile to Asha's face. They had been put there on purpose, whether it was for her arrival, or for the arrival of a new batch of survivors, it was still a sweet gesture.

Looking ahead to the mainland, Asha could see a small gathering of people waving white flags with bright smiles on their faces. The group huffed and shuffled under the weight of their stuff and the memories of the past few months, but every step they took, Asha felt lighter, less burdened; free.

Max strode ahead of them arms open to a man who wore a button-down shirt comfortably against his slightly fuller body. The man had thick rimmed glasses, grey hair that had been slicked back with a side parting, and a thick grey stubble to match. He had a kind looking face and as he approached Max with an even bigger arm span, it was clear to Asha that he was a man who could be trusted. The man must have been Noah, the man Max talked about.

Just behind Noah, stood a woman around the same age as him. She had a bob cut of silvery blonde hair, and her crow's feet showed prominently as she grinned. By her side stood a girl who looked to be around twenty, she had the same coloured hair as the lady and her thin nose matched hers too. Asha quickly came to the conclusion that they were a family. A family was a rare thing, it was often that Nox would take at least two thirds of a family, but here they were, perfect and together. And they seemed to be important; they stood more than twelve feet in front of the rest of the crowd.

Max embraced Noah with a hard hug and a brief pat on the back before pulling away and gesturing for Asha to step forward.

The smiling grey-haired man looked expectantly to her; it made her feel embarrassed and vulnerable. But she complied and joined him, forcing a smile to hide her nerves.

Noah stuck out his hand towards her. "Asha, it's a pleasure to meet you," he beamed, a thick French accent decorating his voice.

She smiled bashfully yet shook his hand firmly.

"Asha, this is Noah, remember I told you about him?" Max introduced, giving her a gentle wink and a grin.

"I remember," Asha replied, looking from Max to Noah, a small smile on her face.

"Well," he began. "I am very excited to have you here and trust me everyone else is too. But first things first, we need to take you on a tour of Harbour, and we need to get you and your friends into your houses."

"These flowers are so pretty! Did you make them?" Boe piped up, toddling to Noah with a bunch of flowers even bigger than her head gripped in her chubby fingers.

Noah immediately bent down to her level and placed a palm on her shoulder. "Yes, I did, and I made them especially for *you*! I'm so happy that you like them!" He said, his voice an octave higher than before.

"You made them for me?" Boe giggled, her face blushing.

"Of course! For such a special girl, I'll do anything," he assured her before standing himself up.

Sunny came to Boe's side and pulled her against her, holding her perfectly in place.

"Such a joy to see more children," Noah almost said to himself as he looked down on the pair. He then looked up to the group, arms up in the air. "Welcome to Harbour! We hope that you'll live long, happy lives here, like so many of us have begun to," he then looked to Max with a narrow stare. "Which one is Finn?" He asked.

It was pretty clear who Finn was, but still, Max pointed to the fragile, broken boy who looked like he'd died not long ago. He stood clutching his bag instead of carrying it on his back, which only made him seem smaller. He looked nervously up to Noah, like he was in trouble with the head teacher.

"Finn, we're going to be working very closely with you, and don't worry, you're in very safe hands," he soothed, turning his head to look at the blonde lady. "Claire!" He called with a pull of his head.

She gave her daughter a rub on her shoulder before bustling over to the group, a shy yet strong grin on her face. "Hello everyone," she ducked her head in an almost bow. She too had a French accent.

The group nodded their heads in acknowledgement and that was enough for her because she then turned her attention to Noah for further instruction.

"Finn, go with my wife, Claire. She will get you acquainted with the 'others' and run a few tests. We want to make sure that the serum is working as effectively as it can be with you. It's all about research and bettering ourselves, and the products that we make. You will be very helpful to us, and I hope that we can be as helpful to you. To help you to live a somewhat normal life, with your friends, and with us at Harbour."

Finn let out a deep sigh and nodded his head slowly, looking unsure.

Claire beckoned him with a gesture of her hands and he followed her, glancing back once to the group and to Asha before disappearing into the now parted crowd.

Asha felt like she wanted to go with him, not wanting him to be alone. But she couldn't go anywhere, not now. She was in the prying eyes of everyone at Harbour now, she wouldn't be able to do anything without at least one person knowing. The pressing thought of the end of her privacy made her stomach churn uncomfortably. This would be her life now. She would be under a magnifying glass, prodded with needles, looked to for a future. But she was safe, she didn't have to run anymore; she could deal with the imperfections of Harbour, because it was a hell of a lot better than being out there.

"Adella, *venir!*" Noah called to the young blonde girl whose hair curled at the end of its long bob.

She walked over with a saunter in her step, her arms folded and a smile that accentuated the bags under her eyes. Everything about her was soft, elegant and wistful. She had an air of clarity around her and as the breeze passed her, the smell of roses came with it.

"Bonjour," she said with a voice a little deeper than Asha had expected.

"This is my beautiful daughter, Adella," Noah beamed as he gave her a squeeze on the shoulder. "She works very closely with us; she's learning the ropes."

"I'm happy to meet you all," she smiled, she had a nose ring that glinted in the sun.

"So, Adella, Max. Take the others around, show them their houses, they need to see everything!" Noah instructed. "Asha, you'll come with me, you're getting the extra special tour," he grinned, beckoning her under his wing.

Asha turned to look at Kit who gave her a reassuring nod and a wave goodbye. She didn't have to be concerned about being split up anymore, they were safe, she could let him go.

And breathe.

Noah led her away from the group with a palm on her shoulder blades, something that she had to pull away from instantly; ever since Jude's pin injected her there, she couldn't stand it being touched. He didn't hesitate and he removed it straight away, noticing her discomfort. They strode side by side for a few seconds in silence before Noah turned, beaming to her.

"Asha, are you ready to save the world?"

Chapter Thirty-Nine

Harbour truly was a sanctuary; but anything would seem like heaven compared to roaming around the desolate streets of a country gone by. Noah talked and talked, every word said with enthusiasm and pride, but Asha found it hard to listen. The overwhelming sight of it all stunned her. Just seeing a bustling place of living sent her into a state of shock.

The majority of the people on Harbour were between the ages of sixteen and forty, with a few exceptions. One thing that Asha noticed in all of them was a sense of freedom and ultimate contentment. They had nothing to worry about, they were protected from the Nox-filled world on an island of pure paradise, a clean and disease-free zone.

Another thing that she noticed was that all the people had a small tattoo on the inside edge of their wrist; it was a small and delicate anchor. She learnt that everyone who lived on Harbour got the same tattoo, representing solidarity, hope and safety. A homage to the island. Many people had lots of tattoos, and most of them had them done once Harbour became Harbour; the taboo of tattoos became meaningless as creativity and carefreeness soared.

Noah also explained that there was no such thing as money on the island. They stocked every penny and note away in an underground bunker that was being saved in the event of worldwide regrowth. But in reality, it seemed that that currency was over.

Even if the world got back on its feet, it was highly unlikely that it would start off in the capitalist, money hungry way that it used to be. It would rise from the roots of civilisation, where bartering and goods were how you made a living, where helping each other was a priority and not a favour.

As they walked around the streets and open areas of Harbour it was clear that everyone had something to do. Men and women were carrying fresh fruit and vegetables, piles of fresh laundry and flowers in abundance. There was also a large amount of scientific and medical personnel who walked around in a rush, papers in hand and brilliant white lab coats covering them.

"It's a blessing to have so many young people eager to help. A lot of them only had a college education before all of this. But now, they are budding scientists, nurses and doctors, learning fast because they know the urgency of the task at hand," Noah said as they rounded a corner to a large building where a red cross stood grandly by its entrance. "This is the main headquarters; you'll grow very accustomed to her. She is a big beauty, waiting to birth that cure," he grinned, beholding the building.

There was a large open space in front of the hospital where a large, intricate stone fountain sat proudly, spouting out water from its many flower-shaped appendages. Around the rim of the pool of water sat a few tired, but accomplished looking medics, fruit in their hands and water in bottles near them. It seemed to be break time. The sun shone down on the whole area and the sound of the water splashing down, paired with the scene of normality warmed Asha to her core.

They moved on, and as they walked through the heavy glass doors to the building, Asha was met by a girl who was around her age.

But she wasn't met with a handshake, she was met by her running full throttle into her, knocking her backwards into Noah's ready arms.

"Oh shit! I'm so sorry!" The girl exclaimed before hurriedly sinking to the floor, gathering all the papers and things she had dropped on impact.

"No, no, it's fine." Asha brushed it off with a smile, bending down and grabbing the name badge that she had dropped. "It's fine... *Harper*," she smiled, and handed it to the girl, forcing her to look at her.

Asha's breath caught in her throat as Harper stared at her with her almond eyes.

Everything stopped for that slight moment. Harper had deep chocolate iris's that were swimming in light, her hair was hip length and golden in colour, her skin was caramel and it was flawless. She bit her full, pink lip nervously as she looked at Asha, which only made the dark-haired girl force her gaze away, bringing herself out of her trance.

They both stood abruptly, and Harper quickly pushed past the pair, but gave Asha one last confused glance before she hurried off, papers threatening to spill from her grip in the wind. Asha watched on for a second, swallowing hard, heart thumping.

What the fuck was that?

"You've just met Harper Berry. Our clumsiest intern. I've never seen a student drop so many precious samples, but still remain in study," Noah chuckled softly as he gestured for Asha to keep walking.

"*Harper…*" Asha tested the name on her tongue quietly and let out a deep sigh, shaking herself awake from her moment, despite the throbbing in her chest and the blush on her cheeks. "Is she *your* intern?" She asked as they continued to walk through the building, the smell of antiseptic and bleach taking over her senses.

"Unfortunately, yes. I can't bring myself to send her away, she's like a little puppy, always there, always ready, but always messing things up," Noah laughed, leading Asha into a vast room.

There were rows and rows of pure white desks topped with tubes, microscopes, folders, test tubes, whirring machines and charts. Each section was manned by a person, busy looking at samples with concentrated stares, scrambling words onto paper or experimenting with different concoctions.

"Welcome to the room of miracles!" Noah beamed. "…*Team Harbour!*" He shouted, catching the attention of everyone in the room. But all eyes went to Asha, and she squirmed internally. "This is Asha, our key."

An immediate burst of applause sounded around the room, and every one of the scientists had a huge smile on their face and a hope in their eyes. Asha's face flushed even redder, but she stood herself proud and tall. They looked to her with enough strength to push her into a false state of it. It did feel a little odd to have a whole room full of people clapping her, congratulating her for existing, essentially.

After Noah's introduction, he allowed each person to come and shake her hand, which again, felt alien and undeserving to Asha. But she played along, shaking each hand and showing her black scar to those who had the courage to ask.

However, it didn't take her long to feel a little more comfortable with it all, in fact, she found she liked the attention, only a touch.

Once the team had had their fill of the immune girl, Noah escorted her out and to another room which had no-one in it. What was there was a hospital bed and a collection of small-scale medical equipment. It was decorated with bright artwork depicting beaches and seashells. There was a large window looking over the fountain outside, and Asha could see the ocean, glistening through a gap in the buildings.

"What is this room?" She quizzed, her stare out to sea.

"This will be your room," Noah said, leaning against the door frame.

"Mine? Don't I get a house?" Asha whipped around, feeling a little spoilt for asking, but also feeling a sense of fear of being trapped in a small room again.

The Frenchman shook his head with a light laugh from his lips. "Of-course you're getting a house," Asha relaxed. "But this will be your room when you're in the hospital. Some procedures will need more recovery time than others, so this will be your mini sanctuary. Also, I know the dramas of teenage life. This can be your home away from home. You're welcome to stay here any time you'd like. Is that okay?" Noah asked, rubbing his grey stubble.

"That's more than okay," she sighed happily, gazing around the room, it had a certain charm and safety about it.

"Speaking of your house... shall we go to it?" He smiled widely, excited.

"Yes please," she replied with a grin.

---

*

It only took them five minutes to reach the road, which was named Dove Grove. It was true what Max had said, they kept everyone very close to town, a tight knit circle of life; safe. The road was lined with pretty little houses, all different colours. It was a long street stretching on in all its pastel shades. Each house had boxes of flowers hanging from the windows and white shutters, wide open. It was so picturesque it could have been plucked from a postcard.

"We've kept you all near each other as best we could," Noah explained as they walked through a flimsy iron gate and stepped up the stone path to a house painted in a sage colour.

Asha nodded her head and took in the beauty of what she assumed was her house. Her very own little nook in the world. She felt immediately protective over it. It was attached on either side by houses in pink and orange. The flowers on her house were pale pink roses and ivory white daisies, which complemented the colour of the walls perfectly. She couldn't believe her luck, how everything had changed so suddenly from when she was standing on the boat to right now.

She couldn't quite deal with the drastic change in emotions. She had been so used to feeling afraid, hardened and ready to attack, for so long that she almost forgotten how to feel normal. Here, she was able to breathe properly, she was able to let her worries fly away in the comforting sea breeze; she could finally stop fighting.

Uncontrollable tears pricked at her eyes, blurring her vision. She had only cried in happiness once in her life; when she found out her mum was pregnant. And now she was filled with the same tear-inducing joy that made her melt and crumble into her emotions, with no say, no choice.

Standing in front of a quaint and pretty place she could call her home was just the icing on the cake of the island.

"Are you okay?" Noah asked, a reassuring hand on her arm.

"I just, I never thought I'd have any of this. To be alive and be given a house, a haven... a *purpose,*" she practically whispered. "I'm sorry, I'm not usually this emotional."

"Don't you dare apologise for feeling," he said sternly, raising a grey eyebrow at her, his eyes bright.

"Yeah, I've been working on that," she chuckled lightly.

"So, over there is where we put Kit," he said, pointing to an off-white house opposite hers. "Next to him is Daisy's place," he motioned to a lavender house. "And next to you will be Finn, when he's deemed safe enough," he gestured to the house in question, the orange one attached to hers.

"When he's deemed safe enough?" Asha enquired, folding her arms and resting her weight on one leg.

"Yes. But with a bit of luck, he'll be moving in very soon."

"Thank you. For everything you're doing here. I thought the world was over, I thought whatever life we had left was going to be painful and full of death."

"It still is, dear Asha."

"But you're ending it."

"No, you are."

Chapter Forty

Noah left her to get settled in, and when the front door closed behind her, Asha suddenly felt strangely alone. She realized she hadn't actually been by herself for six whole months. She wasn't quite sure what to do with herself, so she just slipped off her shoes and breathed in the clean air.

She took in the small hallway that was in front of her, the wooden floors and worn stairs to the right. She glanced down to her feet, noticing a shoe rack laying bare next to her. She bent down and neatly stacked her shoes on it, like it was important.

She then padded along the hallway before entering the room to the left. It opened up to a bright and cheerful living room with cosy sofas covered in intricate tapestries. There was a tall, thin bookcase up against one wall and it was filled with books of all shapes and sizes. Asha skimmed her fingertips against their spines as she walked past them, feeling a smile grace her lips.

The next room was the kitchen, fit to purpose with everything she could have asked for. The laminate flooring around the cooking area was still a little damp, telling the freckled girl that they must have done a deep clean to get it ready for her. When she opened the fridge, she was shocked to see fresh tomatoes, lettuces and cucumbers, along with jars of homemade jams and chutneys. She hadn't seen such a sight in so long. It made a change to the mouldy, disintegrated food she'd grown accustomed to seeing.

She closed the fridge and looked out of the long, horizontal window showing the back garden. There was a little pond in the top corner of the small area outside. There was also a white iron table with matching chairs and a happy blue striped umbrella sitting in the centre of it.

The air inside the house smelt of sweet vanilla, and the culprit was a warming candle sitting on the top of the dining table to the side of the kitchen. It was a quaint area, made for living a quiet, content and tidy life. The ceilings were low and the whole place almost felt like a dollhouse, made especially for her.

On one of the cabinets lining the dining room, there was an old-fashioned radio. It was ruby red and it was begging for her to turn it on. She wasn't sure if it would work, but she turned the dial until it clicked. The sounds of a song jumped through the air for a moment before fading into silence. Asha didn't quite catch the tune, but she kept listening until the voice of a lady came through.

"That song always reminds me of the one time I was lying on the pebbly beaches of Brighton and Alan Carter decided it was a great time to try and discover my mouth with his. Needless to say, he left the beach with a black eye and I'm sorry if that's too much information folks, but Noah, you can come in here and escort me out of this radio tower if you really want to! Anywho, as if you need reminding, this is Dottie with the daytime swing, and this is a song to remind you all of that very special, first time. Or at least, it was special for a lucky few. I have a story on that too, but my goodness, let's just listen to the blasted song," The bubbly, aged voice from the radio swam around the air and Asha found herself laughing along to it.

451

A relaxing and soft song began to ring around the room, and Asha let it play as she walked back through the kitchen, rounding the stairs. She walked up them slowly, analysing the artwork that followed her up. They were all nautical themed with anchors featuring heavily. When she reached the top landing, she clocked three doors.

The first led her into a bathroom and toilet, spotless, blue and cool. The next door opened to a tiny room with a desk and an old beaten armchair, a place to sit and reflect. And the last door led her to her bedroom.

The walls were a pure white and there were two arch shaped windows that let all of the sunlight in, bolstering the room into beauty. There was a large double bed with clean, white sheets and a patchwork throw draped at the end of it. The wooden floors were a washed down white colour, and a large grey, fluffy rug rested near the bed. An antique dresser and mirror combination took up one corner of the room, and a bright orange bean bag took up another.

"This is mine," Asha whispered out loud, her voice echoing in the quiet room.

Grinning to herself, she shifted her backpack off and sat down on the bed with it. Her bum sank slightly into the mattress and soft duvet. She thought about how much of a good sleep she was going to have as she brought her bag to sit on her lap.

As the bag moved onto her leg, she was suddenly aware of Jude's gun that was tucked away in the front pocket. A tiny part of her felt obliged to hand the gun over to Noah, she had no need for it, and they probably weren't big fans of weapons on their perfect island.

But another, much greater part of her, told her to squirrel it away without the knowledge of Noah, just in case something went wrong and she had to go back into her 'kill or be killed' mantra.

She scooped it out and held it firmly in her hands before checking the ammo, four bullets. She sighed and clicked it back together, turning the safety on before hopping down to the floor and looking under the bed.

There were a few boxes and a wicker basket filled with bed sheets and linens. Asha pulled out the basket and peeled away the folded sheets before slipping the gun in underneath. She would find a better place for it in time, but for now it would do.

Once she was satisfied, she climbed back onto the bed and grabbed her bag again with the mind to unpack her measly number of belongings. But as she did so, she spotted the blue folder that she'd acquired earlier, and any thoughts of settling in scattered, leaving only her curiosity brimming, and her hands shaking.

She gingerly removed the thick folder from her bag and held it for a moment. She shook her head of any negative thoughts. Kit was probably overreacting, there was most likely nothing of interest in the folds of the blue card in her hands. But she had to make sure, she had to delve in, she had to uncover what could be.

Her fingers worked slowly to lift the flap and reveal a bunch of papers, all with too much writing on to decipher at a glance. She quickly grabbed the pile and discarded the folder. Bringing the papers up to view, her eyes scanned over them, shuffling them behind one another, getting the full scope of what was written.

Her heart started to hammer as words like 'ancient disease', 'accountability' and 'GPC', were sprawled across the countless pages.

They were letters and confirmations all pertaining to the infection, Nox. Not observations, but documents talking about covering something up, detailed analysis of the Antarctic.

Letters with official stamp marks and footnotes from various worldwide medical companies and government outlets began to form the harrowing picture in Asha's crumpling mind.

The papers held a chronological confession to Nox.

She sat frozen, her breathing out of control, her eyes jumping in and out of focus.

One sentence on one piece of paper stood out like a nail in wood; 'The world's governments are to be kept away from this."

But most damning of all, and what made Asha feel like the floor had been whipped from under her feet, her clothes ripped from her body and the walls snatched from around her, was the name that was written over and over again in print and signature.

Dr. Maxwell Bennett.

Printed in Great Britain
by Amazon

22648511R00260